stay

a BLEEDING STARS *novel*

A.L. JACKSON

NEW YORK TIMES BESTSELLING AUTHOR

A.L. Jackson
www.aljacksonauthor.com
Cover Design by RBA Designs
Photo by Wander Aguiar Photography
Editing by AW Editing

Print ISBN: 978-1-946420-01-5
eBook ISBN: 978-1-938404-97-9

stay

MORE FROM A.L. JACKSON

Redemption Hills
Give Me a Reason
Say It's Forever
Never Look Back
Promise Me Always

The Falling Stars Series
Kiss the Stars
Catch Me When I Fall
Falling into You
Beneath the Stars

Confessions of the Heart
More of You
All of Me
Pieces of Us

Fight for Me
Show Me the Way
Follow Me Back
Lead Me Home
Hold on to Hope

Bleeding Stars
A Stone in the Sea
Drowning to Breathe
Where Lightning Strikes
Wait
Stay
Stand

WILLOW

We rarely know when our lives are about to change. When the direction we have been traveling will shift. When the stagnant comfort we've cut out for ourselves will take a sharp turn south, or when everything we know will come to an abrupt, excruciating end.

Maybe I should have known it then. When the bell jingled above the door.

I guess I'd been too absorbed in my work to note the moment. Lost to the feel of the wood beneath my hands as I shaped and sanded away the rot and decay to expose the true beauty hiding underneath.

Maybe I should have taken the way my heart suddenly sped as a premonition. As an omen. As a warning to steel myself for the debris littering the road ahead.

Instead, I took it head on. My eyes squinted against the blinding rays of late-afternoon sun that spilled in like a flash flood behind the man who suddenly took up the entirety of the doorway.

A concealed figure cast in shadows and silhouettes.

A mystery rimmed in the brightest fire.

Maybe I should have braced myself for impact.

For the collision I never could have anticipated.

He took a single step forward and into my direct line of sight.

He stared at me for the longest time, taking me in as if he knew me, before he tilted his head and slanted me the cockiest grin. One that had the power to plow through me with the force of a speeding truck that'd lost its brakes.

Maybe I should have prepared myself.

Maybe I should have been stronger.

Maybe I should have clung harder to the promise I'd made to never allow myself to get burned.

Not ever again.

Little did I know I was now standing in the flames.

ASH

I prided myself in being about the nicest guy you'd ever meet. Spreading the love wherever I went. Liking damned near everyone who crossed my path.

Which was why this shit going down was so not cool.

Adrenaline pumped hard through my veins and pounded in my ears. The hairs at the nape of my neck lifted in warning.

I peered back into the shadows of the dark, humid night. Bugs droned in the trees, the sleepy silence only broken every so often by an engine whirring in the distance.

The road I'd decided to walk after I'd left the bar was locked down tight, the small shops and restaurants closed for the night. A dingy haze glowed from the streetlamps lining the main road about half a mile away.

My phone burned in my pocket, but I knew even if I managed to make a call, there was no chance any of my boys would show in time.

I lifted my hands in the air in a placating fashion and took a single step backward. "Have no clue what you're talkin' about," I promised, going for cool and casual.

Only I did. I totally remembered the chick he was talking about climbing all over my dick two nights ago. Of course, she'd conveniently failed to mention anything about Billy or whatever the fuck this asshole's name was.

Normally, I could hold my own. Scrap it out when fists were warranted. It was no secret I'd been partner to a brawl or two. I was used to coming out on top. Hell, most of the time, one glance at me was all it took for fuckers to bow out and back away.

Wasn't so sure that track record would land in my favor tonight.

Dude who'd first confronted me back at *Charlie's* about an hour ago, and I'd told him to go straight to hell?

He'd just rolled up behind me and hopped out of his big ass truck.

And he hadn't come alone.

Four of his friends loomed behind him, good old country boys who'd clearly had a few and were eager for a fight.

"You callin' me a liar now, after you fucked my girl?" he spat.

I wanted to do him a solid and tell him he should probably wise up and get himself a new girl if he and I were actually having this conversation. But I was pretty sure that wouldn't be winning me any points.

"Hey, man, I'm sorry if your girl stepped out on you. But I don't take anyone home if I know they've got someone waiting on them back at theirs. Totally not my thing."

At least that little bit was the truth.

I pressed a fist into my opposite palm, widening my stance. Figured he'd either get a clue and get on his merry way, or I was gonna have to fight this one out. I jutted my chin in the direction of his idling truck. "Now, I'd suggest you get back in your ride and go sort this out with her, because it doesn't have anything to do with me."

I spun on my heels, putting my back to them, and started to walk away.

They say hindsight is clear.

Twenty-twenty.

Actually, I'd say she was a bitch because she just never seemed to be around when I needed her most.

Because I'd been playing the streets long enough to know better than this.

Acting cocky when there wasn't a soul around to take up my back.

Do you know another thing they say?

They say pride comes before the fall. Seein' as how I wore pride like a brand, it really shouldn't have come as a surprise.

A whoosh sliced through the heavy air just as something like dread slicked the surface of my skin. I heard the crack before I registered the actual blow to the back of my head.

I roared when an earth-shattering pain cut into my consciousness.

Blackness swam through my sight.

Murky and blinding.

Sucking me under.

I fought it, blinking through the searing torment.

I stumbled forward, but I managed to find my feet. I attempted to whirl back around, hands fisted and ready to go flying.

Because if I was going down, then I was taking the bastard with me.

Second I turned, I caught the gleam of metal right before a rod came crashing down.

Agony blazed as it connected with the side of my face.

With the impact, my head rocked to the side, body following suit as my knees gave.

I flew.

Pavement came up fast, the air nothing but a pained wheeze

in my lungs when I slammed into pitted asphalt.

Blood gushed, cutting a web across my face and dripping to the ground.

I struggled to get to my hands and knees.

To get up.

To fucking do something.

A heavy boot connected with my gut.

A strangled sound shot from my mouth when I slumped back down, and I knew things weren't gonna end well when a clamor of footsteps descended around me.

Hands and feet and that metal pipe.

"Asshole," another voice gritted. My attention darted toward it, my eyes going wide before his fist connected with my face.

That was the last thing I knew before my world went black.

WILLOW

I stepped from the tiny coffee shop. The door drifted shut behind me, and I lifted my face to the sky, which was just breaking with day, that misty hour that cast the world in a woven blanket of grays and purples and blues.

Warmth and hope.

God knew I was clinging to it, hanging on by a quickly unraveling thread.

Wise old oaks strained toward the heavens, spindly branches stretching out as if protecting the solitude of the old buildings lining the street in the Historic District.

Inhaling, I breathed in the invigorating scent of my coffee, the air already thick and bound with the Savannah summer heat. I took a tentative sip of the steaming hot liquid and trudged on toward my little shop as the sun slowly climbed the horizon.

My home.

My sanctuary.

I would do whatever it took to keep it that way.

As I rounded the corner and started down the quaint, narrow road, I dug in my pocket for my keys. My phone rang, and I shuffled my drink and my keys into one hand and dug it free from my purse.

I sighed.

Emily.

But what do they say about counting your blessings? At least it wasn't Bates. I wasn't sure I could handle his expensive brand of manipulation today.

I accepted the call and pushed the phone to my ear. "Hey."

"Are you up?"

"Of course I'm up."

Her voice was light. "The early bird gets the worm."

My laughter was wry. "Not if someone cut off her wings."

Silence crept into the line before she released her own sigh. "You remember the meeting is at three."

Sorrow spun around me. "How could I forget? I'm just...I'm not sure I'm ready to take this step."

I needed more time.

Okay, the truth was, I needed a miracle.

Since I stopped believing in those right around the time I stopped believing in just about everything, time seemed to be about the only thing I could ask for.

When I was a little girl, I'd had so much faith. Believed in dreams and wishes and fate. Believed even the darkest night would eventually bloom with light. What stung the most was the things I'd dreamed of were what most would consider modest.

Simple and right.

Even though I hadn't asked for much, it was everything I'd wanted. Needed.

I'd waited on it.

Counted on it.

But that was before all the most important things in my life had been slowly stripped away.

One by one.

My daddy.

My sister.

My mama.

Lash. Lash. Lash. Until my flesh was raw and wounded, heart bleeding out.

Two years ago, Bates had dealt the final bitter blow.

Belief blown.

"You have to make a decision, Will, or someone else is going to make it for you, and I know you don't want that."

"I know."

She exhaled, and I could almost see my oldest friend pacing her floor. "I'll see you then, okay? Just…think about the options."

The problem was none of the options were ones I wanted to entertain.

"Okay," I promised before I ended the call and turned toward my storefront, key in hand, metal grinding as I slid it into the old lock.

A deep, guttural sound curled through the air.

Quiet.

Stagnant.

Pained.

I froze. A sense of dread took hold of me when in my periphery I registered the darkened heap discarded on a small thatch of grass just off to my left.

Another incoherent moan.

Fear crept down my spine in a chilling wave. Cautiously, I turned. From afar, I searched the man who lay sprawled on his stomach on the lawn, face turned away, dressed all in black. Slowly, I inched that direction, my heart coming as a thunder within the confines of my too-tight chest.

I hoped maybe, maybe it was just a bum, a vagrant who'd scored himself a bottle, spent the night indulging, and was paying for it severely this morning.

That was until I saw blood caked in dark blond hair. The torn, ripped up tee.

That thunder in my chest managed to speed as I took another step forward, keeping my distance as I edged around him.

I gasped.

Blood covered his entire face.

A cut gaped open on his cheek, bottom lip busted wide, beard saturated in oozing red and pebbled with dirt and debris. Bruises littered the muscled arms that were covered in tattoos.

The man was a shattered picture of mayhem and trouble.

God knew it'd found him.

When he whimpered again, I dropped to my knees beside him. My hands were shaking uncontrollably as I frantically dialed 911 and continuously whispered, "It'll be okay, it'll be okay. I promise, it'll be okay."

"911, what's your emergency?"

"I...uh...there's a man in front of my store. He's been beaten. Badly. There's blood everywhere."

"Can you tell me your location?"

I rattled off the address, my knees scooting forward, my eyes peering down.

"Okay, we have an ambulance in route. Is he breathing?"

"Yes," I said immediately, even though my trembling fingers were reaching out, pressing to his neck, his pulse thready and sparse.

He groaned and his eyes fluttered open. Stark against the thick, dark red.

Blue.

So blue and intense they pierced straight through me, their confusion penetrating that vacant, wary place in my heart.

Jesus.

Even with the wounds, the terrifying beauty that stared back at me was striking.

"It's okay," I said again, letting my fingers brush just the side of his face, careful not to touch one of his injuries as I offered him the comfort I somehow knew he needed.

He winced and muttered something that sounded like, "Please."

A siren screamed from the main road and grew louder as it turned down the normally quiet, peaceful street.

"Shh," I said. "It's okay. I promise it will be okay."

ASH

*S*tark *white light blazed from above.*

Blood.

Splatters.

Handprints.

Smears.

Grief, horror, and shock.

A sob wrenched free, and I dropped to my knees, gathered her in my arms, rocked her and rocked her while I begged and pled.

No.

Body cold. Face ashen.

Agony. Agony. Agony.

"No. Anna, no. God, please, no."

I shot up to sitting. Disoriented, gasping, sweat slicking my skin as I struggled for my missing breath. Frantic, my eyes darted around the darkened room.

Bleeps of monitors. The hospital bed I was lying in and the IV tube stuck in my arm. The faint hustle of nursing staff on the other side of the door.

"Shit," I hissed, trying to shake the nagging dread of the dream. One I hadn't had in fucking years. One I wouldn't ever be able to stomach.

So I shoved it down.

Where it belonged.

Forgotten.

Because some realities should never exist.

"Oh, hell no, I'm not getting in that thing. I can stand on my own two feet." I struggled to stand from the hospital bed, wincing like a bitch when stabbing pain shot down my side.

Fuck.

And here I thought Savannah was supposed to be relaxing. A safe haven away from all the craziness of Los Angeles.

"You sure about that?" A smirk ticked up at the corner of Baz's mouth, dude taunting me with a wheelchair like I was some kind of invalid, popping it into a wheelie where he rolled it back and forth in the middle of the room. "Been looking forward to taking you for a ride for the whole day. Payback for the shit you put us through over the last three days."

I forced myself to stand straight. "Ha. Not a chance am I giving you the reins to that sled. You'd probably *actually* break something." I lifted my arms out to the sides. "Besides, I'm good as new."

Okay. That was a goddamned lie. I actually felt like I'd been run over by a Freightliner. But I wasn't about to let a few assholes keep me down.

I raked a hand over my tender head and looked around. "You bring me clothes?"

He tossed a duffle on the bed. "Yep."

"Thank God. The last three days my ass has been playing peek-a-boo with the nurses. Poor things didn't know what to do with themselves."

I mean, seriously, I might as well have gone buck for all the good this ridiculous gown did me.

I turned and started pulling clean clothes out of the bag, talking to Baz over my shoulder as I did. "The worst part of the whole bit was bein' out of commission. Now that shit was painful. All that deliciousness walking in and out of here, doting on me, and not being able to do a damned thing about it." I shot him a wink. "Tragic."

Baz scoffed. "I would have thought that ass kickin' might have taught you a lesson or two. Hope that chick was worth it."

Yeah, no chick was worth that shit. Especially not one that'd been lying through her teeth when I'd asked her square about the ring she was sporting on her finger. Her grandma's, my ass.

I forced a wide grin, fighting the bit of bitterness wanting to take root in my chest. "She was a straight ten on the crazy/hot matrix. Men just don't have the capacity to resist that kind of disaster."

Baz shook his head. "Whatever, dude, you just go on tellin' yourself that."

Something somber filtered into the room, and I paused, setting my favorite tee down on the bed. I pushed a weighted breath from my lungs. "I fucked up, man. I'm sorry. Last thing I wanted was to let you guys down."

Sunder was supposed to be hitting the studio next week, which was why we were in Savannah in the first place. Three years ago, I'd purchased a big old house here. My home away from home. A quiet place to take a break from the insane pace of Los Angeles. Figured I'd need a killer pad where I could kick back and entertain the ladies whenever I was in town, considering this was going to be Baz's home base. He and his wife, Shea, had shacked up here permanently since this was where they wanted to raise their kids.

Though it'd been a long time coming, Baz had officially stepped down from the band last year, and his baby brother, Austin, had stepped up to take his place as lead.

Baz had bought our manager's place out on Tybee Island. The mansion was already equipped with a kickass recording studio, so it only made sense Baz would be the one to produce our next album rather than standing out front.

Yeah, he wanted out of the limelight and tours, far away from the chaos and revelry that surrounded this crazy lifestyle, but that didn't mean he wanted distance from the music. Least of all, distance from us—this awesome, mismatched family that had come together back when we were nothin' but punk teenagers and somehow had managed to create something great.

Each of us had gotten a place out here in Savannah for the months we spent recording.

Baz cocked his head like he was trying to get a read on me while a wave of guilt hit me hard.

It was no secret *Sunder* had endured a whole ton of shit. We'd barely made it through addictions and jail sentences and the death of our drummer, Mark. The whole world had pretty much been waiting on the final pin to drop and the threads that held us together to finally completely unravel. Truth of the matter was, the fate of *Sunder* had been in limbo for a whole lot of years.

Now that things were finally coming together again? I'd thrown in yet another wrench, and I was out of commission for at least six weeks.

Regret curled in my stomach.

Me fucking up the band hadn't exactly been on the agenda.

Baz exhaled heavily. "I know, Ash. I know. But you gotta know you scared the hell out of us. Your sister's been beside herself. Our girls are freaking the hell out, and all the guys want to go hunt the motherfuckers down. You and I both know that's the last thing the band needs. Can't afford more trouble, man. One of these times, you're not gonna be so lucky, and I'm gonna wake up to a call I don't want to get. This was bad enough."

Lucky.

A strange sense twisted through me. A flicker of a memory. Chocolate eyes. Soft, soft touch. Peaches.

Guess maybe that concussion had fucked up my mind worse than I'd thought.

I blinked through it, forced out the words, "Here on out, I'll be more careful. Promise you."

He and I both knew that was a whole ton easier said than done.

I chose to live my life like every day might be my last.

Reckless.

I embraced the chaos and the nonstop women and the endless nights.

Live fast and die hard.

Didn't want it any other way.

My devotion? It was wholly reserved for this family, and this family only. The boys and the band. Their wives and their kids. My baby sister.

Other than that?

All I wanted from each day was a little fun. To reach out and take all the pleasure the world had to give. Embrace it instead of laying all my days to waste, without the morbid consequence of getting tied down.

I'd leave that bullshit for my brothers.

As far as I was concerned? That was safer than getting a taste of *peace* and having it stripped away. Only fools put themselves on the line. Fell in love like it could last. Shouldered the responsibility and burden before it became all too clear they couldn't stand up under the weight.

Learned that lesson the hard way a long time ago.

A fist rapped on the open door. I turned to find our drummer and my roommate, Zee, standing there. "Lyrik and Austin have the Suburban idling out front. You ready to hit it?"

"Yeah. Just let me change real quick. Unless one of you assholes wants to give me a sponge bath before I go?" I tossed out the tease, hoping to lighten the mood. Hated I was the one responsible for making it heavy.

That shit was totally not my thing.

But I could see the worry written all over their faces as they wondered what I was going to do now. Because like Baz had said about the boys—right about now retaliation was sounding really damned good.

I inclined my head toward the door. A clear request for them to step out.

A scoff shot from Baz's nose. "Like we haven't seen your naked ass a million times? Now, you're gonna get shy?"

"Just need a minute, man."

Truth was, I didn't want either of them to see the mess hiding beneath this gown.

Baz frowned before he nodded like he got it. They both stepped out to give me some privacy.

I changed slowly, trying not to look at the bruises covering every inch of my body, the stitches tying up the cuts, the big bandage covering the staples from the surgery on the lower left side of my abdomen.

Proof I wasn't invincible.

Funny how I'd refused to think twice about the end until the end was staring me in the face.

A couple minutes later, Baz clicked open the door. "You good?"

"Yup."

He and Zee helped me gather my things then Baz jutted his chin to the wheelchair. "You sure you don't need that? One of these nurses who has been 'doting' on you is bound to have a fit."

I laughed. "Hell no. Can't keep a good man down."

Zee cracked up. "Good? I'm thinking there are probably a few thousand ladies scattered around the world who would be eager to call you something other than *good*."

I rocked my hips, the motion not quite as enthusiastic as normal. "You're right, man, they would all be claiming I'm the *best*."

He shook his head, muttered under his breath, "Always such

an asshole." Of course he couldn't hide the smile climbing to his face.

I hobbled my way down the hall and to the elevator, letting the guys lead me out. It was just the way they were. Always there. Standing at my side. Taking up my back.

Automatic doors slid open as we headed through the exit, the bright Savannah sun blinding as I stepped out into the light for the first time in three days.

I breathed in the hot, humid air.

A swell of gratitude grew in my gut.

The fact I had another day to live.

This crazy life to embrace.

A thick intensity wrapped me whole.

Energy shimmered through the air.

The hairs at the nape of my neck stood on end.

Not like they did the other night. But in a different kind of awareness.

I turned my gaze to the small silver SUV idling across the lot and the big chocolate eyes that stared back at me. Even through the window, there was no mistaking them.

So fucking familiar.

My chest tightened so painfully it almost felt good.

"Let's get you out of here." My attention slid to Baz as he opened the front passenger door. I nodded and glanced back at the car. Couldn't kick the fascination drawing me that way.

Because whoever she was?

There was no question she saved my life.

And that was a debt I didn't have the first clue how to repay.

WILLOW

The harsh Savannah sun lit up the bank of windows that overlooked the street running the front of my tiny store.

Not a soul had come through the door for the entire day, which was a huge part of the problem, but I couldn't help but find comfort in the solitude.

From where she was in the back office, I could barely discern the soft, hushed movements of Emily as she worked. The steady *clack*, *clack*, *clack* of the keyboard, a muted slide of metal as the file cabinet opened and closed, the drone of an obsolete fan.

Humidity draped the dusty atmosphere, the motes thick and sluggish as they danced through beams of light that sliced through the windows. The old swamp cooler whirred, doing its best to compensate, but not coming close to making a dent in the heat.

A calm quiet filled the space, broken only by the soothing sound of sandpaper as I ran it over the wood again and again.

Scratch. Scratch. Scratch.

Revealing the beauty hidden underneath.

Behind the counter, which was painted a rustic teal, I sat hunched over the antique piece I'd found abandoned beside a dumpster. Left like rotted garbage without worth.

It was almost funny how I found my greatest solace in broken-down relics that had been left for decay. But my mama—she'd taught me how to recognize the value in discarded objects. To find what was concealed by peeling paint and splintered cracks.

To look deeper than the surface.

Hit with a wave of sorrow, my chest clenched painfully. Searching deeper had been what I'd done all my life. Believing the best in the ones I loved.

Pouring out my support and encouragement.

My faith.

Bit by bit, that faith had been chipped away.

For a beat, I mashed my eyes closed against the assault of memories. My teeth gritted, and I increased the pressure against the grains of the wood, rubbing the corrupted away to expose the good underneath.

Finding the beauty I knew.

The beauty I trusted.

I got lost in it, entranced in my work. So engrossed I gasped when the bell above the door jingled. Startled, my head jerked up and my heart sped—an erratic pound against my ribs.

My eyes squinted against the blinding rays of late-afternoon sun, which spilled in like a flash flood behind the man who suddenly took up the entirety of my doorway.

He was cast in shadows.

A darkened silhouette of mystery backlit by a burning ring of flames.

Fire.

I could feel it sparking in the air. Energy and power and heat.

Just as real as the humidity that clung to my sweat drenched skin.

And I knew.

I knew with the way my pulse stuttered and a prick of fear needled across my flesh that this was the man I hadn't been able to rid from my mind for the last week. The one who'd stolen my sleep. The memory of his battered face had left me with a deep-rooted sense of worry and the terrifying beauty beneath had overwhelmed me with an intense sense of intrigue.

Finally, he took a single step forward.

Fully exposing himself.

My breath got locked somewhere in the back of my throat, and that fear kicked up an extra notch, just as a rush of attraction slipped like liquid steel through my veins.

I didn't move. I just froze with my hand still clutching the sandpaper brick as I stared.

As if he were a piece of morbid art.

A statue of broken stone.

Captivating.

Magnetic.

Imposing.

Throat dry, my eyes wandered. Like a primal need spurred me to search out his wounds. Tracing the line of stitches running just beneath his eye, the deep bruises surrounding it, the lacerations and discolorations that marred the intricate riddle of ink woven like a puzzle on his strong, strong arms.

Heat flared.

Thinking it felt like a sin, but it seemed the only thing the inflicted trauma had managed was to make him appear like a conquering warrior who'd returned home from battle.

Every sculpted inch of his big body bristled with strength. The rippling, defined muscle was only accentuated by the black tee, which stretched tight over his wide, wide chest.

I'd seen him from a distance. In that moment, when I'd finally succumbed to the need to see him again, I'd convinced myself I just needed to know he was okay. Because God knew, this man had affected me some way, seeing him there, fractured and broken.

Seeing him now?

It was overwhelming.

The intensity that swirled around us as he stood there, those blue eyes taking me in as if he were searching me the same.

Then he tipped me the cockiest smirk I'd ever seen.

Dimples peeked out from both of his cheeks, deep and dancing with the promise of mischief. In that second, he almost looked…cute. No doubt, that made him a hundred times more dangerous than I'd ever imagined.

"Hey there, darlin'." His voice was just as deep as those dimples. Rough and raw and skating my skin like a rugged caress.

What was wrong with me? This wasn't me. But I knew where it was bred. This crazy connection I felt to a man simply because I'd stumbled upon his darkest hour. Like I'd become a partner to him. Cared for him in a moment we never should have shared.

I gulped, slowly stood, and attempted to brush some of the dust and debris from my work clothes. My smile was timid as I tentatively rounded the counter.

"You're here." It wobbled from my mouth on a breathy whisper.

He stretched his arms out to the sides, a full-blown smirk taking hold, tone taking on an edge of playfulness. "What? Don't tell me you aren't excited to see me. I mean, I'm kinda unforgettable and I figured by now you'd be missin' me. So here I am."

He tossed it out like a casual tease. Just by that grin, I would guess easy-going to be his normal MO if the situation he'd found himself in wasn't so serious.

His tone deepened. "Tell me you didn't miss me."

I gulped.

Apparently, his ego was about as big as the rest of him.

He must have sensed my struggling, because that smirk slipped and grew into something genuine, dipping into a smile that tugged at me from all sides. "I'm Ash. Ash Evans."

I knew his name. The policeman had used it when he'd questioned me, asking what I knew and any information I could give, which had been about zero, considering I'd never seen the man before in my life.

"I'm Willow. Willow Langston." It came off unnerved. Because that was the way this boy made me. Shaky and shy.

His head cocked to the side and his grin only grew, those eyes roving fast, up and down my body. As if he were attempting to find something hidden inside me.

"It's nice to officially meet you, Willow. Seems I owe you a thank you or an apology or maybe both."

I wrung my hands together. "You don't need to thank me. I did what anyone else would have done. I'm just glad to see you standing."

He chuckled, though it sounded with disbelief. "Don't owe you a thank you? I owe you a whole lot more than just a thank you. You saved my life."

My brow pinched. "No…I…I was just coming to work. If it hadn't have been me, someone else would have found you."

"Yeah, and they might have been a second too late. Or maybe they would have looked the other way. It doesn't matter that it *could* have been someone else. Only thing that matters to me is that it *was* you."

Energy spun. Filling up the space. I nodded slowly. "Okay, then, you're welcome."

Laughter shocked me as it bounded through the dense air— sudden and loud and free.

As if he were astounded by the simplicity of my statement. As if he thought it were the cutest thing he'd ever heard. The air surrounding him went light, a stark, jarring contradiction to the fierceness he ushered in moments before.

My head spun and that thunder stampeded in my heart.

"Oh no, Willow. Here I was, acting the asshole, mucking up the front of your pretty store, lying out there like a piece of trash for you to find in the morning. Pretty sure I might have derailed whatever plans you had for the day. Might have turned your stomach, too, because that shit wasn't pretty. I'm here to make it up to you. Anything you want. Name it, and it's yours."

Wow.

"That's an awful lofty promise you're making there, Mr. Evans."

"A promise I intend to keep."

My stomach tightened. I didn't know this guy. But what I did know? He was so much more than I could handle. Everything already felt fragile and brittle. Ready to crack. And here he was, shaking me up more.

"Like I said, it's not necessary." My refusal felt like nothing less than a defense.

His head tipped and his teeth raked across the scab on his bottom lip. Dark blond hair flopped to the side. Hair that was shaved on both sides and longer on top. It only added to the vibe that he was some kind of glorious avenger with a wicked smile and a wayward tongue.

"How about we start with dinner and we can go from there? Least I can do."

A scatter of butterflies lifted in my belly and frantically flapped their wings. Because I was attracted to this man in a way I'd never been with anyone before. Not even with Bates. Bates had been a slow love. The kind I'd grown into. The kind that was supposed to be permanent.

That right there was reason enough for me to step away.

"That's a bad idea."

"Bad idea, huh?"

I nodded.

Yep. Terrible, horrible, bad idea.

Because I didn't have any place left inside myself to get ripped up and torn to pieces.

And somehow I knew this man would tear me to shreds.

His eyes narrowed before he turned away. He began meandering through my store as if he were just another customer browsing the selection, his presence bold as his big hands reached out, fingertips running the wood and fluttering over the designs of the reclaimed antiques that hung from the walls.

Contemporary Comfort had been my mother's dream. She'd always wanted a tiny antique store tucked deep in the heart of the Historic District of Savannah, and had opened it on her forty-sixth birthday. I'd been four. My sister and I had basically grown up surrounded by sanders and paint strippers in the back room that acted as wood shop and storage.

This place had always been my comfort and my play before it'd become my everything.

It was the last thing I had left.

Anger vibrated in my spirit.

And now Bates would be responsible for taking it away, too.

He tugged at an old fashioned price tag tied to a rocking chair with a piece of thin twine. I'd painted it a country red then sanded it down until dappled spots of smooth white wood peeked through.

A frown pulled at his brow, and he continued on, doing the same, piece after piece. For whatever reason, I felt uneasy watching him browse. It felt as if by digging through my art, he were sifting through my mind.

I had this pain in my gut, an intuition that urged me to beg him to stop, but I found I was unable to form the words.

Ever so slowly, he turned and stared back at me. His question sounded like an accusation. "Why's everything half off?"

"Because I'm trying to weed out some things."

Lie. Lie. Lie.

I was sure it was obvious, too. I'd never been any good at hiding things. I wore my emotions on my sleeve for everyone to see. It was why I'd pretty much hidden out here where it was safe for the last two years.

His forehead twisted. "Where does this stuff come from?"

I attempted to clear the rawness from my throat. "I find it and then resell it."

He stared in my direction, those blue eyes ablaze as they narrowed to slits. Heavy boots echoed on the hardwood floors. My pulse lit up in a steady *bang, bang, bang* the closer he came.

"Then why does everything...look the same? And I don't

mean the *same*. Looks like it all came from the same place. The same hand."

Shock stilled me. I was completely surprised this man who seemed larger than life would take the time to actually notice something like that.

I hesitated, before the admission scraped free. "Because I find what's broken and put it back together."

Awareness hung between us, before something significant tilted his head to the side. "Huh. Finding the broken and putting it back together seems to be your specialty, now doesn't it?" he said, voice dropping with the implication.

The man inched closer.

Shivers rolled.

God, I needed to get him out of here. Because he was clouding my senses. Distorting my judgment. Making me entertain thoughts I had no business entertaining.

Whoever this man was, he lived a million miles from my world, and I clearly had no place being a part of his.

Besides, I recognized his type. And his type definitely didn't want what I had to give.

Trouble was written all over him in broad streaks and bright lights.

His lips pressed together in contemplation as he approached.

I blinked toward the ground, wanting to run and hide, yet my feet were pinned to the floor.

"Tell me why you're sellin' out."

"She's selling out because she's going under."

We both jerked our attention to the intruding voice. Emily stood in the doorway to the back, tossing out my business as if it was hers to give.

My mouth dropped open. "Emily," I reprimanded, hard and fast.

"What?" she said, shaking her head as if she were disappointed in me. Her blonde ponytail swished behind her as she stepped out behind the counter. "It's nothin' but the truth, Willow. Maybe if you stop lying to everyone around you, you might stop lyin' to yourself."

I loved her.

I did.

But right then, I wanted to throttle her for embarrassing me this way—right in front of this man who was already ruining something inside me.

Ash looked back at me before turning away again, eyes skating the store. "Yeah?" he uttered like an inciting question. "How much?"

His attention turned back to the woman who was supposed to be my best friend. The one who'd been there for me through thick and thin. And here she was, ratting me out. "Fifty thousand."

"Done," he said as if it didn't cost him a lick.

Anger spiraled through my body, and my hands clenched into fists at my sides. Who I was angriest with, I wasn't sure. "Oh no…there's no chance on God's green earth you're giving me a dime. I'm no beggar, Mr. Evans."

"Owe you," he returned, blue eyes flashing white fire.

"No way. My mama taught me to work hard for what I have." There was a chance I stomped my foot like a petulant child. "And I promise you, that isn't about to change now. Any trouble I've gotten myself into, I brought on myself, and I'll be the one working myself out of it."

It was out before I could stop it.

"So, you're telling me you need to work it off?" That flirty tease was back in full force, and damn it, my heart did that crazy thing, that battering *bang, bang, bang.*

My own eyes narrowed. "I'm no one's whore."

He laughed. Laughed so hard he howled. "Oh, darlin', make no mistake, taking you to my bed sounds about like the best idea you've ever had. Looks to me like you might need it, too, and I promise, I don't disappoint. But I had something else in mind."

Dumbfounded, I just stared, waiting for him to explain.

"You see, I have this big old rambling house that just might fit your flare. Most of it has already been renovated. All except for my bedroom that's been waiting on something extra special to come along. Think I might have found it."

My head shook. "I don't—"

"What do you say you come to my place and pour all the love you obviously pour into this place into that room? Decorate it. Paint it. Fill it with the furniture you've restored. Leave your touch all over it. My budget is *big*."

The innuendo was blatant.

"And believe me, I'll sleep better at night."

I sucked in a breath.

"And you'll pay her fifty thousand plus renovation costs?" This from my best friend who seemed to have no issue throwing me under the bus. But I knew her intentions. They were good and she was only trying to help out. But I got the feeling she was only making matters worse.

"Gladly," he said. "Upfront and in full."

"This is a bad idea," I whispered again, but this boy just took one step closer. He was so close that I was breathing his air, all man and sex and danger.

He wound a single lock of my hair through his fingers and lifted it to his nose. He inhaled deeply then exhaled the words as a whisper against my cheek. "Peaches…just what I thought."

He stepped away, grabbed a pen from the counter, and scribbled his address on a scrap of paper.

Then he strode out the door, tossing out a casual, "I'll see you Monday, darlin'," as he went.

He left me a gaping, confounded mess in the middle of my store.

ASH

I sat staring up at the wooden sign hanging out beside her door. It gently swung on the metal hinges.

The wood was carved with the store's name.

Contemporary Comfort.

Chiseled next to the words was the store's logo. A dandelion that had gone to seed. The stem was curved and a portion of the little white tufts swirled up from the floret like they'd been lifted by the wind. They danced across the top of the carving, getting smaller and smaller before they disappeared.

A frown pulled between my eyes, and I squeezed the steering wheel.

Couldn't help but feel shaken.

Staggered.

Like I owed this girl more than I could ever give.

It didn't help that just looking at her knocked the breath from my lungs.

Fuck.

She was gorgeous.

Big chocolate eyes.

Face like one of those classic heirlooms displayed in the cases on her counter.

Body a temple of seduction that had me shakin' at the knees.

Not to mention the hint of a honeyed drawl. Every word that dropped from those full, red lips shot straight to my dick.

All of it was wrapped in this mind-blowing talent I'd recognized the second I'd stepped through her door.

The sum of it amounted to this fascinating girl who was shy and sweet and fierce.

It took about all I had not to bury my face in those mahogany locks and get a real good whiff of peaches. That scent had been haunting my mind since I'd woken up in that hospital bed. It'd required all my restraint not to let my nose go trailing across the expanse of creamy skin I was betting would be sweeter than sugar.

I was well-accustomed to reaching out and just taking the things I wanted. Used to having them laid at my feet like an offering.

I both loved it and hated it that her first reaction was to shoot me down. Thing was, I usually liked easy and, in my world, there was plenty of *easy* to go around.

Not this girl.

What got me most was this familiarity that wouldn't let go. It was a sense of being tied to her in some fundamental way.

Knew it was the fact she'd saved me.

She'd bound herself to me in a way I was sure neither of us could quite understand.

They said traumas did that to people. Tangled their souls together, and I couldn't stop feeling like mine was tangled with hers.

More than that? I'd seen it—blazing hot in those molten eyes. That same unsettled intrigue she was feeling for me. That pull that had ricocheted between us.

Combustible.

Mix the two together, and I was sure we'd be a flash fire.

It'd be really stupid for me to even consider going there. I got the feelin' I wasn't the only one who couldn't afford it. My boundaries hadn't been set in stone for nothing.

I cast one last glance at the big windows, which glittered and gleamed with the reflection of the sun. Somehow I knew she was still standing there, staring out.

Resolution took hold of my spirit.

At least saving this place was one thing I could afford.

WILLOW

*T*he expensive dark gray SUV pulling away from the curb seemed to snap me back into reality. A rush of disordered anger came sliding back.

I turned all my attention on Emily, who was reorganizing some trinkets behind the counter as if she didn't have a care in the world.

"What were you thinking?" I demanded, taking a step her direction.

She looked up, blinked back at me with feigned innocence in her light blue eyes. "What do you mean?"

"You know exactly what I mean. How could you have told

a complete stranger that? You made me look desperate and pathetic."

A scoff climbed from the back of her throat. "In case you hadn't noticed, Will, you *are* desperate. I've gone over the books a hundred times. Looking for something…*anything* that would help you. And come next month, you aren't gonna have the money for your mama, the house, and the store. The foreclosure *will* kick in. There are no more extensions. You've taken the last of what they're willing to give. And you know what they say, desperate times come for desperate measures, and that *measure* just walked out your door."

Emily Matsy and I had been friends since second grade, and she had stepped in to help me when things had gone south.

Way, way south.

She was the only person left alive that I trusted. The fact she'd basically been working for me for free for the last two years to keep this place afloat promised me where her loyalties lay. I knew she was just looking out for me, trying to find a solution I'd begged her to find.

She shrugged as if that solution was plain as day. "You saved him, Will, and now he wants to save you. That right there is what they call fair. This isn't you being needy or getting a handout. That boy walked in here wanting to repay you, and he couldn't have found you at a better time."

She tipped her head to the side, all coy and cute. "I'd go so far as to call it kismet."

Kismet.

I suppressed bitter laughter.

Well, I'd already established a long time ago fate wasn't my friend, so her argument wasn't winning her any points.

Frustration tugged at my forehead. "That wasn't your choice to make. I'm not even qualified to do a job like he's asking me to do…let alone one he's going to pay me *fifty thousand dollars* for."

That in and of itself was insanity. Madness.

"What if I mess it up? Disappoint him? Besides that, I don't even *know* him, and I'm supposed to show up at his house on

Monday?"

Panic and intrigue and some of that attraction I didn't want to feel took turns doing backflips through my belly. I blinked, almost begged the words. "God, Em, who has fifty thousand dollars just lying around? I mean, did you *see* him? He could be a drug dealer or a hit man or maybe one of those bikers…like…like in that show you forced me into watching?"

Yes. Yes. That had to be it. No man could be that recklessly gorgeous without having some dark skeletons lurking in his closet.

Her eyebrows disappeared behind her bangs, the words a disbelieving mutter all mixed up with an incredulous chuckle. "You really don't get out much, do you, Will?"

"What does that have to do with anything?"

Laughing quietly, she shook her head. "You honestly don't know who he is? All last week when you were completely distracted and on edge—and don't pretend like you didn't give me a reason to notice—you didn't look him up?"

Nervously, I rubbed the pads of my fingertips against my thumb. "Of course not. That's rude."

Not that showing up at the hospital because I couldn't stop thinking about him wasn't.

Of course, I'd stayed in my car, unable to force myself to get out of it and just go inside. I had sat for almost twenty minutes, debating back and forth over my foolishness, but then he'd come striding out.

He'd robbed me of breath when he'd stood there, that hypnotizing gaze searching, as if he felt me.

Right then was when I knew I needed to stop entertaining dangerous thoughts about a clearly dangerous man.

And then he'd just turned around and come waltzing through my door.

On a sigh, Emily turned to the back counter, grabbed her iPad she'd left sitting there, and tapped something into it. She slid it across the counter in my direction.

"What is this?"

"See for yourself."

Tentatively, I took a step forward, then another, eyes peering down, wary to find the secrets revealed on the screen.

My stomach twisted and that fearful allure flamed.

Sunder.

The man who'd been haunting my days and stalking my nights stood in a group of men on a stage. Each of them gorgeous. Brilliant and intimidating. Bad and bold and confident.

But the only one I could see was the man who stood to the right with a bass guitar strapped around his big body, power in his stance and an arrogant smirk riding his too-attractive face.

Ash Evans.

I was such an idiot. I should have seen it from a mile away.

The entirety of Savannah had been abuzz over its new larger than life residents that had taken the city by storm three years ago. The band from LA had rolled into town and ignited an uproar of gossip and speculation.

Paparazzi had descended, and all of a sudden, things around here had become far more interesting.

These boys had been both a blemish and a gain.

But never in a million years would I have imagined I'd cross paths with one of them because I wasn't exactly the type who stepped out and into the places these types of boys frequented.

And of course the one that stepped into my lane had to be the one who made me tremble and question and want.

A crash collision.

Beautiful chaos.

Ash Evans was famous for all the things I despised. That over-the-top, seedy rock star lifestyle. Easy sex and squandered days.

I wasn't sure *rock star* was any safer than any of the other options I'd tossed out.

"I don't know if I can do this." It was a whisper.

Emily slammed the old-timey register shut. "No, Will? You really think you can't? You want to let your mama's dream go? That dream she instilled in you? Give up and give in when you have a solution staring right back at you? Fine. Go ahead. But I promise you, you're gonna regret it for the rest of your life. You're the one who told me you'd be willing to do just about anything to save this store. It meant *that* much to you."

She was right. But this felt...different. Terrifying and exhilarating. That seemed a hazardous combination.

Blue eyes narrowed as they stared me down. "But before you decide to throw it all away, I think you'd better answer yourself a couple questions...like why it is you're actually sayin' no."

On the other side of the counter, she took a step my way, her tone pointed and severe. "Because yes, I *saw* him. And yes, I saw the way he was looking at you, too, and I sure didn't miss the way you were looking at him."

"I..." That one word was a fumble of my own doubts and reservations. In myself. In this mysterious man that elicited something I didn't want him to. In all the choices I'd made up to this point in my life and the ones I wanted to make for my future.

They spun around me like an approaching storm.

She swallowed hard, her attention darting to the wall before she looked back at me. "I know you're scared of stepping out of your bubble. Of moving on. But it's time. You've lost so much through these years, and I know it feels like more than you can bear."

"Em—" I pleaded.

She cut me off with a sharp shake of her head. "What makes it even worse is Bates trying to weasel his way back into your life after everything he did. But it's been two years, Will. Two years of you barely getting by after he betrayed you. Two years of you barely breaking the surface. You keep on this way and you're gonna drown."

I looked to my feet as I absorbed the words she said.

She moved toward the back-office. She paused in the doorway, hesitating, before she looked back at me. "And do you honestly think for one second you're not qualified for that job? All those interior design classes you took? Those dreams you had? You were so close to finishing, Will. Bates somehow manipulated you into thinking it wasn't important. That you weren't good enough. Are you gonna let all the bullshit lies he fed you *matter*? Because not a word he's ever said to you matters unless you let them."

A rush of air left my lungs as she disappeared into the back, and I pressed my hands to the counter, trying to get my senses. To find a solution. All the lessons my mama ever taught me floated around me, just out of reach.

Chase your dreams.

Loneliness swamped me, and without another thought, I grabbed my purse and flew out the door.

"Hi, Mama," I murmured quietly as I brushed back a lifeless curl of gray hair from her forehead. I pressed a lingering kiss there. Breathed her in. Filled my lungs as full as they would go with the familiar scent of baby powder and lilacs and a vestige of this awful place.

She flinched and blinked up at me in confusion as I interrupted her journey to whatever faraway time and place she'd gone.

I sat back, giving her space, while my eyes traced the portrait in front of me. A portrait drawn in a patchwork of wrinkles and lines, her weathered face the story of an age and laughter and years of hard work.

She'd always been my rock. My firm foundation. My definition of strength. Maybe that's why seeing her body and mind taken hostage by her disease hurt that much worse. The slow deterioration that had ultimately left her confined to this bed.

Her glassy, brown eyes lit up in her own recognition, the words barely formed on her dried lips. "Willow? Is that you, sweet one?"

Pain wrenched through me like a blade, and I smiled a sad

smile, willing my tears away as I brushed my fingertips tenderly down her cheek. "Of course it's me."

One side of her mouth tweaked, before her eyes grew distant, and she got lost in her mind.

I hated seeing her this way.

Each day whittled away by the diagnosis she'd gotten right after my sister was born. Growing up, I'd always known my mama had multiple sclerosis. It was a common phrase in our home, something my sister and I fearfully whispered to each other in those times when she'd hug us and her eyes would seem so sad when she'd whisper, "It's just a bad day. It'll pass."

She always got better.

Until the day she didn't.

Stress makes it worse.

That's what the doctor had said.

It sure didn't help things when my daddy had up and left us when those "bad days" came closer and closer together.

After we lost Summer? My mama had spiraled fast and she'd never gotten out of bed again.

End stage.

That's what they called it.

Maybe I'd been a foolish child, but I hadn't prepared myself for this—for this ultimate outcome—when her arms and legs would no longer cooperate. When the painful spasticity would set in and her muscles would lock in spasms that would never let her go.

On top of that, I'd had to sit and watch helplessly as her mind also gave, her lucency coming and going with the disease and the medicines they gave her to make her comfortable.

I gently shifted her arm where her fist was pressed up too tight to her chin, my voice just as gentle. "How are you feeling today, Mama?"

I got no response, just her distant eyes. Tears gathered in mine, and I pulled the chair up close next to her, my words quiet as I confided in the one person who had always understood me.

"The store's been in trouble, Mama." I bit my lip, glanced away, before I turned back to her. "I didn't mean to let it happen.

I'm so sorry. I never meant to be careless with your dream."

Her dream that had become my own.

I brushed my fingers through her hair. "Sometimes love gets in the way, doesn't it?"

She'd always taught me love was the most important of all the things we'd ever be given in our lives. I just didn't know how to reconcile the two, choosing to love and what it'd cost me in the end.

My throat felt scratchy when I continued, "But I have a chance to make it right. Save the store. I want to, Mama, I want to so bad, but I'm terrified I'm going to turn around and mess everything up again."

Change was always a risk, and after Bates, I'd spent the last two years making sure to encounter the fewest *risks* possible, isolating myself from the world that seemed intent to gobble me up until there wasn't anything left. Funny how I still stood to lose it all.

"What do you think, Mama? Is it worth the risk?"

I didn't expect a response, but her glassy eyes were on me, soft and filled with the love and belief she'd always had in me. "When is the answer to that ever anything other than *chase your dreams.* Always, Willow. Always."

A tear slipped down my cheek, and her smile trembled as she struggled to stay focused on me, but her eyes began to flutter as she started to fade away.

I felt desperate to hold on to her for one moment more.

I wrapped my hand around her tightened fist, squeezed. *Mama…you're the only one I have left. Don't leave me. I need you so much.*

My silent plea was left unheard as her raspy, labored breaths slowed with her sleep.

I gasped around the grief that crashed through my body and tried to subdue my cries, feeling lonelier than I had ever before.

Piece by piece.

Heart by heart.

Why did everyone important to me get ripped away?

It's crazy when the last thing you want is to be alone, yet

you hide away so there's no chance of ever having someone else stolen from you.

My sister's face whirled behind my eyes. So vibrant. So full of life.

Gone.

But my mama...

I looked down at her weathered face.

My mama had always taught me if something was important enough, you never gave up or let go. I stood up and pressed a kiss to her forehead. I whispered against her skin, "Always."

seven

ASH

"*A*ssholes are still out there, man." Lyrik raked a tattooed hand through the crop of his pitch-black hair.

"Yeah."

"So, what are we gonna do about that?"

"Not sure there's anything to do…don't even have a name to go on."

Just five fucking faces taunting me in the recesses of my mind and a litany of scars to show for them.

"And what happens if you run into them again?"

I cracked a wry grin. "Hope to God you're with me."

"*Pssh*…you think you need me to back your ass up? Big burly fucker like you? I'm disappointed you couldn't handle them. That shit's embarrassing." His mouth twisted with the razzing I totally deserved, considering I was normally the one meting it out.

"Sometimes a man just has to admit when he's outnumbered."

He eyed me with those dark eyes, his favorite guitar settled across his lap. His fingers pressed down, and he strummed a single chord, flashing his upper knuckles that read *Sing My Soul*. Though now his left lower knuckles read *Blue* and the right *Adia* since the guy had finally found something real to sing for.

"You sure you don't want to try to press the police to track them down? You weren't exactly helpful when they questioned you."

I let my fingers glide along the strings of my bass, plucking out a few notes. "Nah, man, you know that's not how we take care of shit."

He shook his head. "That's exactly what I'm afraid of."

"Before I step through your door, I need you to understand I'm not qualified to do what you're asking me to do."

Energy pulsed between us.

A fucking live wire.

All weekend, I'd been questioning if I'd imagined it. Would be no surprise if the bash to my head had made me a little bit insane. But I was thinking now it just might be this girl who was the culprit.

So maybe I'd spent the last three days wondering if she'd actually show.

Wondering what that would mean.

Second-guessing why I insisted she'd come here in the first place.

God knew I could have cut her a check and let her off the

hook.

So what if it was relief I felt when I found her standing in my doorway, wringing her dainty hands, a bag slung over her shoulder? She wore a pair of fitted jeans and a super thin, loose sweater that slinked over her in all the right ways, all mahogany waves and chocolate eyes and sweet sunshine.

I wanted to put my mouth on her and take a good long drink.

"Says who?" I demanded low.

She shook her head with a flustered huff. "Says the fact I have no degree and not a whole lot of training. I've never even attempted to tackle a job of this size before."

I gave a harsh shake of my head. "Says the girl who has a store full of kickass furniture she refurbished herself. Wouldn't ask you inside if I didn't have the confidence you would give me exactly what I'm lookin' for."

I lifted my arms out to the sides, gesturing to the massive house towering around us. "This here's my baby, darlin'. Second I passed her by, she called out to me, and I knew I had to have her. Been fixing her up ever since."

My entire crew had told me I was crazy when I'd laid down cash for the run-down mansion the same day I'd stumbled on it.

Finding the sprawling plantation had felt like I'd tripped into another age.

A time that was simpler.

Figured it'd be my refuge. Home away from the glitter and glam of Los Angeles. My sanctuary away from that unending blur of roads and stages and shows when we were on tour.

Here in Savannah, where it was hotter than Hades and the limelight had been dimmed. Where there weren't cameras shoved in my face every time I stepped out a door and sleep came a little earlier than the all-night affairs full of women and booze and the sun breaking the horizon before exhaustion finally set in.

Hell, even I needed a breather from the crazy lifestyle I lived every once in a while.

"I'm not saying I don't believe in my work, Mr. Evans. I just need you to tell me you understand I haven't taken on something of this magnitude before. You're paying me a lot of money, and it feels a whole lot like you're doing it out of obligation rather than because of my ability."

I lifted a single shoulder, figuring honesty was my best bet. "Maybe. But what I do know is after you gave me back everything, I have something I can offer you, so please don't take that from me. Besides, all that stuff in your store? It blew my mind. You're crazy talented, and I know you know it, too."

A shy smile tremored around her delicious mouth, and she looked at the wooden planks of the porch. "You're ridiculous."

Laughter rolled up my throat. "I've been called far worse things, darlin'."

Those eyes gleamed when they peeked up at me. "Why don't I doubt that?"

"I'm guessing because you're a smart girl." I shot her a wink, loving the ease between us that seemed to tumble in with it.

I widened the door. "You should come in."

Sucking in a breath, she stepped inside. Her gaze bounced all over the foyer. Her eyes traced the grand staircase that curved as it crawled its way to the second floor and bounced over the ceilings that were recessed and edged in thick crown molding.

The place was completely kickass, if I said so myself.

Her voice filled with awe. "Wow. This is incredible. This place could be in a magazine."

"You like it?"

She slanted me a wry smile. "Only a liar would say they didn't. Probably someone who was jealous and wished they were you, *rock star*."

She mouthed the last as if she were offering up a deep, dark, dirty secret. Letting me know she knew exactly who I was when it'd been clear as day when I'd stepped in her store three days ago she didn't have a clue.

I took a step in her direction then another.

That electricity lit up between us.

She backed into the wall.

"Well, I'm glad to hear you're no liar, *country girl*." I leaned in real close to those red, plush lips as I said it.

What was I doing? This was so not my gig. Stepping into dangerous terrain like this. I needed to get back to *easy*. Step away from this girl, who was so obviously sweet.

Modestly confident.

Timidly strong.

Good.

Boys like me wrecked girls like her, because we never stayed.

But I couldn't help my eyes from tracing her stunning face. Couldn't keep my fingers from twitching with want.

Just a little taste.

She cleared her throat, breaking the intensity. I forced myself to take a step back.

"Shall we head upstairs?" she asked.

"Come now, darlin', do you really need to ask? You know that would be my absolute pleasure." I said it with all the mischief I could muster, hoping to cover all the seriousness riding out beneath it.

"Boundaries, Mr. Evans." She was already moving to the staircase as she spoke. "If we're going to work together, you're going to need to figure out what they mean." She hooked a thumb over her shoulder, her words slanting into that lust-inducing Southern drawl. "I saw a dictionary in one of those bookshelves back there in the sitting room. You might want to use it."

I started up the stairs behind her. "I understand the word just fine, darlin'. I just think your boundaries might run a little high and wide. Doesn't leave you a whole lot of wiggle room, now does it?"

"Oh my word...you are..." She cast a smile over her shoulder, chocolate eyes widening with the tease. "Ridiculous."

I laughed.

Hard.

This girl.

There was just something about her.

Something different from the women I met in seedy clubs and dank bars. So different than the one's hanging out after a show, waiting for that coveted invite backstage. At the ready to give it up. Carnal greed.

Easy.

I guided her left at the top of the stairway. Her contemplation was almost disbelieving as she quickly examined the area. "How big is this place?"

"Big. Eight bedrooms to be exact. Just shy of six thousand square feet."

I'd always been drawn to excess and extravagance. To taking more than I needed.

Possessions.

Women.

The high was what I longed for.

Whether it was the literal shit I used to pump myself full of before death and a loss so brutal proved I couldn't continue on that path or the insane high I got from being on a stage.

Wild.

Reckless.

More.

That was just me. I'd accepted that fact a long damned time ago.

"Here we are." I stepped around her and pushed the double doors open wide.

She seemed cautious as she stepped into the enormous room that took up almost one whole side of the upstairs. The hard wood floors were unpolished and worn. My huge bed sat like an island in the middle of it, a mess of pillows and rumpled sheets and tangled comforter.

I scratched at the back of my head. "Like I said, this is the one room I haven't had anyone touch. It's just as bad as the day I moved in, except for the layer of dirt I had scrubbed away."

"It's gorgeous," she whispered as she spun in a slow circle, taking in the aura of the room. Like she were allowing the old walls to speak to her.

Her striking face held an expression that was serene and soft and awed.

So goddamned intriguing.

Her roaming gaze traveled to the dramatic view out back.

Sometimes it still even got to me. The sweep of windows overlooked the sprawling backyard, out across the expanse of lawn, all the way to the small creek that weaved along the edge of the thicket of trees that grew up like a living wall to enclose the property.

She dug a notebook from her bag, settled it in the crook of her right elbow, and grabbed a pencil. Her left hand began to fly furiously across a sheet as she took in her surroundings.

Absorbed. Almost enchanted.

"Beautiful," she mumbled, entirely to herself. The flow of her hand and the inspiration pouring from it seemed to whip up her own energy, turning it into something fierce and powerful that glowed in the thickened air.

I just watched.

Finally, she jerked her head up. Thought maybe she'd just remembered I was still standing there. "There's so much to work with here. It's…stunning. These floors and the crown molding. The space in general. But what I want to know is what you want this room to say about you? What do you want to see when you come in here at night and what do you want to feel when you wake in the morning?"

Could feel the smirk slide to my mouth.

"Wouldn't mind some sexy pics of you on the walls. Big ones."

Problem was I wasn't sure if it was truth or tease.

I waved my hand in the direction of the big, blank wall that faced my bed opposite the bank of windows. "Pretty much cover this wall right here. I'd definitely like to wake to that in the morning. Go to sleep with it, too. Let's start there. My own personal Feng Shui."

At least the delivery was all flirt and play.

Beneath her breath, she laughed but remained focused on scribbling something on her notepad. Sure. She was lookin' down, but that didn't mean I missed the shy, affected grin playing all over her mouth. "You're ridiculous. Completely ridiculous. You know that's not going to happen, right? But what I'm hearing is you want sex."

Yes, yes, I definitely wanted sex.

"For the room to have a seductive edge?" she clarified, arching a single brow my way.

"Yeah. Sexy. A little dark. But I want it fun, too."

She frowned. "I'm not sure I follow you."

I slanted her a grin. "No question a bedroom needs to scream peace and comfort and all of that, but you're missing out on an important factor. A bedroom should also be where a person has the most fun."

"I can only imagine the type of fun you're implying, Mr. Evans." She cleared her throat, trying to hide that sweet little giggle.

"Oh, don't get me wrong, darlin'. I'm a real fan of *that* kind of fun. Like I said, sex it up. But I don't think you're letting your imagination run wild enough for this project."

I lifted my arms out to the sides. "I'm a guy who's prone to outbursts of fun. I want this room to accommodate that. Last thing I want is for it to feel stuffy or like I can't let loose in here if I want to."

"And what exactly might that entail?"

Slow and predatory, I closed the distance between us. Maybe I was lookin' for any excuse to get a hand on her. Who the hell could blame me? "Let's say I want to dance…"

Pulling the notebook and pencil from her hold, I set them aside and took her by the hand.

Nerves shimmered around her. Awkward and excited. Clearly she wanted to step out and play while that shy strength told her it'd do her wise to run away.

Those chocolate eyes warmed, curious and wide. Open. Like she'd give anything to see inside me. Like maybe she wanted to dig through my demons. Discover my sins. Find out if there was any good to uncover.

Again I got that crazy feeling of familiarity. The bizarre sensation that I knew her in some way, or maybe it was my gut telling me I needed to know her better, all the while that same *gut* was warning me to keep her at a distance.

Fuck distance.

I tugged her hand and made her stumble forward. Our fingers were woven and locked between our chests. My other palm glided down to rest on the small of her back. I pulled her closer.

Heat shocked through the air.

Electricity and fire.

I could damn near feel it shivering across my skin.

Swaying her gently, I held her close, my voice a gruff mumble against her cheek, "Maybe I wanna dance slow."

I guided her to step back before lifting her hand above her head. "Or maybe I want to cut loose and take up the whole room."

Quickly, I twirled her around.

She squealed in surprise. Her hair fanned around her like a dark halo, a bright, bright smile on her face when I brought her back into the well of my arms.

"Or maybe, I wanna get a little wild. Do cartwheels across the floor. Jump on the bed. Whatever feels right."

She was laughing free while we danced and swayed, me twirling her and dipping her before I suddenly had her backed against the wall, that sweet body all up close to mine.

Urges hit me from every side. An overwhelming compulsion that had me aching to press my nose to the exposed flesh running along the delicate slope of her neck. To inhale her all the way from her tiny ear down to that sexy collarbone.

Could almost smell the honey coming from her skin.

My mouth watered.

Shit.

Here I was, just beggin' for trouble.

Our mouths were a breadth apart. That short-lived, easy atmosphere was replaced with the suddenly harsh breaths panted from her mouth.

Everything rippled and shook.

She stared at me, searching my face, looking at me a little like the way she'd been looking at my house.

Like maybe I was one of those broken bits she wanted to sculpt and shape. Like she saw something buried that needed resurrected. But this girl didn't have the first clue there was no chance of *fixing* me.

Tucking her bottom lip between her teeth, she tentatively reached up and let the warmth of her blunted nails go scratching through the beard lining my jaw. Her touch was softer still as she trailed up, barely brushing the brand new scar marking me just below the eye.

My dick jumped, and my chest squeezed.

It felt so damned good.

So right and so fuckin' wrong.

Her voice was a rasp. "Did you know I worried about you? When they took you away in that ambulance, all I could do was think about the man they'd carried away. I couldn't stop picturing you strapped to that stretcher. A stranger who'd touched me without saying a word."

Something foreign shivered through my senses, rising up from that place I'd long ago locked up tight. I wanted to fucking trample it. Instead, I was giving in and brushing my nose across her forehead. I buried it in the fall of her hair.

"Peaches," I murmured.

Did she know it'd been exactly the same for me?

That hint of a memory stalking me. Day and night.

With shaky, unsure hands, she caressed over my shoulders. Tentative and slow.

Her breath hitched as she trailed farther down my arms.

And those eyes. They were soft and warm and curious as her fingers began to trace over the lines and shades of the tattoos covering the entirety of my arms.

I flinched.

It wasn't like chicks didn't touch them all the time. But it was never done for any reason other than some girl taking the two things she could get from me.

A night of wild, unbridled sex and a name to drop.

And shit, I'd always counted that a win. The detachment. Skin on skin without a thread of intimacy.

Willow's touch almost felt like she was weaving herself into the fibers of my being. Like that crazy creativity that poured from her brilliant mind was passing through her fingers and becoming one with the art that covered my skin.

I could feel it etching me like a slow burn.

I heaved out a shuddered breath.

With the sound, her eyes flicked back to mine.

Her lips parted, and her expression churned in confusion.

Lust. Need. Want. Fear.

All of them played out across her delicate features.

I shouldn't have. I knew I shouldn't. But there was nothing I could do to stop myself.

Always, always in the moment.

That was me.

I pressed her harder against the wall, my straining cock eager against her jean-clad pussy.

Desperate for friction.

Anxious for relief.

Everything sparked, and I could have sworn the room spun, the ground shifting below our feet.

She gasped out in surprise, eyes so damned wide. Her nails pricked where they dug into the flesh of my shoulders.

Hanging on.

What was this girl doing to me?

I leaned down, my mouth close to her ear. My voice came on a rough murmur. "Do you want me?"

Didn't have to wait long for her answer.

Horror suddenly stole her expression.

Grief and sorrow and guilt.

She jerked free of my hold and turned to face out the windows. Rays of Savannah sun were shining down around her as she dropped her forehead to the pane, shoulders heaving with each breath she took.

I edged up behind her. Set both my hands up high above her. Caged her in.

"Peaches," I murmured again, trying to coax her out of the regret she was obviously riddled with now.

Her words flowed with fortitude. "I don't believe in love at first sight, Mr. Evans."

Confusion struck me, before a dark growl rumbled in my chest—my chest I was pressing to her back—letting all my hard get mixed up with all her soft.

God. I wanted to sink straight inside.

Leaning forward, my mouth brushed at the shell of her ear. "Who said anything about love, Peaches? This? This is lust."

I dropped a hand from the window, set it against her belly that shivered and shuddered against my touch. "Do you feel that? Everything simmering around us? Threatening to boil over? A flame just waitin' for a match."

That lust stampeded through my veins, gaining speed. I could feel her heart battering her ribs against the thin fabric of her sweater.

My voice dropped an octave. "Tell me you want me. Tell me you feel this, too."

She sucked in a breath, and I could feel the hurt threaded through the question. "Is that what you brought me here for?"

The distress in her tone struck me hard, and I forced myself to edge back and give her some space. Seemed like a lifetime passed as she seemed to gather her resolve. Slowly, she turned around to face me. "Is it?" she demanded.

The uncharted spun around us. Questions and confusion and uncertainties. "I don't know," I finally admitted.

Anger and disappointment twisted her expression. "You don't know? You offer me *fifty thousand dollars* to come redecorate a single room in your house, which of course just *had* to be your bedroom, and you don't know? Tell me, Mr. Evans, did you bring me here to actually *do* something for you, or did you just want to sleep with me? Maybe you just needed to get a little guilt off your chest so you decided you might as well get something for yourself in the process? Which is it?"

"Willow," I mumbled, knowing my truth completely contradicted my actions. "You've gotta know it wasn't my intention to upset you."

"It wasn't your intention to upset me?" Her hands fisted against her chest like a cross of protection. "This…what you do…" She waved her hand to the spot where I'd just had her pinned against the window. "It might not be a big deal to you, but it's a big deal to me."

Moisture glistened in her eyes, and I wanted to fucking kick myself for backing her into a corner.

She fumbled to quickly gather her things.

"Willow," I attempted as she slung her bag over her shoulder.

"I think we're done here," she said.

"Come on, Willow."

She ignored me when she all but ran out my door.

I gripped my hair, shouted toward the ceiling. "Fuck!"

Because that was me. Reckless in the moments that should be cared for. The ones that so clearly should be taken in caution. I knew the moment I met her she was different.

Guilt squeezed my chest. I'd hurt her and I hated being *responsible* for it.

Scariest part of all was I didn't know why I gave a fuck.

ASH

"*H*ey there, sugar, what can I get for you?"

I glanced up at the hoarse voice of the older lady slinging drinks behind the bar. She tossed a napkin in front of me where I sat on a stool, my knee bouncing a million miles a minute. My attention darted around the small dive where I'd never before stepped foot.

"Guinness would be nice."

"Coming right up."

So yeah. I was supposed to be lying low. Staying out of sight. Not knowing when I might stumble upon one of those assholes from the other night.

stay

Call me *reckless*.

But there was no chance I could sit tight at my place for a second longer. After what went down with Willow earlier, I'd spent the whole day feeling like I was gonna go out of my mind.

I was antsy. Anxious. Needing the thrill. That *high* of carnal pleasure shooting through my veins.

No doubt, it was time to step back into my safe zone. Get firmly back into the realm I'd sentenced myself to years ago.

No better place to rid Willow from my system than a place like this.

"There you are," the bartender said as she set the mug in front of me. "Bad day?"

I chuckled as I wrapped a hand around the handle. "Something like that."

I was an ass. No wonder Willow had hightailed it out my door. I'd pushed her when I shouldn't have. But that sure as fuck didn't give her the right to try to have the 50k I'd transferred to her account wired back to me.

I'd sent it right the hell back.

It was hers. Job or not.

"Well, let's just hope we can make it better. No happier place in the world than *The Hideout*." She gestured around the shabby, grimy, rundown bar, the woman chuckling at her own joke.

A smile ticked up at the corner of my mouth, and I lifted the mug her direction in a salute.

She was right.

This place would do just fine.

I took a swig of the beer, before I turned away and got down to business. Hunting as I looked around the dark, dank space littered with a few small tables and a row of worn down pool tables at the back. Traditional billiards lights hanging from above cast the area in a yellow haze. The place was sprinkled with just a handful of people out shooting a round and a couple scruffy old guys at the bar who probably considered this place home.

She found me before I even found her.

Easy.

The chick sauntering up to me would probably slap me

across the face if I were to actually speak the word aloud.

Not sexy or hot or all kinds of fuckable. Which believe me, she was all those things.

But the God's honest truth? I didn't mean it offensively. Meant it as a compliment to us both.

No strings attached.

Zero consequences.

Who the fuck would count that as bad?

Not me.

The leggy blonde didn't even hesitate to run her fingers through my hair.

Apparently I had *easy* written all over me, too.

"Ash Evans." It was all a purr in the back of her throat.

Second nature, my smirk kicked up, and I was chewing at my bottom lip as I let my hand cinch on her waist. "In the flesh," I told her.

She let her fingertips crawl along the collar of my tee. "I'd like to see more of it."

"Is that so?"

"Mmhmm."

Coy apparently wasn't her thing.

This chick was so my speed.

So much my speed that I was on my feet and hauling her toward the short hallway that led to the restrooms, where I was pushing her up against the wall and shoving my fingers in her hair, my mouth diving to meet with hers.

Seeking relief.

To get back to who I was.

What I knew.

Because *Peaches* had invaded my mind.

And this girl was all floral perfume.

That kind of thing never bothered me.

Not ever.

But I couldn't shake the feeling something was off.

Something sour settled in my stomach. I tried to pour that frustration into this girl.

I mean, come on.

I was the goddamned life of the party, and for this kind of *party*, I was usually the world's most obliging host.

But it wouldn't come. My aggressive kisses turned shallow. Finally I let my forehead slump against hers as I pushed out an exasperated groan.

God.

What the hell was wrong with me?

The poor girl I had pinned against the wall tilted her head back in confusion. "What's the matter?"

That was a good damned question.

"It's just...been a weird couple weeks."

She quirked a brow. "Not in the mood for living up to your reputation?"

Short laughter rocked from me, and regret had me shaking my head as I took a step away. "Guess not."

I prepared for her to rail on me for being a total dick. Instead, she patted me on the chest like she felt sorry for me. "You don't look so good. You should go home."

What bothered me most? No doubt she was right.

ASH

The doorbell echoed against the old walls of the house, rousing me from sleep. I blinked against the emerging day. Considered tossing the covers over my head and ignoring the intrusion, but when it rang again, I hauled myself out of bed, pulled on a pair of jeans, and snagged a tee from the floor.

I jogged downstairs, opening the front door as I was pulling the shirt over my head.

Then I froze.

Bright morning light poured in through the doorway. In the middle of it was Willow, standing there looking totally unsure and somehow confident, too.

My chest tightened in that crazy way, in relief and regret and something I didn't want to contemplate.

"Willow." Caution filled my tone.

Honestly wasn't sure if I'd ever see her again.

She peeked up at me. "Can we talk?"

"Of course."

I stepped back, giving her space to enter. She didn't say anything. She just went directly for the stairs, climbing them with the same work bag she'd had yesterday bouncing against her hip.

I followed her lead, trying to come up with the right kind of apology, wanting to reach out and touch her just the same, hating the fact this girl had me so off-kilter I was having a hard time recognizing myself.

She headed straight into my room. She rounded on me as soon as she was in the middle. She lifted her chin. Fierceness took hold of her posture, all mixed with distinct apprehension.

Confounding.

This shy girl who exuded a quiet strength.

"You returned that money to me," she accused.

I sighed. "Of course I did. It's yours."

Her gaze bounced around my room. "But I left."

My nod was reluctant. "Yeah. You left because I was pushing you a direction you didn't want to go. That's on me. I'm..." My gaze dropped, before I looked up at her, wading in my own unease, because I sure wasn't used to this shit. "I'm fucking sorry, okay? Really sorry. And I want you to have that money, one way or another. I guess I just thought..." I trailed off because I didn't want to say it.

She'd been right yesterday. I'd wanted to take a little something for myself. How could I not? She was goddamned stunning. Intriguing. Different. That familiarity was like a drug.

She inhaled deeply and turned to face the window. Those mahogany locks spiraled in soft waves down her back. But her body? It was dripping with hesitation. Her voice was a whisper when she spoke. "I'm a private person, Mr. Evans."

She looked back at me from over her shoulder. Like she wanted to see my reaction.

"I get that."

"Do you?"

I gripped the back of my neck, muscles tight. "Maybe not wholly. But we all have secrets, Willow. Things we don't want people to know. Some of us just hide them differently than others."

Her eyes narrowed. Assessing. Before she seemed to come to a decision she worried might cost her everything. "How many women have you slept with?"

The question hit me out of left field. That was about the last thing I'd expected her to ask.

My brow drew tight. "What?"

"You heard me."

I scrubbed both hands over my face. "Is that really what you want to know right now?"

"It is."

"What does it matter?"

"You and your friends riding into town didn't exactly come without rumors. I want to know if they're true."

Exhaling heavily, I shook my head with a shrug. Wasn't about to start spouting lies.

"Rumors are all true. I am who I am, and that's who I'm always gonna be. And the fact of the matter is, I can't honestly answer that question, because I have no clue. Stopped keeping track a long damned time ago."

Out on the road, belts ran out of notches real fast. All those faces and names and bodies morphed into an obscured image. Like an old black-and-white movie that'd been set to fast forward, just blinks and blips in time.

Disconnected.

"The reason…" She hesitated, before she pressed on. "The reason I found you beat up outside my store? It was because of a girl?"

A shock of that bitterness tightened my chest. That chick made me something I promised myself I'd never be again.

A cheater.

I nodded. "Wouldn't have touched her if I'd known she

belonged to someone else. But that didn't matter to the assholes who hunted me down."

Willow flinched with the information, and she wrung her hands. "And you want me to be another one of them…another of the girls you touch and it doesn't mean anything?"

I knew I was traversing uneven ground. Toeing that line.

Caution filled my explanation. "The only thing I know is I can't stop thinkin' about you. Wanting you."

"You don't even know me."

"Yet, here we are."

She stared back at me. Everything about her seemed so apparent in that moment.

Innocent. Decent. Honest.

Something that felt a whole lot like grief fisted in my chest, and this sick part of me wanted to wrap her up and steal whatever that emotion was that dimmed her bright eyes.

I could feel her warring again. Deciding just how far she was willing to step out with me. What she was willing to give.

She clasped her hands against her chest.

"If I'm going to do this job, I need you to understand something about me, Mr. Evans." She waved a hand at the spot where I'd had her pinned yesterday. "That may be you…casual sex. So many women you can't count them. But it's not me, and it's not ever going to be. I don't do one-night stands or flings, and I don't have a three date rule or a five date rule or even a ten date rule."

She hesitated, before she seemed to gather resolve. "I'm a forever kind of girl. If I share my body with a man, it's because I love him and he loves me. Because I want to share my life with him. I'm not ashamed of it…not at all." Rapidly she blinked and her teeth caught her lower lip. "But somehow, standing here in front of you, it makes me feel small and foolish."

Her throat bobbed.

I took a pleading step forward. "Peaches."

Somehow I got her sharing that with me was huge. That she was trusting me with something I hadn't earned.

With a shake of her head, she took a step back. "Let me

finish. I've been with one man my whole life. My ex-fiancée. His name...his name was Bates."

A jolt of pain seemed to strike her when she uttered the name. Grief from every direction.

Out of nowhere, anger billowed up in my chest, something protective rising up in the middle of it. My hands fisted at my sides.

"My *whole* life. He was my first, and he was supposed to be my last. *My only.*" Frantic, her eyes darted around the room, lingering on the door just a second longer than anything else. Got the feeling she'd do about anything to escape this conversation.

"Two years ago, I found him with a woman he'd introduced me to. You know...for years he'd tried to convince me that my store and my art were silly. That they meant nothing because he was going to be the one to take care of our family. Then all of a sudden, he was dead set on me going into business with her."

She shook her head. "I should've known better. I should've. He convinced me to sign my savings over to her for a new business venture. He told me it was the only way we could finally afford to start the life I'd been dreaming of since I was a little girl. A life he'd been pushing off for more years than I could count. The thing was, I would have given up anything for him."

That intensity flamed and lapped between us. It strangled me in a way I didn't quite understand. A sticky, hot feeling coated my skin.

I wanted to wrap her in my arms.

Tell her it was okay.

When it was obviously not fucking okay.

Pain hitched her breath. "He betrayed me in the worst way a man could. He stole everything from me. Broke me. Treated me like a doormat, and I might have fallen for it then, but I won't ever fall for it again. One thing you should never do is mistake broken for weak."

Fuck. Me.

This got deep and fast. I was having a hard time deciphering up from down. Inside from out. Who I was supposed to be and what this was supposed to mean.

And hell, I guess I was the one who was weak, because I couldn't stay away a second longer. Slowly, I erased the vacant space separating us.

She looked at me as I stood towering over her. My voice was grit. "And now you're waitin' for the kind of guy this Bates was supposed to be to come along."

Surprise flashed in her expression before she offered the slightest nod. Clearly, she hadn't expected me to get it. But with this girl? It was hard to miss. That sweet, soft innocence. The goodness that radiated from her like the goddamned sun.

My gaze jumped all over her face. "Dude is an idiot."

Anyone who could let a good thing like her go was a straight idiot. A selfish motherfucker who needed a good lesson. Wanted to hunt down the little prick and teach him some manners.

Which was precisely why I didn't normally get mixed up in this kind of bullshit. Yet, here I was, standing there wanting to ask her a million questions…find the solution for every single one of them.

"I was the one who was the idiot."

I hooked her chin with my index finger and forced her to look at me. "Don't fucking say that, Peaches. You're beautiful and smart."

Unlike any girl I'd ever met.

The frown on her mouth wobbled.

I cupped her cheeks in my hands and made sure she was looking at me before I spoke again. "That guy's out there. Promise you, darlin'. He's out there looking for you, and one day, he'll find you. He'll find you because you deserve him. Don't you dare settle for anything less than him. You got me?"

Chocolate eyes softened.

So goddamned sweet.

I tucked a loose strand of hair behind her ear and sent her a smile while everything inside me was a jumble of confusion.

The disappointment this girl had officially become off-limits.

Underlying that was an assault of searing hate. Hate for the bastard who'd done her wrong.

Not to mention the twinge of jealousy I felt for some metaphorical, abstract guy I'd just finished promising was out there waiting for her.

I knew with every part of me this girl was incredible.

Special.

Call it gut, I didn't fucking know.

All I knew was I was compelled to show it to her.

Make her claim it by the time that lucky-assed guy came knocking at her door.

"You still want that truth? Why I brought you here?" I asked. Squeezing her face tighter, I drew her an inch closer.

She nodded in my hands.

"Because a little more than a week ago, I was discarded like a piece of garbage on the side of the road. Body mangled. Bleeding internally and going into shock. Minutes from death. I can't remember a time in my life when I was more terrified. I could *feel* myself slipping away, and I couldn't do one goddamned thing about it. Then, I opened my eyes...I opened my eyes, and I saw these brown ones staring back. And right that second? I knew I was gonna be okay. And now it's really fucking hard to look away."

I smiled at her. Softly. Honestly. Without any pretense. Hoping she'd get that I understood her. That I respected who she was.

I told her what it all amounted to.

"I like you, Peaches."

Sweet, somber laughter slipped out into the room. "You're ridiculous," she said again.

"You have no idea."

I stepped away and inclined my head toward to the room. "You gonna take mercy on me and do this room?"

"What if I'm just here for the money?" Her response felt like both a test and a tease.

"Are you?"

"I'd be a liar if I said I didn't want to save my store," she admitted, before she reached out and set a soft hand against my cheek. "But I want to do this for you, too. Even wild souls need a place to rest."

Jesus.

This girl.

I forced lightness into my tone and put some space between us before I went and fucked this up all again by giving into the overwhelming urge to kiss her. "Then we'd better get you busy, hadn't we?"

It wasn't so hard to fake the grin I slanted her. "And just so we're totally clear, you do realize you're insanely gorgeous, right? Wasn't joking about needing those pictures on my walls. We're gonna need plenty of time to set up for a big photo shoot. I'm talking epic. You name it—Exotic location. Hair and makeup. Super sexy wardrobe. FYI, I like black. *A lot*."

That energy still roiled around us, though it'd calmed to a quiet, sated buzz. "Oh, and you totally need to drop the whole 'Mr. Evans' thing. It's Ash, baby. Ash."

"Only if you drop the whole 'Peaches' thing."

"Not a chance."

"Ridiculous," she huffed out, and I just grinned.

And somehow, in that second, I liked her a little bit more.

I knocked my shoulder into hers. "Now about that shoot…we can't forget the lace. Never, ever forget the lace."

WILLOW

"How is she today?" I asked as I pulled up a chair next to my mama where she slept.

Sheila busied herself around her, shifting her frail body in an attempt to keep her from getting the bedsores that were starting to seem inevitable.

Sympathy lined Sheila's expression, and she turned away, tucking the blankets in around my mama's body. "Fever's been spiking again. Trying to keep it down. Looks like she's getting another kidney infection."

Worry compressed my ribs. I gave her a tight but appreciative nod. "Thank you."

Her only response was an encouraging squeeze of my shoulder, before she headed from the room and snapped the door shut behind her.

I turned to look down on my mama, brushed my fingertips softly over her hand tucked up under her chin that was forever clenched in a fist. "I did it, Mama. I stepped out. Took the job that's going to save the store."

A smile wobbled at the corner of my mouth as something heated in my belly. "Ash Evans. That's his name. He's the man who hired me to renovate his bedroom. You should see it, Mama…his house. You'd absolutely love it."

I held her hand a little tighter, chewed at my lip, confided the words. "He makes me nervous, because he's not like any man I've ever met. He's not close to bein' my type, and I'm pretty sure I'm not his, either."

I suppressed the laughter working in my belly.

Hardly.

I'd seen a few of the tabloids proclaiming the type of woman Ash Evans liked. And that type of woman came from a different world than the one I knew.

"But there's something about him. Something that has me wanting to be in his space. To know him better."

And it had nothing to do with the fact it felt like my biological clock was ticking fast. It wasn't about snagging a man, because that had never been my thing. Ash was the one who'd nailed it, head on. The fact I was waiting on the man who was my match.

One who'd love me the way I'd love him.

One who wanted a family and a home.

Devotion and loyalty.

But that didn't change the fact every time I was in the same room with him I felt shaky and needy. Wanting something I could never let myself have.

My voice tightened. "I'm not giving up on those dreams,

Mama. I'm not. I promise you. Do you remember them? Do you remember…?"

Above, blue skies stretched on forever. Tufts of pure, white clouds floated on the endless breeze. Birds flittered and chirped, passed from tree to tree.

Tinkling laughter rippled through the heavens as her big sister, Summer, chased Willow through the field.

She tackled her from behind.

Both of them squealed, laughing free as they tumbled on the ground.

"Got you," Summer almost gloated.

Willow used both her hands to push back the messy locks of hair that'd fallen in her face, grin free and wide. "You always catch me."

Summer was seven, only a year older than Willow, but she always seemed to be faster. It didn't bother Willow all that much, except she was afraid one day she might not be able to keep up. She didn't ever want to get left behind.

Their mama came and settled next to them, watching them in the way she did, so protective and full of love that it made Willow's heart feel like it just might burst.

Their mama turned her face toward the sky, returning to their game. "Your turn, sweet one. What do you see?"

Willow peered at the clouds sailing above. "A knight. I see a knight who's come to slay the dragon that's hiding right there."

Willow pointed her finger at a puffy cloud rimmed in a bright blaze of sunlight. "See….he's in his lair. He's stolen the princess's jewels and is guarding them with his life. But he's not bad. He thinks that's what he's supposed to do."

"And why is that?"

"Because no one took the time to teach him what's right."

Affection flitted through her mama's chuckle. "That's a sad story, my Willow."

Willow didn't think her stories were sad. They always had a happy ending. But her mama told her she was the serious one. The timid one with romantic notions and simple wishes. Her stories were so far removed from the wild, magnificent dreams her sister had just spun.

Sometimes she wished she could be like her big sister.

Braver.

Prettier.

Older.

"They're not sad," Willow disagreed. "The knight is going to grant him one wish, and his wish will be that he finds love. The true kind."

Light laughter fluttered from her mama and she looked at Willow adoringly. "That's your gift. You see the beauty in the old. The beauty in the bad. The beauty that's hidden in all things. It's always there, we just have to look hard enough for it, don't we?"

Willow nodded enthusiastically, like she might understand.

"Who are you gonna be?" her mama asked her.

Willow could feel her grin splitting her face. "I'm gonna be a mama and work in your store forever and ever."

Her mama ruffled a hand through her messy hair. "Of course you are."

"Oh…oh…and I'm always gonna be Summer's best friend!"

"And how about you, my glorious Summer?" their mama asked.

Summer lay on her back with her arms and feet stretched out as if she were making a snow angel in the grass. She stared up at the sky, her black hair strewn all around her. "I'm gonna be a dancer. Maybe move to Paris or maybe New York. Yes, that's it, New York. And I'm gonna take Willow with me because she's always gonna be my very best friend."

Willow stretched out on the ground beside Summer and linked her pinky finger with her big sister's. It was their special sign they'd always be together.

Her mama reached down and plucked two dandelions with white heads from the expanse of grass where they sat at the creek's edge. She held one out to Willow's sister.

"Mmm…that sure is a big one, and I don't doubt it a bit because my girls can be anything they want to be. But just to be safe, I think you might want to wish on it."

Summer's face got that dreamy look, and she blew hard.

Their mother looked at Willow, the way she always did, breathing all her belief and inspiration.

"Your turn, sweet one."

She held a dandelion out to her.

Willow squeezed her eyes shut.

I want to be just like my mama.

Willow leaned over and blew it into the air.

Yearning pressed down all around me, and I swatted at the tears streaking from my eyes. I stood up and pressed a kiss to my mama's forehead, whispered the words. "Always, Mama, always."

She moaned from somewhere deep.

And I could only take comfort in the fact she knew I was there.

ASH

"That's a really bad idea."

Why did people keep telling me that?

Baz leaned one hip against the big island that took up a ton of space in my even bigger kitchen. The kitchen area opened up to the cozy entertainment room that overlooked the sprawling back yard. I loved the whole great room vibe, the room's one large space closed off from the rest of the house, giving it an enclosed, secluded feeling.

He took a sip of his beer, that stare of his hard, like he was driving home a point.

"How is this *not* a good idea?" I defended, trying to bite back my laughter. "I think this just might be the best idea I've ever had."

"I think we already established all your ideas are bad."

"Hey now, hey now, that's not very nice. You're really tryin' to rip me up here, aren't you? And I can't think of a better way to let the world know Ash Evans isn't going anywhere than getting back on a stage."

"I thought you were supposed to be out for six weeks?" Austin frowned from across the kitchen as he tossed a bottle cap into the trash.

"He is," Baz said, widening his eyes at me as if to say, "See, everyone knows your ass is supposed to be sitting this out."

"Yeah, and the fucking paparazzi has been speculating my demise ever since. Lurking out on the street in front of my house, trying to snag a pic. Hell, half of them think I'm actually dead and are sitting around waiting on my publicist for the confirmation. One chick wrote some blog post about her life ending because mine had. Not cool, man. Not cool. I need to rectify the situation."

Baz pointed at me. "You know you aren't supposed to read that shit."

"And what the hell else am I supposed to do during the day? I'm bored as fuck over here by myself. I mean, except for Zee over there…" I hooked my thumb at Zee, who was lounged back on one of the double chaises set up in the great room. "But considering boring is the dude's middle name, he isn't helping matters any."

The dude was as cool and casual as they came, and he'd been my roommate ever since the rest of the band had started branching out and finding lives of their own. Putting rings on their girls' fingers and starting families.

Not once had I ever seen him hook up with a girl. Or a guy for that matter.

Zee scoffed. "Whatever, asshole. You know you can't live without me. And don't pretend like you haven't had 'company' over here every single day this week."

Lyrik, our guitarist, chuckled. "Ah yeah, I think it's about time you filled us in on this whole 'redecorating project' you have going on."

Asshole had the balls to toss up air quotes.

"What? My bedroom suite is the last spot in the house that needed to be redone. I had a need, and I found someone to fill it."

"I bet you did," he shot back with a salacious grin.

"Not like that." I gave a shake of my head. "Went over to the girl's shop to thank her—"

It was beginning to come like second nature—the sudden rage that vibrated my spine when the onslaught of images hit me. Those five faces were getting harder and harder to forget. I was so accustomed to bein' that easy-go-lucky guy. Built my life on it. But there was just some bullshit that was impossible to ignore.

My throat felt tight, and uneasiness had me scratching at the back of my neck with my index finger. "Honestly, it felt odd going back over there, where it happened. But the second I went inside, I knew this girl was talented, so I figured what the hell."

So maybe I left off the part about how I couldn't get her out of my mind. That was ammunition none of these assholes needed.

"Oh, come on, Ash," Austin said, crossing from the counter and leaning his forearms on the island. "Fifty grand just for someone to come in and give you design suggestions, which doesn't include any of the actual costs? That's insane. Hell, I'd do it for twenty-five." He clapped his hands together. "*Boom.* Bargain. It's a win-win."

"Right, like your lazy ass would lift a finger around this place."

Laughing, he arched a brow. "All I'm sayin' is I don't believe for a second there isn't something else going on."

"I've got the money to spare. Besides, she's working some original pieces herself. Doing the painting. Ordering supplies. Managing. All that shit. Room's gonna be kickass."

"I don't know," Baz baited. "Seems to me my baby brother might have a valid point. Let me guess how this went down…super-hot savior chick rescued your ass, you got a good look at her, and you decided fifty grand was a good trade for dipping your dirty hands in the honey pot for a couple of days."

Normally, I'd laugh it up with my crew. Because nothing they said would be anything but the truth. Because it was all in fun. No harm, no foul.

Not this time.

Protectiveness swelled. It was a feeling that was so foreign, so unsettling, it made me grit my teeth together. My voice was harsher than I intended. "Doubt very much I'd be standing here today if it wasn't for that girl. Found out through the grapevine she was in a bit of trouble. And if there's anything I can do to help her out, then I'm going to do it. I owe her."

The smiles slid off their faces, and something heavy took to the mood.

Baz hefted out a sigh and worry cut a path across his forehead. "And how are you gonna be sure this girl isn't going to take advantage of you? I mean, don't forget where that got you last time."

Panic rushed me.

What the fuck?

Baz knew well that was a topic not to be broached. Considering he hadn't brought it up in all this time, he knew it, too.

Still, I went for light. "Nah, man, it's nothing like that. I promise you, she's one of the good ones."

The double doors leading to the great room suddenly swung wide open and Shea strutted in, carrying a bunch of bags.

"Who's one of the good ones?" she asked.

A tumble of all the people I loved most in this world followed in behind her.

Kallie, Shea's daughter who Baz had adopted, bounded in with a mess of those blonde ringlets flying all around her, and her baby brother, Connor, struggled to keep up.

Of course, Brendon, Lyrik's son, was at the helm, hollering over his shoulder for them to *try* to catch him.

Leader of the pack.

Because that was just the way the kid was.

Tamar came in behind the kids, holding Adia, her and Lyrik's daughter. The kid was all wild black hair and big blue eyes and adorable smiles.

My baby sister, Edie, was the last to step through the swinging door.

At the sight of her, affection and regret swirled through my spirit.

It damned near gutted me every time I saw her, even though I did my best to keep it contained. To pretend I didn't want to come unhinged every time I thought back to that night. The night when I'd set her at the wolves feet when she was fourteen—little more than a baby—and let them sink their razor-sharp teeth into her.

Even worse, I hadn't found out until last year. That night seven years ago? I'd been too wrapped up in my own damned mess. That same brutal night when my sister was being destroyed was the same night my world was coming undone.

Guilt rose up like a storm.

I bit it down, shook off the morbid thoughts, and forced a smile and lightness into my voice. "Oh, hell yeah, day is made. All my favorite people are here!"

I lifted my hand out to the side for Brendon and Connor to give me a high five as they ran through my kitchen. Brendon jumped up, slapped my hand, and shot me one of his badass grins.

That one was bound to be a heartbreaker.

Connor did his best to keep up, stopping right in front of me and focusing on his jump. "Got you, Uncle Ash!"

Of course because Shea and Sebastian couldn't keep their damned hands off each other, they'd had Connor about the second they'd gotten hitched. The three-year-old basically spent his days trying to keep up with the "big kids."

"Heck yes, you did. You got me good."

Brendon started running circles around the island, stirring up trouble.

So damned much like his dad.

The three kids took off again. My house may as well have been a playground, but you sure as hell wouldn't hear me complain.

"How about we take this game outside?" Shea's voice held a tinge of reprimand, though her face was easy-going smiles.

I moved across the space, dipped down, and pecked a big smacking kiss to her cheek. "Hush it up, fun sucker. What do you think this big house is for? Fun and fun. Oh, and more fun. Isn't that right, Kallie O'Malley?"

"Yep, yep, yep!" she hollered from the other side of the island. Her hand was now all wrapped up in Brendon's.

Shea pointed at me. "Now, don't go calling me fun sucker, mister. Who is it who came to feed y'all, while the rest of you run around—"

"Having fun," I supplied real quick, cutting her off with another kiss to her cheek.

Baz chuckled. "Watch yourself, man. I see you over there, kissing on my wife."

I held one hand up. "Hey now, hey now. I'm just spreading the love around. Shea looked a little lonely when she stepped through the door, so I figured it was on me to step in and make sure she wasn't missing out on the good things in life."

He lifted an eyebrow before chuckling low and embracing her from behind. "Oh believe me…she's not missin' out on anything."

Lyrik took Adia from Tamar. He lifted her up high in the air, making the six-month-old baby girl laugh and flail.

With a grin, he pulled her down and set her protectively against his chest. The man was nothing but a sappy puddle of goo when it came to his family. This was the first year he got his son, Brendon, for an entire month during the summer. Thank God, he'd manned up and went back and made things right with the kid's mom a few years back.

I let my attention slide to where Austin moved toward my baby sister. Finding out they were hooking up was a bit of a shock, but they were perfect for each other.

Edie pulled herself out of his arms and moved my direction.

Eyes the same color as mine brimmed with worry. "How are you feeling?"

"Perfect."

She scowled. "Come on, Ash. There is no way you feel *perfect.*"

"Yeah, claiming that shit isn't gonna win you any spots on the stage, either." Lyrik grinned. *Asshole.*

I lifted my hands, palms out. "Better, okay? Way better."

A soft smile pulled at my sister's mouth. "Good. Now I can kick your ass for being so stupid to go and get yourself in a brawl."

"Not necessary, I plan to do it for you, Edie," Baz added, cocky smile on his face as he stared over at me.

I pointed his direction. "Watch yourself, man, you know I can take you in a second flat. Besides, I just might need to enlist your help one of these days."

Lyrik stepped forward with his daughter cuddled in his arms. "Which is just another reason to keep you out of *Charlie's.* Last thing we need is for you to go looking for trouble. God knows you know exactly where to find it."

"Says the pot to the kettle." I added all the teasing affront I could find.

Lyrik chuckled. "Touché, my friend. Touché."

"Um, there will be no enlisting my man's help in any of that business," Shea said. "And don't think you distracted me with all this crazy talk. I want to know who's one of the good ones."

Of course she did.

Tamar's red lips stretched into one of her signature sexy smirks. "I'm going to guess this has something to do with Willow. Ash's guardian angel."

"Oh, my Tam Tam." I said it like a warning with a glare her direction.

Tamar hiked a single shoulder. "What?"

Shea rubbed her hands together. "Ohhh...I like this talk of guardian angels. Is she pretty? Nice? A cowgirl or a city girl?" Her attention darted to the ceiling. "You know all those rooms upstairs are begging to be filled. Still got my hundred bucks on you needing to paint them pink and blue instead of those lavish extra rooms you've got up there. Total waste."

Did my best not to let her razzing hit me in the wrong spot. No.

Not ever.

I'd never let myself feel that way again.

I kept that smile plastered to my face.

"Think I might have to up my ante on our bet. Blue and pink bedrooms. *All. Of. Them*," she issued like a threat. "Double or nothing. There are these super cute boots I saw in the window of *Tomgirl's* last week. Come to momma. Pretty sure my man here would appreciate them."

"You do remember you tossed out that bet more than three years ago? How long am I going to have to wait for the pay up?"

"Until I win, of course."

A sound of disbelief drifted out with my smile. "And just how is that fair?"

"Oh, it's fair. Believe me, it's fair."

"Not gonna happen," I said.

Crazy how women assumed just because I wanted to live my life without a bunch of bullshit attachments they thought I was missin' something. They couldn't imagine anything different than me having a big hole in my soul aching to be filled.

Well guess what? Those attachments were what created those holes in the first place. No thank you.

Austin butted in, "Yet you have the girl you've been chasing decorating your room. Sounds pretty domestic to me." He smiled. All teeth.

"Not chasing her."

Almost sounded like a lie.

Because, shit, a part of me wanted to chase her. Catch her. Hold her. Just for a little while.

A huge crash shook the walls in the next room where the kids were playing. Glass shattered, and the little voices that had been shouting went suspiciously quiet.

"Oh my goodness, you two are gonna tear down this house," Shea hollered.

Brendon peeked his head through the doorway. Eyes just as dark as his dad's brimmed with worry and guilt. "Momma Blue, we need your help in here. STAT."

Tamar laughed and shot Shea a smile before heading into the sitting room.

Baz tossed a disturbed scowl Lyrik's way. "Dude…our kids…put them together and those two are nothing but trouble."

"Thick as thieves, brother. Just wait till they're teenagers. Just wait. Gut tells me we're gonna have to keep that shit under lock and key."

"Don't even go there, man, don't go there."

Lyrik laughed. "We'll know to get concerned when they figure out they're not actually cousins. But hey, that's a good lookin' kid and he's got my blood flowin' through him, so…" Lyrik delivered the last with a cocky shrug.

Austin laughed as he crossed the room, snagged a chip from a bowl, and popped it into his mouth. "You really think Kallie Bug fell for that shit, Baz? She's a whole ton smarter than you give her credit for."

"What are you talkin' about, smarter than I give her credit for? Little Bug's as smart as a whip, which is precisely why she'll have zero interest in boys until she's at least thirty. Maybe forty."

Shea giggled, hiked up on her toes, pressed a soft kiss to his mouth. "Oh, Daddy Bear, you have a lot of lessons coming your way."

He grunted. "Don't break my heart, baby."

"Hey, I thought that was my line…you coming and stealing My Beautiful Shea right out from under my nose. Heart. Broken. I still can't believe you went and done me that way. The atrocity."

I jammed my fist against my chest, driving in that imaginary knife and pitching the guy who was one of my best friends in the world—one of the few people in this world I was wholly devoted to—a joking grin that was purely that.

A joke.

He punched at me, refusing to let go of his wife while he did

85

it. "Watch yourself."

Laughing, I moved out of his line of fire.

I always, always watched myself.

I knew the boundaries.

I knew where a good time crossed into the land of the perilous.

I might have toed that line. Walked beside the flames.

Didn't matter.

I never allowed myself to get close enough to get burned.

I smacked my hands together. "Now, about that show..."

WILLOW

*H*ow he'd convinced me to come tonight, I didn't know.

This was so not my scene.

I was in knots. Tied up, twisted knots. Knots of confusion and want.

Blue eyes flashed when he looked down at me and wrapped his big hand around mine. Blue eyes the color of the Caribbean.

Endless.

Bottomless.

A rush of chills shivered down my spine, and I clung tighter to his hand as he led us through the throng of people packed in the dark, hazy bar.

He'd told me he and his band were going to play at a place called *Charlie's*, which wasn't all that far from my shop. I almost declined. Almost. Then he told me he *wanted* me there, for me to be a part of the first show he'd play since what'd happened.

There was nothing I could do.

I'd simply nodded and said I'd be here.

This man made me…unstable. Shaky and irrational. He was making me desire things I'd never desired before.

Things I knew would wreck me if I gave up and gave in.

He was steadily gaining the strength to splinter me into a million unrecognizable pieces.

Kindling for a devastating fire.

Ash parted the crowd without a word.

It seemed there wasn't a single person in the massive, ancient building immune to his presence.

To his power.

I was sure I felt it most.

He was met with hellos and claps to the back. Not to mention the hungry gaze from women obviously eager to sink their claws into his skin and devour him.

Jealousy stabbed me in the chest.

God.

It was an emotion I couldn't afford.

Not with this man.

But tonight, with my hand wound in his protective hold, I felt that way—as if he were mine.

Now he just smiled wide as he shouldered his way through.

Confident.

Strong.

Gorgeous.

He tossed one of those grins at me from over his shoulder. "Right this way, darlin'. And you need to take a breath and relax. Don't pretend like I can't feel you shakin'. Promise you, my friends don't bite."

Little did he know I was shaking for an entirely different reason.

His grin widened to one of those arrogant smirks. Pure flirt and tease and sexy temptation.

"I mean, they might look like it, but you'll be completely safe just as long as you're at my side." He spun around, dipping down so his mouth was near my ear. "Thinking you better stick close, anyway…you do look delicious tonight. Someone's bound to want to eat you up."

Tingles coated my skin.

A flash of attraction.

A rush of need.

He led me to a secluded horseshoe booth hidden at the very back. Extra chairs had been set up around it to give more seating for the large party that had taken control of the area.

As if they owned it.

Belonged.

The men of *Sunder* were kicked back against the plush maroon cushions. An intensity unlike anything I'd ever seen surrounded them.

An unmistakable aura.

Severe, dark, and deep.

Each of them had an arm draped around a beautiful woman, pressed to their shoulders as if they'd been carved to fit.

All except for Zee, who was the only one I'd previously met.

Nerves skittered through my body, and I sucked in that breath Ash had suggested I take. Turned out I needed it after all.

What I hadn't anticipated were the smiles and the welcome that moved across their faces, even if there was no missing the curiosity in their eyes when they looked back at me.

Ash made quick introductions, helped me into a seat beside him, and ordered us drinks. All the while excitement gleamed from him, getting just a bit brighter as he peered over his shoulder into the throng. "Can't wait to get on that stage."

His friend Baz took a sip of the amber liquid that swirled in his tumbler, his hand curled around the glass as he pointed his index finger at Ash and spoke to me. "Did you know your boy here always gets his way?"

Baz sent an affectionate look in Ash's direction, and Ash just smiled back.

That was all it took for me to be thankful I came.

We'd shared a couple of drinks. The mood had grown rowdy, the group of friends having the best of times.

I thought I'd feel awkward.

Out of place.

As if I didn't belong.

I'd been completely wrong.

I tried to hold back the riot of laughter that wanted to burst free as I watched the man who was sinking deeper and deeper into my bones tell a story.

Clearly, he was buzzed.

His grin was messy, and his voice was loud enough for everyone at the table to hear since he was standing beside the booth rather than sitting.

"And Baz boy here, he just starts running down the alley, bare ass shining in the moonlight, trying to keep his pants from falling down around his knees."

Lyrik pounded his palm on the table, cracking up.

"Hey, man," Baz defended, hugging his wife a little tighter. "That was totally your fault. You're the asshole who let those chicks on the tour bus in the middle of the night."

Ash shrugged. "What? I figured you could use a little unwinding. You'd had a really long day."

A brow quirked, and Baz took a swig of his beer before he pointed the neck of it in Ash's direction.

"And I needed ten chicks to do it? Here I was, fast asleep, and my eyes dart open to a herd of screaming girls jumping on the bed in the back of the bus. Felt like I had a hundred hands on me, yanking and tearing at my fly, trying to get my pants down. Woke up to squeals and smeared lipstick and fangirl eyes. Freaked me the fuck out. I went flying down the aisle and out the bus door."

He hooked a thumb in Ash's direction. "Of course, this punk right here, he's standing right outside the door in the parking lot, laughing his ass off like it was the funniest thing he'd ever seen."

"It *was* the funniest thing I'd ever seen. You seriously should have seen your face when all ten of them came running out after you. Dude, the whole lot of them might have been ghosts with the way you went running. Might have told them you like to play chase."

Shea pressed her hands over her ears. "Eww…eww…eww. Stop right there, Ash. I don't want to hear anything about my man and a bunch of girls trying to get him naked. You should know that subject is totally off limits."

Ash feigned offense. "Oh, come now, Beautiful Shea, that was long before you went and broke my heart and started keeping this sucker warm at night. Had to have been at least ten years ago. Ancient history."

"Um, news flash, no woman wants to hear about her husband's conquests…like…ever."

Sebastian buried a kiss in the curls on her head. "Don't worry, baby. Didn't let any of them touch me." He lifted his brow at Ash. "Although, if I remember the story correctly, Ash was all too happy to step in and take my place."

"Hey, I didn't want to go disappointing any fans. That's just not cool. A man's gotta do what a man's gotta do. Sacrifice and all."

"Oh my God." Ash's younger sister, Edie, covered her eyes with both her hands from where she was sitting on her fiancé, Austin's, lap. "My brother. Sometimes I can't even," she said.

Zee flicked a bottle cap at him. "Always such an asshole."

Ash swiveled to the side and deflected it like an old pro. I was betting that was the case.

"What?" he defended, totally playing the serious card even though everyone who looked at him could see the smile pulling his lips.

Tamar rolled her eyes and snuggled closer into her husband. "Uh, how about the fact you throw out these stories like they're normal behavior?"

Ash held his hands up in the air. "Hey, these were *normal*, everyday occurrences until the two of you"—he pointed at Tamar and Shea—"came barging in and busted up all the good times. Couple of sexed-up fun suckers, that's what you are.

Bewitching my boys with all that hotness, taking them by the dicks and bagging their balls. So not cool. Not cool at all."

A part of me wanted to cringe at the way he talked about sex so casually. As if it meant nothing. But a bigger part of me couldn't find it tonight. I was too wrapped up in the easy affection that passed between them all.

The comfort.

The loyalty.

The way it was supposed to be.

That kind of devotion was precious. Priceless. And it was so vivid in this side of him, even if it was done with all his reckless, gorgeous ease.

"I keep Lyrik's balls zipped up in the front pocket of my purse, thank you very much," Tamar taunted with a red-lipped, sassy smile she canted at her husband.

He looked over at her. The guy looked so bad. Almost mean. But there was no question this woman was the center of his entire world.

My chest clutched in old agony. In loneliness. I shoved off the depressing thoughts. I wanted to experience this. To be in *this* moment rather than in the one's threatening to drag me down.

Lyrik shot a menacing smirk at Ash. He lifted his chin, flashing the tattoo stamped on his neck. "Kinda like my girl's hand on my dick, anyway, so don't really have too many problems with her leading me around by it."

Baz busted up laughing, spewing beer across the table. Shea leaned around Lyrik, hand going up for a high-five with Tamar. "That's what I'm talking about."

Ash smacked his forehead with the heel of his hand. "Every last one of you have lost your damned minds. Someone save me from the madness. Now all I have is Zee in my corner, and since the guy is some kind of celibate or some shit, he's of absolutely no help."

A giggle slipped free. I tried to cover it. But it was there. My teeth raked back and forth on my bottom lip, fighting the smile that wanted to break loose beneath his brilliant light.

Because he looked over at me.

Smiled this smile that cut me to the core. One that was soft. Kind. Almost adoring.

My stomach twisted and flipped, and a lump grew heavy in my throat.

Without a doubt, the ground beneath me was getting slippery.

Perilous.

Baz drained his drink and slammed the empty down on the table. "All right, if we're actually gonna do this, we need to do it."

All the guys followed suit and downed their own drinks.

Ash smacked his hands together. "Hell yeah, it's on. Time to give the paps something to actually talk about."

A surprise show.

That's what *Sunder* had planned. This was a band that typically sold out shows around the world and, here they were, taking the stage in front of an unsuspecting bar crowd.

All the guys climbed out from behind the booth. Adorning the cheeks and foreheads and mouths of their women with tender kisses.

I looked down. Away. Feeling as if I were violating something private.

And then he was there. That powerful man stood in front of me, hand stretching out to help me to stand.

He palmed my cheek.

Softly.

God.

I couldn't breathe.

"Thank you for being here, darlin'. Means more to me than you know."

I nodded against his touch.

Fire and light.

I fought the well of consuming emotion that threatened to take me hostage.

Shackle me.

Chain me.

A willing prisoner.

Zee clapped Ash on the shoulder, breaking up the moment. "Let's go, man. You wanted this and we delivered."

"Coming."

Reluctantly, Ash began to back away before he pointed at me. His expression quickly morphed into something cocky and sure, a contradiction that seemed to be the heart of this confusing, chaotic man.

"You are in for a treat tonight. Promise you, you won't regret stepping through that door."

I could only muster the smallest nod as I watched him disappear into the fray. Uneasily, I settled back down onto my chair.

In that moment, I could feel the quiet sanctity of my world crack as I fell into another. It was a world of mayhem and confusion and lawlessness. A world that belonged to Ash Evans.

Warily, I peeked over to the three women left at the table with me.

All three stared back as if they'd witnessed a miracle.

Edie was the first to break as she shifted forward. "I'm glad we have a minute alone. I want you to know how thankful I am for what you did for my brother."

Bright blue eyes, so much the same as her brother's, glistened beneath the lights.

"I was just doing what any other person would do."

"We like to think so, don't we?" She shook her head. "But we know that's not always the case. This world can be so cruel. I think that was evidenced by the ruthless jerks who left him there in the first place."

Tamar and Shea grunted their agreement.

My eyes narrowed in sincerity. "I could never look away from someone who needed my help that way."

The memory of his words I couldn't shake pushed into my mind.

"And now it's really fucking hard to look away."

God knew I'd spent more time than prudent trying to decipher what they meant.

Wondering why I felt the exact same way.

How I'd become inexplicably tied to a stranger I felt desperate to know.

Shea smiled. "That's why we're all so thankful it was you who found him. That it was you who was there at the right moment. Our lives are an endless string of what-ifs and what could have beens, and the reality is that you saved him." She angled her head. A soft, prodding question. "And now you're here…with him."

I fidgeted again, glancing to the riot that had struck up at foot of the stage. All the guys climbed the two stairs to the right of the risers. It ignited a ripple of interest and excitement in the dense, hazy air.

"He asked me to." It almost sounded like a defense.

Tamar grinned. "He seems to be asking you to do a lot of things lately, doesn't he?"

The implication was clear.

My brows squeezed together. "It's nothing like that. We're just…he went through a lot. And I'd be here for him even if he weren't doing what he's doing for me."

The truth of the matter? I'd needed a little saving, too. And somehow in the process, I felt like he was offering me something different than just the cash flow to save my business.

It felt like *more*.

Shea smiled a genuine smile.

These women were so different than what I'd anticipated when I'd seen their pictures. So different than the tabloids made them out to be.

Apparently, it was true what they said. You shouldn't believe everything you read.

"That boy's a handful, though, isn't he?" Shea asked, affection in her tone.

I stared in the direction of the stage.

It seemed impossible to look away.

"That he is," I mused, mostly to myself. I was distracted by the crush of the crowd that seemed desperate to get closer. By the vibe that lit in the air. Intense and severe.

Ash bent over, fiddled with something on the stage.

I struggled to breathe.

I tore my attention away, catching the grin that played across Tamar's face. "Do we need to rein him in for you? Because I'm pretty sure that boy is more than just a *handful*."

Redness flamed on my cheeks.

Instant.

Unstoppable.

Just as unstoppable as the salacious fantasy that took hold of my mind.

It came unbidden.

Unwelcome.

All except for that hidden, secret place inside that simmered and shook with dark curiosity.

"Ohhhhhh," Tamar drew out. Her mouth stretched into a perfect 'o'. "So that's how it is, huh?"

So maybe I wanted to crawl under the table and hide.

Shea's eyes widened, and she jumped in with the ribbing. "No need to get self-conscious about it, Willow. The boy does love to brag about it. If you hadn't noticed, the guy isn't exactly shy or modest."

"Pssh, he likes to brag about everything," Tamar added, laughter in her voice. "Ash's ego is as big as his—"

"Gah!" Edie slammed her hands over her ears. "I think this conversation might be as bad for me as Ash talking about Sebastian in front of Shea. Stop right there, thank you very much."

"I was going to say his heart, Edie. His heart. Your brother has a really big heart. Almost as big as my husband's."

Tamar winked at me when she said it.

Pure innuendo.

Redness flamed and heat licked across every inch of my body.

Oh my God.

I didn't know if I wanted to laugh or cry.

If I wanted to get up and run for dry land or cling to these women forever.

If I wanted to freeze up behind my fears or for a few blissful minutes let go.

Allow myself to live. *To feel.* I hadn't felt much of anything but pain and sorrow and worry in so very long.

"I...I don't..."

Sobering, Shea sat back in the plush booth. I thought maybe she was able to read every single one of the insecurities that had flashed through my mind.

"Hey, it's okay. Honestly, Willow, we get it. It's scary to feel something we aren't sure we should feel. Scary to feel something new. Especially when we know it might just break us even though our heart is telling us to give it a shot anyway."

"Ash isn't—"

She cut me off with a sharp shake of her head. "Ash picks up women, Willow. He doesn't bring them with him. Not in all the time I've known him. Not once."

I struggled to process what she was implying.

Her smile was nothing less than a sympathetic frown. "And Ash...there's a complicated man underneath all that happy-go-lucky, easy-going guy. He doesn't show it to a lot of people, but I know it's there."

Her frown deepened. "But the one thing you should know, he does have a huge heart, Willow. Ash just might have the biggest heart of them all. And I think maybe that's what terrifies him most."

Her words felt like both a buoy and a warning.

Encouragement and caution.

He might wreck you but it just might be worth it.

A deep voice was cleared in the mic.

The crowd thundered and stomped their feet. Whistles and cheers ricocheted from the old wooden walls of the massive building.

I expected to see Austin out front.

But no.

Standing out front and center was the man I couldn't expel from my mind.

One I could feel slowly but surely seeping into my skin,

soaking into my spirit, where he would take me whole.

Invade and inundate.

I knew if I let him, I wouldn't ever be the same.

"How's everyone doin' tonight?" Ash's rough voice tremored over the space, shackling every soul with his words. He pushed a casual hand through the long pieces of his hair, his grin wide.

Though something about it held a predatory vibe. Body so big. Strength bristling in every bulging muscle.

No doubt, it was the warrior who had taken to the stage.

"Oh my God," I heard Tamar mutter from behind me. But I was too entranced to look for her reaction.

Instead I watched his gaze skate across the enraptured faces who stared up at him.

"Seems there've been some rumors about my well-being floating around. So yeah, I might've gone and gotten myself into a bit of trouble after leaving this fine establishment a few weeks ago."

He chuckled low, and I thought he was going to play it off as something simple with the way he smirked at the crowd.

Insignificant.

The incident just another blip in his day.

But instead those blue eyes raced across the faces gathered at his feet until his steely gaze tangled with mine.

Turbulent.

Relentless and sincere.

The room spun.

"Now I know I'm usually the one standing up here, livin' life large and without a whole lot of thought about the consequences. But I want to be real for a second."

He paused, found my eyes again. "The truth is, I'm not sure I'd be standing up here tonight if it wasn't for the care of one single girl. All those rumors that've been flying around? Well, they wouldn't be rumors and instead my band would be telling a very different story tonight."

Blood hammered through my veins.

"She saved me, and I don't think she's quite yet grasped what that means to me. But I'm hoping there's a chance she'll realize it tonight."

His eyes held me for the longest beat, before he jerked his attention away, turned it back on the waiting crowd. "I know I normally don't stand out front with a guitar and we don't normally play covers, but I'm bettin' y'all would be willing to hang with me for a bit, yeah?"

Shouts and cheers vibrated the walls. A thunder of approval. My racing heart skipped a wayward beat.

God.

I was in so much trouble when he began to play. When he opened his mouth and the most seductive voice came sliding out.

He jumped into a cover of Snow Patrol's "Chasing Cars."

But he was playing it gritty and raw. Like a tortured, perfect plea. It slammed against me with a direct shock to every single one of my senses. All of it was wrapped up in the man at the center of the stage.

A spotlight.

A beacon.

Sensuous and alive.

Standing up there, I saw a man consumed by the secrets he held in the recesses of his mind.

Gone to a depth he'd only barely let me glimpse.

But I knew it was there. Hidden beneath his own intimidating, striking exterior was something dark and shadowy and pained all mixed up with a goodness I thought maybe he didn't even know was there himself.

He sang the song as if it might be his last.

With everything.

By the time he trailed off at the end, my throat was completely locked tight. Questions swirled through my spirit and mind. The confusion he incited in me had never been greater than in that single moment.

Because I got what he was saying.

But somehow it felt like he just might be saying more.

He stepped back and took his bass before the band

continued with their set.

Tonight's style was so far removed from the loud, thrashing music I knew they normally played. Each song raw and unplugged. I floated and swam through the intensity.

Wave after wave.

Lost to the vibe and the music and the lyrics.

Lost in the man.

I almost felt shocked when the set suddenly ended to a roar of applause echoing from the old walls.

And by the time Ash set his bass aside and jumped down from the front riser of the stage as if he'd never been injured at all, I was a complete, utter mess.

The DJ took over, and a dance beat started pounding through the overhead speakers.

Erratic, my heart sped harder and faster when Ash shouldered through the crowd, offering thank yous and smiles as he passed.

But he clearly had only one target in his sights.

The man was so dangerous and alive.

Compelling.

Magnetic.

A bright, bright flame.

As he burst through, he cast out a cocky smile intended only for me.

I swore it touched me from across the distance. There was absolutely nothing I could do but climb to my shaky feet.

Wings fluttered in my belly. Anticipation and warmth.

I blinked through the realization. I was excited. Excited to get close to a man I had no business getting close to.

What did I think I was doing? Setting myself up yet again to play the fool?

He'd made himself perfectly clear. Our lives were heading in opposite directions.

Polar.

For these few short months, they would intersect in the middle. But that didn't mean we'd ever end up in the same vicinity.

But there I stood, helpless as he came straight for me. He didn't slow. His long strides ate up the ground, his muscles straining beneath his shirt, the color etched on his skin dancing and playing like a tease.

He didn't stop.

And my breath was gone when he dipped down and wound those big arms around my hips, scooping me up as if I weighed absolutely nothing.

He spun me round and round, his face turned up with all that easy joy as he laughed.

No shame.

No worries.

All I could do was hang on to him. "Ash, you're going to hurt yourself."

That smirk. "Nah, baby, you'd never hurt me."

I grappled to take control of my emotions, which were quickly spinning out of control as he slowly slid me down the planes of his hard, hard body.

"What did you think?"

I think you're amazing.

I think the real you is someone no one really sees.

I think I could fall for you.

Too easily.

So stupidly.

"You were brilliant," I whispered, feeling brave as I reached up to touch his face. I searched that sea of blue, the way his eyes tossed and turned and played. "Thank you for bringing me here," I said.

His big hands gripped me by the outside of my thighs and he tugged me close.

"Peaches." He sounded almost confused, as if he couldn't make sense of this, either.

At the contact, I gasped, my hands twisting into fists in the fabric of his shirt. The words left me before I could stop them. "What are you doing to me?".

ASH

*T*hat was the fucking problem. I didn't have the first clue what I was doing. Had no grip on the direction my intentions were heading.

Because shit.

Standing there with her wrapped in my arms? That scent flooding me and her soft body tucked against mine?

I wanted to keep her.

Just for a little while.

But I knew doing that would be nothing less than a sin, taking this sweet, innocent girl and marking her...corrupting her.

She wanted all the good things in this life that I didn't have to give. Those things? They were out there somewhere, waiting to find her.

God knew, that bastard wasn't me.

But that didn't stop me from drawing her closer, murmuring, "Dance with me," as I led her deeper into the throng. A riot pitched and throbbed with the heavy dance beat. It vibrated the floor and shocked through our bodies. Strobes glinted and those chocolate eyes flashed.

Goddamn.

She was beautiful, staring up at me as if she were seeing something that just wasn't there. It was a part of me that had been buried a long time ago. It was the part that wanted to reach down and wrap her up and hold on forever.

Somehow, being in her space made me almost remember what that was like. The glimmer of hope that would spark in my belly, a fear that terrified me with the thought of ever letting go.

That familiarity.

It was always there, nagging at me from somewhere in the recesses of my brain.

I was so close to recognizing it.

Sucking in a breath, I let my hand glide to the curve of her slender waist. She trembled with the contact, and my fingers twitched, itching for more when I knew damned well I couldn't have it.

The thrumming crowd swallowed us. We were lost in the middle. To the flashing lights and the spellbinding darkness and the hypnotic sound. Rocking my hips, I encouraged her to match me. She swayed, breathed out a breathy sigh, let me barely edge my knee between her thighs.

What the fuck did I think I was doing?

Problem was, I didn't quite know how to stop myself.

The only thing I knew was I wanted her to be free. To feel what it was like to be unchained. Unbound. Loosed from the bullshit betrayal of that asshole, Bates. So, we danced this delicate, confused dance in the midst of the grind of bodies and the heady pulse of pounding blood.

The entire scene was like a prelude to sex.

Foreplay.

Hot and heated and uncontrolled.

I could almost smell it.

Taste it.

I moved, inching in closer, my knee wedging deeper between her thighs.

She stiffened.

My mouth was at her ear. "I've got you, Peaches. Let go."

She warred, but I could feel it, the tension bounding through her muscles. Pulsing then giving.

I cinched my arm around her waist, hugged her closer, my free hand on that gorgeous face.

"Ash." She exhaled it. Needy and deep.

It was the first time she called me by my first name. It slammed me like an electric prod, and I pulled her closer. My hips were up tight against hers, beat to beat, my nose lost in the lush, silky fall of her hair.

She was so fucking warm.

So fucking soft.

And those legs.

Those long, long legs.

She was wearing the shortest damned dress, beige and flowy and loose, the hem and sleeves trimmed in this lacy ruffle that screamed country, and I was sure it was supposed to come across as demure and sweet.

It didn't.

It was sexy as hell.

Sinful.

And here I was, the bastard in me itching to get wicked.

Fantasies assaulted me. Those legs wrapped around my waist, my tongue licking them up and down.

Suppressing a groan, I did my best to will my cock into submission. To keep every drop of blood hammering through my veins from sliding south.

Fucking impossible.

Not with the steady brush of her heat against my thigh. Not

with the slow sway of her hips and the unsteady heave of her chest.

I could feel her breaths coming shorter and faster, the pitch of them matching mine.

Shit.

I should get laid and do it fast. Tuck this girl in a cab and send her safely on her way. Grab myself one of the willing fangirls that overran the bar. Reach out and take my pick.

Doing it would serve both of us well. The problem was the only thing I wanted right then was her. It had only been her since the morning she'd saved me.

"You have me so spun up, darlin'," I murmured at her ear. "So spun up I don't know if I'm comin' or goin'. It's me over here wondering what it is *you're* doing to *me*."

She exhaled a breathy sigh I felt rather than heard. "Ash, I…"

"I know, gorgeous, I know."

But I didn't, not really. I could feel us slipping off that line I liked to toe. Tripping over it…and I didn't know if I wanted to run back to safety or let myself fall.

But getting close was dangerous.

Reckless in a way I refused to be.

But none of those nagging thoughts stopped me from burrowing my nose in her neck, inhaling the scent at the soft skin behind her ear, tracing down to the silky slope of her neck.

Peaches and cream.

Sweet.

Intoxicating.

My lips pressed against the flesh over her pulse. My dick hardened painfully and my heart crashed in my chest.

My tongue slid out for a taste.

Just a little taste.

Her fingers dug into my shoulders, and I jerked back to look down at her, knowing once again I'd pushed this wholesome girl over all those invisible boundaries that were set between us like a trap.

Though, unlike when I'd done it in my room, this time her

expression didn't reflect hurt. It was flushed and flickered with desire and doubt and this crazy need that brewed between us like a storm.

"Ash." It was a whimper.

Lust slammed me. I wanted to kiss her. I wanted to kiss her so bad my mouth watered and my gut fisted.

"Think it's time I took you home, darlin'."

Before I did something stupid.

Something we'd both regret.

And shit. It killed me to think of this girl regretting me.

"Promised you I'd bring you here, you'd have a good time, and then I'd get you home safely. That's exactly what I intend to do."

She blinked, totally shocked out of the trance we'd both been under.

She nodded, though it looked like a tiny bit of hurt that flashed through that warm gaze. "Okay."

I wound her fingers in mine.

Flames licked up my arm.

Fuck.

This was bad.

A wise man would just keep his mouth shut, but I couldn't stop myself from needing to say more, to wipe away that flicker of rejection I'd seen flash through her eyes. I yanked her back to me. "Before we go, want you to know one thing. I want you to know you're the prettiest girl in the whole damned place."

I let the pad of my thumb run down the angle of her cheek.

Motherfucking sparks.

"Did you know that, Peaches? Did you know you're the most gorgeous girl here? So fucking sexy and sweet. One look at you and I don't wanna stop."

It was precisely why I needed to get her the hell out of here. I should have been granted sainthood when I turned and led her back toward the table. Because my body was screaming and my mind was shouting all the reasons taking her would be okay, when I knew without a shadow of a doubt there would not be one thing *okay* about it.

It'd be nothing but selfish.

Vile and base.

By the time we got back to the table, my crew was standing to head out.

"There you are, asshole." Lyrik punched me in the shoulder a little softer than he normally would. "Thought we were gonna have to come hunt you down, because we sure aren't about to let you have any run ins with any douchebags tonight. Last thing we need is you inciting another rumble."

"Nah, man, all's good. You don't need to worry about that."

At least for another day.

"You ready to hit it then? Only have the babysitter till one, and mommy and daddy duty is gonna come really fucking early in the morning."

Still was so weird hearing those words come out of the dude's mouth.

I chuckled. "Ah, the big bad Lyrik West has turned into a straight pussy."

"A pussy who'd be happy to drop you flat."

"You wish you could take me, asshole," I said with a playful taunt, just smiling as I squeezed Willow's hand, the girl looking between us as if we were completely crazy.

Admittedly, we were.

Just a little bit.

"Let's go," Baz said, leaving a fat stack of large bills in the middle of the table.

With the way the guy tipped, you'd think he'd be broke.

And I was supposedly the one who was heedless with my dough.

We left as a group, a rowdy cluster that weaved back through the thick crowd. We shouted out goodbyes, shouldering through as we received compliments and claps to the back, quick to dodge the hands of chicks who were all too eager to get friendly for the night.

Some of these girls? They had no fucking shame. Didn't think twice about doing it right in front of Shea, Tamar, and Edie, either, which pissed me right the fuck off.

Apparently, a ring on your finger meant absolutely nothin' if you were a prisoner to fame.

But Baz, Lyrik, and Austin...they'd become pros. The only thing they offered were tight-lipped smiles and a glare that screamed *fuck no.*

Every time someone would try to grab my attention, Willow would steal a cautious glance my way. Obviously wondering what'd I do.

If I'd bite or abstain.

Like I'd pull some asshole move and ditch her for a one-night stand.

Like I could stomach one right then, anyway.

Outside, the night had cooled. Darkness hung like a smoky drape from above, the endless canvas splattered with a spray of stars. Streetlamps jetted up at the edge of the cobblestone walk. They cast spikes of light into the hazy fog that rose up from the Savannah River.

There was something haunting about this place at night. Comforting in a dark, mysterious way.

I reveled in it.

I thought maybe I'd feel out of sorts, have some reservations stepping out into the deep, dense night after what'd gone down three weeks ago.

But no.

I felt...good.

Right in a way I hadn't in a long, long time.

I looked over at Willow, who was walking next to me. Her hand was in mine, her stunning face upturned toward the sky, eyes closed as if she were breathing the beauty in. As if she were a part of it rather than just a gorgeous observer.

My chest tightened.

Shit.

Light laughter echoed off the worn exterior bricks as everyone chatted quietly. The mood had taken a turn into the subdued as we left the noisy bar behind. Couples snuggled into each other as they ended their night away, Zee out front ambling along, hands stuffed in his pockets.

Peace.

Didn't have a lot of it in my life. But right that moment? I floated in it.

Good nights were shared, and everyone slipped into their cars.

I unlocked my Navigator and helped Willow inside, trying to ignore the way my body lit up in awareness when I did.

I rounded the front and hopped in, turned over the engine, headed back to the tiny house where I'd picked her up earlier that evening. Silence swam between us, just as complex as the night.

Quiet and brimming with the unanswered.

Finally, I broke it. "Thank you for coming tonight."

She slanted me one of those gentle smiles. "Tonight was incredible." She chewed at her lip that threatened a tremble. "Sometimes we get so comfortable behind the protection of our walls, we forget we need to step out from behind them to actually live."

I glanced at her. "Is that what you've been doin', Willow. Hiding?"

She seemed to contemplate a moment before she spoke. "I don't think it was conscious or any sort of a decision I made. But it seemed like it all came so fast. Seemed like every time I turned around, I lost someone I loved. My daddy. My sister. My mama. *Bates.* One loss after another until I got to the point where the only thing I was doing was breathing pain. I guess I folded in on myself as my world folded in around me. It was easier to stay there."

A million questions whirled through my mind.

She looked over at me. Open. Honest. "But that's not where I want to be."

My gut clenched. "Peaches."

"Don't feel sorry for me. Remember what I told you. Don't ever mistake broken for weak."

I swallowed past the lump that suddenly grew prominent in my throat, overcome by the fact this private girl was allowing me in a little deeper. A little further.

"What do you say you tell me about it?"

"That would be an awful long story to tell on such a late night."

My brow rose. "If you didn't already assume that about me, I'm kind of a night owl. All ears, darlin'. All ears."

That smile widened just a bit before it fell flat, and she inclined her head to the street we passed. "Okay then...my mama. She lives down that street."

Guess when she'd said she'd lost her mother, I'd assumed she was *gone*.

At a loss, I peered over at her.

"She lives in this cute historic house that's all done up in antiques and relics. She would absolutely love it if only her mind and body were there to enjoy it. It's a long-term care facility that's dressed up as a quaint home." Her smile was faint as she explained. "As if the surroundings might conceal the fact she won't ever get out of bed again."

Sympathy gripped me, my voice tight. "What happened to her?"

"She has M.S." She shook her head. "I never imagined it could consume her the way it has. Sometimes I feel guilty the hardest part for me is watching her slowly lose her memory. Seeing her confused and agitated."

No doubt, this girl was confiding things in me I was certain she rarely confided in anyone.

I should stop her. Knew I should. But I just sat there like the goddamned bastard I was, silently asking her to share more of herself.

Her voice drifted in sadness. "It kills me to go there because she seems to be stuck in the past most of the time...in her dreams. Dreams she had for me and my sister that never came to pass. Most of her dreams were simple. Just like mine."

I reached across the console and squeezed her hand. "I'm really sorry."

She smiled over at me. "Me, too."

"And your sister?"

I was pushing it. But I couldn't stop myself. Couldn't stop

this exchange or this feeling she was giving me. Like maybe just by being there I was offering her some kind of comfort.

Instantly, I regretted the question.

Because Willow physically flinched.

A full-body blow.

Like I'd struck her in the face.

Her voice was rough and forced. "She died a long time ago, and that's something that's really hard for me to talk about. To anyone."

Fuck.

I roughed a hand through my hair.

"That's horrible, Willow. I'm so fucking sorry." I glanced at her, wondering why I couldn't just shut the fuck up. Why this girl compelled me to splay myself open wide. "It's hard for me to talk about my sister, too," I admitted.

She frowned. "Edie?"

I knew what she was thinking. Edie looked just fine. Happier than could be. Which I got the inclination she really was, and that made me so goddamned happy, too.

But still…

Both my shoulders lifted with the confession. "I was responsible for some bad shit in her life. Shit I wish I could take away. Go back in time and stop. Change. But I can't and that kills me."

Willow's attention got lost out the windshield, in the spray of dingy lights that spread out in front of us, the intangible guiding the way. Her voice was subdued. "I wish I could go back and change so much. I've made so many mistakes."

My smile was somber. "I've made a few myself."

A million.

Too many to count.

Mistakes I'd spend the rest of my life paying for.

Gut told me Willow felt the exact same way.

I pulled up at the curb in front of her house, the heavy rumble of the engine the backdrop behind the silence that descended, darkness encroaching from all sides.

That strange connection simmered in it.

Comfort and peace.

After a few seconds, she shyly peeked over at me. "Do…do you want to come in?"

Shit.

Shit. Shit. Shit.

I wanted to bang my head on the steering wheel. Maybe dunk myself in a bottomless vat of ice cubes and water. What I really wanted was just to give.

"I think that'd be a bad idea."

Who would have thought it'd be me dishing out that kind of wisdom?

But if there was ever a high road to take, this was it.

Hurt sliced through her delicate features. Like I'd just deepened the cuts she already suffered. Like she was fumbling, wanting to heal them, willing to hurt herself all over again in the process.

"Okay," she whispered before she cracked open her door with the intention to escape all that was left unsaid.

Without thinking through all the ramifications, I reached out, hand greedy as I weaved it into her hair, deep enough so I could palm the back of her neck.

I forced her to look at me.

Fuck. She was gorgeous, all wild eyes and sharp breaths and broken spirit.

"I want to," I amended with the truth, edging farther into her space.

Nose to nose.

Breath to breath.

"God, I want to."

My tone hardened with the raging need the girl had constricting every cell in my body.

"If it's what you *really* wanted, Peaches? If it's what you really wanted, I'd follow you right into your house. I'd toss your hot little body over my shoulder, carry you upstairs, strip you down, and lay you out. I'd spend the entire night making you beg and scream my name."

The words dropped even lower, grating from my throat,

filling up the cab like arrows of delirious torture. Striking one after the other. "I'd make you come. Again and again."

Her breaths were short, needy rasps that I inhaled, every part of me wanting to suck her in as I had my way.

"But you know that's not close to being what you really want, Willow. Not close to being what you deserve, because I'm not close to being that guy. In the end, only thing I'd do is end up hurting you. So, right now I'm gonna pretend like I don't want to fuck you so bad I can hardly see, so I can do exactly like I promised and walk you to your door and leave you there."

Awareness sparked between us like a short-circuited plug.

A frenzied energy that zapped and popped against our tingling skin.

It threatened to take us places she couldn't go.

Threatened to make me feel things I wasn't sure I'd ever felt.

Things I couldn't.

Not like this.

Not this way.

Needing to break the spell the girl had me under, I cleared my throat, drew my hand away, and killed the engine. I let myself out, rounded the front of the SUV, and helped her down.

We said nothing while I led her to her door, both locked in our own struggle for control. When she stopped, key in hand, I dipped down and pressed my lips to her forehead, breathed in the sweet and the innocent that only reinforced my resolve. "You deserve better than what I have to give."

She fisted a single hand in my shirt until I reluctantly pulled away.

Then I left her there like I promised, fighting the itchy, angsty feeling burning up my blood. It took about all I had not to turn around and go running for her when I heard her door creak open and then closed behind her.

Warily, I peered back over my shoulder. A light flicked on in an upstairs window and her shadow danced behind the drape.

I stood there staring at it. A tremor shivered down my spine. Spindly tendrils stretched out and sank their teeth into my skin.

Because right then?

A.L. Jackson

Gut told me this girl might shine too bright.
And I was worried both of us were going to get burned.

WILLOW

"So, I have good news and I have bad news. Which do you want first?"

I wavered in his doorway with my heart in my throat, not sure where we'd stand this morning, but sure at the very least it would be awkward.

Apparently not.

He stood there, all smiles and smirks and that sexiness, all but guaranteeing that whatever his "bad news" was couldn't be bad at all. Easy warmth pulsed from him in waves. Just as bright as the sun that climbed the sky, striking him in rays of shimmery light.

He stretched his arms out to the sides, and I swore the intricate web of tattoos was singing all his songs. Songs I felt almost desperate to know the words to. Those colors tugged and pulled against the hulking muscle, his shirt so tight, just as tight as his jeans and every inch of his toned body.

I shouldn't stare.

But that had become an impossible feat, especially after the way he'd twisted me inside out last night.

He made me want to experience things I was sure I'd never experienced before. It was unnerving.

Last night, I'd barely slept. I'd tossed and turned in the vacancy of my bed, like a fool longing for the salacious, scandalous promises he'd murmured to me like threats. Part of me had wanted to shut him up and shut him down, while a rebellious voice hidden inside had piped up, whispering, *you know you'd really like to know what that's like.*

The scariest part was I'd been so close to begging him to make good on all those warnings. I just wanted to feel *something* good and have the guts to step out and take it.

Nervously, I scraped my teeth over my bottom lip and forced a smile that didn't feel so wrong. "Don't you know the answer to that is the bad news comes first? You always, *always* give the bad news first."

He stepped back with a smile, didn't hesitate to take my hand in his. As if it'd belonged there all along. "I really guess I shouldn't have asked then, because I'm pretty sure the good news comes first in this case."

It was all easy tease.

"Now, don't go and get yourself too worried, because it's honestly not that big of a deal. All just part of my life, darlin'. And since you've been hanging out with me, that makes you a part of it, too."

Curiosity peeked out from deep inside me as a shot of unease rustled. "Okay," I drew out as I allowed him to lead me into the depths of his stunning house.

He hauled me all the way down the expansive hall that cut down the middle of the bottom floor and dipped us through the swinging doors and into the kitchen and great room, which was as big as my entire house. The kitchen was black stainless steel and white marble countertops. The cabinets and wood accents were carved to keep the country flare.

A perfect contrast of old and new.

He spun in the middle of the kitchen and walked backward as he spoke, clearly wanting me to follow. "So, like I said, we have some good news and some bad news. The good news is I totally gave the paps something real to talk about. They're all abuzz this morning with a bunch of pictures that were snagged of *Sunder* on stage. We laid to rest all the bullshit speculation that *Sunder* is going split or that they were gonna have to replace me."

"That's good," I said, nodding emphatically, still wringing my hands as I waited for the other shoe to drop.

"Yeah. It is." He hesitated, pulling in a deep breath that widened his chest before he began to speak. "See, thing is, they just love to twist things to fit their own agendas. Slant the stories whatever direction is going to win them the most hits. Create the most buzz. Lies have followed us around pretty much since the second *Sunder* made it big. And I'm not gonna stand here and pretend like I haven't been part of some shady shit in my life, because I'm pretty damned sure you're well aware. But let's just say sometimes those stories get contorted."

I could feel the bewildered frown pulling all over my brow. "What are you saying?"

"I'm saying, they saw the two of us together last night, and apparently that seemed way more intriguing than the actual show." He roughed a hand through that mess of hair. "Hell, it's always that way. Things are far more interesting off stage than on."

"Okay." I was still waiting, still wringing my hands.

He watched me with those potent eyes. "This is just the everyday for me, Willow. Something I pretty much have to deal with every time I step out of the privacy of my house. But I didn't know how you were gonna react."

He glanced to the floor before he looked back at me. "Think you might have had me a little distracted last night to consider it."

He said it like it wasn't taboo or a subject we needed to avoid.

"What did they say?"

Grabbing my hand, he tugged me forward. "Take a look for yourself."

He turned me toward his laptop that was open on the island.

My heart rate spiked and stuttered. I couldn't discern if it was because of nerves at what I'd find or because I'd entered Ash's space.

Because I'd begun to orbit his atmosphere.

That big body moved up close behind me. His breath breezed through the loose strands of my hair and brushed my neck, and he set both his hands on my shoulders, as if he were bracing me. At the ready to support me in whatever I might see.

A shiver rolled before a shock of air jolted from my lungs as my eyes focused on the screen.

The tab was open to a celebrity site. One that kept voracious fans and insatiable gossips apprised of the dirty deeds of their favorite superstars.

There were two pictures of the band on stage. But that didn't seem to be where the focus was directed.

No.

It was aimed at the grainy image filling most of the page. The picture was dark and shadowy, but unmistakable.

It was an enlarged picture of Ash and me, on the dancefloor, and clearly snagged by someone in the crowd nearby.

We were chest to chest.

His hands were on my hips and his face was buried in my hair.

I didn't know whether to be horrified or to shift on my unsteady feet when I looked at the erotic vision presented for all to see. I was certain I'd never once worn that kind of expression before as I was wearing in this picture.

It was as if I'd been lifted to some kind of rapture I'd never felt.

To a place where I was free and alive.

Sexy.

Wanted.

My mouth went dry, and with a shaky hand, I reached out and scrolled down. There was another below it that had captured everyone when we'd filed from the bar. Fuzzy halos of light streamed down through the haze, illuminating the group in a yellowy glow, *Sunder* looking so big and bad and beautiful in a wealth of power and dark mystery in the deep night.

But it was the last that had been zoomed and cropped that hitched my breath.

Ash squeezed my shoulders, a gentle reminder that he was there.

This picture was blurrier than the rest, and I thought maybe it should seem so much less interesting.

Dull and boring.

Because it was so simple. The act mundane.

Ash and I were holding hands as we strolled down the cobblestone walk.

In the moment, it'd felt innocent. Natural.

Seeing it now…

My head was tipped back as I drank in the endless expanse of stars, and I remembered I'd closed my eyes to imprint that perfect moment in my brain. So I'd forever remember the way I'd felt standing there at his side.

And Ash…Ash Evans was gazing over at me.

Emotion twisted through me like a tornado.

Men didn't look at me that way.

Bates surely never had.

This had to have been captured by chance. Interpreted wrong.

It wasn't real.

The scariest part of all was I realized right then I wanted it to be.

My attention traveled to the headline.

Has the ultimate bad boy been tamed?

Sex, drugs, and rock 'n' roll.

119

Ash Evans, of *Sunder* fame, is no stranger to any of them, so it was no surprise when the notorious rocker recently found himself in more hot water when he was assaulted in the early hours of August 23rd near his vacation home in Savannah, Georgia. The altercation occurred outside *Contemporary Comfort*, an antique store in the Historic District. The owner discovered him badly beaten and alerted the authorities.

Rumors the bass player had met his demise were shredded when he joined *Sunder* for an acoustic set last night at a local bar in downtown Savannah.

It's no secret the bad boy has had more than his fair share of women. He recently told *Wise*, "I love women and women love me. I make no apologies. Simple as that."

Although what's always remained most apparent is how he loves to leave them.

But we'd be hard-pressed to find him looking as cozy as he did after last night's show with none other than Willow Langston. Yes, the owner of *Contemporary Comfort*.

Is this a classic case of obligation, or has the unapologetic bachelor finally met his match? Sorry ladies, only time will tell.

Silence hovered around us as he let me catch up to what the article implied.

"Are you mad?" He released the mumble of words against the crown of my head.

"How could I be mad at you over this? We were just dancing.

Celebrating that you were able to get back on a stage."

That's all it was.

Right?

But my tremoring heart thought maybe it recognized the difference.

The breath he released was almost pained, and he pressed his fingers deeper into my shoulders. Massaging. Coaxing. Demanding. As if he wanted to dispute the statement I had made.

"Willow," he uttered my name carefully. "Know you're private, darlin', and I know I promised this was no big deal, but like you pointed out before, just because something might not bother me doesn't mean it won't bother you."

God, he had such a conflicting, confusing heart.

So indulgent and nonchalant.

So thoughtful and kind.

"It's just…" I struggled to make sense of my own confusion. "Someday…I want what those pictures are suggesting. For someone to really look at me that way. Your friends…the way they love each other…the way they talk about their families. Their *kids*." My words dropped to a yearning whisper. "To me, there's nothing in this world more beautiful than that."

Slowly, he turned me to face him. No doubt, he recognized what was in my expression.

Longing.

That commanding stare chained me. Tied me in a way I didn't understand.

I felt trapped. Exposed. Vulnerable. As if every single wish I'd ever ushered into the heavens had just been laid at his feet.

"Willow." His voice was a raw scratch at the back of his throat. That beautiful body inched closer and closer. Stealing what little air was left in the room.

His presence swirled through my head, the quiet yearning getting all mixed up with a bold shock of desire.

My chest heaved.

Tentatively, he reached out, that big hand resting on my cheek, coaxing my eyes to look up at the brilliance of his. This mesmerizing, intoxicating man.

Exhaling hard, he edged in a fraction, so close I could feel the hammer of his heart.

He brushed his thumb beneath the hollow of my eye.

"Peaches." This time when he said it, his voice fluttered with some kind of unknown grief. "So that's really what you've been waitin' for." He said it without a hint of doubt. "The family part."

Moisture gathered in my eyes. I couldn't stop it. This man saw straight through me, to all those places that were raw and aching. "I've been waiting on all of it. Love. A family. It's the only thing I've ever wanted."

"That dude was such an idiot." Those dimples almost peeked out with his tender smile.

I choked out a shot of laughter as I looked up at this man who was doing something to me he shouldn't have the power to do. "Bates stole everything from me, Ash. My money. My mama's house. All the things I was saving for. But most of all...what hurt me most? He stole the family we were supposed to share."

I angled my head as I studied this man. One who should have been nothing more than a stranger. I was sharing things with him that were intensely private. Yet somehow I knew he'd protect that knowledge in his big, capable hands. "All I ever wanted was to be a mama. Since I was a little girl...playing and dreaming, conjuring up stories with my sister of who we were going to be. Her dreams were wild. Big. Adventurous. And mine...they were simple and small."

Bringing her into the story almost felt like a dirty confession. Thoughts of her life brought me so much sorrow. So many regrets. But I was tired of keeping it all buried inside. Tired of going at it alone.

"I'm twenty-eight, Ash." It almost sounded like a plea. "Ten years ago? I would have sworn by now I'd have a house full of kids. Running wild. It'd have been hectic and messy and I would have cherished it with everything I had. Sometimes I stop and look around, and I wonder where did I go wrong? How did I end up in this place I never imagined I'd be? Instead of building a family? Every time I turn around, it seems like I just lose someone else. And I know I'm only twenty-eight, but there are days I wake up and wonder if I'm ever going to find someone who'll truly love me. Someone who won't leave me."

"Peaches." It was a whisper. His own plea.

My mouth trembled with the sad smile. I knew it made me sound a fool, but I knew this boy would somehow understand it all the same. "My high school reunion is in two weeks, and I can't even bring myself to go. Part of it is knowing Bates will be there. But more than that? It'll be a reminder of everything I've lost. A reminder of the things I was so sure I'd have achieved by now."

Not money or financial or material things.

The precious things I wasn't sure I'd ever have.

I dropped my eyes. "God...I sound so pathetic. Weak."

His head slowly shook. "Not weak, darlin'. Just broken."

Choked laughter rolled out on a rush of sorrow, and I found the smallest smile.

Because that's what this boy did to me.

He made me hope.

Sparked something inside that'd been missing for so long.

Maybe forever.

Big hands framed my face. "Maybe it's time someone returned the favor. Put your broken pieces back together."

Everything felt so tight, the air and his hold and the moment that seemed bound between us.

Waiting to trip into the unseen.

His heated gaze flashed.

"Willow," he murmured, eyes searching. Hesitating before something gave.

And I wasn't prepared.

Not at all.

But that dangerous mouth was suddenly on mine.

Lips and warmth and blinding light.

A needy gasp left me and my heart rate kicked.

My hands clutched his wrists as he kept my face in his steady hold, refusing to let me go.

He kissed me softly. Carefully. Like that single touch might restore something inside me.

I melted against him. That powerful body pressed me harder against the counter, and I let him. He must have taken it as an invitation because the demand of his mouth became urgent.

His teeth nipped at my lips, and his big hands slid into my hair. He gripped it tight, urging my head back.

On a breathy sigh, my lips parted.

His hot tongue slanted against mine.

Flames.

I felt them everywhere. Burning me up from the inside.

My skin was alight.

His hold possessive.

Kiss merciless and claiming.

Devastating.

Mind-rending.

He kissed me and kissed me until my spirit thrummed and my soul thrashed. His needy hands tangled in my hair while our bodies rocked and pitched and churned.

The only thing I wanted was more.

And more with this chaotic man was the very last thing I needed.

He would wreck me.

I knew it.

I welcomed it all the same.

He edged back a fraction. His hands slid across the slope of my cheeks. He gripped me there and let his forehead drop to mine as he panted for a breath. "Pretend with me, Peaches. Pretend with me."

Confusion distorted my already clouded judgment, and I clung tighter to his wrists to keep from falling to the floor. "What?"

"Pretend with me. Pretend that everything that article said was true. Pretend that you're mine and I'm yours. That you tamed the ultimate bad boy. Let's show up at your reunion and show that bastard exactly what he lost. What he's missing out on. Let him know he's the loser at his own game."

He swept his tongue over his swollen lips. "And after two months, when you finish this job, when you leave your mark on my house with your amazing talent, you can publicly break up with the world's most notorious rock star. Because you and me both know he doesn't come close to bein' good enough for you. Let's go. Let's show Bates and that bitch they can both go fuck themselves."

He squeezed his eyes closed and nearly begged it. "Pretend with me."

What if you hurt me?

What if I fall in love with you?

What if I want you to stay?

All my reservations howled and roared.

All I'd ever wanted was to be loved.

Wholly.

To amplify that love as I gave it in return.

To take that love and form it into something brilliant. To feed it with life.

This man was offering me a counterfeit version of that.

"That won't change the fact those pictures are a lie." The words were tight when I forced them from between my lips.

"So it'll be our lie. Ours. I want to try. Let me try to put some of those broken pieces back together again. Make you remember who you are. Shake you out from that battered shell so you'll be ready when that guy comes looking for you."

The last of those reservations screamed.

What if I want him to be you?

His lips touched mine.

Soft. Sweet. Fire.

"Please," he said.

"Okay."

I gave before my self-preservation could have a say.

Because God, if I were being honest, I wanted a little of what this boy was offering, too.

Then he put that mouth back on mine.

Marked me with the magnitude of his kiss.

A spark of hope glowed bright.

And I knew no matter how this ended, I would never be the same.

WILLOW

I sat back in the chair and closed the book on my lap.

Sheila sent me a caring smile. "She loves when you read to her. The best sleep she ever gets are the nights after you've been here reading to her. She hears you, you know, whether if she's answering you or not."

I gazed at my mama, her mouth wrenched open, jaw angled to the side. Grief constricted my heart. "I know."

Sheila gave a pat to my shoulder. "You're a good daughter, Willow. Not a whole lot of people take the time to do this."

That was something I couldn't fathom. Because sitting there? I felt helpless. Wishing I could change her world and there was absolutely nothing I could do.

Mama stirred in her shallow sleep, moaned my sister's name. "Summer."

Every cell in my body clenched. "Shh…" I murmured as I brushed back her hair. Giving her comfort the way Summer and I had always wished we could.

Summer rocked Willow in her tiny twin bed. "Shh…" she said. "It was just a bad dream."

Willow gulped around her sobs, trying to keep them quiet, knowing her mama would want to come. That she'd worry and fret and try to pretend everything was okay.

"I don't like it when she's sick."

Summer kissed her on the temple, brushed her fingers through Willow's hair. "Mama doesn't like it, either. She hates it. So that's why we've got to be strong for her. Stick together."

"But you're gone so much…I don't like it here, bein' alone. Especially when Mama's sad."

Their mama had been sad so much since their daddy had left, since her hands had stopped working the way she needed them to. Even though their mama tried to hide it, Willow still heard her muttering, worrying she didn't know how she was going to keep up with the shop.

"I'm tryin' to help every bit as I can," Willow promised.

"I know you are. You're mama's angel. You know that? Working in there beside her. She's proud of you."

"She's proud of you, too."

Silence hovered thick in the air, Summer's disagreement held back yet still apparent. "I want to make her proud. I'm just not sure I know how to do that anymore."

Since she'd turned thirteen, Summer had been gone a lot. Leaving Willow alone. More and more. But Willow had always understood everyone's dreams were different. It wasn't her place to ask her big sister to change hers.

"Mama just wants you happy," Willow said.

Summer linked her pinky finger with Willow's, her voice going quiet like a secret. "I'm trying to be. I just don't know why I feel like I've forgotten what that's like."

ASH

*O*n all things holy.

The woman was a sweet temple of temptation.

I held my hand out to help her from the low seat of my car.

So yeah, I'd pulled my favorite one out of the garage especially for this occasion. Because if we were showing a fucker up? We were showing a fucker up.

But my Maserati didn't have anything on the girl who glanced up at me with a shy smile as she swiveled and let those lust-inducing legs slide out, so damned long and toned and adorned in these super high, strappy heels that were a straight shot to my groin.

I pulled her the rest of the way to standing with a little more force than necessary. Okay, maybe with just the right amount, because she fumbled a step into me.

"Hi," I teased, a smirk kicking up at the corner of my mouth.

"Hi," she whispered so low I could barely hear it.

Or maybe I was too busy taking in a good whiff of peaches, loving the way her hair was pulled up high at the back of her head in some kind of sexy, messy twist, the length swishing down her back.

Neck exposed.

The girl was rocking some kind of black romper, the neckline plunging down the middle to land like a kiss right between her gorgeous tits.

Oh yeah.

I'd spent the entire ride over imagining the fastest way to peel it from her body.

"You've got this," I told her, pulling at her hand to edge her closer, our lips close to brushing.

"I've got this," she reiterated.

I thought maybe I felt her promise all the way to my soul, because it jolted through me, this pride I couldn't help but feel for this girl.

I wound an arm around her slender waist, tugged her against me, and tried not to moan when I pressed my mouth against hers.

Pretending.

Seemed *pretending* wasn't so hard to do when you had a girl like this by your side.

So maybe I'd spent the last five days practicing for all this pretending we'd be doing tonight. Kissing her long and slow every chance I got. Stealing her breath. Wading a little further into the murky waters of her mind.

Through her loss and the sorrow I was barely just beginning to understand.

Wishing I had the power to eradicate it all.

Knowing I didn't stand a chance.

I set my hand at the small of her back. "Come on, let's go

show these assholes who the real Willow Langston is."

"The real Willow Langston? I think we might be presenting the fake, souped-up version of Willow Langston. I'm not sure there's a lot of *real* happening tonight."

Laughter rumbled in my chest. "Oh, darlin', this is definitely the sexed-up version, but from where I'm standing, I don't think there's anything *fake* about it."

I let my gaze slide up and down the length of her mouthwatering body. Tonight was going to be a long night. I had to remind myself I was only pretending she belonged to me.

Because this girl deserved more.

She deserved everything.

Problem was, my dick didn't seem to know the difference.

She gave one of those soft, mischievous swats to my chest before she snuggled closer. "Are you teasing me?" she asked, looking at me from where she had her head resting on my shoulder, those chocolate eyes so full of warmth and unexpected ease.

Like my being there had a direct bearing on her mood.

Like maybe I was actually giving her something back.

Doing something good.

That energy blazed.

Awareness stretched between us.

A tethered, charged high wire.

Because here I was, toeing a dangerous line.

But it was that familiarity that spun through my deepest senses, in that place that was dark and quiet and reserved, that incited me to take another step.

"I do believe you have the whole teasing thing turned completely around. Did you look at yourself in the mirror before I picked you up? Do you not know you're what fantasies are made of? One look, baby, and you bring me to my knees."

Redness touched her cheeks. Something sweet and tender and shy. Dizzying to my mind and overwhelming to my senses.

"You don't look so bad yourself there, rock star."

"Yeah? Thought you might like it." I tugged at one of my suspenders.

Of course I'd dressed up. I'd dug through my closet and found some kickass black slacks, rolled up the sleeves of my white button-up to show off my arms, just in case this asshole needed another reason to be jealous, threw on some suspenders, because—let's be honest—I totally owned that shit.

Didn't think we had much to worry about with the way this girl looked tonight, anyway. Chances were the dude wouldn't even look my direction except to wish he were me. Well, that and to hope I didn't have a mind to kick his ass.

Anger pulsed.

God knew I did.

Wasn't sure how I was going to control myself tonight. How I would rein in the rage that boiled hot in my blood every time I thought about what the bastard pulled. Betrayal was a bitch. Disgusting. Something I hated and one of the reasons I chose to play it solo. But the truth of the matter? Cheating scum were in no short supply.

It was the other shit that made my mind spin.

The fact he'd stolen.

Destroyed.

Desolated.

Would be lying if I denied wanting to take the guy out. Permanently. Couldn't believe he and that bitch had gotten away with that kind of stunt. Swindling her out of her savings. Scamming her out of her childhood home.

Couldn't fathom that kind of inhumanity.

Made me want to show him *just* how brutal this world could be.

Willow ran her fingers along the row of buttons on my shirt, toying with the one at the top.

God, this girl was going to be the death of me.

"I do like it," she murmured all seductive like, pulling me from the lethal direction of my thoughts.

I pressed her palm flat against my chest. "Good. Because you're stuck with me. All. Night."

Wishful damned thinking.

But hey. A guy could dream.

She pulled in a deep breath as we approached the entrance. "Promise?" Nerves rolled down her spine. Palpable and real. She looked up at me, pleading with those soulful eyes. "Promise me you won't leave my side. Okay?"

I ran my nose along her jaw. Inhaled. Fought the fire that lit in my veins.

Surely we had to look like the happiest damned couple on the face of the earth.

Right?

"Promise, darlin'. There's no need for you to be nervous. Tonight, it's just you and me."

See.

Pretending was easy.

And pretending never hurt a thing.

seventeen

WILLOW

"Do you know when you just know? That's the way it was for Willow and me. Second I opened my eyes and saw her? *Bam.* Love at first sight. Never believed in any of that shit before…but sometimes all it takes is one woman to turn your entire world upside down. Isn't that right, darlin'?"

Strands of tiny twinkle lights glittered from above, pushing at the cloak of darkness draped across the balmy night. A cool breeze rustled through, drawn from the waters where we stood in the trellised rose gardens at the edge of the quiet river. Gas fire pits sparked and blazed from beds of colorful glass, their reflections projecting a glimmering dance along the streams of calming waves.

Ash had one of those hulking arms wrapped around my waist like a permanent fixture, his grin so easy, shining full of that blinding light.

Magnetic.

I swore, he had every girl here wrapped around his finger.

Including me.

Like the fool I was, I played along. Standing there beside him felt far too real and way too nice. Leaning in closer, I set my palm right over his heart, loving the comfort of the steady thrum.

"That's right." I stole a look at him before I glanced back at five pairs of star-struck eyes. I patted that strong chest. "This one *is* kind of hard to resist."

From across our little circle of old friends and acquaintances, Emily rolled her eyes and buried her knowing smile in her martini glass to keep from slipping up and throwing the game.

I'd long since gotten over being angry with her for putting me on the spot that day in the shop. How could I regret it now? Not with him wrapped around me and me wrapped up in him, the night cool and calm.

So what if I'd fessed up to her about this charade. Confided in her how this man twisted me into a million intricate knots I wasn't sure could ever be undone.

How he'd kissed me.

Then done it again and again.

How he made me feel something I hadn't touched on in all my life.

"Ugh. I'm so jealous," Maddie almost whined, though it was done with a smile. "Your boyfriend is like…the hottest guy on earth. This is so not fair."

I could feel Ash trying to subdue his laughter. Leave it to Maddie to talk as if he weren't standing right there. As if he weren't made up of flesh and bone and blood, but rather a figment of that glamorous, untouchable world that seemed almost imaginary.

"I would have to agree," I said, maybe a bit too readily

myself. This man was magnificent. A rare creature to be found.

His arm tightened around the back of my waist, his fingers gripping my side, voice so smooth. "Ah, now that's sweet, but y'all don't have to go tryin' to overinflate my ego. We all know who's the lucky one around here, and that'd be me."

"Hmm." Kimberly mulled as she frowned. "I would have bet my house ten years later it would have been you standing here with Bates. And now you're standing there with some famous guy? It kind of blows my mind." Kimberly almost scoffed it as she took a sip of her beer.

Always so brash.

Kayla smacked her in the arm. "Kimberly."

"What?" She looked unrepentant. I knew she had no clue it still felt like razors were scraping my skin every single time I heard his name.

That mention of his name? It automatically had me back on guard.

On high alert.

The same way as I'd been when we first stepped through the doors.

We'd been here for two hours. He hadn't shown. In that time, I'd eased into the safety of the night.

Maybe I should have taken that as my own warning. A sign to step away. To put some space between us.

Instead, I sighed in comfort when Ash gave me a reassuring squeeze, as if he knew I might need my confidence restored. I sank deeper into his hold. A hold that felt as if it might mean something.

He pressed a kiss to my neck.

Chills scattered, free and fast.

"No, honestly it's fine." It seemed crazy how true it sounded. "I got over him a long time ago."

I was over him.

Maybe I wasn't over what he'd done.

But I was definitely over *him*.

Ash nuzzled the side of my face, playing his part so damned well I could almost believe it.

I hummed. "Believe me, I found something much better to take his place."

Ash nipped at the sensitive flesh of my ear.

Desire.

It rushed so real, a thunder pounding through my too-tight veins all too vivid. Tugging and pulling at my insides. Throbbing between my thighs.

God, what was this man doing to me?

Ash chuckled.

Whatever it was? He knew exactly how to wield it. How to control it.

That arrogant boy slanted a smirk at my friends. "Ahh...y'all are talking about the little cocksucker who thought he could possibly do better than my girl?"

"Umm..." Kimberly stammered, their eyes wide as they looked at each other as if they had no idea how to answer him.

Emily busted up laughing, finally breaking into the conversation. She laughed so hard she buckled at the waist. "Oh my God. If Willow ever decides she wants to get rid of you? Please. Come find me. I think I love you."

But it was all soft affection, and there was nothing serious about it except for her gratitude for what he'd done. An unexpected peace took hold of me that I hadn't felt since I was just a little girl.

Not since I'd sit with my momma and my sister and dream.

Dream big and small and everything in between.

"Sorry, love, but my heart's already taken. But I'm sure we can set you up with one of these fine country boys. That one over there has been making googly eyes at you all night."

He pointed in the direction of Freddy, who was most definitely not making eyes at Em. Ash shot Emily a wink when he did. She just shook her head with an exasperated smile and took another sip of her drink.

The night grew deeper, and we all chatted and laughed and sank into the warm comfort. Ash and I wandered the small gathering as if we were one. I caught up with a few people I hadn't spoken to in years.

Some I'd lost touch with after I'd lost Summer.

Others had faded away with the years.

Then there were the one's who I'd shut out when I'd finally shut out the rest of the world.

When I'd hidden away because it'd been so much easier than facing the day.

And now Ash was making me stand out in his light.

He doted on me, filling me with his praise and his words and steady belief. Like he promised, he never left my side.

"I have to use the restroom," I whispered in his ear.

"Is that an invitation to follow you in, darlin'? Because if it is, I'm totally game."

A smirk took over the whole of that flirty mouth, the boy totally at ease, in his realm.

"Don't you wish."

"Uh…yes, darlin', I definitely do *wish*."

And I was getting confused about the pretending. Especially when he guided me inside and started us down the hall, spun, and pressed me against the wall.

He kissed me hard.

Surprised, I whimpered, before I gave, clutched at the collar of his shirt.

For the first time, he palmed my ass in one of those big hands.

"Peaches," he mumbled so low. He grew hard in his slacks, and that foreign feeling was back, rushing beneath the surface of my skin.

Suddenly he jerked back and sent me a tummy-tilting grin, though he was panting for his own air. He pecked a close-mouthed kiss to my lips.

"Go, before I follow you in there. And I know you don't want that."

Searching for breath, I peeled myself from the wall and fumbled the rest of the way down the hall on my too-high heels, trying to straighten myself out as I went.

I shivered, feeling the heat of his gaze eating me up the entire way.

I pushed open the door and stepped into the restroom. I met my reflection—swollen, red lips, wild brown eyes, and pink, heated cheeks.

I saw someone who was bold and brave.

I'd forgotten what that girl looked like. The scary thing was I no longer could remember exactly when she'd gone missing.

I used the restroom, washed my hands, applied a coat of sheer gloss. That smile was still firmly on my face when I tucked a stray lock of hair behind my ear then eagerly stepped back out in the hall.

I gasped out a shocked breath as I did, having to brace myself against the wall to keep myself from falling to the floor.

Fear and hurt and rage slammed me like a rogue wave.

Bates was there, at the end of the hall.

Backed against the wall.

Because Ash?

Ash had him pinned to it.

ASH

I watched her flounder her way down the hall in those heels, those shorts so short and those legs so long I couldn't look away. When the door closed behind her, I dragged a frustrated hand through the top of my hair and blew out a strained breath, choking back a chuckle.

I could feel her wanting to peek back. Itching to look. To find what my expression would be.

Knew if she did hers would be all wide eyes and confused smiles and affected blushes.

God, I liked it.

I tucked my hands in my pockets and rocked back on my

heels to settle into waiting.

That was when I felt it.

An awareness that prickled across the back of my neck like nails scraping a chalk board. My gut churned with the instinct that warned things were about to take a sharp turn south.

Slowly, I shifted to look over my shoulder.

Every cell in my body froze.

I never forgot a face.

Except, he wasn't looking at me. He was looking at where my Peaches had disappeared into the restroom. That was right before his jaw clenched tight and his glare slid to me. Like he were adding it up. Figuring it out.

It hit me so fast I was certain my heart was pumping nothing but pure adrenaline. Crushing rage spun through me like a tornado, catching me up in its mind-rending rotation.

Still, everything moved deathly slow. So goddamned slow as I turned the rest of the way around on my heels and faced the bastard.

I saw it.

The second he recognized me, he blanched and took one shocked step back.

My hands clenched into fists at my sides. I did my best to stay cool. To keep calm because life goes on and all that shit. Because I was about two seconds from coming completely unhinged, and I doubted this was the best place in the world to enact revenge.

I pressed a fist into my opposite palm. Exactly like I'd done that night. Unlike before, though, it wasn't five to one. It was just him and me.

He'd been the one to hop out alongside his buddy. The one who'd descended on me with fists and feet and fury. The one who'd delivered that last blow that'd knocked me unconscious.

Like I said, I never forgot a face.

Only tonight, he was wearing a suit like the asshole had just come from the office, tie loosened and jacket unbuttoned, all kinds of puffed-up ego and unwarranted pride.

A gush of air pushed from his lungs before his face twisted

in a sneer.

That was all it took for my reserve to snap. I flew forward and had him by the collar before he could make sense of it.

I slammed him up against the wall.

He grunted with the impact. He struggled against my grip, flailing around like a little bitch as he grappled with my wrists. It was pathetic and completely pointless.

He wasn't going anywhere.

"Well, what do you know? It's a small fucking world, isn't it? Remember me, asshole?" My words were delivered with bone-chilling calm and laced with the promise of my retribution.

Could feel the fear radiating from him just as sure as I saw him trying to keep it under wraps.

"What the hell are you doing here?" he strained, breaths short and rasping. "And what the hell are you doing with Willow? You piece of shit…what are you doing with her?"

Confusion jarred me back an inch, before a slow, knowing dread leached into my skin. Into my consciousness. Into my reality.

Bates.

This prick was Bates.

Of course he was. I really shouldn't have been surprised. Once a scumbag, always a scumbag. And this one actually had the audacity to show up and act like he had a say in her life.

I shot the asshole my cockiest grin, only imagining the scene he'd unwittingly walked in on between Willow and me a few seconds ago. All that "pretending" we were doing right in this very spot.

Dude had impeccable timing, that was for sure.

"What am I doing with Willow? Think the better question would be what am I *not* doin' with her, now wouldn't it?" I shrugged like any fool should have known. "Mostly living inside that tight, hot body every chance I get."

He thrashed all over the place, fighting with all his might to break loose. Pussy didn't even move me back an inch.

"She's quite the wild one, isn't she? Fucking insatiable. Woke me up three times last night because she just couldn't get enough." I frowned, all kinds of feigned enraptured confusion. "Or maybe it was four."

"Willow would never touch someone like you." He said it like the thought was vile.

Someone like me?

Anger cinched down on every cell in my body.

Yeah. I wanted to rip him to pieces. Tear him to shreds. Give him a little taste of what he and his friends had dished out that night. But seeking retribution for myself was not what I'd come here for tonight.

I was here for her.

Besides, I figured shoving my and Willow's "relationship" in his face would be the exact kind of punishment he deserved— the kind of penalty that hit him where it counted most.

Because this girl? This girl was obviously the ultimate prize, and tonight I was accomplishing exactly what I came here to do.

Willow and I were showing this fucker up. Knocking him down about a hundred notches or two.

I laughed a taunting, impetuous sound, laying it on thick. "You sure about that? Because you and I both know you were just standing right over there playing peeping Tom, getting an eyeful of what was about to come. Think it'd do you best to keep your eyes off my girl. Because next time you and I meet on a darkened street? I promise you, I won't be alone."

"Willow's not your girl," he growled.

I growled right back, tightened the collar of his shirt around his throat. "See, I'm pretty sure that's where you're wrong. Funny, isn't it? How you and your boys hunting me down brought me and Willow together."

He all-out shook when I uttered what they'd done aloud.

Maybe he saw it in my eyes. Payback was coming.

I grinned up close to his face, and he tried to jerk away. The only thing he managed was to smack his head into the wall. I shifted, getting back in his line of sight. "Didn't take me long to figure out the best way to repay her kindness, either. But you know, that sweet girl isn't all that hard to please. Though, you might not know all that much about that, now would you?

Satisfying her?"

My voice dropped low, like I were sharing a dark secret. "She did tell me her past experiences were a *little* disappointing."

I wiggled my pinky finger in his face, my expression one of total mock sympathy.

His face blistered with rage, so damned red I thought he might have an aneurysm right there on the spot. His teeth clenched so hard they had to be grinding to dust.

"Fuck you," he spat.

Like a bomb had been detonated, I felt the hurt that suddenly came bounding down the hall.

Willow.

I was praying she'd be good with this. That she'd play along. Stand strong when I knew she would want to fall apart.

I'd do my best to pick up the broken pieces later.

I looked at this girl that literally knocked the breath from my lungs. The one who tied it up tight and sent my pulse into a scattered frenzy. It was this mixed-up battering that throbbed and vibrated, a cocktail of my rage and lust and this strange devotion I couldn't shake.

I pushed all of that aside and sent her my biggest grin, begging her with my eyes to catch on to what was going down before I turned back to the bastard who was fighting my hold. "Nah. I think I'd rather fuck her."

Lifting his feet an inch from the ground, I rammed him against the wall. Not hard enough to hurt him. Just hard enough that I figured he'd be about ready to piss his pants.

Without giving him time to recover, I let him go and took a step back. Caught totally off guard, he stumbled forward. He bent in two, inhaled a bunch of harsh, wheezing breaths into his lungs that were no doubt aching from fear and violence and jealousy.

I stood there like the cocky bastard I could be. Smug look on my face while he leaned over, hands on his knees while he struggled to gather himself, his violent gaze glaring me down before he turned it on her.

"Willow." He said it like he owned her when he saw her

slowly approaching.

I knew it. Saw it all over his seedy expression.

He thought he could snap his fingers and she'd come running.

Hell no.

"Hey there, darlin'." I snagged her around the waist and pulled her into the safety of my side. A silent promise I would hold her up. "Looks like the dirtbag ex decided to show up after all."

I said it like he wasn't standing right there.

She smoothed herself out and lifted that courageous chin. "Well, I guess it's perfect timing, since we were just leaving."

I shot the asshole the biggest, gloating smirk I could find. "See ya around, Bates. My girl and I have some *business* to attend to, don't we, baby?"

He stood there raging as I began to lead her out. Second we turned our backs on him, his low, grating voice pelted us from behind. "I came here to talk to you, Willow. I've been trying to get in touch with you."

She stopped but didn't turn to him right away. She glanced at me for strength before she slowly turned to look at him over her shoulder. "Well, that's too bad, Bates, because I have no interest in talking to you. Everything that needed said was said a long time ago. Believe me, I got your message—loud and clear. Signed and stamped. Set in stone. So you can drop the texts and messages, because I don't have anything to say."

This fucker had been messaging her?

A fresh round of possessiveness ricocheted through the boundaries of my chest.

"That was years ago," he spat.

Bitter laughter ripped from her throat. "And you think that changes a thing? Because it's been years since you took everything from me. You're truly a fool if you think it does."

She glanced around. Resentment and old hurt trembled around her mouth. Her voice hardened with the accusation. "Where's Chastity, anyway? Did you leave her at home to wait for you?"

"We aren't together anymore."

She laughed a scoff, her head shaking as she struggled to stand her ground. "Isn't that a tragedy." Her entire body quivered her own suppressed rage. "Things make so much more sense now."

I stepped closer to her and lowered my mouth to her ear. "Come on, darlin'. Let's get you out of here."

Furiously, she nodded.

I turned her away, and we took another step while the bastard took a desperate one behind us. "You can't seriously be leaving with that guy."

She didn't look his way. "Yeah, I am."

He scrambled behind us. Took about all the strength I had not to turn around and lay this guy flat out in front of the audience steadily gathering around us. "Do you even know who he is?"

She ignored him.

"He's dangerous, Willow."

I scoffed. Damn right I was, and I was getting more dangerous with every offensive word that fell from his corrupt mouth.

We kept right on moving. I had to get us out of there before I lost it.

Snapped.

I could feel my control splintering beneath the pressure.

And this was not the place.

"Did you know he fucked Billy's girl? Did you know they broke up over it? Wedding's off."

Like it was my fault that bitch lied when I asked her straight up.

She inhaled a sharp breath and stumbled on her feet as she came to a stop. I tried to urge her to keep moving, but her heels dug in. She didn't understand how close I was to losing it on this asshole in the middle of this reunion.

She blinked what seemed a million times before gritting out four clipped words. "What did you say?"

Slowly she turned around to face him.

Emily was suddenly there. "Willow," she said, her voice damned near as protective as I felt. Her attention darted between each of us, worry and angst plastered all over her face.

Bates just stood there looking smug.

Like he held all the cards and he was getting ready to lay down a straight flush.

"I said he fucked Billy's girl."

Emily gasped at the mention of the name and Willow swallowed hard. "Billy? Your best friend, Billy?"

"Yeah," he said.

She started nodding, but it was shaky all over, sliding through her shoulders and heaving her chest. "You were a part of it."

Her statement punched the air like a gavel strike.

He paled. Obviously, he was expecting a total different reaction from her than the one he got.

Her eyes moved to me. Horror filled her own recognition.

Sorrow. Regret. Empathy.

All of it this twisted protectiveness over me.

Slowly, her focus moved back to the rat bastard still standing there like he had something to prove.

"You did this? You and those worthless jerks you call friends? You attacked him? Left him in front of my store to die? How could you?" It was all an appalled accusation.

"He had it coming."

"Oh my God," Emily wheezed, both hands pressed to her mouth.

Shock rippled through the gaping crowd.

Rage curled through my muscles, and I bounced on my toes, giving it my all to restrain myself. Because if anyone had it coming, it was him.

Instead it was Willow I was restraining as she moved to get in his face. From behind, I hooked my arm around her waist and started hauling her back.

Her voice shifted to a whisper. "I can't believe I ever loved a man like you. You disgust me."

She turned into my hold, and I started striding toward the door when the bastard reached out and grabbed her by the arm.

She yelped.

In a flash, I had him by the throat.

It was instant.

The violence that skimmed across my flesh. My teeth gritted and strain pulsed through every muscle. A rustle of anxious energy billowed through the room. People closed around us, eyes wide in morbid curiosity. I only saw him, my narrowed sight tinged in red and violence and hate.

"Don't touch her. Not ever again." I tightened my fingers and yanked him close. "If you do, I'm gonna make sure that meeting in a dark alley happens, and I promise next time, you aren't gonna like the outcome. Do you understand what I'm tellin' you?"

Not giving one flying fuck if he understood, I tossed him from my hold, making him fumble back. He landed hard on his ass, sliding across the slick marble floor.

Fury raced through me on a circuit of destruction I felt desperate for. I wanted it. Whether I wanted it more for me or for her, I couldn't tell. But it was there. Burning hot.

I grabbed her, hid her face in my shoulder to protect her from the mess playing out in front of us. I hauled us out of there before things got uglier than they already were.

My gaze remained vigilant, watching over my shoulder while we waited for the valet to retrieve my car. Willow kept breathing all her breaths into my neck, filling up my lungs with peaches and sweet and honey every time I panted for that elusive cool.

The valet pulled up. I helped Willow inside and was quick to round the front and get into the driver's seat. I gunned it, taking to the street with a peel of tires, getting us out of there before I did something that couldn't be undone.

I jammed my finger at the sunroof button. Needing air.

It slid open to the night and ripping wind and glimmering stars.

While I took all my aggression out on the road and steering wheel I squeezed in my hands.

Fuck.

I wanted to pound something to pieces.

Taking in a steeling breath, I chanced a glance at the girl I could feel staring at me from the other side, knowing I probably looked a madman.

Vicious.

Savage.

She was pressed sideways to the door.

And I thought maybe she'd be scared by my outburst back at the resort.

But her chest was heaving, expression wild as those long pieces of hair whipped around her gorgeous face.

She stared back at me with big chocolate eyes.

Molten.

Her gaze washed over me like lava.

Burning up everything in its path.

"You are so beautiful," she said, voice hoarse.

"Peaches," I whispered as a warning. Wasn't sure I trusted myself with her right then.

"You are. Did you know…did you know the first time I saw you…when you were lying covered in blood and you opened your eyes and looked at me, that I saw it? Something so beautiful and raw and powerful. Even when you'd been broken. The way you looked at me shook me straight to my bones. And then tonight…what you did for me…I don't…"

I roughed a hand through my thrashing hair, a perfect mirror to my thrashing heart. "Peaches."

Another warning.

I didn't deserve the way she was looking at me. Like I was good and right when I was no better than the bastard we'd left lying back there on the floor.

So slowly, she reached out, shaking fingers gentle as she traced them along the scar that marked that night beneath my eye.

A tremble took me whole.

Energy pulsed and shivered and shook.

Shit.

I gripped her by the wrist and pressed the underside to my nose. "You're killing me, darlin'."

149

"And you're saving me."

A hard frown hit me. "It was you who did all the saving."

Sitting back a fraction, she shook her head. "If it weren't for you, I'd be home tonight, hiding in the dark." Her tongue darted out to sweep across her lips. "I never would have been brave enough to go there or to stand up to him. To say those things."

"But that's where I think you're wrong, darlin'." This time it was my turn to reach out and touch her. I cupped the side of her face, glancing between her and the road. "I think you're so much braver than you've been giving yourself credit for. I see it there. Feel it every time I look at you. You're incredible, Willow. Every time you walk through my door, I know it. So good that I know I shouldn't be doing whatever the fuck it is I think I'm doin' with you."

She was still panting those breathy pants, and she leaned into my touch.

"I…" she attempted before she looked down, averted her gaze. Even with her head downturned, there was no missing the blush creeping to her cheeks. She hesitated before she spoke. "When you kiss me…it doesn't feel like pretending. It feels like the best thing I've ever felt."

I swallowed hard, crossing a line. Pushing into the boundaries that should have been firmly set in place. "That's because when I kiss you? It's not pretend. When I tell you you're gorgeous—the best thing I've ever seen? I mean it. And when I look at you…"

I touched the center of my chest, feeling ripped open wide. Exposed. Maybe telling her the truth when it wouldn't do either of us any good was wrong. But there was no hiding when this girl was looking at me that way. "I feel it right here. We might be pretending, but you can't fake this."

Like she didn't trust herself, she pressed farther against the door. "You make me want things…things I know I shouldn't want."

"And what is it you want, Peaches?" I prodded low, knowing full well I was pointing us in the direction of no return. "Told you when I came into your store that I'd give you anything."

"I want…" She tucked her bottom lip between her teeth, nervous or unsure whether to give me the truth.

Blood pounded mercilessly through my veins. Thickened with lust. All of it clouded my judgment, knocking loose my center of gravity.

Because I knew the look on her face. Desire was written across her like a musical score.

The way her body rocked and trembled and silently pled.

Desperate to be played.

I knew I should close my mouth. Shut *this* down. Drop her at home. Instead, I let the words slide free. "Tell me, Peaches."

The needy rasp fell from between her lips. Quietly. Honestly. "I want you to touch me. I…I don't…know what it's like…"

That blush was back full force, eyes wide and telling.

"Shit." I hissed it almost silently while a shot of lust kicked me in the gut. Realizing what she was saying. What she was implying.

"You want me to make you come?"

Her mouth dropped open and she nodded slow. "I've never…"

I rubbed a hand over my face, hoping it might help me see straight. All the resolutions I'd ever made gurgled to the surface, vying for me to take note, and that tiny spec that was left of my conscience was screaming at me to see reason.

For once, not to be the bastard who was at fault.

This girl was good.

Pure.

Waiting on what was right.

And *right* was most definitely not me.

But none of that seemed to matter to my subconscious that had already jumped into action. Before I even realized it, my car had changed direction and was blaring down the sleeping, desolate road, headed toward my house.

I struggled to find a balance.

Looking for boundaries.

Maybe asking for a wider line because toeing this one was becoming impossible.

"Never?" I asked.

She just shook her head.

"Just how far are we taking this pretending, Peaches? Because I can't go messing you up. Refuse to. You and I both know you deserve more than that. I know you want more than what I can give you."

"Just…let me feel something. Something different. Something better. Something *good*."

She twisted her fingers so tight I was sure she was cutting off blood flow. "I'm not…I'm not very good at these things," she quietly confessed.

Mother. Fuck.

"Idiot." I gritted it out into the torrent of air that ripped between us. I couldn't begin to imagine the bullshit that asshole had fed her for all those years. If she were even capable of thinking it was her who was lacking, Bates must have done a bang-up job fucking with her head.

I took a sharp right into my driveway, a little faster than necessary. The tires kicked up a storm of dust as we barreled up toward my house. I jammed on the brakes as I slid into the garage, threw it in park, and killed the engine. Half a second later, I was holding that gorgeous face in the palms of my hands, forcing her to focus on my words.

"Listen to me, and listen good. He's nothin' but an idiot, Willow. That bastard didn't have the first clue how to take care of you. How to touch you right. How to make you feel good. Only a selfish prick would turn that blame on you."

Her eyes fluttered in doubt, in want, and I pressed a soft kiss to her mouth. "Come on…let's go show that fucker up."

She giggled the softest giggle. So sweet. So perfect and light. It managed to weave its way in to take hold of that dark, dark space. That space that was hidden deep inside. One that for years I'd tried to forget. One I hardly recognized anymore.

Yet, somehow, it recognized her.

My chest tightened. All that shame I'd stuffed so deep, the regret and remorse begged me to take heed, to watch what I was doing. To check my intentions.

This wasn't some groupie looking for a one-night stand.

You're shaking her from that shell. Showing her that she's beautiful. Reminding her of all she has to offer. So when that lucky bastard out there finally finds her, she'll be ready to demand it in return.

That seemed to be enough of a reason to have me climbing out of my car and rushing around to her side. Helping her out, I took her by the hand, hauled her inside and up the stairs, and flung the door open to my room.

Instantly, I could feel her nerves ratchet high, the way her urgent steps slowed as she followed me in. I needed to slow the fuck down. Keep my cool when all night it'd been slipping away. I released her hand, thinking maybe she'd choose to bolt, knowing it'd be for the best.

Instead, she moved over to the line of windows, staring out at the night.

That energy pulsed around us.

"You sure this is what you want?" I asked from where I stood by the doors.

She slowly turned around to face me.

Moonlight filtered in behind her, illuminating her in shimmering shadows and soft, milky light.

She was fucking stunning.

So stunning I couldn't stop the lump from forming at the base of my throat or the heaviness that suddenly weighed down on the center of my chest.

"I shouldn't, but I do."

I started for her, my footsteps measured as I approached. I slid the suspenders from my shoulders, the words rumbling from my mouth, "I'm gonna make you feel good, Peaches. Give you what that asshole was too selfish to give. Then, it's going to end right there. If you feel uncomfortable for even a second, you say it. *You say it.*"

She dropped her gaze to the floor.

I touched her chin, gave it the gentlest nudge, urging her to look at me.

Chocolate eyes stared back. They swam with trust and desire and lingering fear.

Anger fisted my spirit.

I wanted to slaughter that bastard.

I got the feeling he'd never lifted a hand against her. His abuse? His abuse was all the words he'd clearly spewed that'd cut her down. Insults that had made her question.

I set my palm on her cheek, tilted my head, made sure my voice was sincere so she would know I meant every single one of the words that I let roll from my tongue. "This is for you, Peaches. Because you want it and you chose it."

I let my hand slide down the slender, delicate slope of her neck. My skin burned against her pulse point that ran wild beneath my touch.

"So beautiful," I said, filling her with the truth. "So kind. So good. Did you know those are all the things I see when I look at you?"

I ran my hand around to the back of her neck and pushed my fingers into her hair where it was twisted into a tie. I freed it from its hold, letting that beautiful mess rain down around her.

She exhaled a needy breath.

I inhaled it. Like it might draw her closer to me. I was such a fool, wanting more of what she had to give but knowing I had so little to offer in return. Praying the whole time that this might be enough.

I edged her back toward my bed. "And this body," I murmured as I was undoing the knot of material at her waist that acted as a belt. "Every time you walk through my door, my mind heads straight into the obscene. Wondering what you look like underneath all those clothes. Knowing it's spectacular and only my fantasies to vouch for it."

She shivered.

I backed her up another step. "And now, I'm gonna know firsthand."

Chills skated across her flesh.

Palpable.

My stomach twisted in a whorl of heated knots.

Shit.

I had no fucking clue how I was going to make it through

this in one piece. I was dying to get messy with this girl. Filthy. Touch her everywhere. Fuck her every way.

If we were pretending, I was gonna be all her fantasies.

I steeled myself as I set my palm against her flat belly, told myself to go slow, to take it easy. The only finish line being crossed tonight was hers.

I ran my nose along her cheek to her ear as I rounded her to the back, murmuring the whole way. "Tonight belongs to you. I'm going to touch you until you're dancing somewhere with the stars and then I'm going to catch you when you come back down. Then, I'm going to send you flying again."

She whimpered and pressed her thighs together, and I knew I already had her where I wanted her.

Shivering and wet and ready.

Needing this so damned bad her nerves wouldn't get in her way, the girl so worshipped by my words that Bates' would be deleted, one by one.

I brushed the mass of her hair aside. It uncovered the long zipper that held her outfit together. My fingers fluttered along the top of it at her nape. My touch lifted a rash of goose bumps across her exposed flesh.

"Do you feel that, Peaches? I'm barely touching you, and you're already shaking."

"Ash," she whispered.

"Tell me, darlin'."

She wet her lips. "I don't…please."

A dark chuckle slipped free, because this girl was just too good. Too innocent and sweet. Never had I been with a woman like her. Not in all my life.

Slowly, I slid down the zipper. The sound of it ripping free echoed like a promise against the barren walls.

"Gorgeous," I whispered across her skin.

I set both of my hands on her shoulders, massaging light. I pressed a lingering kiss to the back of her neck before I moved to her side, kissing her under her jaw as I glided around to the front.

Standing in front of her, I watched her expression as I

slipped both hands beneath the material on each side.

A sigh parted her lips and she stared up at me.

Trusting me to take care of her.

Carefully, I began to peel the black fabric away, my hands flat on her silky skin as I guided it down.

It was like the unveiling of some priceless, precious piece of art. One that had never before been on display. One that every bastard in the world wanted but not one of them could afford.

She trembled, and I all-out shook.

What the hell was she doing to me?

She inhaled and exhaled these quivering, harsh breaths as I let the single piece of material glide down her stunning body.

Her outfit dropped to the floor. A puddle at her feet.

Kinda like me.

She was exactly what I expected.

A masterpiece.

All toned, long lines and subdued curves. The girl was tall and sleek and slender. Just as willowy as her name.

Gorgeous.

Awe-inspiring.

It felt like if I got too close I would sink right in and disappear.

Maybe forever.

Her tits were all pressed up, swelling over the sexiest black bra I'd ever seen, purely lace with a few flimsy straps, underwear to match.

I let my fingertip trail across a strap. "I like this. A lot."

Self-consciously, she chewed at that lip. "You said you like black…"

She trailed off with the severity that lit up between us.

Energy spiked and pulsed.

Every cell in my body was set to high alert as she and I moved through the dense intensity that swallowed every drop of air.

Barely touching.

Yet, I felt closer to her than I had to anyone in so many years.

My dick strained, begging at the sight set out in front of me.

Obviously, he'd be getting none of the action tonight. And it was so messed up, so at odds with who I was, that I could be okay with that.

But it was my spirit that hitched when I caught a hint of what was marked on her skin.

It was hidden beneath a thick, mahogany wave that cascaded down her bare shoulder on the left side.

Almost wary, I brushed back the lock of hair to reveal the obscured. My fingertips tapped along the tattoo she had etched there, always before hidden by her clothes. My eyes jumped between the design and the intense pain that struck in her eyes.

It was a dandelion. An exact replica of the logo hanging on the sign over her store.

She trembled, her voice abraded with something brutally sad. "My mama...she loved them. She believed they guided the paths of our dreams. We just had to have the courage to chase them."

"Peaches." My murmur struck the weighted air, and she smiled this wistful smile that cut me to the core. How was it possible this girl could touch me this way?

But she was, and I just stood there while she got that expression on her face. The expression like she wanted to know me. The real me. The parts that were nothing but skeletons and bones hidden at the very back of a padlocked closet.

My insides were shaking by the time she found the hem of my shirt and started working through the buttons. A needy sound came from the back of her throat as she took her turn to reveal me, inch by inch.

Her throat bobbed as she swallowed. "It scares me...the way you make me feel."

Hot hands landed on my stomach, and I suppressed a moan, couldn't stop myself from letting it go when she began to slide them up the planes of my abdomen that jumped and ticked at her touch.

She pushed the material over my shoulders, and I shrugged the rest of the way out of it.

And I wondered what the fuck she would think when she saw the tattoo hidden on my side.

But it was like she already knew it was there.

Her attention went straight to it, though she seemed almost leery to caress across the dandelion I had imprinted there so long ago. Though mine? Mine was warped. Rotted. The flower head was completely barren of seed. It looked like a limbless, lifeless stick figure where it was marked deep in a chaotic rush of colors and whirls and despair.

Inscribed like a home for the deranged and broken.

A place I'd reserved for those who'd never make it back.

All the things Willow wanted most? I'd plundered them away. Too much a coward to face the obstacles head on. So I'd let them crash. Obliterated. Gone.

The words were grit where they scraped from my throat. "Funny…because I always thought they were your dreams floating away. Escaping you. Leaving you standing there to watch them drift out of reach."

Her face pinched in sorrow. "Or maybe they're just out there waiting for us to find them."

The smile that hit me was the furthest from feigned. Almost sad and flashing with that bit of old grief I never showed. But this girl managed to pull it from me. I touched her trusting face. "Yours are, darlin'. They're out there, waiting for you to catch up to them. Think you're closer. You just have to step up and let it go."

"How do I do that when I have so much holding me back?"

"I say we start right here. Right now, you start taking back all the things you lost."

"Some are lost forever."

Disquiet spun, and I forced it down, pushed forward an inch, erasing all the distance that separated us.

Skin to skin.

Chest to chest.

Her heart beat so wild. A stampede that had raced out of control, beating a mile out ahead of her. I pressed my hand there.

A sizzle lit in the air.

I explored just a little, my fingers brushing the lacy fabric of her bra, tracing across the swell of her perfect tit, before I was cupping the weight of it in my hand.

She gasped out like she'd never been touched that way before, fingers sinking into my shoulders.

My mouth pressed to hers, softly a first, reminding myself to take it slow. To handle her with care. Treat her the way I knew I'd never treated a single girl before.

Not even *her.*

That dark place ached with the thought, and I shut it down, closed it off, focused on the velvet of this girl's lips, the soft pants that were escaping between them. My tongue flicked out to get a tiny taste before I was licking into her delicious mouth.

"You taste so good." It rumbled free as I kissed her deeper. Harder. Fighting the frenzy that steadily built inside of me.

Begging for the chance to get a little closer to the kind of beauty I'd never experienced before.

To brush up against it.

Take some of it with me after she went.

She whimpered, and I completely lit.

Everything sped.

Her heart and my mind and the world that started spinning out of time.

Her tongue stroked and explored and begged.

While mine danced and promised and provoked.

My cock throbbed. So fucking hard. Dying to dive into all that silky flesh. To get lost in this sensation that was winning me over.

I moved her back another step, wrapped an arm around her waist. "Hold tight."

She locked her arms around my neck, and I crawled with her onto my bed until we were in the middle.

I kissed her mad, just as mad as she was driving me. I rose up on my hands and knees, arms caging her in, my head dipping down as I delved into the well of her hot, hot mouth.

Her tongue was chaos. Her touch insanity. And I thought, right then, that I had surely lost my mind. Every rational, logical part of me screamed to stop. But I couldn't. I was barreling ahead into that dangerous territory where I couldn't afford to be. Feeling a flicker of something other than lust when I rocked my pant-covered cock against the lacy seduction that rested between her thighs.

She lifted up. Begging. Searching for friction. "Oh my God," she whimpered. Her head swished back and forth like she could feel the world slipping out from under her and she was trying to take hold.

Like she'd never felt anything so good.

And I was just getting started.

I knew it wouldn't take more than a brush and this girl was gonna go off. That thought was really all it took for me to let my hand go sliding down, caressing over the crop of her underwear that was soaking wet, her body keening for release.

"This, darlin'? Is this the way you were wanting me to touch you?" I voiced it like a question when I slid the scrap of lace aside, fingertips slicking into her lips and kissing across her clit.

Her hips jerked from the bed.

"This…please," she nearly begged.

I shifted so I was entirely on my knees. I watched down to catch her expression as I pressed two fingers into her pussy, the girl so snug and right.

Her mouth parted, and her eyes sparked.

I groaned.

"Shit, baby…you are indescribable."

And that was all I could take before I was leaning back on my knees and peeling her panties free.

Masterpiece.

I wasn't lying.

Pink and pretty and tight.

I wound my arms under her legs and gripped her by the thighs and dove right the hell in.

My tongue plunged into all her heat.

She bucked, fighting the sensations, but I tucked her closer.

I licked her up and down before I set to lapping at her clit and my fingers returned to sliding deep.

"Ash." It was all a surprised gasp when her hands flew into my hair like she needed something to hang on to. I focused all my effort on showing this girl exactly the way she was supposed to feel when a man touched her.

Tension wound her up fast.

Pleas panted from her mouth. Growing thicker. Needier. Deeper.

Willow rode an edge she'd never ridden.

I could feel it influencing every cell in her body. Tightening. Wringing. Shimmering bright.

I twirled my tongue and tipped her over.

She arched from the bed.

Begging my name like it was a song.

I fucking loved that she wasn't reserved or shy about it. That she kept chanting my name in mumbled whispers as she squeezed her thighs around my head. I continued to eat her up, milking every last drop of pleasure I could find from her body.

Her walls pulsed around my fingers, and I slowed my assault, easing and easing until she stopped throbbing and the tremors took over.

I kissed her gently on the inside of her thigh.

And she lay there, gasping as she stared at the ceiling.

I smirked her way. "Yeah?"

Was it wrong that I felt a little smug?

She touched my face. Softer than she should. "Stars."

My guts twisted with the way she looked at me, and I backed off her to give her space. Or maybe I needed it for myself.

She sat up, her hand on my chest. Chocolate eyes blazed. A liquid mixture of curiosity, fear, and want.

"I want to feel you." The words scraped across the dense air.

I shook my head while my dick screamed yes please. "Told you tonight wasn't about me."

She climbed off my bed and stood before me covered in nothing but her lacy bra, body insane and still shaking with the afterglow.

She took my hand, so brave and confident where she was looking down on me. "But what if this is for me?"

I looked up at her.

My mind and heart and spirit at war.

Problem was none of them knew what they were fighting for.

She pulled me to stand, and I didn't resist. And I didn't stop her when she dropped to her knees. Her shyness was back, all the questions and uncertainty returning.

I caressed her cheek. "Peaches. You don't need to do this. You've got nothing to prove."

She traced her fingertips over the scar on my side, her eyes so sincere when she gazed up at me. "I can't believe he was a part of this. That he did this to you. I…"

"Fuck him," I said.

Her lips danced with the faintest smile. That blush struck up on her face when she let the words fall from her pretty mouth. "You definitely know how to show a man up, don't you? The two of you? You don't even live in the same stratosphere."

I thought maybe it was that second that I fell a little bit for her. The moment when a dead piece lit.

Because I swore I could feel my spirit climb into my chest when she started fumbling with the button of my fly, her nerves rippling free like they had wings when she pulled my zipper down.

My cock twitched. Way more eager than he should be. Neither of us should be getting this involved in the first place.

Especially when a gush of shocked air rushed from her mouth when she pulled me free.

Those eyes were wide and so damned wild as she stared at me. Her fingertips came up to barely brush along the swollen, sensitive skin.

"*You* are indescribable." She barely managed to murmur back my praise as she peeked up at me before testing me in her hand. Unsteady and apprehensive.

"Willow," I said. Half warning. Half plea. Because here was this girl trying to figure out how to get her hand around my dick while I could feel her sinking into every inch of me. She finally lifted the other, gripping me right in the middle in both hands, lightly, like she didn't know if she would hurt me.

Then she…

She closed her eyes, sat up on her knees, and leaned forward.

She set the gentlest kiss against the very tip.

So damned sweet.

Fuck. Me.

And I knew with her eyes squeezed tight she was looking for courage. She was somewhere in her head, trying to unearth the boldness I saw so plainly inside her. She must have found it, because between one breath and the next, she was using her hands to test me against her lips. They parted and pulled me inside.

I moaned, twisted my fingers through that mass of mahogany, the girl just as intricate and complex as the pieces of wood she brought to life. She began to suck me, gaining a shaky confidence as she took me deeper with each stroke.

Somewhere in the back of my mind, I knew I'd had better head in my life. That this was a little fumbly and awkward because this girl was so timid and unsure.

But not one of those faceless girls stood out, and I knew without a shadow of a doubt that I'd never experienced anything better in all of my pathetic life.

And that right there scared the fuck out of me.

WILLOW

"Did you let him kiss you?" Summer knocked her shoulder into Willow's.

Willow couldn't help but drop her head to try to hide the hot flush that climbed her cheeks. Her fingers played through the high grasses where they sat. Warmth filled the Savannah air, the sky so blue and bright above, the trees waving with the gentle winds and dropping their leaves, the sound of the stream trickling through.

"No."

Summer laughed her carefree laugh. "Oh my, Willow, what am I going to do with you? Don't you know that's what boyfriends are for? Kissin'?" her sister teased.

"I'm not like you," Willow admitted.

Summer feigned offense with a gasp, and her hand slammed over her heart.

Willow's eyes went wide. "Oh my goodness…you know that's not what I meant, Summer."

She meant she wasn't bold and daring like her sister.

Her mama told her it was her thoughts and ideas that were bold. It was the way she looked at the world that would leave her mark.

Laughter filtered through with the breeze again. "I know, I know, Willow. You'd never say a negative word about me. Even if they might be true."

"Don't say that," Willow urged.

Summer just shook her head and looked toward the sky. "Some things are just what they are, baby sister. Even if I never meant for them to be."

Her sister's tone turned that sad way it had so much lately. "That's why I can't wait to get out of this small town with even smaller minds. I can't wait until I'm free of it all. To live my life the way I want to."

Dread curled through Willow. The thought of her sister leaving her, too. Just like their daddy had not a year before. Not with their mama getting sicker and sicker. Being alone was her greatest fear. "What would I do without you? I hate the thought of you not being here."

Sadness filled her sister's sigh. "I hate the thought of leaving you, too. Of leaving Mama. But I don't know if I can stay, Willow. I don't belong here. I don't fit in. Don't you see that?"

She turned and faced Willow, expression pleading for her to understand. "You and me. We're different. All the beautiful things you've been creatin' at Mama's store? You shine here. Your happiness is here. And I need to find a place where I shine."

Willow linked her pinky finger with her sister's. "You'll find it. I know you will."

Hope that seemed marred by disbelief glinted in Summer's eyes. "Yeah. I will."

Plucking a dandelion, Willow held it out just the way their mama had always done. "Make a wish."

Summer's chuckle was both disbelieving and slow, her voice soft with affection. "See…that's what I'm saying. You are all the good, thoughtful things I'm never gonna be."

I jerked awake, thoughts of my sister lingering in my spirit. Sunlight slanted in through the windows. Disoriented, I started to panic, before I settled into the comfort surrounding me.

This couldn't be real. Wrapped up in the strong comfort of a strange man's arms, his big body so warm and secure, legs tangled with mine.

A man like Ash Evans, nonetheless.

He hugged me closer, as if from within the confines of his sleep he felt me stir. His mouth was gentle where he pressed it to the back of my head. His nose was in my hair as he mumbled a contented sigh.

Memories from last night came tumbling in.

"I should go."

His hand cupped my face. He guided me to standing from where I'd knelt before him.

He tilted his head and his mouth lifted in a satisfied smirk. Full of dark promises. "Darlin', you think that was it? I'm just gettin' warmed up. You should most definitely stay."

I trembled. Body. Mind. Soul.

Stay.

The night passed in a blissful blur. His touch and his tongue and his body pressed to mine. Time and again. Pushing boundaries without ever breaking through. My body spent and wrung out, he carried me to his bed. Big hands so tender as he worked his tee shirt over my head before pulling the covers over us and whispering, "Sleep."

I could almost feel the blush light on my face. How was it possible to feel both embarrassed and bold?

Naïve and beautiful?

Careful not to wake him, I unwound myself from his hold and slid from his bed. My feet landed on the warmth of the worn wood below me, at this place he'd entrusted to my hands. It looked so much different in the light of the day.

So much like him.

I glanced down at his hard, hard beauty, that broken, perfect statue cut of precious stone that rolled to lay on his stomach. His bare back was exposed, pure muscle and strength, wide,

wide shoulders and narrow waist, the sheet just barely coming up to cover his perfect round ass.

Redness flushed and my teeth clamped down on my lip.

So maybe I was a voyeur. Stealing the private minutes.

When he wasn't standing over me in that magnetic, imposing way, but instead lost to his own dreams. And I wondered...wondered if those dreams traveled any further than his love of being on a stage. If he wanted more or something different or if he would forever be satisfied with the same.

Needing to clear my head, I looked around the room at our clothes strewn about the floor, down to my bare legs that peeked out from beneath the huge tee shirt I was swimming in.

So that didn't help.

I blew out a breath, cast one last glance back at the boy, and tiptoed out of his room and downstairs.

After last night, coffee was a necessity.

Yes, yes. Coffee.

Suddenly full of purpose, I swung open the kitchen doors.

Then I shrieked and skidded to a stop. I slammed my hand over my mouth to muffle the horrible sound from leaking out. Or maybe to cover up my embarrassment while I wished my hand was about a hundred times bigger to cover up so much more.

Zee flipped around from where he was standing in front of the coffee maker.

"What in the world, Willow?" He gasped out a breath. "You scared the shit out of me. What the hell are you screaming for? It's just me."

I attempted to steady myself, my trembling hands yanking the hem of Ash's shirt down a bit more. "Scared you? I think it's the other way around. I didn't..."

His brow lifted. "Tell me you didn't forget I live here. Am I really that indistinguishable up against the rest of the guys? Now, that's just sad."

Not even close. He was gorgeous. Incredibly. But it was his spirit that seemed quiet. A fly on the wall who absorbed it all.

I frowned, hoping I hadn't offended him. "Of course not. I

guess you're not around a lot when I'm here…and I…"

And I was totally distracted. Still floating through that dream of last night. Wondering when I was going to come back down. When that bubble was going to burst.

Redness flashed, and I started to back away. "I should…" Self-consciously, I waved a hand toward the door behind me.

God. This couldn't get any more awkward. Was this what they called the walk of shame? Because I was feeling it, all over, lighting up my skin and crawling through my nerves.

Zee laughed. "Don't worry, Willow. You aren't the first girl to come roaming into this kitchen first thing in the morning. Maybe the first one to come in screaming. But definitely not the first."

I flinched.

Okay.

That hurt.

It shouldn't have. But it did. Another reminder that I needed to watch myself. Watch where I was stepping and what I was getting into. Because it already felt like maybe I was getting in too deep.

Summer had always told me to be careful. That I had a special kind of heart. The kind that was easily crushed.

Zee's smile was kind. Soft in his easy, understanding way. "Hey, I didn't mean anything by that. What you do with Ash is your business."

I wrung my hands out in front of me. "But we're not…we didn't…"

The doors swung open from behind. The presence that gusted in with it swallowed all the air.

I shook.

Oh God.

This boy affected me. Too much.

From behind, he wrapped both arms around my waist.

Fire, flames, and light.

A shudder ripped through me from head to toe.

He chuckled like he knew he wielded all the power. "What do you mean, we're not?"

I could feel the satisfied grin he tossed at Zee from over my shoulder. As if it were plain as day when what we were doing was the most confusing thing. Then, he set to leaving a dizzying trail of kisses along the slope of my neck.

Spellbound.

That could have been the only reason I melted against his hold in the middle of his kitchen in front of his friend.

Zee laughed quietly. He had to be accustomed to humoring his over-the-top friend. "Looks like that's my cue to leave you two to whatever it is you are, or aren't, doing."

Goose bumps blazed.

"Thanks, man," Ash mumbled.

"No problem. Coffee's done."

Zee grabbed his cup and started across the kitchen. I got an almost sympathetic smile as he approached. The one he leveled on Ash was hard—almost a warning—as he disappeared out the swinging door.

"What was that?" I asked. It came out breathier than I intended with those lips against my skin.

"It means he likes you." Ash kept kissing along my neck, nose going deeper into what had to be a rat's nest of hair. "Basically, he told me he'd be all too happy to kick my ass if I hurt you, all without saying a word."

He swung me around, and my heart stuttered before it took off at a sprint. The longer pieces of his hair fell forward across his forehead, his face defined angles, his jaw wide, and his nose sharp. A perfect, broken statue. My glorious avenger lit up in the light.

A secret part of me thrilled. That part that was going to get itself trampled to pieces by being so foolish to do what I was doing now. Because I'd told him no lie.

I only shared my body with a man if I loved him. And bit by bit Ash kept taking pieces of me for himself. My heart and my spirit and my body.

If I wasn't careful, it was all going to belong to him.

He would wreck me.

Something severe flashed through his expression. Pained and

promised. Delivered rough as he took a menacing step toward me. Stealing air and sanity. "But there's no risk in that, seein' as how we're just pretending. Right, darlin'?"

I got the unnerved feeling he might be saying it for his own benefit. That maybe there was a chance this felt different for him, too.

"You can't hurt what you don't hold," I told him. Maybe my own warning to take a step back.

He gripped my hips in both his hands. I yelped, then gave, welcomed the hard heat as his body connected with mine. His voice was both raw and smooth. "Even if I wanted to hold you…keep you…it's all wrong, baby. It's all wrong because I'm wrong. I'm ugly in all those places people can't see. That's a place I can't let you go. Won't let you go. You deserve so much better than what's waiting there."

He said it as if he were trying to convince himself. But there was something about him offering that truth. Confirming the reality of that spot inside him I'd only ever glimpsed. This beautiful, broken boy hadn't just been cut down on the outside. He had some of those scars littering the inside, too.

"I never asked to go there."

Defense.

That was all I had.

He smiled, and it was both sad and arrogant. It should have been impossible. But not for him.

"No need to say it." His thumb brushed the hollow beneath my eye. "It was written all over you last night. These eyes, Willow."

I watched the heavy bob of his Adam's apple as he swallowed. "It's like they have their own soul. Like they know things they shouldn't. Hold all the secrets they were never told. And I want to give you everything they're begging for. Anything. But there are some things I just don't have to give."

Emotion welled. Tight and hot. "What are you saying?"

"I'm saying that when we're done? I want to have given you something rather than have taken from you. I want you to be ready to face this world, take it in the palm of your hands, and demand all you deserve. I want to spend every day we've got showing you how goddamned beautiful you are. It means I don't want to hurt you. Not ever. Need to know you can handle that."

"You make me feel like I can."

It was both my greatest truth and my biggest lie.

He edged closer. "What's your greatest fear?"

I didn't need to search all that deep, and my mouth was whispering the secrets I held. "Being alone." I squeezed my eyes with a sharp shake of my head before clarifying. "Not of being alone physically. But of being lonely."

I wound my arms up in the space between us before touching my chest. "Of having all this love in here and having no one to give it to."

Guarded, I eyed him, his gaze so intense.

"It seems everyone I love the most gets ripped away. One by one. And I'm terrified that one day, I'm going to turn around and the only person standing there is going to be me."

"That guy's out there," he promised again. Emphatic. "I bet he's riding out there on one of those dandelions your mom issued into the heavens when you were just a little girl. Out there floating in the air…waiting on you to catch up to him."

What if I want him to be you?

That greedy, vacant voice screamed through me, howling with the all-consuming loneliness that only this man had had the power to touch when he was touching me last night.

Bates had never come close.

I shushed it and stared up at this striking man, the words merely a breath. "What's your greatest fear?"

He didn't hesitate. "Falling in love. Being responsible for it. For the happiness of another, knowing one day I'm liable to let them down."

The look on his face nearly obliterated my heart. It was there for the briefest flash of a second. Gone before it could be discerned.

The cruelest kind of grief.

A fake grin cracked his face. "Tried it once…didn't end all that well. And I'm not sure I'd make it through something so horrible again. I've wrecked a lot of shit in my life, Peaches. I don't intend to repeat it."

I nodded slow, trying to process this man. His big, bleeding heart and his callused soul.

He edged forward, forcing me to back up until the sharp edge of the counter was pressed into my back. "We good then? We agree I'm gonna spend the next couple months blowing your mind…everything but sex, Peaches. Because like I told you last night, I can't go messing you up like that. Know what that means to you. But I'm going to teach you to demand what you want. What you need. Then when we're finished, you're going to walk out my door ready to find that guy who's going to blow me out of the water."

Impossible.

I didn't say it.

I nodded instead.

A smirk sprang to his lips. "Good. I think the next thing on the agenda is changing the order of business in my room, because waking up at the ass crack of dawn with the sun rising through the bare windows is not exactly my favorite kind of morning. Especially when I woke up to an empty bed when you were supposed to be in it."

He feigned a pout.

A giggle slipped free. "What, you think just because you got me into your bed I'm all of a sudden going to start doing your bidding? You get no curtains until the walls are painted. It's not like you don't have six other rooms to pick from."

He shifted faster than I could make sense of it. He pinned me against the counter. A predator caging me in. At the ready to pounce on his prey.

Was I a fool for wanting him to?

An arrogant smirk quirked on his flirty, flirty mouth, and he leaned in close. "Hmm…if I recall, it was you who was doing all the 'bidding' last night," he rumbled.

"I think it was you who told me never to be afraid to ask for what I want."

The truth of it was that I had been afraid to ask for it all.

"And what is it you want?" he coaxed.

"I want you."

I gasped when he had me by the waist, hiking me up onto the counter, hands on my knees as he was pushing them apart.

I whimpered, shocked and so turned on I couldn't see as I braced my hands flat on the counter behind me.

This. This was what I'd been waiting for. The feeling I'd been desperate for. What I knew had been missing.

His grin was devious, and his tongue darted out to wet his lips. A single finger teased through my wetness.

The entire world turned electric. Every atom, a synapse of need.

"Still bare."

I swallowed around the lump in my throat. "Yes."

He groaned. Barely touching along my sensitive, swollen skin, still tingling from last night. My stomach tightened, and those places throbbed with a want I'd never known.

His words abraded across my skin, like the sandpaper I raked across wood. Exposing what was underneath. "What was your favorite part?"

He circled the tip of his finger around that spot I wanted him most.

Sparks.

"I—"

I couldn't breathe. Couldn't think.

He added a finger, teasing and exploring me from front to back, touching places I'd never been touched.

I gasped. "Ash..."

"I know, baby, I know," he whispered. Before he even started testing me, he already knew the answer.

He pressed two fingers deep inside, and I felt sweaty and hot, flames licking and dancing and curling. Pleasure spread and gathered. Taking me whole. Higher and higher. I flew up to sitting, my bottom barely clinging to the edge of the counter.

I kissed him hard.

The seconds our lips met, he devoured me.

Mouth, tongue, body, soul.

He pulsed his fingers hard and deep, swirling his thumb in that magic way, knowing exactly what I needed. He sent me soaring again. Shooting me to that place he promised. Where the stars danced and bled. I stayed there for forever, for too short a time, before I came crashing back down.

And like he promised, he was there to catch me in his arms.

Without a thought, I slid from the counter and dropped to my knees. "This...this was my favorite."

After what he had just done, it should have been a lie. But this...this was what had chased me in my dreams. Exploring and experiencing this magnificent man. A fantasy. My own flawless delusion.

He groaned from somewhere deep in this throat. His features twisted in a mess of confusion and shock and lust.

"Touching you. Tasting you."

And maybe it really was all the orgasms that made me crazy.

Because the shy, shrinking girl would have thought this was demeaning. Probably because Bates had told me I was horrible at it. He made me question every touch, every need and want I had. But sinking to my knees in front of Ash Evans made me feel as if I held all the power. Seeing the intimidating man stand above me, the bulge of his biceps and pecs, the flat, rippled planes of his ripped stomach, jaw clenched so tight.

The warrior.

But I could feel him shaking.

Brimming with need.

Something I'd created in him.

I peeled down his briefs. Exposing him the way he'd exposed me.

The man was huge. I had the wayward thought that Tamar had been right. It had to be just as big as his heart.

"What are you down there smirking about?" he asked with one of those grins. "I think you might have been hanging out with me too much. Seems I'm rubbing off on you."

Boldly, I took him in my hand.

Because Ash Evans rubbing off on me was exactly the point.

WILLOW

Downstairs, the doorbell rang. Excitement shivered down my spine. I took one last glance at myself in the mirror, smoothed out the cute beige dress that I'd coupled with a pair of sandals. I gave myself a reassuring smile and turned away to grab my little bag and head downstairs.

A date.

Apparently Ash Evans was taking all this pretending seriously.

And God, I loved it. Chose to cherish every second of it until the moment it was gone.

I hit the landing of my small house and went straight for the door. I swung it open. Caught off guard, I stumbled backward, my insides feeling as if they might twist me in two, when I found who was waiting on the other side.

Bates.

Anger gathered like a storm.

"What are you doing here?"

"Aww, now is that any way to welcome the love of your life?" He said it with every ounce of the condescending sneer he'd always happily reserved for me.

Resentment rippled and roiled. "That's because I don't have any welcome left to give. You used it up. Which means you aren't welcome here…so you need to go."

"I'm worried about you," he said, the contempt suddenly missing from his tone.

That was Bates. Cunning and sly. Always using words to get his way.

My laughter was nothing less than a scoff. "You're worried about me? That's rich."

"That head of yours was always full of fairy-tales, Willow. I can't help but feel responsible to step in when I see you letting yourself get carried away by one of them."

Outrage bristled through my nerves. "That's funny, considering you're the one who showed me firsthand not to believe in them."

"I've changed."

Scorn wove into the words. "You've changed?"

"Yeah."

My gaze traveled over his shoulder, to the street where a truck was parked at my curb. I barely made out the silhouette of the man sitting in the driver's seat.

It didn't matter. I recognized him.

A quiet wrath saturated every cell in my body, this hatred I couldn't quite fathom that built in my spirit. "You have the nerve to show up at my door, with Billy nonetheless? After what the two of you did?"

"I told you before, he had it coming. The last thing I'm going to do is sit aside and watch you get tangled up with a man like that."

Sickness clawed at my belly. "A man like that? Are you really that clueless, Bates? You really think after what you did to me, you have a say in who I see or what I do?"

"I love you. I made some mistakes, but I'm here to make up for them. Can't you see that?"

Mistakes?

He ruined my life.

His words soured on my ears. I hated them. Because maybe it was that moment when I realized I hated him. Wholly. There were no parts left inside that secretly wished we'd found a different outcome.

"My love died for you a long time ago. Now you and Billy need to be on your way. I have plans."

His eyes traced my body, the dress I wore. His nostrils flared. "I'm not giving up on you, Willow. I promise you that."

I shook my head. "Well, that's too bad, because you're wasting your time."

ASH

I turned onto Willow's street. Anxious. Eager. Which was probably about the damned most ridiculous emotion to be experiencing. But none of that seemed to matter. Because there it was, growing stronger the closer I got to her place.

That grin slid off my face when I saw the big ass truck pulling from her curb.

A surge of something fierce and lethal slicked like ice through my veins. Every nerve in my body fired with a hatred so thick I was sure I would choke on it when I made eye contact with the bastard at the wheel.

Fists, feet, and that rod.

My glare coasted to the fucker sitting in the passenger seat.

My hands tightened on the wheel and my teeth grated in unspent fury, the anger on my chest crushing so tight I was at a loss for air.

Rage spun my head.

Both our vehicles slowed as we passed. Glares locked down in a silent, impending war.

Maybe Lyrik had been right. Maybe I should have pressed the cops. Taken care of this bullshit the way rational, normal people would. Because the reckoning I was itching for now had disaster written all over it.

The second he passed, that asshole Billy gunned the engine, and I was left with this protectiveness that swelled up to consume my spirit when my gaze traveled to the girl standing in her door.

God damn it.

Why'd she have to affect me this way?

Make me feel crazy and different and better and worse.

But I couldn't stop it. Couldn't stop the desperate need to get to her when I flew into her drive, threw my SUV in park, and cut the engine.

I jumped out like some kind of deranged madman, stalking toward her and doing my all to control the anger seething in my muscles as I climbed the two steps to where she stood.

"Peaches." My hands landed on either side of her neck.

Relief.

"You okay?"

She was heaving her own angry breaths. "Yes."

"What the fuck did he want?"

"Me."

I choked out a laugh. Of course he did. Who wouldn't? Sometimes even idiots came to their senses.

"And?"

"And I told him he needed to leave because I had much better things to do with my life."

I laughed again. This time something soft wove into the sound as I dropped my forehead to hers. "Good girl."

She smiled up at me. "Hey, I have an infamous rock star to tame. This is serious business. I don't have time for any of his nonsense."

Why'd she have to be so sweet?

"Peaches…what am I gonna do with you?"

"Kiss me."

I groaned, kissed her deep and long and slow, my hands on her jaw and my heart beating far too fast. She clung to my wrists, kissing me back. Soft and tender. Delicious. Delirium.

I pulled back. A sharp edge of seriousness stole into my tone. "Need you to tell me if that asshole is bothering you, Willow. I don't want him anywhere near you."

"And I don't want him anywhere near you. Either of them. What they did…"

I swallowed hard. "Don't worry about me."

Her brow drew together. "I hate that he was a part of it. I hate him so much for hurting you."

I shook my head. "I promise you, I'll handle it. For both of us. Understand? I don't want you dealing with that asshole."

She nodded, but it seemed reluctant.

"Tell me," I demanded a little harder. Because shit. I wasn't joking about this. Not with her. Not with someone like him.

"Okay," she said.

"Good. Because you were right…we have much more important things to get on with. Like this date."

I slung my arm around her shoulder and began to guide her toward my Navigator. Could feel the tension drain from her as she cuddled against my side. I pressed a kiss to her forehead before I slanted a smirk at the couple of paps waiting to snag a pic on the other side of the road.

"Seems you're getting awful popular, Ms. Langston," I muttered with a gesture that direction.

She buried her face in my chest, and I could feel her smile fluttering over my heart. "It's a small price to pay to get these moments with you."

I grabbed the picnic basket and blanket from the seat behind me and quickly rounded the front of the Navigator. Opening her door, I dipped into the most exaggerated bow I could find. "At your service, madam."

Willow giggled, that free, tinkling sound that wrapped around me like an embrace. "Well, aren't you the gentleman?" she said in her cute little country drawl as she slid out of her seat.

God. That sound alone made me want to eat her up.

And that dress…

The woman was trying to kill me.

I quirked a brow. "And whatever gave you the impression I'm not a gentleman?"

This time, she laughed. "Um…hello, mister *spread the love everywhere you go*. That in itself should be proof enough."

I threaded her fingers with mine. "How in the world could spreadin' the love ever be considered rude? Sounds pretty *nice* to me." I leaned down, whispered at her ear, "And I always say please and thank you. See. Gentleman. Through and through."

She rolled those pretty eyes. "You just keep telling yourself that, rock star."

Chuckling, I tugged her a little closer as I led her up a bank of small dunes. Sparse, high grasses grew up from the sand, swaying in the breeze that moved with the mellow waves that tumbled and crashed on the shore of Tybee Island.

"How's this?"

Locks of mahogany whipped around her as she took in the display. She gave my hand a squeeze, glanced over at me. "It's perfect."

I spread out the blanket and set the basket on top, unpacked everything tucked inside, wine and cheese and crackers. So yeah. I'd had to suck it up and call Shea to ask her advice on what to bring, while the girl had squealed over the phone, proclaiming her win on our bet was just on the horizon.

She just didn't know that shit was impossible, so I'd let her goad and tease and harass, wondering again what the hell it was I'd gotten myself into.

But seeing Willow standing there? That delicate dress clinging to her thighs and her hair whipping in the wind? The adoring expression on her face? Knew it was worth it, to give in just for a little while.

We kicked off our shoes, sat on the blanket, fed each other little bits of food while we laughed and sipped on our wine like we were a normal couple sharing another peaceful evening. Our conversation easy and relaxed. Our touches playful and sweet while the air cooled a fraction as the day slipped away, the heavens growing darker and darker by the minute.

Content.

I wasn't sure I'd ever felt it so strong.

Willow suddenly jumped to her feet, that free smile turned at me from over her shoulder as she went running down the bank and onto the deserted beach. She went straight for the water.

I was right behind her.

Laughing as I chased her.

She splashed me and I splashed her back, the thin material of her dress getting soaked through at the hem, thoroughly clinging to those thighs.

God.

She was stunning.

Different in every way. We romped and played for what seemed like forever, until my chest felt too full and my cock was begging for attention.

And I knew I was getting in deep. And for just this little while, I chose not to fucking care. Because this kind of pretending felt like the best thing I'd ever done.

She yelped when I suddenly grabbed her and tossed her over my shoulder.

"Ash...what do you think you're doing?" she begged, all panted breaths and a growing hunger that was impossible to miss.

"Carrying your sweet ass up to that blanket so I can get a

taste of you." I gave that sweet ass a good swat. "What does it look like I'm doing?"

"Oh my God, Ash, put me down."

"Not a chance."

Her giggle was nothing less than seduction. "Oh, watch yourself, Mr. Evans, I don't belong to you."

I laid her out in the center of the blanket, caged her on every side.

Her hips rocked up, seeking friction, her shoulders pressed firm to the blanket as she writhed. I gazed down at her with the shadows playing across her face, the faint glow of the moon that'd taken to the sky striking on her creamy skin.

My dick throbbed. I leaned down and rubbed myself against her sweet, sweet heat.

Bliss.

Willow shivered and gasped, then gave a little giggle when I nipped at her jaw, my voice rough. "Right now, you're mine. All. Mine. And there's nothin' you can do about it."

"And what if that guy I've been waiting for suddenly comes walking over the hill, looking for me?" It was all a raspy tease.

"I'd tell him to turn right the fuck around because I'm not finished yet. We still have some lessons to learn."

"Oh, we do, huh?"

"Mmhmm…all kinds of lessons."

One's that were sure to test my limits.

Good thing, because I was up for the challenge.

I let my hand slide up the outside of her thigh, slinking beneath her dress, and palmed her ass. She moaned.

Laughter rang through the air, voices carrying from the beach.

We both froze and Willow's eyes went wide.

She pressed her face into my neck, hiding her self-conscious laughter there, the sound working through me like a caress, neither of us willing to move until the voices faded away.

I pushed back onto my hands, smiled down at the girl. Softer than I meant to. "Think we'd better save this until we get back to my place. We don't want to give the paps too much to talk about now, do we? Last thing that lucky bastard is gonna want is a picture of you going at it on the beach with me."

Kind of choked on it, because I was hating the thought of that more and more.

Low laughter rolled from her, before her eyes filled with something deep. Adoring. She brushed her fingers through the long pieces of my hair. "You deserve to be loved, too, Ash. I hope you know that. I hope you open up enough to find it one day."

I stilled, before I shook my head to refute it.

She ran her palm down to that spot on my side where all my mistakes haunted me before it traveled up, her hand set flat against the thud of my heart. "Do you know what I think? I think this giving heart is frozen in time. A prisoner to the past."

My mouth opened to stop her, but she continued, cutting me off, "I think somewhere along the way you got your heart broken and now you're terrified of allowing it to happen again."

Grief spun around me like a whirlwind. Like it rose up from the depths of the sea and crashed over me like a devastating wave.

A wave that unveiled the spot I wanted to keep buried forever.

"Who broke your heart, Ash?"

I cupped her cheek, the admission rough. "I broke it, Peaches. *I did.* And I won't ever do it again. You need to remember that."

ASH

"What the fuck? And you didn't call us?" Baz flew forward from where he sat on the couch, while Lyrik shot from it and started pacing the room. Austin sucked in a rigid breath, and Zee's jaw locked tight.

Hostility was palpable in the confined space.

It ricocheted between all of us.

We were down in the basement of Baz's place where the killer studio was tucked in the back.

We'd been down here for the last couple of hours, going over shit, rehashing some lyrics, and working through some riffs.

So, yeah. Technically, I was still supposed to be sitting on the sidelines. But like I said, those assholes weren't about to hold me back or shut me down.

Assholes who'd become the focus of our conversation.

I blew out a strained breath, still trying to work through the reality of it. "Asshole walked in that reunion like he owned the place. Like the world owed him something. Until I got in his face. Get a guy one on one and suddenly the douchebag isn't such a badass. Go figure."

Lyrik gripped both his hands in his hair, raging through the room. Typical. "Yeah, until you rolled up on two of them. Those odds are heading less and less in your favor. Told you, you can't be out there wandering around by yourself. This is bullshit, man. What if that'd turned into a repeat of the first time?"

"Had it handled."

"Yeah, but what about the rest of his friends out there? Now you've got two dickbags running around pissed that their girls chose you. And I'm betting after that encounter at the reunion, you didn't exactly leave him with a warm, fuzzy feeling."

I scoffed. "He might have been red, but I wouldn't exactly call it *warm*."

"I bet."

Baz clasped his hands where they dangled between his knees. "So, what are we going to do about this?"

Lyrik pretty much sneered, bouncing an amped-up beat on his toes. "Know exactly what I want to do about it."

Austin flicked the pick he was fiddling with into the air, caught it in a fist, and flicked it again. "I'm game. I say hunt the fuckers down. End this now before you get yourself in a situation you can't get out of. They've already proven they're the kind of lowlifes to gang up on one man. Or maybe you need to get the fuck out of Savannah. Head back to LA and lay low until things cool down. We can hold the album a bit. Already a couple of weeks behind. A few more aren't gonna hurt."

"Yeah. I vote LA." Zee wasn't about throwing blows. Not his style. But if push came to shove? He'd be right there with gloves on, climbing into the ring.

I gave a harsh shake of my head. "Hell no. I'm not tucking tail. And seriously? Lay low in LA? That's like some kind of twisted oxymoron. This right here is where I'm supposed to come to relax."

And Peaches was here.

I tried not to let the fact that was my first thought penetrate too deep. But I'd made her an offer—a promise—and I intended to keep it.

I sat forward. Anger kept ripping at my chest, trying to chain me down. I looked toward the ground, raking back the long pieces of my hair that were falling forward. "I don't know what the fuck to do. Fact he's Willow's ex...it..."

A ball of rage clotted off my words.

Fuck.

I wanted to erase him. In so many ways.

I blinked. "It complicates things."

Lyrik frowned. "This isn't about her."

I flinched, and his words dropped to a hiss. "Shit. It *is* about her?"

I flopped back in my chair. "You know it's not."

It couldn't be.

"You sure about that?" Lyrik pressed.

"Don't even start with that kind of bullshit. You know I don't get tangled up like that."

I shot him a warning glance. He knew better. He was heading into that dangerous territory where he knew he wasn't allowed.

"Yeah? And why was it when I was all twisted up over Tamar, thinking I couldn't have her, you were right there to pull my head out of my ass? Forcing me to face what was right in front of me?"

I tried to keep my voice light. "That's because you thought you didn't deserve her, man. I made a *choice* to live the way I do. Chose to go it alone. And I don't need any one of you telling me that choice was wrong. You were a miserable fuck, and I'm as happy as can be. Big difference."

I wondered when that started to be a lie.

"We've all got histories, man," he prodded, voice dropping

lower because he knew he was skating thin ice. "When are you going to learn you don't have to be a prisoner to yours?"

The vision slammed me before I could stop it.

Blood.

Handprints.

Smeared.

Cold.

Agony clawed at my chest, and my hands fisted on top of my thighs. "Don't."

Baz started pushing, too. "You do know you've been feeding us your own brand of bullshit since we were like nine? I smell it from a mile away, and from where I'm sitting, it smells real bad. What went down was a long damned time ago."

A long time ago when time fucking stopped. Like any amount of days or years could erase it. Change what I'd done.

Zee laughed, totally unaware to the insinuations Baz and Lyrik were dropping. "Seriously…I'm used to waking up every morning to this asshole sending a different girl stumbling out the door. Damned near trips me up when Willow comes slinking in the kitchen for a cup of coffee at the ass crack of dawn every morning, all mussed up and red-faced and shy. Think it's time to fess it up, brother, because she's not even close to bein' your flavor, and it seems to me you can't get enough. I mean, not that I can blame you. If I had a girl like that, I'd want to keep her, too."

Keep her.

That unseen place inside me tugged.

I forced out an uneasy chuckle. "Whatever, assholes. Nothing like that."

Except it felt everything like that. I liked her being there. *Staying.* Falling asleep in my arms and waking up in them in the morning.

Guilt spun. Hard and fast. Shouldn't even be entertaining those thoughts. Refused to shoulder that kind of burden. To take on that weight. The joy of someone else.

"Still doesn't solve anything." Lyrik stood in the middle of the room with his fingers threaded at the back of his head.

Trying to hold it together. "We need to either push the cops on this or take care of it ourselves. You know where I land, but it's not that simple anymore. There's a ton more for all of us riding on the line. Families. Kids."

Baz grunted his agreement.

"Wouldn't ask that of any of you."

Austin sat forward. "But that doesn't mean we wouldn't be there, either. Because that's right where you've always been. Taking up our backs. Next time, I promise you I'll be there to take up yours."

Baz exhaled heavily. "Just…lie low, okay? Don't be heading out on the town or putting yourself on the line the way you like to do. We'll figure this shit out. Chances are it'll just blow over."

"Problem is, I'm not sure I want it to."

"We get that, man. We get that. You've just got to decide if going after them will be worth it in the end. You decide yes? You know where we'll stand."

Baz glanced around at everyone, seeking agreement.

Each of them nodded their allegiance.

The way it always was.

All in.

All of us.

Every time.

Edie had pulled me out into the privacy of the hall, the rest of the party a rowdy rumble from the other side of Baz's house.

She watched up at me. "We wanted you to be the first to know before we made the announcement."

"No way," I muttered as a bit of shock rippled through my senses. Didn't quite know how to process this kind of news.

God's honest truth, I couldn't be more grateful that my baby sister had found love and happiness. Knowing all the while her announcement was at the root of her sorrow.

Another fucking tragedy I'd been responsible for.

Austin had his arms crossed over his chest and was watching her with an adoring expression written all over his face.

"Are you happy?" I asked her.

"So happy."

I pulled her into my arms, hugged her tight, whispered a thousand more silent apologies for that night I'd do anything to take back, while I murmured the here and now against her head. "You're going to be the best mom in the world, Edie. Know you will."

She nodded and pulled back. "Thank you," she whispered.

"There's absolutely no thanks to me."

She glanced over her shoulder at Austin, and he slowly approached.

I looked between them. "I'm truly happy for you both. That you both took the chance and found something better. Something good in each other. Don't ever let that go."

Edie stepped back. She let her fingers flutter down my chest, her voice a mere whisper, "We won't."

She blew me a kiss as she and Austin stepped back into the fray that was her birthday party.

I followed them, but kept a dozen steps behind.

Willow was at the island, laughing free at something Tamar had to say, the sound coming from her mouth like the breeze through the trees. Rustling through. Touching me to my bones.

Her eyes found mine when I walked in. Like she felt me there looking at her. That crazy familiarity lit me up. That recognition growing stronger every day.

Edie clinked a fork against a wine glass. "All right, everyone…bring it in…we have an announcement to make."

I eased up behind Willow, wrapped her body in my arms, and hooked my chin on her shoulder. I threaded our fingers together, clasping her in the front, somehow knowing I needed to be there to hold her tight when my sister uttered her joy into the world.

Everyone clapped and cheered.

Willow stilled, for the flash of a second her entire body going rigid.

I knew she didn't want to. This bright, brilliant girl was the furthest from unkind. But when someone else was favored with what you wanted most? News like that would always just hurt.

An hour later, I was sitting in Baz's recliner nursing at a beer when she walked in. As natural as breathing, I opened my arms, and Willow climbed onto my lap, weaving her soft fingers through my hair.

My chest fisted and my blood took off at the simple touch.

"You okay?" I asked.

She peered back into the main room where the rest of my family was hanging out, laughing and talking and loving on their kids. Tamar was snapping what had to be about a gazillion pictures as she aimed her camera at all the smiling faces scattered about the room.

"Yeah," Willow murmured quietly.

She turned back to me, her voice low and reverent. "Sometimes the best thing we can do is find joy in other people's happiness. And I'm so happy for her." She brushed her fingers through my hair, expression sincere and soft. "Happy for you."

God.

This girl was so damned sweet.

"C'mere." I tugged her against me, and she curled up on my lap, resting her head on my shoulder. She fit there perfectly.

My life always moved at the speed of light.

Blips of faces and endless nights.

I was always hungry for the excess to fill me up.

For those few erratic moments to give me some semblance of being whole.

Right then, my chaotic world felt set to pause. This girl a reprieve.

I kissed her on the top of the head and brushed my fingers through her hair.

She sighed.

Had anything ever felt so good?

I glanced up, almost startled when I saw Tamar in the

archway, camera poised.
   Click.

WILLOW

*T*he sun was bright and high. Spikes of glittering light streaked in like arrows and struck across the floor where I sat in Ash's room. I was sitting on a burlap tarp, which was spread out to protect the worn, wooden planks as I worked on a battered, neglected dresser that rested on top.

Stretching my legs around it, I leaned in and ran the sandpaper brick over the coarse, gritted wood. Slowly... Carefully... Gingerly revealing the beauty that waited underneath.

I knew it would be there.

The second I'd seen it, I knew this shoddy piece of forgotten furniture had been made for Ash's room. Masculine and robust. Colossal. Substantial. I knew as I poured my love into it, it'd turn around and give another hundred years of love in return.

I drifted through the quiet solitude, immersed in my work and elevated to a type of peace I only ever attained when my focus was tuned solely into my art.

A shock tremored through the tranquility.

I fumbled for a deep breath and held it in my lungs. Energy stirred through the dust-laden air, and I looked up from my work.

He stood in the doorway, watching me.

No longer was I entranced. I was intoxicated.

Both his arms were stretched out, hands pressed to each side of the jamb. He wore nothing but a faded pair of jeans that rode low on his slim waist, the grooves and divots and defined cut of his flat stomach making me shake. Chest stretched with that intimidating strength.

His presence potent.

A drug.

Slowly, he walked into the room. He dragged that intensity in with him like a destructive storm that built in the distance. Clouds and thunder. Fire and ice.

He looked at me from over the top of the dresser as he ran his index finger along the top of the smoothed wood. A small smile worked his face as he came the rest of the way around and settled himself on the floor behind me. He stretched out his legs wide and slid up to envelop me in his warmth.

I shivered.

His breath blew through the tiny strands at my nape that had escaped my ponytail. "What are you working on?"

"A dresser."

"Mmm...I think I like it," he mused. The antique was a long, short piece, three drawers high and three drawers wide. Unlike anything you would walk in a regular store and find today.

Perfect for this indescribable, unconventional man.

"What color are you staining it?" Even his most mundane

words sounded like seduction.

"Dark gray, almost black."

That would be the motif—dark, dark floors and dark, dark furniture. White and black and gray. Bold pieces on the walls. The monotones broken by a splash of red.

"Sex and comfort," he muttered what had become the room's mantra against my neck.

That spot quivered between my thighs. "Sex and comfort."

It was becoming harder and harder not to seek the sex part from him. I could feel the boundaries between us becoming flimsy and frail.

He kissed a greedy path up my neck. An avalanche of sensation tumbled through me. I gulped for a breath and tried to focus, to keep grating against the wood. "Stop," I almost giggled like some kind of giddy girl. "Can't you see I'm trying to work? I'm never going to get this project done if you keep interrupting me every five seconds."

He mumbled the words in the crook of my shoulder, "What if I don't want you to finish?"

Hope.

It sparked to life right along with the desire that rode in with a simple brush of his hand.

"Then I'd say this is a really expensive job to just leave incomplete."

"Sex and comfort." He said it like a deliberation. "Sounds to me like a work in progress."

I huffed a laugh. "I guess you could call it that."

I kept grinding at the wood. The sound wound between us. The steady build that promised a crescendo. He set his hand over mine and began to grind the wood with me, his other arm wrapped just below my breasts.

A quiver pitched through my body.

He pressed his cheek to mine. His voice floated out around me, touching me like a caress. "So, tell me when it is we're setting up that photo shoot. I'm most definitely looking forward to that."

My eyes flicked his direction. "You're ridiculous."

"You wouldn't love me any other way."

And I wanted to gasp around it. To hold it. To both rejoice in it and deny it.

Instead, I froze, then completely gave when he shifted us. He slowly lowered me to my back. He climbed over me, caging me against the hard floor, his hands planted on either side of my head where he held himself up above.

The sun shone down around him. A fiery halo for a dangerous man.

"You're so beautiful." His voice was rough, as if he weren't immune to all the things I was feeling. "And your work…it's just as beautiful. Incredible. You know that, don't you?"

"Sometimes it feels like the only thing I have."

"Magic," he said.

I touched his face. My fingertips ran through the rough coarseness of his beard, gliding across his full, full lips.

He nipped at my fingers, before he pressed his nose to the sensitive skin of my neck.

Desire keened on a tightly strung bow.

A fever.

Fire.

I moaned a tiny moan.

"Magic," I whispered up at him, returning his praise.

He groaned in the back of his throat. The sound vibrated down my throat, picking up a path and trembling through my veins. Sweet arrogance surged to his smirk. "I make magic, baby. And you've barely even felt me."

Emotion pummeled me from all sides. Roiling, unsettled waves. Lust and longing and a disintegrating sense of fear. I was overcome by the wonder of what it might feel like. How it would feel to have this man pushing into me.

Taking me whole.

Filling me full in every way. Body, spirit, and soul.

He was fast stealing it all. Taking me piece by piece. He'd touched me places I'd never been touched. Showed me it was okay to demand what I wanted when I'd never had the first clue I'd needed it.

Fingers illicit. Tongue criminal.

Taking me prisoner.

Soon there would be nothing left of me.

He dipped down, stealing some more, controlling me with the power of his kiss. Demanding and hard and deep.

My phone rang from my pocket.

He stilled with a frustrated groan.

"Don't stop," I pled, because when it came to him, I was getting needy.

A beggar who had no claim.

It rang again.

"You better get that, darlin'." He edged back. Those Caribbean blues sparkled, danced with his light and mirth. "Now that we've got a slew of people talking about you taking on this house, seeing the talent you've got displayed in your store, that thing never stops ringing. Not to mention the tabloids are eating up the fact the prettiest girl in all of Savannah swooped in and conquered the infamous Ash Evans. Now you're gonna be in high demand. We're going to have to hire you a bodyguard to keep people from knocking down your door."

I fumbled a grin. My teeth bit down against my lip, the action a poor attempt to stop the constant redness from flushing to my cheeks. Maybe contain some of the belief this boy had pouring out from within me.

I dug my phone out while he was still braced above me.

I glanced at the number illuminated on the screen.

Panic slammed into my spirit, and I pushed on Ash's chest so I could sit up. I rushed to answer the call. "Hello?"

"Willow? It's Sheila."

"What happened? Is she okay?"

My heart was hammering in an entirely different way.

Fear. Grief. Sorrow.

Ash settled back on his heels, worry thick over his expression. He gentled his fingers through my hair in silent encouragement.

"It's just been a bad day," Sheila explained. "She's been crying. Calling for both of you. Think it might be best if you come over and put her at ease. You know how seeing you settles her down."

Agony twisted through my racing heart.

"Okay, I'll be right there."

I ended the call, attention cast low as I fiddled with an errant strand of my hair. Dragging myself from the clouds and down into reality.

"Hey. What was that? Are you okay?" His words were pure concern. Soft affection.

This hard, intimidating man with the most merciful heart.

"My mama…she needs me. I need to go. I'm sorry. I'll finish this up tomorrow."

Ash climbed to stand and held out his hand. "Well, we'd better get going then."

ASH

Willow rushed into the room ahead of me. Warily, I hung back in the doorway. I roughed a hand down my face, wondering what the fuck I was thinking coming here. But that was the problem when I was with Willow. I stopped thinking.

Dread curled my stomach as I slowly made my way into the room. Hushed voices echoed against the walls as Willow received an update from a woman named Sheila.

But I couldn't focus on them.

My attention was chained to the frail woman lying on a hospital bed, her arms tweaked at an odd angle, fists clenched tight, her mouth drooping open as she groaned incoherently.

Fuck.

I only had the information Willow had given me. I wasn't prepared for this.

"Thank you," Willow told Shiela, and the woman gave her a nod before she slanted a parting glance at me as she passed by and silently clicked the door shut behind her.

Sorrow wound through the room.

Willow's grief.

My sympathy.

Her mother's torment.

Willow edged around to the side of the bed and pulled a chair up close to her mother. "Hey, Mama, it's me. I'm right here."

"Summer," her mother whimpered low, hardly decipherable, but there.

Willow winced, leaned closer, brushed her fingers through her mother's hair. "Shh...I know, Mama, I know. It's okay."

Her mother cried it again. Willow wrapped her hand around her mother's tightened fist.

"You want me to tell you a story, Mama? Tell you about Summer?" Willow was so damned tender when she brushed back the white hair from her forehead, struggling not to cry when she looked at her.

That right there was why I was here. Why I couldn't just up and let her go when I'd seen the anguish fill up her soulful eyes.

I'd wanted to...

Fuck. I'd just wanted to be there for her.

Support her in the ways I knew I shouldn't.

Show her she wasn't alone.

Willow's voice dropped to close to a whisper, something so intensely sad and adoring fueling her words that it made me want to fucking weep. "Do you remember, Mama? Do you remember it was your birthday...it was beautiful out. The sun was warm but not hot. You, me, and Summer, we packed up a lunch and headed out to your favorite spot." Her eyes pinched together. "That meadow off of Staley? Hidden by the trees? Do you remember all the dandelions? We danced in them all afternoon.

Casting our dreams in the air."

One side of her mother's mouth tweaked. A semblance of a smile. A memory. Recognition.

Sorrow whipped through Willow.

A dark, battering storm that rained hope.

"Do you remember Summer's, Mama? She said she wanted to be free. She's free now. You don't have to be sad."

But it was sadness that glistened in Willow's eyes as this selfless girl poured all her love into her mother. Giving and giving and giving.

I wanted to stand up. Stand behind her. Press my hands to her shoulder like some kind of silent advocate. Give something back. But how the fuck was that my place? It wouldn't ever be.

Attachments always felt good in the beginning. That feeling you got that you might just belong. Fit. Until you figured out all the wrong pieces were trying to come together and they started working at odds. Just vicious teeth in a cog snapping at the other.

Yet, here I was.

Following her here like a fool. Acting like I was some kind of goddamned knight in shining armor when I knew with all of me I was nothing but the dragon.

The destroyer.

She sat there, living up to her name. A strong, stoic willow. Graceful and elegant while she waded through the turmoil.

Her mother's smile widened a fraction, her scratchy voice laden with affection. "Sweet one."

A tear streaked free from the corner of Willow's eye, and she swatted it away with her free hand. "You make me feel that way, Mama."

"Sweet one…still chasing yours."

Willow blinked like she was trying to gather herself, keep it together. Finally, she glanced at me, almost pleading, before she looked back to her mother. "I want you to meet someone, Mama…someone who's really important to me. He's the one I was telling you about. The one who saved the store."

Anxiety raced through my nerves, and I swallowed hard when I decided to suck it up and edge forward instead of standing in the corner like a pussy.

I moved behind Willow, right to that spot where I'd wanted to stand.

Like her supporter.

Her advocate.

Like someone who might love her the way she deserved.

I set my hands on her shoulders, squeezed, while my heart beat like a hollow drum. "It's an honor to meet you, Mrs. Langston."

Her mother's attention flicked to me.

Aware.

Lucid.

Pleading.

Good. God.

I needed to get up and go. Get out of this mess. Could feel myself sinking in, getting deeper and deeper and deeper. Could feel the weight pressing in around me. Responsibility I knew nothing other than driving right into the ground.

Instead, I moved to the other side of the bed, pulled up a chair. Because for a minute I just wanted to take this burden off of Willow. Do some of the comforting Willow Always gave.

I leaned forward while I felt something inside crack, this place open up just as I opened my mouth and began to sing before I could stop myself, my voice so damned rough and low.

Lay me down
Say your peace
Come what may
But you can't hide
The pain behind your eyes

The room spun around me, the walls too tight, but I couldn't keep the words from coming.

So stay with me
I don't mind
Find your comfort

stay

Right here by my side
I've seen it all before
Want to take it away
So stay with me
I don't mind
Find your comfort
Right here by my side

The song broke off, and I stared down at her mother who'd drifted to sleep.

Everything itched, my skin and my throat that raced with that sickly feeling.

Finally I looked up. Pinned to my chair by that potent stare, her mouth slack and her eyes bleary as that awareness spun.

Familiarity and need and every damned thing I couldn't have.

Fear bubbled up from that spot that was supposed to be forgotten. Under lock and key.

Screams.

Blood.

Loss.

I gasped over the flashes. I flew to my feet. Willow jumped at the sudden, jarring movement.

I needed air. Breath. Sanity.

I could feel each of them being sheared away.

I couldn't even look at her when I said, "I'll be outside."

I hurtled down the hall. This house that was decorated to exude solace and peace reeked of death. I needed to escape it. I flew out the front door and into the light, searching for breath.

I paced and questioned.

You can't do this.

You can't do this.

Not again.

All the while, some part of me screamed it wasn't close to being the same. It was the foolish part of me just begging for trouble. The kind I didn't have the strength to fight my way out of.

I felt like such a prick when Willow finally stumbled out five minutes later. She wrung her hands, trying to look into me the way she did. Deeper than I wanted. "I'm sorry I brought you here. That it was too much."

And there she was. Apologizing when it was *me*.

Always fucking me.

Still, I couldn't say a thing when I turned and started across the street to where I'd parked. I ignored the single fucking pap hiding out behind a bush, one of those creepy, stalker kinds who'd been trailing us for days, waiting to snag a little dirt.

No doubt I was kicking plenty of it up as I tore across the lot.

Willow climbed into the passenger seat, the silence dense and dark as I drove her home.

I could feel her hesitation when I pulled to her curb, the things she wanted to say that I couldn't afford to hear.

So I left her there like a total prick with little more than a mumbled, "See you later."

Because I couldn't stay in her space for a second longer. Couldn't get myself any deeper. Not when this girl kept pulling me closer with the promise of all the good I could never have.

Without looking back, I gunned my Navigator and did my damnedest to ignore the way my insides trembled like a bitch the whole ride home.

WILLOW

I watched him drive away, feeling as if he were breaking off some piece of me as he went.

I knew better. But knowing better never helped anything when it already was done.

They say the danger in pretending is it becoming real.

And this afternoon it'd become far too real. Too close and too hard and too good.

For the both of us.

It was obvious the second he sat forward and did more of that pretending with my mama.

This terrifying, intimidating man who was so wickedly kind. I'd saw him sitting there, desperate for a way to take away some of the constant fear, anxiety, and confusion that haunted what was left of my mama's troubled life.

But offering her that tiny semblance of peace had somehow stolen his.

I saw it.

In the twitching in his muscles and held in his rigid jaw as we'd driven the short distance in silence. Then, he'd just left me at my house rather than taking me to his, where I'd left my car. It was as if he couldn't handle being in my presence for a second more and he was looking for the fastest route of escape.

He'd been riddled with his own questions he couldn't answer. So, he'd pushed me away, and Ash pushing me away right now was the one thing in this messed up world I wasn't sure I could handle.

Instead of heading inside, I rounded to the back to my little shop where I sometimes worked at night when I couldn't sleep, where the feel of the wood would soothe and relieve.

Quiet my racing soul.

This evening it wanted to scream and shout and plea.

In the far distance, thunder rolled, deep and melodic, the Savannah summer still thick with the waning day. The smell of rain held fast to the air, stirred by the short gusts of wind that whipped at the trees.

Wrenching open the lock on the double sliding doors, I pushed them aside and flipped on the little swinging light above my work bench. Unfinished pieces were stacked against the walls and littered the dusty floor, tools scattered wide. The place was an utter mess, but somehow, it provided me with the greatest peace.

I pulled my stool in front of the vintage apothecary cabinet I'd been working on for years. The one my sister had started with me on one of her whims and never had finished. One I'd never had the heart to finish myself.

I squeezed my eyes closed and began to sand. Slowly. Methodically.

It was like welcoming an old friend and the loneliness at the same time. Prying open old wounds and covering them with balm.

I got lost in it, and at some point, the day faded away and twilight took hold. The storm grew and gathered strength. A few fat droplets tapped at the roof, steadily increasing until rain began its free-fall to the earth. The intensifying rumbles approaching in the distance only added to the peace.

A shiver of awareness prickled across my skin.

With him, it was always the same.

Turmoil and mayhem.

Chaotic comfort.

Disordered relief.

Guarded, I slowly turned, fearful there would be nothing left of me if I did.

My breath hitched in my throat, and my rebellious heart thrummed a wayward beat.

He stood at the opening of the sliding doors, rain pouring down around him, his hulking arms stretched out on either side of him and clinging to the doors. His big body was drenched, clothes clinging to every inch.

He stayed that way, fighting for air.

Finally, he lifted his face an inch and stared at me from beneath the shadows of his strong brow.

Staggered.

This man…

He staggered me.

That terrifying beauty I'd witnessed that first day was there, potent blue eyes ablaze.

The conquering warrior.

His expression was fierce. Carved in stone. Chiseled with the same doubts and uncertainties he'd left me with this afternoon. As if the man had built up his own walls. Barriers of protection.

I felt the desperate need to know why they were there. To get over them and beneath them and within them. To know this man the way every part of me ached to know him.

Wholly.

"Ash." My own confused whisper.

Rain ran in rivulets down his cheeks and through his beard, droplets clinging to his full, full lips.

A gust of wind whipped through, stirring the rain. Shivers raced across my flesh and it was desire that soaked me through.

I watched the thick bob of his throat as he swallowed. "What have you done to me?" He stared across at me, tone demanding. "Tell me, Willow. Tell me you want me. Tell me I'm not goin' crazy. Tell me this isn't all just on me. Tell me that every time I touch you, it feels like something more."

A wheeze pushed from between my lips, my breaths coming harder and faster. I swiveled fully on the stool and slowly climbed to my trembling legs.

My heart stampeded a path out in front of me and cut down all the obstacles in my path. Plowing through them as if they meant nothing. As if they posed no harm.

Is the lamb innocent if it knows it's being led to the slaughter?

A willing volunteer?

Because here I was, signing up for the position.

I lifted my chin. "I've never wanted anything the way I want you."

Whatever thread of control had been holding him back snapped.

He erased the space between us in the flash of a second, hands fisting in my hair at the same second his mouth slanted over mine.

Possessive.

Powerful.

His wet lips demanded as they nipped and sucked, pushed and gave. He tugged at my hair, angled my head, controlling our movements.

"Peaches." He mumbled it as he edged back for a frantic breath before he dove back in. Deeper this time, seeking a way inside.

He slid one hand down my spine and twisted the other hand up tighter in my hair. His fingers sank into the flesh of my bottom, and he yanked me against him. Against his wet clothes and the heat that burned from beneath, his cock so hard and big where it pressed against his jeans, begging for friction against my belly, my body begging for it in return.

I gasped, and my fingers latched on to his shoulders. "Ash. Please."

He spun us, knocked me back into the piece I'd been working on. I hit it with a grunt, his or mine, I couldn't tell. We were a frenzied tangle of moans and hands and desperate bodies.

Tools tumbled and metal clattered and the storm gained intensity. Wind ripped at the thin walls, rain pelted the roof, and I couldn't find it in myself to care the doors were still open. The only thing I registered was *this*.

His hands gripped me by the waist, and he set me on the top of the cabinet. My legs locked around his waist.

Instinct.

It was there from the moment he first touched me, though I'd grown bolder in it, demanding what he gave and giving it in return.

I kissed him hard, and he kissed me harder.

Wild.

Raging.

"What have you done? What have you done?" he rumbled as he rocked his length against me. Warmth spread like a flood. Lust and greed and the tight emotion that welled up to take hold of my chest.

I angled back from the force of his attack, his hand holding my head to keep me upright, the other palming my breast. My nipple hardened, and his hands were gone, mine braced on the edge to hold me up as he ripped the buttons of my shirt.

I whimpered as he exposed me, my chest heaving with every lust-filled pant.

"Fuck." It scraped from his throat, the word just as raw as the hunger in his gaze when he stared down at me. He rushed to get my shirt free of my arms, and his hands were back to my lace-covered breasts. He pressed them together, his hot, hot mouth closing over one.

Fire rocketed to my core. Streaked through my nerves. Flying fast. Lighting me up. Everywhere. Every inch. That heated spot ached a needy, empty throb.

"Ash." His name was a gasp. A plea. Everything. Because I could feel myself falling beneath the demand of his touch. Sinking into the sacred space where lives were either made or forever shattered.

"I know, baby, I know." He slipped a hand around my back, flicked free my bra, and dragged the straps down my arms.

He leaned back, his eyes wild when he dropped the fabric to the floor. "God…you are a masterpiece, darlin'. So fucking gorgeous I don't know how to make sense of you sitting there. The things I want to do to you."

Goose bumps lifted at his words. Dark, dark promises.

"Tell me," I murmured, my head rocking back on a gasp when he pinched a nipple between his fingers and took the other between his teeth.

Pretending.

I knew better because I knew I was only fooling myself, but right then I was just the fool who was happy to be deceived.

He laved and lapped, his tongue working its magic as it wound me tight. He licked between the valley of my breasts, taking a sharp turn north, delving into the hollow of my neck.

I whimpered, and his voice drew near, a shower of a breath at my ear. "I want to own you, Peaches. I want to awaken what's been lying dormant. Bring it to life. Watch you glow."

He kissed at my jaw, at my chin, a hungry lash at my mouth before making his way down the other side. His hands dug into my hips as he tucked me close and grunted the words, "I want to get so deep in you I won't ever make it back. Make it to the place where neither of us knows where one starts and the other begins."

He'd been singing me that same song like praise since the first night when he'd opened my eyes.

And I knew this boy would tear me to shreds.

Crucify and slay.

But this time I was coming as an offering.

I gripped tight to his hair before I was tearing at his drenched shirt, yanking it over his head and getting straight to work on his fly.

"Take it." It was an appeal.

He froze.

Jerked back to look at me.

"Take it." I whispered the demand.

A puff of air shot from his nose.

A charge of lust and desire.

A crackle of intensity.

We lit.

This fury and passion and mania neither of us could seem to catch up to. He popped the button on my jeans and dragged them down my legs, taking my panties with them.

He pushed down his underwear, tossing them off as he was wedging his way between my thighs. His hands ran up and down the outside, trembling and trembling with his penis that was far too big nestled between us.

My mouth parted and desire spun.

Ash swore between his clenched teeth and pressed his thumb into my mouth. I sucked it the way he seemed to want me to, my tongue playing across the pad as I fisted him in my hand.

He shuddered, and his taut stomach flexed as I pumped him up and down, my mind a blurred whirl of colors and lights emitted by this man.

I needed him. So bad. And I was mumbling it aloud as his thumb brushed across my bottom lip. "I need you. Ash, I need you. Want you. More than I've ever wanted anything." I scooted to the very edge of the cabinet, the man still in my hand. And somehow I was in control. Delirious. Mad with the need.

Or maybe it was him.

Because I was guiding him to my center, the head of him pushing into my folds.

And I didn't care that I was crossing a line I swore I'd never cross. Giving myself to a man when he wasn't really mine.

But that didn't matter. Because I wanted to weep with the feel of him, barely there, so big that when he took me by the hips and surged forward, I screamed against the full intrusion, my rejection nothing but a soft cry, "Yes."

Consumed.

Incinerated.

"Fuck...Peaches...you feel...you're the best thing I've ever felt."

He burned inside me. Too big. Too much. Not enough. Because I wanted more. For him to fill me up and take me and never let me go.

He started to rock, snapping his hips, slamming into me again and again. Each of his breaths came on a throaty grunt, the warrior in his eye as he stared me down.

He fucked me like he promised.

Owned me.

Possessed me.

"Ash."

He brushed his thumb over my bottom lip once more, dipped it into my mouth, before he pressed it against my clit. Stroking and circling.

His touch building and inciting and ruining.

Because I would never be the same.

Our bond might sever, but mine would never break.

Our movements were frantic. Desperate and consumed. I clawed at his chest while he annihilated me.

Laid me to waste.

I had no chance.

No reserves.

Pleasure sparked in my nerves, gathering fast to the tiny pinpoint of bliss. Where the man sent me soaring, floating with the stars. Lost in darkness. Blinded by light. I shuddered and shook as he did the same, the man gone with me as he jerked and twitched inside me.

He gasped out a strained breath, mouth open at my chest.

His arms slid around my waist, and he hugged me tight.

He'd walked into my store and told me he'd give me anything. To name it and it was done.

And the only thing I wanted? I wanted him to stay.

ASH

I pressed my face to the bare skin of her stomach that was slick and wet. Just as slick and wet as the skin between her thighs. I gasped for breath. For some kind of goddamned clarity when it was nowhere to be found.

"Peaches," I mumbled, squeezing her tighter as the girl I was wound around began to shake. Draining of adrenaline and filling right up with regret.

If I share my body with a man, it's because I love him and he loves me.

Her assertion from all those weeks ago raged through me, all the while reality settled slow.

Hard.

Painfully.

Fuck.

Wincing, I eased out of her body. A part of me wanted to vomit. Give my own damned self a beat down.

Or maybe climb right back inside her.

Shit.

I didn't know.

All I knew was I'd fucked up.

Fucked up bad.

I swallowed around the jagged rocks lodged at the base of my throat, words so rough when they came out they cracked on my tongue. "I'm clean. I swear."

My head gave a bare shake of my shame as I met the churning expression I couldn't quite read in her eyes. "I'm so sorry. Never meant to get carried away. Lose control. Not with you."

Here I'd been the fool who'd thought there was no harm in pretending.

She started shaking all over the place. Like she was the one who'd been standing in the driving rain, cold taken to brittle bones.

If I share my body with a man, it's because I love him and he loves me.

What the hell did I do?

Guilt ate me whole. A panic unlike anything I'd ever felt rose, a wave ready to drown and destroy. My eyes darted around the dusty shop, landing on what I was looking for. I reached out and snagged the old blanket that was folded on a shelf off to my left, shook it out with a hand and wrapped it around her, covering that gorgeous body.

I tucked it tight up under her neck like a shield, not that it would protect her from the depravity I'd just dealt her.

I should have known better. But like always, I was the reckless bastard, bingeing on the good. Taking what wasn't mine to take.

I kept one hand tight to keep the blanket closed, and I fumbled into just my jeans. I left them unbuttoned, quick to sweep an arm beneath her back and another under her knees. I lifted her against my chest.

A sigh filtered from between her quivering lips. She hid her face under my chin and snuggled close.

The scent of peaches and wood and honey glided into my already muddled senses.

Ruining me a little more. I carried her from the shop, hugging her tight as we stepped out into the rain. It poured down around us, and I ran toward her house.

"Back door," she managed, and I carried her up the three tiny steps. I leaned my side against the wall to keep her propped against me so I could fumble with the knob.

The door swung open. I slammed it shut with my foot behind us, the sound of the storm muted within the walls. The house was dark. Quick flashes of lightning blanketed the windows, guiding my path.

It seemed crazy that I'd never stepped foot inside her house. It was warmth and beauty, new and old, comfort and ease. Perfect, just like this girl.

A feeling I didn't want to recognize tightened in my chest. But it was there, present with her weight in my arms, her heart this thunder where it beat against mine.

I carried her out the small archway, into the main room, and straight up the stairs that rode the side wall.

There were only two doors at the top, and I took the one on the right, figuring it had to be the same room where I'd seen her silhouette taking up the window that first night I'd dropped her here. Walking inside, I headed straight for the attached bathroom.

Carefully, I set her on her shaking feet, keeping one hand on her for support while I turned the showerhead hot and high. Steam filled the confined space, and she kept flicking those chocolate eyes my way. Searching.

That familiarity clung to me stronger than it ever had before.

Making me feel like I might just lose my mind because I was fucking terrified I was losing my heart.

What did I do?

I peeled the blanket from her body. So slow. A shiver wracked her whole.

God.

She was so damned beautiful.

Stunning.

She watched me while I shucked out of my jeans before I laced my fingers with hers and led her into the glass-encased shower. Steaming hot streams fell from the showerhead. It hit my cold skin like a million fiery needles.

I breathed out when I began to get used to it, and I wound my arms around her, pulling her to my chest, turning us both so the shower fall was mostly on her. I nudged her head back, getting that mass of waves wet, kissed her forehead because how the fuck could I not?

Once the sharp prickles of heat turned to a relaxing thrum, I grabbed a sponge and squirted it with soap. I massaged it over her body, starting at her shoulders and neck, down her sides and belly. I sucked in a stealing breath when I leaned down and pressed it between her thighs like maybe I could rub myself off her.

She shivered, clutching my shoulders for support.

I glanced up at her. "You're not on the pill, are you?"

The unreadable expression flashed tighter, harder, and she slowly shook her head.

"I'm so sorry, I'm so sorry," I was mumbling again. My mind was racing for an *easy* fix. But this girl was the furthest thing from easy, and I couldn't even begin to form the words. Instead, I was soaping up her body. Gently. And she was doing the same to me.

And the expression I was having such a hard time deciphering grew soft. This girl undoing me.

I made sure we were both rinsed and then shut off the water. The old pipes screeched, and I reached outside the shower for a dry towel on the rack. She stood still as I wrapped it around her, only moving so she could hold it closed. Then I grabbed one for myself, twisted it around my hips, and picked her back up.

"Ash." She said my name like confusion, the girl staring up

at me as I carried her to her bed.

I pulled down the blankets and lay her in the middle. When I backed away, she stretched out her hand. "Stay."

And God. A wise man would go. Stop this bullshit right then. But there I was, dropping my towel and sliding in behind her.

Tucking her against my body.

Why did she feel so good?

She sighed.

"I'm sorry," I said again.

"What are you sorry for?" She reached up and threaded her fingers through mine that rested just above her head. "I told you what I wanted. I told you I wanted *you*." She murmured it out into the stillness of her room.

I snuggled closer and kissed the back of her head. "See? That's what I don't get. I'm no good for you, darlin'. Can't give you all those things you really want. What you really deserve. Things I want you to have. But in the back of my mind, I'm getting stingy. Want to keep you for myself. Then I go and..."

Fuck.

"I wasn't thinking about anything but getting inside you."

She squeezed my hand. "It's okay."

"It's not."

Silence spun around us. Minutes. Hours. I didn't know. "What happened this afternoon?" she finally asked.

"What happened?"

I'd always prided myself on being the nicest guy you'd ever meet. But my conscious wouldn't let me get away with that lie. Because that was always on my terms and never if it came at my own expense. That kind of cost was something I just wasn't willing to pay.

"You want to know?"

Still facing away, she nodded against her pillow.

I buried my nose in her damp hair and offered the confession there. "You terrify me, darlin'. Make me want to do things I just don't do. Like step up and be a real man when someone needs me. It terrifies me that I'm fool enough I just might offer it, knowing the only thing I'm gonna do is turn around and break your heart. That's what I do, and that's why I don't get attached. When I was sitting there beside your mother, I realized just how fucking attached I've grown to you. How much I wanted to take care of you."

She rolled to face me.

Muted light glanced across the curves of her face. So goddamned sweet. She touched my cheek. "I'm terrified of you, too."

"Tried all afternoon to stay away. I should have."

She shook her head. "I needed you."

That, right there, was the problem.

"What was the song?" she asked, so tentative, knowing she was pushing against those raw places I didn't want her to see.

I swallowed around the grief that bottled at the base of my throat. "Wrote it a long time ago."

Desperate to change the subject, I brushed my fingers through her hair. "Tell me about your sister."

Pain lashed across her features as she drifted someplace far away. "She was the best. So full of life. The kind of person who walked in a room and lit it up. The dreams she shared with me and our mama were always so big. She was always laughing. Teasing. She loved so much."

I played with a strand of her hair. "Sounds like you two were close."

She barely nodded, before her brow pinched. "But she was sick, too, Ash. So sick. She'd always been, and it got worse as she got older, or maybe it was just that I'd gotten old enough to recognize it. Always so high then so low. Happy then couldn't get out of bed. My best friend then someone I couldn't even recognize."

I swam through her sorrow, held her close as she whispered her grief against my neck. "I begged her not to go, but she left when she was eighteen. And somehow I knew I'd never see her again."

My throat constricted. And it scared me a little more how badly I hated this for her. How I'd do anything to go back and change something for her I didn't come close to knowing anything about. Protect her from the pain. "I'm so sorry."

She chewed at her bottom lip. "You keep saying that."

"That's because I'm the bastard lying in bed with you when I don't have the right to be in your space. Shouldn't be touchin' you. Not like this."

"What if this is right where I want you?"

"Peaches." It felt like a warning. For her. Or maybe one for myself.

I'd fucked up. Bad.

I was such a damned fool.

Because even I was wise enough to know it was a fool who learned no lessons.

I rolled her to her back and climbed between her trembling thighs.

Then I turned around and fucked up all over again.

WILLOW
SEVENTEEN YEARS OLD

"Summer." Frantic, Willow dropped to her knees where her sister was on the floor, her back pressed against the wall and her knees hugged to her chest. Rivers of black streaked her face from her tears and her face was splotchy as she wept.

And her room.

Her room was torn to pieces. Clothes strewn and furniture overturned.

Carefully, Willow touched her sister's shoulder, fear trembling all the way to her bones. "Summer...what happened?

Are you okay?"

Her sister looked up at her, eyes glazed over. Faraway. Before they slowly came into focus. She shook her head. "No, Willow, I'm not okay."

Willow felt the ache all the way to her soul. More and more her big sister had been like this. Frantic and raging. Lost.

"But what about the medicine?" Willow almost begged as she scooted forward. "I thought it was helping."

Helpless, Summer stared at her. "I can't feel on it, Willow. Don't you get that? I don't feel anything, and I'd rather be dead than feel that way."

"Don't say that."

Her smile was somber. "I hate this, Willow. You know that, don't you? Hate being who I am?"

Willow shifted to sit down beside her, their backs resting side by side. "Of course I know you hate it. Your sickness isn't any different than Mama's. Neither of you asked for it, and I'd take it from both of you if I could."

Summer tapped her temple. "But mine's all here. I should be able to control it. Change it. And I don't know how to stop."

"It'll get better," Willow promised. Even to her, it sounded like a lie.

Sadness rimmed Summer's mouth. "I'm scared that's not gonna happen here. I've got this feeling like I've got to get out of here before I come out of my skin. Before I completely lose it. I can feel it…me coming unhinged. And that's not something I want Mama to see. It's bad enough, some of the things I say to her when I don't mean them. But every time I swear to myself I won't let it happen again, it does, and there's nothing I can do to stop it."

Fear curled through Willow's spirit. "Please, don't leave me."

"You've got Bates and Mama's got you."

"But what if I need you?"

Summer linked her pinky finger with Willow's, lifted it between them. "You'll always have me, baby sister. But I've got to find myself before I get smothered. I can't breathe, and I feel like I'm gonna die if I stay here for one more day."

She pressed a fist against her chest. "You've got to understand that, Willow. You're going to stay here and have that big family you want and you're going to be happy. Tell me you want that for me, too. To find happiness. Because I'm not going to find it here."

That was the only thing Willow wanted for her sister. She nodded, a lump so big in her aching throat when she tried to speak. "Just…just promise you'll come back to me."

Her sister squeezed their pinky fingers tighter. A bond. Unbroken.

"Love is never cut and dry. It's messy. Confusing. Sometimes it's ugly and sometimes it's the most beautiful thing you've ever seen." Summer looked at her, so sincere, like she was trying to convey a message Willow couldn't quite understand. "But no matter how much it might hurt, it can never change the fact it's real. That it's worth fighting for. And the real kind of love will always come back to you."

WILLOW

"What the hell were you thinking?" Emily hissed her horror and shock as she scrambled along at my side. We had just left our favorite coffee shop, which wasn't that far from the store, and we were strolling down the sidewalk.

That was the problem. Neither of us had been thinking.

I ducked to miss a low-hanging branch.

"I don't know what the hell I was thinking."

"God, Willow…this isn't like you. You've been waiting and waiting for a guy who would step up and be the kind of man you want. And then you go and jump in bed with a rock star?

Without a condom? That man is likely to give you some kind of disease."

I cringed with the brash assumption.

"He told me he was tested."

Of course, that was completely after the fact.

After I'd already gone and done all the things I couldn't take back.

"Convenient," Emily scoffed, before she huffed through a sigh and slowed her pace. "I mean…" She blew out a breath that made her cheeks puff. "I don't even know what I mean. I like the guy, Willow, I promise I do."

"You were the one who pushed me his way. You told me I had to take the job or I'd 'regret it forever'."

She blinked. "I was talking about the job, Will. It was time for you to step out of your comfort zone. To get back on your feet. See a great opportunity when it was offered to you. And yeah…I saw the attraction, and I thought maybe that would be good for you. For a man to flirt with you and make you remember what it felt like to be beautiful and wanted."

She wet her lips. "I just never thought it'd go this far or that you'd be so reckless about it. And I hate saying it, Willow…*I hate it*…but you know he's not the type of guy who's going to stick around, and you know as well as I do it's going to wreck you. You're standing there, and I see that expression on your face. I *see* what you're feeling. I *know* you're going to get your heart broken all over again."

Her words struck me like knives. Tiny daggers cutting me in all the places that hurt the most.

Wrecked.

I was well on my way.

It wasn't as if her assertion was breaking news. I knew he wouldn't stay. That I couldn't have him in the way my heart already claimed him. My foolish heart that had grown prone to so many foolish, rash things.

She looked me straight on, eyes reeling with disappointment, voice a reproach. "You want it so bad that you're willing to get it this way? A baby? Because you keep on with this kind of foolishness, that's exactly what you're gonna get."

Pain squeezed me all over.

Shame and regret.

A wheeze of words tumbled from my tongue. "Of course not."

Of course not.

I staggered a step and slumped down onto a bench.

I pressed a trembling hand to my mouth. "I don't know what I'm doing, Em. I just…when I'm with him…when I look at him? He feels like what I've been missin' all along. What I've been searching for my whole life. And when I'm with him, every worry slips away and I forget the man he keeps promising me he is. It's not the way I see him. *I forget myself.*"

She sank down beside me, sympathy edged into her expression. She brushed her fingers through my hair and gave me a sad smile.

"It's easy to forget ourselves when things feel right. I get that, Will. I do. That doesn't mean I'm not worried about you."

My phone buzzed in my hand. I cringed when I saw the sender.

Bates.

Emily caught it, her silence prodding me to flip into the message. For the last week, he'd been texting pictures of Ash in a world I just couldn't comprehend. Ones of him in dark, seedy clubs. Draped in women. Backstage. Doing things I didn't want to imagine.

This one was of Ash, obviously somewhere backstage, sipping at a drink with a woman on her knees between his legs. His apathetic expression promised he barely even registered her presence.

I'd wanted to avert my eyes and shield myself from the brutal reality of the man I'd grown to care about so much. Too much.

It only made me hate Bates more.

This was him not giving up on me? Taunting me? As if him showing off those pictures could ever forgive what he'd done?

Never.

Emily looked at me with something akin to pity.

"It hurts, Em," I admitted, chewing at my trembling lip. "Is this what they call dumb love?"

She wound her arm around my shoulder, and I slumped into her hold. "You might be acting dumb," she said with the hint of a tease before her tone went serious. "But no, love isn't for the dumb, Willow. Love is always, always for the brave."

WILLOW

"Where are we going?"

I rested my cheek on his bicep. Because why wouldn't I if I could? He had our fingers threaded together and was guiding us through the crowd that leisurely strolled the quaint Savannah street.

Sunlight streamed through the leaves on the big shade trees.

Families were out and about exploring and the tourists checking out the sights seemed to be subdued.

Being with him made me feel that way, too.

Like there was nothing in the world better than this.

Being at his side.

He slanted me a cocksure grin—arrogant and sexy and the hottest thing I'd ever seen. Just that look was enough to make me flush.

God. The things this man had done to me.

"What, don't you trust me, darlin'?"

I snuggled closer to his side. "Trust you? That's an awful lot to ask of me, rock star. You do kinda have a bad reputation."

He laughed, so loud and free that people turned and stared.

How could they not?

The man was a magnet.

A force.

One that had completely knocked me off my feet.

He leaned down close to my face, voice dropping low. "I thought it was my 'reputation' that you liked best."

Pure insinuation.

More heat. This time in my belly and spreading lower. "I do kind of like that 'reputation'."

He hiked a brow. "Kind of? You start talkin' like that, and I'm gonna have to double my efforts."

Shivers.

Yes, please.

"Why do I get the feeling that's not just a threat but a promise?"

"Because you're smart."

I laughed, lightly smacked his strong, strong chest, and snuggled even closer, letting myself get swept away in the freedom that came with confidence. Something I'd almost forgotten. So grateful to this man who'd taken the time to show it to me.

Honestly, I'd been terrified to return to his house that morning two weeks ago after the night he'd taken me. I thought maybe he'd shut himself down.

I was completely taken by surprise when he'd met me halfway across his yard with a searing kiss. One that'd weakened my knees and caused me to fall a little further. I'd been falling ever since.

He pressed his mouth to the top of my head. "What am I going to do with you, Peaches?"

Stay.

We rounded the corner.

I gasped a tiny breath that wasn't really shocked at all, my grin so wide when I stepped out ahead of him and turned to face him as we walked, our fingers still bound. "You brought me to a flea market?"

Feigned offense parted his flirty lips. "A flea market? Don't break my heart, darlin'. That's just a straight insult. This here is the finest antique show to ever grace the East Coast. Treasures galore. Vintage heirlooms. It's a good thing your man has a few extra bucks in the bank. You know, so he can take you on all these lavish, extravagant dates."

My man.

God.

That was all I wanted him to be.

Mine.

Still, I smiled at the amusement swimming in his eyes, floating in that calm, mesmerizing sea. "I couldn't imagine a better place to be."

"Uh…I'm pretty sure the correct answer to that is my bed."

"Right. There's that."

Always, always that.

His indulgent smile shifted to soft, and he was tugging me against him and kissing me tenderly right where we stood in the middle of the sidewalk as people moved around us.

"Come on…let's go find some of those *treasures* I promised you."

For hours, we browsed and laughed. Soft touches and quick kisses stolen between our easy conversation. He humored me while I rummaged through every stand, digging through all the treasures that most would see as nothing more than garbage and junk that Ash knew I'd see as priceless.

I returned the whole *humoring* favor when a woman recognized him and started fangirling in the middle of the market, squealing and fumbling over her words. I offered to take their picture while he mouthed, "I'm sorry." There was nothing I could do but smile and snap the picture of this star-struck girl who couldn't seem to fathom she was in Ash Evans' space.

I understood her pain.

Thankfully, she moved on, and Ash and I ducked into a large, tented stall that was full of eclectic art and plastic crates that held prints of every kind.

"We have to get this." I gestured to one of the paintings stacked in the back. It was narrow and taller than me. Painted in reds, blacks, and shadowy grays. Musical notes were hidden like obscured art, just the innuendo of a song coming to life. "It will go perfect in your room. Against the big wall."

This afternoon, we'd already found a huge mirror, big enough to be set on the floor and leaned up high against the wall. I'd re-stain the thick wood frame but planned to leave the warbled mirror tinged with age, something to give depth and texture and contrast.

"I didn't bring you here to get stuff for me, and I'm pretty sure every single thing you've picked out today has something to do with me."

That's because you've consumed my mind.

"That only makes sense, doesn't it? I'm working on your room. That's where my thoughts are going to be."

"But I brought you here to get something for you."

I quirked a brow, biting back my laughter as I stepped closer and narrowed my eyes. "You brought me to get used junk?"

Horror took over his face. Genuine. A split second later, it slanted into amusement. "Oh, Peaches, you are so going to pay for that," he murmured the last in my ear, another one of those threats I wanted to take head on. "You think I don't know you?"

My hand fisted in his shirt, clinging to him as he bent me back. I could feel the world falling out from beneath me. Because he knew me better than anyone else.

"Thank you," he suddenly said.

My eyes moved all over his face. Searching. Memorizing. "For what?"

"For being you. You're..." He trailed off and tucked a strand of hair behind my ear, as if he didn't know what to say. Then, the man was kissing me again.

ASH

Sometimes you have to wonder if it's worth the gamble. Stepping out and taking the risk. The problem was when you didn't know who to bet on. If you were deserving of the pot. If the roll of the crooked dice landed you with a pair of snake eyes, who was it that was really going to lose? And if you did manage to throw sixes? Just what the fuck was it that you hoped to win?

Yet, here I was.

Putting it all on that quickly fraying line.

Playing stupid.

Reckless.

I was pretty damned certain neither of us would come out on top.

Tinkling laughter rang out against my walls. The kind that caused mayhem to wind in my already twisted gut.

"Be careful," I warned. Why the hell did I let her talk me into this?

"Quit being such a baby, rock star. We totally have this." Humor ridged her straining voice as we struggled to maneuver the bulky mirror up my staircase. She was up top because I'd convinced her that was the heaviest part. That in and of itself was a damned miracle, considering the girl started off by insisting she could get it upstairs herself.

Without my help.

Really, I'd taken the bottom because I figured if this bitch of a mirror came tumbling down, it was going to land on me. No chance in hell would I put her in that position.

"Where the hell is Zee when I need him? Asshole's always lurking around until there's work to be done. Then poof. Boy's nowhere to be found."

Light, lilting laughter rang from between those pretty lips again as she sent me one of those smiles that knocked the breath right out of me. "If I were him, I'd be running the other direction, too. I bet you had no idea what you were getting yourself into the day you walked into my store."

No, I definitely didn't have a clue what I was walking into.

"Maybe he went and found himself a girl. Dude's been scarce lately. Or maybe he just can't handle being around and knowing what kind of delicious I have locked behind my door."

I couldn't see the red I knew rushed to her cheeks. But, fuck, I could feel it. Swore I could feel this girl from across the room. The familiarity that urged and coaxed and comforted.

We made it up a couple more steps. Willow's breaths came harder with the exertion. "I think I might have underestimated when we bought this just how heavy this mirror was going to be."

It was hard enough getting it into the back of the SUV.

"Big plans require big solutions. *Big, big* solutions." I couldn't even keep my laughter out. Apparently, I had the sense of humor of a twelve-year-old.

Sue me.

"Aren't you a clever boy."

"You want me to get clever? Is that what I hear you saying? Tell me, darlin', because if you want me to get clever, then you know I'm totally game."

"Oh, I bet you are."

A chuckle rolled free.

Yes and please. I was all for showing her just how talented I could be.

When we finally reached the top of the never-ending staircase, she swiveled, and I followed. She backed the rest of the way down the hall and into my room. "Over here," she instructed.

She guided me to the middle of the room where she'd basically set up shop. "Just lie it down on its back. I'll start work on it tomorrow."

We carefully set it on a drop cloth already spread out on the floor.

"We did it."

"Of course we did. Wouldn't want you to go and get the false impression I'm some kind of sissy boy, now would I?"

Mock horror widened her mouth. "I could never think such appalling things about such a strapping, robust man."

A grin infiltrated her tease, before her expression softened.

Tender.

Sweet.

It clutched me right in the center of my chest. My heart did that crazy thing I kept begging it not to do.

She straightened herself. That fall of mahogany was disheveled where it cascaded around her shoulders and her cheeks were pink from the day out in the sun.

A heavy sigh blew from her lips and she looked around my room that was getting close to being done. All the major renovations had been completed, the fixtures and tile installed in the bathroom, the sanding and re-staining of the floors, paint on the walls. A few pieces of the furniture she'd created were already set in place.

"It's going to look amazing," she said. It seemed more to herself than to me, the girl caught up in her work the way she always was. Like she saw it as something alive. Constantly in transition. As a flow of time and years and memories. This girl was leaving her mark on the moment that belonged to her.

"Sex and comfort," I said, a little hoarse.

She looked up to stare across at me, something unsaid bounding between us, before she seemed to shake it off, turn away. She moved to the big wall opposite the bank of windows and lifted the painting we'd picked up at the market. "I thought we'd put this painting right here above the dresser and the mirror on the floor off to the side."

Her gaze slid down the long, blank wall, like she was imagining what would eventually go there.

"Still don't have that photo shoot complete. Think it's time to make that magic happen. Imagine what that's going to look like...you up there, gracing my walls. Fucking best thing I've ever seen, and I'll be the lucky bastard who gets to wake up to it every morning."

It came across rougher than I intended.

She grinned. But it was soft. Almost sad. Her head just tilted to the side. "You're ridiculous."

She was right. I was ridiculous. Because this was ridiculous, and I'd lost capacity to stop.

I moved across the room with measured steps. Energy lit. A shockwave of electricity. Like a flick of a switch. Instant. Bright. Blinding.

She sucked in a staggered breath as soon as I got in her space, but held my eyes as I cupped her face in one hand. My thumb brushed the curve of her cheek. "Do you get it yet, darlin'? What I see when I look at you? How all my thoughts get crossed and everything goes haywire? Second you touch, I'm lost in a confusion I shouldn't feel because the only thing I feel is you."

A tiny moan bled from that sweet, sweet mouth. I caressed my thumb along her bottom lip and stared down at the girl who had completely rocked my world. Single-handedly crushed the foundation that should have been solid.

Unbreakable.

My heart picked up an extra beat.

Like maybe it'd been missing one before.

"Ash."

I kissed her. Slow, deep, and purposed.

She melted against me.

Her honeyed tongue so damned sweet.

Lust.

It burst in my blood like the breaking of a dam.

Taking me under.

Eating me alive.

Overwhelming need crushed me. The need to get in this girl. To devour every inch.

She kissed me like she would let me. Give it all. Even if it destroyed her in the end.

I edged back, still kissing her while I worked through the buttons on her blouse. I pushed it free of her shoulders, revealing black lace and all that creamy skin.

A groan rumbled free. "Darlin'…you are killing me. Every fuckin' time I touch you, I'm losing breath."

Sanity.

Didn't even fucking know who I was anymore. If all her light was covering up my dark. If maybe she was exposing someone new or maybe bringing to life the old. Or maybe it was all just a twisted, sick illusion. One cast by the hand of an enchanting girl who made me see things I shouldn't see.

Hot hands pressed under my shirt. Greedy. Her palms were flat as she raked the material up. She didn't hesitate when she tore it over my head.

She rocked back, chocolate eyes doing a little of that devouring I was dying to do.

"You are everything." It was a rasp. Fingertips traced across the lines of my abdomen, up over my chest, touching along the ink tattooed on my skin.

Memorizing.

Etching.

Marking.

The girl ruined me a little more with each trembling caress.

"When I'm with you…everything…everything feels right."

Painfully, my chest squeezed. She was wrong. Sick part? I wanted to be.

Right.

Good for this girl when I knew, without a doubt, I'd only fuck it up in the end.

Either that thought didn't come through clear or I was just a selfish bastard, because it wasn't enough to curb my actions. Not enough to stop me from reaching around to flick the snap on her bra. My hands glided back over the caps of her shoulders and down the length of her arms.

Goose bumps trailed in my wake.

One touch, and this girl was shaking in my hands.

I dropped it to the floor.

Air hit her flesh and I watched as her nipples pebbled under my stare.

Pink and puckered tight.

So damned pretty.

Her tits were small, and I cupped one in my hand. I swept my thumb back and forth across the rock-hard peak.

A quiver rolled down her spine.

"Perfection." It was a murmur. Praise.

I edged her back, urging her to climb onto the center of my bed.

She complied. No questions or reservations. Just that sweet shyness that kissed across every exquisite inch of her body.

I removed her socks and shoes, dropped them with a thud to the floor. A smirk ticked up at the corner of my mouth, and I bit my bottom lip when I popped the button of her jeans. "Let me show you just how damned much. How fucking sexy you are. Way I can't control myself the second you step in the room."

She trembled. "Ash."

"You own me," I murmured low, hating the confession but knowing it was true. I was so far out of my element. *Easy* had taken a nasty fall out the window right along with my senses.

Because I had none.

All except for the one's that lit up under her touch. Under her stare. Beneath that tender heart that was slowly undoing me. Cutting right through my reserves and getting to all those places I didn't want her to be.

Because then she'd see. See what I'd done.

See just how fucking vile I was.

Blood.

Smears.

Freezing cold.

Anna.

I squeezed my eyes against the foul images, and I sucked in a breath and focused on this girl as I dragged her jeans down her legs.

It left her in nothing but the scrap of black lace covering her heat as she leaned back on her hands. That mess of hair flowed around her shoulders and brushed at my bed, and she had a single leg bent and slowly rocked it back and forth as her chest heaved with desire.

Fuck.

"Idiot. Any asshole who'd let someone like you go."

No doubt, I'd be just another bearer of that unfortunate title.

"Talk you down. Make you feel like you're any less than you are. Not when you're the best thing that's ever walked into my world."

Shaken it up and shattered it.

"Did you know, Willow? Do you get it yet? You are the sexiest girl I've ever seen."

My words were grit, both hard and soft because this girl made me confused like that. "Did you know you walk in a room and every goddamned head turns your way?"

She frowned, teeth yanking at that lip. "That's because they're looking at you."

I shook my head. "Not even close. That's what you're missing, baby. Just how gorgeous you are. Inside and out. In the places we can and can't see. And there's this part of me that wants to tear every single one of those guys dying to get an eyeful of you to shreds. Lash out. Tell them you're mine when I know I can't keep you."

She shivered.

"Do you trust me?"

A hard swallow.

A resolute nod.

I snagged her blouse from the floor. Setting a knee on the bed, I leaned around her and slid her arms back into the sleeves.

Questions fluttered across her face.

"Trust me," I murmured deep, right at her ear.

I left the shirt open the barest fraction. Just a lust-inducing inch of her skin was exposed right down the middle.

Fuck.

This girl.

And after everything?

This is what that goddamned pretending was all about.

I wanted to show her.

This was what I wanted her to see.

"This is just for me. Just for you. You understand?" I asked when I edged back from the bed and dug my phone from my pocket. "No one else is going to see this. Not ever."

A pant parted her lips.

Surprise, want, and curiosity.

That dauntless spirit up against a sliver of timidity.

Muted light filtered in through the windows. The room spilled over with dancing shadows and bouncing light.

Right in the middle of it, the girl sat on display. Art in motion. A masterpiece.

I thumbed into my camera app.

"Ash...I..." She dropped her head.

"Shh..." I ran my knuckles down the side of her face and hooked my finger under her chin. "Look at me."

She turned her gaze my direction. Watched me with molten, trusting eyes.

I snagged a close-up of her face. "You stagger me."

It was burned on my screen. Her confused, eager expression.

I glanced the pad of my thumb across her plush lip.

She moaned while I snapped another.

Click.

Click.

Click.

"Lie back a little."

She didn't hesitate. She just settled back on her elbows with a needy sigh.

I set to tracing my fingertips down her throat, and I tapped out a trail across her chest where her heart hammered and thrashed.

No question, mine was doing the same as I took picture after picture of this stunning girl.

Capturing her raw.

Vulnerable and brave.

I nudged the shirt aside. Just a fraction. And maybe that was sexier than anything, just the mind-altering tease of the swell of her breast.

A shiver rippled beneath the surface of her skin, and I splayed my hand across the full expanse of her flat belly.

It tremored beneath my touch. Swore I could feel it slide right through me.

Click.

I edged back to get a better view. The girl writhed, coming alive in the center of my bed.

"Do you feel it, Willow? How beautiful you are? All that life overflowing in you? From you? That's real beauty. The kind that can't be contained, no matter how hard someone tries to keep it tamed."

Click.

"Touch yourself. Feel what I feel when I'm touching you." The demand slid out low.

A whimper, and her head rocked back. She barely ran her fingertips across the swell of her exposed breast. She caressed her neck. Her legs. Barely grazed between her thighs.

Sweet fucking torture.

I couldn't help it. I angled my camera in to catch the

expression on her face.

Her body twitched, and my name caught in her throat. "Ash."

She dipped a finger under her underwear, and my world tipped.

There was only so much a man could take.

Any willpower I had left buckled.

Restraint stripped.

I tossed my phone to the bed and shucked out of my jeans and underwear.

I placed a knee on the bed and set to tearing that shirt right back off her tight, tight body.

It yanked her arms back behind her when I did, wrists held hostage.

Her bare chest jutted into mine, and she gulped at the position, her tits pressed and bunched between us and her hands tied behind her back.

Mother. Fuck.

Control's a bitch to lose when you don't have a whole lot of it to begin with.

The last of mine snapped.

Severed.

Gone.

Gone to this girl.

I kissed her hard. Demanded her tongue and her breaths and her heart that thundered against her ribs.

I climbed all the way up and straddled her body. I rose up high on my knees, towering over her as my mouth devoured and my cock rubbed at her belly, her arms still tied behind her back.

"Oh. God. Ash." Her body bowed, trying to meet mine.

I ripped her wrists free of the bind of the shirt. I backed off just enough to get those panties down her long, inspiring legs.

Because if this girl wanted me to get clever, I would gladly oblige.

I didn't miss a beat, and my hands were on her knees, pushing them wide. "Beautiful," I growled. Because it was damned true. Her perfect slit that I parted with my tongue.

A needy breath shot from her lungs, and those delicate hands fisted not so delicately in my hair.

A growl that originated somewhere in my stomach scraped up my throat.

"God...I love the way you taste."

Hot. Wet. Throbbing with want.

No wonder I'd been dying to get a taste.

"Could spend my life right here...buried between your legs."

I sucked and nipped at her folds. Teasing and torturing. Winding her up. While she squirmed and tried to get her sweet cunt closer to my face.

A litany of urgent pleas whimpered from her mouth.

I chuckled and backed off, loving that I had the power to affect her that way. I nearly lost my footing when I looked up and met with the sincerity in her liquid gaze.

If I share my body with a man, it's because I love him and he loves me.

That feeling washed over me. One devastating wave. The kind that took out cities. It took me under where I knew I would drown.

I ran the tip of a finger between her lips. "What was that, darlin'?"

"Please."

"What is it you want, love? You want a little of this?"

I pushed that finger deeper, dipping just into the tight well of her body.

"Yes...more...please. Don't tease me...please....I need you...want you. You're all I want. Everything I want." It fell as an incoherent jumble from her mouth, each word finding its mark like a punch of clarity.

I dove back in, this time delving deep. I spread her with my thumbs, fucked her with my tongue, moved up to circle her clit, and trailed back down again.

Touching her everywhere just like she was touching me.

It was only fair.

She bucked.

I laved and lapped. I moved all the way back to her ass.

She moaned in the back of her throat, loving it but not sure she should. Her fingers were trembling and needy in my hair, as if she didn't know if she wanted to pull me closer or push me away.

"Please."

I flipped her onto her hands and knees.

"Good?" I said it almost like a warning.

Hands fisted in my sheets. "Yes."

I jerked open the nightstand that'd been crafted by this girl's brilliant hand and grabbed a condom.

In all this fuckery, at least I'd progressed to getting at least one thing right.

I covered my dick, grabbed her by the hips, and took her in one solid thrust, filling her so full my body bowed with the impact.

She nearly screamed, but it bled into a moan as her body adjusted to me.

God.

She was so tight. Her walls held me in a needy, throbbing clutch.

No girl should feel this good.

"Do you feel that? Do I come close to feeling how good you feel to me? Is it even possible?"

"Nothing…no one…never, Ash. It's you."

I set a rigid, punishing pace, yanking her back by the hips to meet my thrusts. Her hair was all over the place, her gorgeous skin blanketed in a light sheen of sweat, my name a constant petition falling from her lips.

My fingers kneaded deep. Her lush, round bottom fit perfectly in the clench of my hands.

Confessions tumbled from her mouth. "Ash…God…what are you doing to me? I can't…I need you more than anything I've ever needed."

That, right there, should throw up a stop sign. I should cover this girl back up, send her home with a chaste kiss, and pray I hadn't already done too much damage.

Instead, all my attention turned to my cock disappearing into the tight clutch of her body as I slid in and out of her.

Tingles raced my skin. And I knew I was nothing but a sinner and a liar. I'd chased this. This body and this unnerving feeling I couldn't shake. The needy feeling that tracked my spine and tightened my balls.

"You want me?" I demanded.

"Yes."

I gently circled her ass with my thumb, not so gently pushed it in.

A whine escaped her panting mouth. Her body clenched all around me.

I fucked her faster and harder. She met me thrust for thrust.

Demanding all I could give her.

Right then, it felt like everything and nothing at all.

I wound my other arm around her waist and barely flicked her clit.

She went off like a bomb.

Her hands fisted in the sheets, and she cried out my name. She was making all these sounds that slipped beneath my skin and sank into my spirit, her creamy skin lighting up in flashes of red as pleasure streaked through her body.

Incinerated.

Burned.

I knew it was me who'd be reduced to ashes.

I rocked into her hard. Two erratic thrusts. Before bliss stole every cell in my body.

So goddamned good, so unbearably wrong.

I went back to squeezing her hips, holding her against me while I buried myself as deep as I could get while the world flickered and tremored around me.

Taunted me with *what if.*

Willow collapsed below me, gasping into the sheets as she slowly came back down. I bent closer, peppering her spine, shoulders, and neck with kisses as I struggled to regain my own composure.

"I'll be right back."

All I got was a spent, sated nod.

Climbing from bed, I headed into the bathroom, shucked the

condom, and washed my hands. I stopped at the doorway, just looking at the girl laid out on my bed, lit up in moonlight against the silvery gray sheets.

A bed she'd fashioned from hand. A bold piece she'd reclaimed.

She looked perfect lying in it. Like she'd been carved in with the rest. I couldn't even begin to picture what it might be like without her there.

I roughed a hand through my hair.

What was I doing?

But whatever it was, it was unstoppable, and it had me crossing the room, crawling onto that bed, and rolling her a bit so I could get in behind her.

She sighed and scooted closer.

Seeking sanctuary.

A home.

I brushed back her mussed, tangled hair, and kissed the crown of her head before fumbling for my phone. I thumbed across the faceplate. The bright screen came to life.

Through the images, I watched her expression flicker through uncertainty to wonder.

"This is you." I whispered my praise, my belief.

Silence swam around us for the longest time as she looked at the pictures, my body half inclined to take note and go for another round. For once, I kept the insane need I felt for this girl reined.

"This is what you really see when you look at me?" Her question was quiet. Almost timid.

"The first time I saw you…" A wistful smile cracked my face, and I hugged her closer.

"You nearly knocked me from my feet. Yeah. You're gorgeous. Don't think there's any question about that. But it was more than that. I liked that you were different than all the girls that run in my circle. A little shy but confident. Convictions and principles clear. Right from the start, it made me want to look closer and see what was really hiding inside."

She turned enough that she could look down at me. "What

did you find?"

"Found someone who makes me wish I was someone else."

"What if you're him?" she urged, and I could feel it starting to bleed through. The desperation neither of us knew how to handle. That feeling like the two of us belonged when I knew that was nothing but a cruel delusion.

"I'm not." Could feel that emotion gathering on my face, winding out as the softest smile as I stared at the girl. "Any guy would be the luckiest bastard to get to be him. But I'm not, Peaches."

It seemed the more I told her, the less either of us believed it.

Shadows danced across her face, questions and contradiction. "Because of the life you lead? The band and the traveling?"

I sighed. "Think my boys have proven that theory wrong. Maybe I used to think it, but all of them are better off now than they've ever been."

I set my phone aside and cradled her face in my hands. "The problem is *me*, Peaches. The problem is who *I am*. Yeah, I could lie here and make you a thousand promises and tell you I'm going to be here for you forever. And right this second? I might be just the fool who'd think he might be able to make good on them. But I have a really bad habit of letting the people I love down. Don't want to, but it's what I do. It's who I am. And I hate that person, and I won't ever let that person ruin you."

She sucked in a breath at my careless words.

Love.

My heart capsized.

Because there it was, shining back in those bottomless eyes.

I pulled her face closer. Our noses brushed, my words emphatic where I pled them near her face. "You deserve better than what I have. Better than what I have to give. Better than what I *am*. And I know that guy's out there."

Jealousy surged. A suffocating ache that pounded through my veins, strangling every sense and denying every word.

Couldn't stand the thought of another man touching what

was mine.

"You just have to find him," I promised her, the words thick and sour on my tongue.

Sadness swelled around her. I fucking hated that I was already hurting her.

I knew I would.

She pushed away. I wanted to panic until she turned and lay back on her side so she could wind herself back in my arms.

She grabbed my phone again, and I blinked in uncertainty when she suddenly held it out in front of her, the camera lens angled to capture the scene.

Click.

And fuck. My expression was carved in stone. Hard.

But my eyes—they splayed me wide open.

Cut me down until all the promises waiting inside were exposed.

This picture?

It illustrated a girl looking at a man like he might be her world. Like she held the faith he would stand by her side. Hold her up. The man in that picture was looking down at her, ready to give up his life to protect the goodness in her.

Move mountains to find her.

Walk through hell to save her.

Her voice was a whisper. "This…this is what I see when I look at you."

WILLOW

*T*here are moments in your life you wish you could set to pause. Press a button to delay the passage of time. Maybe have the ability to play them again and again so you could hold onto them forever.

Because you know without a doubt they're some of the best you'll ever experience in all your life. Even when you know they're fleeting. That time is spinning around you, sucking away the blissful days and the rapturous nights.

This was one of them.

Chandeliers sprinkled a hue of shimmery silver light over the long table nestled in an alcove of the posh restaurant.

Smiling faces sat all around me, their chatter and easy laughter echoing in the air. The ambiance one of hope and belief and the kind of love as a little girl I'd always believed I'd find.

Under the table, a big hand squeezed my knee. Ash grinned at me. So free. So easy. It was as if he were promising me this was exactly where I belonged.

He returned his attention to his patchwork family that stitched together so perfectly.

Everyone was there to celebrate finally heading back into the studio tomorrow.

I had the inkling they were old pros at finding any excuse to get together and let loose. The three bottles of wine the table had gone through seemed evidence enough.

"You wish, man. That story is all kinds of backward. If memory serves, it was you who incited that fight. Just begging for it…walking in that bar like you owned the place."

Smug, Sebastian, who had switched from wine to a tumbler of amber liquid, tipped the glass he was holding in Ash's direction and pointed an accusatory finger at him.

Ash scoffed, his voice lifted in that over-the-top, imprudent way. "What in the world are you talkin' about?"

Tonight, the cocky, arrogant boy had come out to play. He'd been that way since the second he'd picked me up at my house. Flirty smirk already firmly set in place. Ease in each powerful step.

He gestured to himself with both hands. "This boy right here? He's a lover, not a fighter."

With as much zeal as Ash poured into the argument, I might have believed him.

Apparently, his friends knew better.

Lyrik sputtered on his wine. "Not a fighter? I think between our crew we could probably come up with about…oh…I don't know…a thousand or two instances that would tell an entirely different story."

Lyrik ticked his chin at me. "Besides, I think your girl here would attest to the fact you are most definitely a fighter."

Your girl.

God.

Was it wrong how much I wanted it?

Palms up, Ash held out his hands. "Hey now, hey now. Get backed into a corner and a man's gotta do what a man's gotta do. Only thing I'm concerned about is getting the fact clear that I enjoy the lovin' part so much more than the fightin'. Let's just say it's so much more…satisfying. Thinking my Willow here could attest to that, too. Some of us are just endowed with…certain gifts. Isn't that right, Willow?"

He cocked his head at me, just as cocky as his grin.

Shivers.

Heat.

I couldn't stop it. Right there in the middle of the restaurant. In front of all his family and friends.

The man had me twisted inside out.

Made me forget who I was.

Or maybe he'd just slowly showed me who it was I wanted to be.

Laughter contained, I forced a shrug and wide, innocent eyes. "You're okay, I guess."

"Goo!" Austin pounded on the table, laughing loud. "Shoot, sink, score. Willow for the win."

Edie cracked up and buried her face in her hands.

Zee howled and hooked a thumb at me. "Oh, dude, now I get why you've been keeping this one around. Think you've met your match, my friend. Glad to see someone finally step up to the plate and put you in your place."

Zee smiled at me, almost soft. As if he knew he were traversing into territory that might sting. His gaze telling me it was all in jest. Part of the constant sparring that went on between all of them.

Ash's mouth dropped open in offense, and he slammed a closed fist over his heart, obviously dying from a mortal stab wound.

"Oh, darlin', you just really know how to break a man's heart, don't you? And here I thought I was blowing your mind every single night…a time or two or maybe four. Guess I'm just going to have to throw in the towel. Give it up. Don't think my fragile ego can take it."

Tamar laughed. "Fragile ego, my ass. Your ego has to be as big as your—"

"Gah…stop…stop right there," Edie pled, falling into a fit of giggles she hid in Austin's shoulder. "I don't even know why I hang out with you all. This is supposed to be my safe circle and every single time I leave with images in my head I just don't want to see."

Tamar shrugged a tattooed shoulder. "What? If we have to put up with your brother, then you have to, too."

"How's that putting up with Ash going anyway, Willow?" Shea edged forward, mischief seeded in her words. "Are his 'gifts' really all that disappointing or are they enough to maybe get you to hang around? Because I have two hundred bucks on this player having to paint all those extra bedrooms pink and blue one day. Think it's about time I cash in."

She meant it to be a tease.

I knew she did.

But it didn't stop the pain from leeching into my insides. Squeezing my spirit.

I forced a wobbly smile. "I don't think there's any threat of that happening any time soon."

I made a valiant attempt not to look Ash's way, hating that I felt vulnerable. Raw.

I didn't want to be that girl.

Not anymore.

Silence fell over the table. Tension thick.

Finally, Shea spoke quietly. "I'm so sorry if I said something I shouldn't have. I would never want to hurt either of you."

I swallowed around the lump in my throat. "It's fine. Honestly."

Was it?

Because I could feel myself at the precipice. Those moments slipping by. Ones I wanted to cling to forever.

Ash slammed his palms down on the table. "Whelp, I think

this party calls for a round of shots, don't you?"

He was all strained, wooden smiles when he stood, pushed out his chair, and strode for the long, elegant bar situated along the far wall just outside the alcove.

"Shit," Lyrik muttered as he rubbed his fingers across his mouth. He and Baz shared a look I couldn't decipher. I sat there twisting my fingers in the fabric napkin, wishing we could go back a few moments to when things were easy and all the questions that seemed to hover around Ash and me didn't feel quite so profound.

But there they were. Shoved in our faces. No question, all this "pretending" was catching up to us. Neither of us seemed to know what was real anymore. What we wanted or how far we could go.

"Excuse me," I said, deciding to stand. To make a claim or a statement, I didn't know. Maybe my only aim was to soothe the man I could tell was set on edge. Tell him I was truly okay. That yes, I had huge regrets in my life, but that didn't mean I wasn't finding happiness in the here and now.

He'd been responsible for so much of it.

Even if this ended right here, right now, I needed him to know that.

I eased around the table, doing my best not to feel awkward or insecure, because I was learning fast that wasn't who I was. I paused at the threshold of the sectioned off room.

Ash sat on a stool at the bar.

He was set in profile, his strong, bearded jaw pronounced and defined, his hair slicked back, a button up casually rolled up his forearms to expose the ink hidden underneath.

God.

He was stunning.

A magnificent, mystifying creature that tore at all my sensibilities.

He leaned in to speak to the bartender, who angled his way, her cleavage spilling out and a seductive smirk slicked across her red lips. She was all sass and tease as she lifted a bottle and expertly poured the dark fluid over a short row of shot glasses and quickly arranged them on a tray. I watched as she then scribbled something on a napkin and slid it to him across the bar.

He glanced down at it, and from the side, I couldn't read his eyes. Couldn't tell what they would say, before she said something else to him and turned to begin making another drink.

Hurt clenched me in all those raw spots before resolve rushed in to take its place.

I moved across the floor and came up behind him. I could see the tension ripple through his body, the apprehension that lifted his shoulders as I approached.

That sensation grew thick. The feeling that I knew him in a way I couldn't possibly know another man. A tether tied. Our spirits bound.

With each step, it just kept cinching tighter and tighter.

He slowly looked at me from over his shoulder.

That sea of blue washed over me. Soft and warm and cautious. I edged closer. He reached out and snagged me around the waist, shifting just a fraction to pull me between his parted legs.

A surprised breath rushed from my lungs.

He searched my face. "You okay?"

I nodded slowly, a smile merging with my frown. "Never mistake broken for weak."

Pride simmered in his gaze, and he set a warm palm on my neck. "Peaches."

I set my phone on the bar, fully turned to him, and fiddled with the collar of his shirt, stalling for just an extra second before I looked back up to meet the intensity in his eyes. "I'm fine, Ash. Honestly. I think I've been holding on to a lot of regrets for so much of my life. For too long. It's time for me to start letting them go and realize I can't go back and change it. I need to accept that no matter how badly I want them, there are some things in my life I might not ever have. It's time to find joy in the amazing things that I do."

Pain lanced across his face. "Willow."

I shook my head. "Come on. Tonight we're supposed to be celebrating with your family. The last thing I want to be is the spoilsport who ruined your party. That's not the kind of 'reputation' I want to have."

He chuckled. "Darlin', are you speaking in innuendos? I do believe I've been rubbing off on you."

My eyes widened. "Oh, I think you've been doing plenty of rubbing. In all the right ways."

"Ahh…so now her tune changes." He gripped my hips. "Thinking I do you a whole lot better than just *okay*."

"Mmm…I'd say you do."

The bartender was suddenly there, pushing back into his space. Eyes full of greed as she looked at my man like she wanted to swoop in and sink in her claws. I grabbed the napkin she'd scribbled her number on and tossed it her way. "He won't be needing that."

Sudden laughter ripped from his throat. He tried to contain it in the bare skin exposed above the neckline of my dress, his lips pressing to the flesh when he rumbled the words. "You are…what am I going to do with you?"

He pulled back and placed the chastest kiss he'd ever given me on my lips. "You make me happy."

Emotion thickened my throat. It spread, sliding slow until it occupied everything. My heart, my thoughts, my spirit.

You make me happy, too.

So happy.

I don't want to let it go.

Please don't let me go.

He leaned in and kissed me deeply.

Softly.

Different than he ever had, as if he were desperate to cherish these fleeting moments, too.

He held me by both sides of my face in those big hands. Hands I'd come to trust in every way.

My pulse rate spiked, thrummed, and churned. I swore I could feel the man beating through my veins and dripping into my bones.

He pulled back and gazed at me. Something tender moved through his eyes.

"When does this end?" I whispered, my mouth dry.

His fingers twitched. "Don't have the answer to that…not when I'm the selfish bastard who doesn't want it to."

My phone dinged and lit up on the bar top. It shocked both of us out of our bubble. Our heads turned in sync, the little box at the top popping up with the notification.

Bates.

God.

I needed to get a new number and erase the stain of him from my life once and for all.

A scowl took Ash's expression hostage. He turned back to me, his voice close to a growl. "What's this?"

I swallowed again, stammered. "He…he keeps—"

He didn't give me time to explain. Ash grabbed my phone and flipped directly into the messages.

A picture took up the whole of the screen.

Another of the offending pictures Bates kept flooding me with as if he might have the chance to win me back.

But this one…this one managed to curl my stomach.

Nausea swirled and tears pricked at my eyes.

Ash was in bed with two women. Face down. Passed out. One of the girls had her phone held out capturing the illicit scene. The obvious aftermath of a night gone wild.

She'd captioned it.

#AshEvans #RockedMyWorld #Threesome #SunderSlut

Her fifteen seconds of fame.

Ash nearly crushed my phone in his hand.

"Motherfucker."

He flew from the stool. Rage bristled.

"Told you to tell me if that asshole was bothering you, Willow. You've been hiding this from me?"

He shook his head as if he couldn't see straight, spun on his heel, and headed for the door, his long strides full of fury. He flew outside without a parting glance.

I stood there staring. Gasping for breath, trying to find my footing. Before I jumped into action. I scrambled after him, dodging a few chairs to make my way through.

I pushed open the door and stepped out into the night.

A hazy gloom stretched across the heavens, the air dense and humid. Thick. My eyes bounced left, but my body was already turning right. Drawn.

He stood in the distance at the head of an alleyway. The intimidating man was nothing but a raging, shadowed silhouette.

His face was upturned toward the sky with both hands pressed to the sides of his head.

I could almost see it radiating from him.

Anger.

Hate.

Maybe a little of his own regret.

Warily, I approached, my heels clicking on the cobblestones. A warning echo in the night.

His back went rigid when I stopped two feet behind him.

He was still crushing my phone in his hand. "You see?"

"What?" I challenged.

"What I've been telling you all along. That I'm not good enough for you. That you deserve someone better."

"You never hid any of that from me."

Bitter laughter rumbled from his chest. "This is barely scratching the surface, darlin'."

"The only thing I know is the man I see…the one you've been showing me. He's the one who's changed me. Woken me up. Shaken me from my shell."

He laughed again, this time softer as he shook his head and slowly turned around. He lifted both his arms in surrender. I wasn't sure the man had ever looked more broken.

"It's always me, Willow. I know you don't get that. On the outside, I look like this guy who doesn't give two fucks about a whole lot of anything. But I'm the one who's always been responsible."

I blinked through the confusion.

He sighed, roughed a hand through his hair, and stared at the dirty ground as he began to pace. "My crew…we've been through so much shit. So much bad stuff. Every bit of it was prompted by me."

He huffed an affectionate sound and jutted his chin back toward the restaurant. "They all make light of it. Laugh it off— the fact that I'm a fighter and am always looking for trouble. The next thrill. They've always taken up my back and never put the blame where it belonged."

"Ash…"

He rubbed the back of his hand that still clutched my phone over his mouth. Like he could wipe away the sour taste. "We were just kids running the streets, learning how to live, finding out who we wanted to be. When we were twelve, guess who it was who showed up with the first six-pack he'd snagged from his dad's cooler? Me. First time we all got high? It was me who had the bag."

Distress climbed into his frazzled words, and he blinked like he was seeing back to that day. "It was *me* who snorted that first line."

His face curled in agony, curling my heart right up along with it.

"I was hooking up with this chick, and one night she brought it to the house. All just fun and games, right?" Disgust twisted his features. "Next thing we knew, things were totally fucked. Slipping out of control so fast. Before we could even make sense of it, we were pumping ourselves full of all this shit. Whatever we could get through a needle or up our noses. *Me.*"

He looked to the sky like he was looking for a lifeline. "Zee's big brother, Mark?"

The shake of my head was short, because I'd never heard the name.

"Used to be our drummer," he clarified. "My best friend. Dead. OD'd. Started out on the bullshit I brought into our house."

He slammed a fist against his chest. "*Me.*"

His head turned toward me, his stare severe. "And I'm the bastard who always seemed to manage to scrape by. The one that never quite got hooked. It was like I was the guy who'd accidentally incited a war but was left standing on the sidelines, watching it all go down, his brothers in arms falling. One by one. And there wasn't a goddamned thing I could do about it."

Harsh, hard breaths grated from his lungs. "My sister...what happened to her...that bastard raping her? It was on *me*."

Grief punched me in the gut.

Ash kept right on. He flung a hand toward the underside of his arm, to that knot of tattoos that screamed of horror and insanity and grief. "I marked them all here. Every strike against me. So I won't ever forget that I always manage to fuck it up. To remember not to get too deep."

My head spun. All I wanted was to wrap him in my arms and tell him I'd bear some of his burden, too. Promise him he was so much more than all of that. I saw it. The goodness and the kindness. Neither of us deserved to be prisoners to regret.

He ground his teeth so hard I could hear them creaking, and he turned away, his hands going to the back of his head as he tried to draw in a breath.

"Did you know I was going to be a dad?"

I collided with a wall of pain. His. Mine. My entire being went rigid with the force of the shock. My legs shook and my stomach twisted.

He turned back to look at me.

His face was written in agony. "*Me*."

"Ash."

Torment poured from him, and I took a tentative step forward.

The shake of his head was harsh. "And after all of that, Willow, after all that, I want to hunt this fucker down."

He lifted the phone a fraction, squeezing it in his hand.

"I want to hunt him down and take him out. And not for what happened that night in front of your store. But because of *you*. Because I'm just that selfish of an asshole that I want to claim you. Tell him you're mine. Tell him he can't ever have you back because I'm not ever letting you go."

He waved the phone. "And this right here is just another reminder of why I can't."

Everything spun. His words and my spirit and his heart. I could feel both of us teetering at the edge. Ready to go tumbling over.

My phone rang.

A crazed shout ripped from him. Incredulous and enraged. He answered it like he was going to do that very thing he promised he wanted to do.

"Listen, motherfucker—"

He froze.

Completely.

His breaths and his body and his words.

A chill slid down my spine.

Fear and dread.

"Yes...I'm so sorry...please forgive me...hang on one second."

He blinked hard, but his eyes went achingly sad. Slowly he held out the phone. "You need to take this."

"Mama." I clung to her lifeless body, begging it again and again. "Mama. No. Don't leave me. Don't leave me. I'm not ready."

I'm not ready.

Anguish burned through me like white hot fire. Ripping and rending. Cutting me in two.

Wails bounced off the walls, the sorrow I expelled having no place to land. No place to go.

"Mama," I cried, hugging her closer, never wanting to let her go.

My rock. My foundation. My strength.

Gone.

I couldn't breathe.

The loneliness cried out.

The vacancy too much to bear.

Hands pressed to my shoulders. As if they sought to pour new strength into me. Gathering me closer. A breath in my hair. Lips to my head.

"Shh…I've got you. I've got you."

A sob tore free from my spirit. Just another missing piece of me. I clung tighter to the woman who'd always made me believe, grief gushing from my plea. "Why, Ash, why does everyone leave me? Why?"

He gathered me closer, and I gave, collapsed into his arms. We slid to the floor and he pulled me onto his lap.

He rocked me. "Shh."

Agonizing comfort.

Tears saturated his shirt. "Why?"

My soul wept.

Mama.

The words tumbled from my tongue. Incoherent and desperate. "Don't leave me. Please, don't leave me. I need you. Ash, I need you."

I need you.

He pressed his mouth to my forehead. "Shh…I'm right here. I'm right here. I'm not going anywhere."

ASH

I spent three full days with her.

I held her for hours. First on the hospital floor. Then, once I'd convinced her she needed to get out of there, back at her house. I wrapped myself around her from behind. Both of us still fully clothed where we lay on top of the quilt on her bed.

I sat with her while she made funeral plans, and I helped her pick out a casket. One that would match her sister's. Her mother was being buried beside her in the next plot.

Today, I stood beside her at the gravesite while she bowed her head and cried.

I didn't think she'd stopped crying. Not once. It fucking slayed me.

I kept an arm wrapped around her waist while her mother's old friends and acquaintances showed up to offer their condolences.

Trees thrashed and flailed and the sky spat its fury around us.

Like the earth mourned with her.

My crew came. Of course they did. All of them were there to offer their support. The girls stepped up with tears shining in their kind eyes and offers that they'd be there for whatever she needed. The guys stood nearby with all that staunch, silent loyalty.

Never once did I leave her side.

And I couldn't pinpoint it.

When it happened.

When my world tilted and every vain promise I'd ever made became a lie. When everything became *her*.

Because somewhere in those three days? Somewhere along the way, I made a silent vow I never would.

"You need to eat something," Emily fretted. She wrung her hands and paced in front of Willow.

Willow was snuggled under a blanket in an old rocking chair in her living room.

It wasn't cold.

Knew well enough sometimes cold didn't go just skin deep. Sometimes it was bred from within. A chill that originated in your spirit and spun out in a frosty web.

Wrapping your bones and numbing your blood. Before it slowly but surely seeped to the surface.

She shook her head. "I'm not hungry."

Emily exhaled heavily. "Fine." She turned and went back

into the kitchen where she could do more of the fretting she'd been doing.

Willow sat there with that huge mess of hair piled on top of her head, expression ridden with sorrow.

And all I felt was her peace.

The peace she'd given me.

The peace I wanted to give her in return.

And I wanted to drop to my knees and tell her I loved her. That I was terrified that I did. Terrified I might turn around and fuck it all up again, but that I was done running.

Because like she told me once.

Even wild hearts needed a place to rest.

And she'd become mine.

But I didn't want that confession coming at a time like this. Didn't ever want her to think I was sayin' it just because I wanted to pull her from her grief because God knew she deserved some time to feel it.

So, instead, I sank to the floor in front of her and framed her sweet face in the palms of my hands. She looked up at me.

Chocolate eyes.

Broken soul.

Spirit so far from weak.

"I need you to eat something, darlin'. You haven't eaten in four days. I'm not telling you to snap out of it or to dry your eyes or that it was for the best. All I'm telling you is I fucking care about you a whole lot and I need you to at least get something in this sweet body before it withers away."

She gave me a trembling half smile.

I squeezed her tighter. "Deal?"

She nodded in my hold. "Deal."

"Thank God." I pressed a kiss to her forehead.

I started to climb to my feet when Emily cut me off, already jumping into action. "Campbell's famous Chicken Noodle or Maude's not so famous tuna casserole?"

Willow laughed, soggy and choppy, but it was there. "I'll take the soup."

"Soup it is."

I turned back to look at her. She ran her fingers down my face, so goddamned tender. "Thank you for being here. You don't know how much it means to me. I'm not sure I could have gotten through this without you."

I gathered her hand that was fluttering along my face and pressed her fingers to my lips. "I don't want to be anywhere else. Not ever again."

Maybe it was shitty to say it then. Making her promises when she was in this state. But I couldn't regret it. Not when she looked at me the way she did. Like maybe I'd given her back a little of her life the way she'd given me back mine.

"You make me happy." She repeated what I'd told her that night, before things had gone to hell.

We both jumped when the doorbell rang. "I'll get that."

She nodded, and I pushed to stand. Roughing a hand through my hair, I headed to the front door. I looked through one of the small windows to the side. Sheila, her mother's caretaker, waited on the other side holding a box.

I clicked it open, raked an uncomfortable hand through my hair, murmured, "Hey."

I felt terrible I'd lit into this poor woman thinking it was that bastard Bates.

She quieted her voice. "I know it's a difficult time right now, but I wanted to drop these things by for Willow. I know she'd like to have them."

I accepted the box, which was filled with knickknacks and pictures. "That's kind of you. I know Willow will appreciate it."

She shifted and warily peeked inside. "I hope she's doing okay."

"She's not right now…but she will be."

She smiled. "Okay then."

"Thank you again," I said before I latched the door shut.

Turning on my heels, I took the three steps back out into the main room where Willow was still sitting. "Sheila brought your mom's things. How about you and I look through them later? When you're ready?"

Emily came in carrying a bowl of steaming soup. "I think

later is good."

She motioned toward the stairs with her shoulder. "Why don't you take that up to the extra room? That's where Will here keeps all the sentimental stuff. We need to be careful or this one's gonna turn into a hoarder."

A tiny scoff managed to work free from Willow's mouth. "I work with antiques. And I'm not above a dumpster dive. Do you really think I'm actually going to part with the good stuff?"

It was almost playful, and a little relief settled on my heart when I bounded upstairs and took a left through the closed door and into the room I'd never been into before.

Emily wasn't joking. It was hoarder's heaven in there.

Natural light filtered in through the window. The drapes pushed open on either side were dated with floral embroidery, the bedspread covering the bed hailing from an era Willow certainly had never stepped into. The floor was covered in stacks of boxes and trunks, an old armoire in the corner.

I suppressed a chuckle.

Because *this girl*.

I fucking liked it.

Liked that she was humble. Modest. A million miles away from the chicks that hunted like goddamned vultures in my world.

I crossed the floor and set the box down on top of another propped against the far wall.

Straightening, I glanced across the big ornate dresser cluttered with trinkets and photos. Couldn't help but smile when I saw one of an adorable little girl. Had to be Willow. She couldn't have been more than six or seven, her arms squeezing around her mom's neck with that awe-inspiring smile already written on her face, hair blowing all around her where she stood in a field.

Her mom was smiling right back.

I trailed my fingertips over a necklace and a ring, drummed them over a tarnished silver cup.

Learning this girl because I wanted to know her in every way.

I stopped dead at the small wooden box situated in the

center. Ashy gray with bronze hinges and hook. The same logo carved on her store's sign, the same written on her skin, was etched onto the top.

Dread curled through my fucked-up, muddled senses.

I blinked what had to have been a thousand times.

Trying to make the picture come out different.

Instead, everything crystalized as all that familiarity crushed me like a rockslide.

My hands fisted in my hair.

No.

Panic hurdled around the room. Ricocheting from the walls and gaining strength. It yanked at my heart and my spirit and nearly dropped me to my knees.

Fuck.

No.

My head shook and dizziness spun.

Still, I couldn't stop myself from reaching up, tentatively lifting the lid and peeking inside, like maybe doing so would come up with a different answer.

Inside was a small scrap of paper folded in quarters.

I stumbled back like it'd burned me, my eyes frantic, attention bouncing around the room at the rest of the tokens.

At the pictures I suddenly processed.

The breath punched from my lungs.

Gutted.

I pressed a fist to my mouth and bit down. For the first time in what felt like a lifetime, I wanted to weep. To fucking get on my knees and beg it.

Why?

Why the fuck did life have to be this way?

Unfair.

I fled the room with panic hounding at my back and grief weighing on my chest.

That's just what I got. Falling in love like a fool.

Knew better all along.

I clung to the railing as I clamored down the staircase.

Willow looked up when I got to the landing.

My chest squeezed.

So fucking tight I was certain it was going to strangle me.

"I…ah…I got a call. I need to go."

She frowned but then gave me one of those understanding smiles. "Okay."

I didn't stop. Didn't kiss her or touch her or hug her. I just bolted out her door.

Stark white light blazed from above.

Blood.

Splatters.

Handprints.

Smears.

Grief, horror, and shock.

A sob wrenched free, and I dropped to my knees and gathered her in my arms.

Cold and limp.

I shook her.

"What did I do? What did I do? No! Please." My wails bounced against the bathroom walls.

I pressed my mouth to her forehead, every part of me trembling. Shaking. "No, baby, no. Anna, no. God, please, no."

I jerked to sitting, sweat slicking my skin and my heart pounding out of my chest.

I roughed both hands down my face.

Fuck.

Knuckles rapped on my bedroom door, and I realized that's what pulled me from the dream.

From that goddamned nightmare that had become my life. I should have known I couldn't run from it forever.

Groaning, I slumped back down and pulled my pillow over my head, cutting off what was left of the evening light. "Go away."

For the last three days, Zee had been riding my ass nonstop. Dude kept striding in here like my own damned room belonged to him, telling me to stop being a pussy and go fix whatever the hell it was I'd fucked up.

He didn't even need to ask if I was to blame. Clearly he knew where that fault lie.

Another knock, and I bit back a slew of curses, because when the fuck had lashing out at my crew been my thing? I groaned a little louder when he didn't take a clue and the door creaked open.

"Goddamn it, Zee, told you I'm not in the mood—"

My rant broke off just as that crazy energy depleted all the air from the room. It lit with that suffocating familiarity. Peace and mayhem. Soft and fierce. My perfect demise.

On a harsh exhale, I jerked up to sitting.

"Willow."

On all things holy. I tried to contain the surge of relief at the sight of finding her standing in my bedroom doorway. I did.

But shit.

She looked so damned good. Like the breath I hadn't been able to catch for the last three days.

Chocolate eyes blinked at me from across the space. The girl clung to the door handle like she needed the support to continue to stand. Her hair was twisted in a lawless mess, tied up high on her head. Errant pieces tumbled down.

Did this hurt her as bad as it was hurting me?

I was hit with the onslaught of emotions that rode through her stare. So many I couldn't make sense of them.

Or maybe the only thing I could read was my guilt.

Guilt for doing this to her.

Guilt for leaving without a word or an explanation. But that explanation? It would only hurt her more. So instead of manning up and cutting things off, I'd hidden away in my room.

This goddamned room where she was everywhere and nowhere at the same time.

Twilight tumbled in through the windows. A duel between night and day. A clash of shadows and streaming, brilliant light.

She was caught in one of them. The girl lit up in glittering fire.

God.

She was gorgeous.

So damned gorgeous my bones rattled and my chest heaved.

How the fuck was I supposed to make it through this?

She lifted her trembling chin. It exposed the delicate column of her neck. My vision shifted course, and there I was, the asshole who was imagining burying my face in silky flesh. Taking a teasing taste before I dipped in and took a good long drink.

My fingers twitched.

The girl was wearing this short, flimsy dress—the kind that drove me straight out of my mind—and those long, slender legs were bare. But the thing that got me? She was wrapped in a sweater, hugging it to her tight, sweet body, like she still couldn't shake the cold.

My mouth went dry, and my heart started at a gallop I couldn't contain.

Peaches.

I wanted to claim it. Instead I shifted, moved so I was sitting up on the edge of my bed. Of course, I was in nothing but my underwear. Didn't know what made me more transparent—the fact she could see my body reacting to her simply standing there or the fact my spirit was screaming out.

So loud I could practically hear it.

Aching in agony.

Guess that's what happens when you toed that line.

You fell.

She edged forward.

I shivered when I felt her stop right in front of me.

I just kept staring at the floor, wishing it would open and swallow me whole.

Because this was me. The coward. The one who couldn't stand to look at her face when I drove the final stake through her heart.

"You left me." It slid from her mouth with a sharp blade of accusation.

269

I forced myself to look up at her.

"It was for the best, darlin'." I croaked out the lame excuse.

Chocolate eyes watched. Gauging and reading. Seeing right through me.

I wanted her to lash out or tell me I was a bastard. Make it easier on the both of us. Instead, this sweet, soft girl set a tender hand on my face. Shivers rushed and warmth spread beneath the surface of my skin.

"Do you remember what I told you?"

Maybe I was lost to the sudden dose of comfort I didn't deserve because confusion pulled at my brow.

She swallowed. "That day in the kitchen downstairs, when you asked me my greatest fear."

Anguish pressed down at the same time understanding came sliding in. I nodded, my voice gravel. "You told me your greatest fear was of being alone. Of bein' lonely. Of having all that love in your heart and not having anyone to give it to."

Her mouth quivered, and the words hitched in her throat. "And for the last three days, every time I turned around…*every time*…the only person there was me. There was no one there for me to give it to."

"Willow." I reached out and clutched her hips. I couldn't help it. Couldn't stop myself from touching her.

Beneath my hands, she shivered, and she traced her thumb along my cheekbone as she continued to speak, "And you told me your greatest fear was falling in love."

Energy shimmered around us. Disorienting and confusing.

She set her free hand on my other cheek, the girl burning into me as she forced me to fully look at her. "And here we are…both of us suffering. Because both of our greatest fears are now our realities."

Air rocked from my lungs.

God. This girl.

This amazing, insightful, brilliant girl.

The girl who'd made me remember.

My hold tightened on her hips, fingers sinking in because I didn't want to let her go.

stay

You don't deserve her.
You can't have her.
You will wreck her.

I groaned when she began to slowly shrug out of her sweater. She pealed it from her shoulders and let it drop to the floor behind her, exposing the dress which was really nothing more than a slip. Her breasts strained at the thin material that caressed every slim curve of her body.

"Willow." I said it as a warning that got locked up in my raw throat.

She toed out of her shoes, before those tender hands were threading through my hair, eliciting a moan, just as the girl edged forward, making a spot for herself right between my knees.

On a shaky exhale, I buried my face in her flat, quivering belly. I gripped her behind the thighs to keep her close when I knew full well I should be pushing her away.

When she eased back just enough to put an inch of space between us, I almost pulled her back to me. A shudder skated across her skin, before she reached down and gathered the material. Ever so slowly, she pulled it up, inch by inch.

The girl just about undid me when she pulled it over her head.

She was bare beneath.

Just a goddamned endless expanse of peachy, creamy skin.

I groaned, fighting for some kind of restraint. But shit. I was just a man. A man dying for the one thing he couldn't have.

She leaned in closer. My breaths became hers. "Pretend with me. Just for a little while, I don't want to feel so hollow. So alone. Pretend with me."

Shame blew through me like a bullet.

If she knew, the last thing she'd do was ask this of me. She'd hate me. Exactly like I deserved.

I gripped her by the side while my fingertips danced across the tattoo on her collarbone. All those dreams. Fleeting. I swallowed the swell of grief and slid my palm to the curve of her neck, fingers spreading wide.

Her pulse fluttered and thrummed against my touch.

I drew her down. Slowly. Slowly. Until that sweet, honeyed mouth met with mine.

This kiss?

It was too tender.

Too deep.

Too soft.

A plea. A second's surrender.

But right then? I couldn't stop from treating her like the priceless treasure she was.

Sex and brutal, vicious comfort.

Because it hurt the most when it was gone.

I shifted her and pressed her down onto the mattress as I climbed over her. I twisted out of my underwear without ever breaking the kiss.

I kissed her and kissed her while her shaking hands trembled across my skin. Gliding up and down my back. Touching my face. Pressing at my heart.

The girl always, always touching my heart.

She managed to in a way no one else ever had.

And I knew that familiarity was real.

That it belonged to us.

That it wasn't some twisted, fucked-up perception.

Without a word, I edged back and dug into the nightstand drawer, quick to cover myself.

Emotion clotted in my chest when I paused to look down at her.

She was shivering in the middle of my bed. Pleading with her unwavering gaze.

Slowly, I crawled back over her and nestled myself between her thighs.

She cast out a shaky exhale full of nerves and need.

I threaded her fingers with mine, kept them held between us when I bracketed her with my elbows that I braced on the bed.

Nose to nose.

Chest to chest.

Our breaths confused.

Our hearts a thunder in the confines of my room.

I could feel her sinking into me when I sank deep into her.

Her lips parted, and her eyes adored while I shivered and shook when I took her whole.

Fire. Flames. An incinerating blaze.

I kept her as close as I could get her. Just for this little while.

Our bodies moved slowly.

In sync.

Quietly.

Remorsefully.

Tears streamed from the corners of her eyes and into her hair while I stared down at her and tried to tell her all the things I couldn't say.

In that moment, I knew I was closer to a person than I'd ever been.

Closer than I'd ever wanted to be. Closer than I *could* be.

And I knew I wouldn't ever feel this way again.

What we were feeling was the furthest from pretend.

She came silently, her mouth parted on a muted gasp, and I just tucked her closer and dropped my forehead to hers when my body went rigid.

And for a moment…Peaches and I?

We bled with the stars.

Where they streaked and wept across the endless sky.

Infinite.

Burning bright right before they quickly burned out.

Ashes.

Squeezing my eyes closed, I kissed her mouth. Relished this girl for a second more. Before I wordlessly climbed from bed. I snatched my underwear from the floor and headed straight for the attached bathroom.

Everything pounded and roared while I shucked the condom and pulled on my underwear. A vicious war between my head and my heart that wanted to hold on to her forever and the fleck of courage that demanded I grow a backbone.

On a strained sigh, I leaned both hands against the counter and dropped my head.

Jesus.

What had I done?

I'd fucked everything up.

Fucked it up bad.

I forced myself to leave the minute's safety of my bathroom. I took a single, wary step back into the storm. I could feel it building.

Willow now sat facing away on the trunk she'd strategically placed at the foot of my massive bed. She'd redressed and was hugging that sweater around her body as she stared at the far wall that still remained blank.

It was the one spot in this room she'd never gotten around to completing before that mind-blowing bliss we'd touched on had gone to shit.

My chest tightened, and I attempted to swallow around the shards of glass that had gathered at the base of my throat.

Fucking torture.

Wistful, subdued laughter rippled from her sweet mouth, and she looked down, exposing the nape of her neck as she picked at a thread on her sweater. "That morning when I found you...I felt you. I didn't just sense you, Ash. But I *felt* you. It was that moment when you opened your eyes. I was staggered. I knew when you walked in my store that day, things weren't going to end well. I knew I should guard myself from the collision I felt coming the second you stepped in my path."

Her head tilted to the side. The breath she pulled in was palpable, tugging at the air. "I didn't know it at the time, but I think I lied to you that first day here in your room...when I told you I didn't believe in love at first sight."

She hesitated before she spoke again. "Because I'm pretty sure a piece of me fell for you the first time I saw you broken on the ground. And I've been falling ever since."

The lump in my throat throbbed.

"Willow." It was raw.

She shifted a fraction, turning to me with that stunning, unforgettable face. Chocolate eyes liquid. Soft and tender. So soft they nearly knocked me to my knees.

She touched her chest. "Tell me you love me...the way I love you." She clutched the sweater tighter, a shield and an anchor. "Because I have so much love. So much, Ash. And the only thing I want is to give it to you."

Those were the words that cut me in two.

Love. Goddamned love. It was everywhere, nagging at my conscience and thrashing in my spirit.

Grief pelted me, and I dragged my attention away, looked to the ground. I ran the back of my hand over my mouth and forced myself to tell her the most blasphemous kind of lie. "I can't tell you that."

I phrased it the only way I could because my heart wouldn't let me form a deception that big.

I could see her work up to acceptance, the way her shoulders jerked and her head bowed, before her spine eventually straightened.

She wiped her face with the long sleeves of her sweater and stood. She glanced around the room, somehow bearing a semblance of a smile.

"It's a good room, Ash. Thank you for letting me share it with you. Be a part of it."

Tears streaked free, and she clasped her hands together right over her chest. "Thank you for *saving* me the way you did. I'm sorry I didn't get to completely finish, but I can't pretend anymore. Not when all my pretending is a lie."

Our lie.

She started for the door.

Let her go. Let her go.

Panic spun. Too fast. Too much…

"Willow."

Still facing away, she hesitated. Her shoulders heaved up and down.

The girl so fragile and so strong.

Drawn, I moved to stand behind her. Her back an inch from my chest, I set my hands on either side of her neck. Her pulse thrummed wildly, a fluttering plea at my skin, and in her own surrender, her head dropped back.

I leaned in and pressed my lips to her forehead, the word the barest plea. "Stay."

Fuck.

I didn't even know what I was asking.

What I was asking of myself.

Because what did I have to give her but more pain?

Sadness danced with the shadows. Slowly she shifted to face me. Her words were soft but filled with resolve. With belief. This broken girl who was the farthest from weak.

"You told me that guy's out there looking for me. That one day he'd find me because I deserve him. You made me promise not to settle for anything else. I want him to be you. So badly I'm dying inside. But I won't settle, Ash. I won't settle for anything less than the match to my heart."

She lifted her arms out and turned her face to the ceiling. Like she were looking for a promise somewhere beyond the room we were in, lost in the night sky she couldn't see. "Maybe he's out there, floating on those wishes my mama had me casting into the air. Maybe I just haven't caught up to him yet."

Tears streaming down her face, she aimed her attention back on me.

She smiled that dizzying smile that did that crazy thing to my heart. It trembled with sorrow and brimmed with hope.

My guts clenched with agony and regret.

I love you. I'd die for you. I'd live for you. But the one thing I can't do is take this away.

I couldn't make any of it form on my tongue.

"I love you, Ash Evans. I hope you know you were worth the risk."

One last time, she brushed her fingertips over my mouth and down my beard.

So goddamned sweet.

Then she turned and walked out my door.

WILLOW

I pressed my hand to my mouth as I ran out his front door and flew down the porch steps. I just needed to keep it together for one second more. I jumped into my car and slammed the door, hands fumbling to get the key into the ignition. I gasped out a relieved breath when I finally turned the ignition over and threw it in drive.

I had to get out of there.

Away.

Tears streamed down my face, my eyes bleary as I strained to focus out the windshield as I took to the street. I swept the back of my hand beneath my eye, struggling to keep in the sob bottled in my throat.

It erupted.

Broke free.

Just like I could feel everything splintering inside of me.

Loss. Grief. Heartbreak.

They churned with the power of a hurricane in the confines of the cab.

How much could I take?

I choked around a cry that climbed my throat.

Ash.

My beautiful, bold, brilliant Ash.

So full of life yet so terrified of living.

I'd seen the fear in his eyes.

Felt the love in his touch.

Heard the truth in his lies.

Maybe that was what had scared him most.

Maybe tonight was the most foolish thing I could have done. I had stepped out on that limb and put myself in the line of fire.

But I couldn't go on without knowing. Couldn't spend one more day waiting for him to return. Couldn't stand to sit alone praying he'd show up and confess whatever had sent him running.

I'd known it when I'd chased him outside the restaurant that night.

This man, all cocky arrogance and flirty tease, kept a well of secrets and pain. I'd felt him so close to giving them to me.

I'd felt his surrender in the days he'd stood at my side. When the man had supported me through one of the most difficult times I'd ever endured. I just couldn't comprehend what had sent him running three days ago. When he'd gone from a man promising not to leave my side to one fumbling out my door.

So I'd stepped out. Taken the risk. Landed right in the middle of a failure I didn't want to find.

Loneliness.

I swore it was a living, thriving being.

Gasping over a sob, I swiped the sleeve of my sweater across my face and tried to focus on the road as night descended.

Ominous. Overwhelming.

I could feel it pressing down on me. Taking me over.

My mama taught me all along I was stronger than this.

My world was mine to hold. Even if it were in pieces.

But tonight, those pieces were scattered so far I wasn't sure they could ever be gathered.

Everyone.

Everyone was gone.

I turned onto my street. Home. Vacant. Empty.

I could feel the last pieces of me sheering apart when I saw the truck parked in front of my house. Anger and hate compounded with the misery that lined my body.

Why was he doing this to me?

I was trembling when I turned into my drive, every inch of me shaking when I put my SUV in park and killed the engine.

I fumbled out.

At my end.

"You need to get off my property." The words grated from my throat.

Bates pushed off from where he was leaned against Billy's truck, Billy still sitting in the cab. "I came here to talk to you."

I turned my back on him, headed for my door, could barely get my hands to cooperate as I attempted to unlock it. "I told you before, I don't have anything to say."

"Oh, I think you just might have something to say about this."

I scoffed, tried to hold back the tears fighting for release. The last thing I wanted to do was cry in front of him. I just couldn't process it, the fact he was here, continuing to do this to me after I'd lost my mama. There was no question he knew, the grapevine in this small city surely crawling its way back to him.

The door swung open in front of me. "Please, just leave me alone. I can't do this with you, Bates."

He grabbed my arm. A shocked breath shot from me, and I tried to shake him off. His jaw clenched as he gripped me tighter, fingers digging into my skin. He sneered. "That guy...the one you've gone and slutted yourself off to? Actin' the whore?"

Whore?

My mouth twisted with fury. "You don't have any right to accuse me of anything. I don't belong to you. Not anymore. What I do and who I see is none of your business. Now go…before I call the cops."

He laughed as if I was ridiculous. As if he held all the control the way he always had. He suddenly released me and I stumbled back into my living room. He pushed into my space.

Fear rose up.

That was just before he drew attention to the folder he had in his hand.

Confusion spun through me, dread pooling in my belly. I couldn't take any more of the cruelty Bates had to offer.

But he had no mercy when he pulled out the first photo. Black and white and blown up big.

Horror slammed me.

I dropped to my knees. Both hands pressed to my mouth.

Nausea spun and the walls closed in.

No.

My head shook. "No. N-n-no."

Bates dropped the folder to the ground in front of me. Pages and pages of glossy, black and white pictures slid out to reveal their brutality.

Ruthless.

Inhumane.

Wrong.

"No."

Bates' vile breath was at the side of my face. "Willow. Always so naïve. Seems you don't know him at all, doesn't it?"

WILLOW
TWENTY-ONE YEARS OLD

Sobs echoed through the line. Frantic and frenzied. Incoherent. They were the kind Willow had grown to recognize in the years before her sister had left, even though there was no chance she'd ever grow accustomed to them.

Dread curled her stomach.

Willow pushed the phone harder to her ear. With the other hand, she fumbled around in the dark to find the switch to her bedside lamp. She flicked it on, squeezing her eyes closed against the intrusive light that cut through her small childhood room.

She still lived with her mama so she could help take care of her on the bad days. She blinked and tried to orient herself. To catch up to that speeding train Summer had seemed to be riding for far too long.

"Calm down, Summer. I can't understand what you're saying."

Since Summer had left four years ago, Willow never knew what kind of call she was going to get. If her sister would be full of life, bubbly and shining her bright, blinding light. Or if she'd fallen to the depths of her sickness where it was dark and bleak.

Willow felt it stretched out between them. The distance. Greater than it had ever been.

"He told me he loved me...he told me," Summer babbled, tears in her harsh breaths. "He's cheating on me. Oh my god...I can't believe this."

More sobs, and Willow could almost see her sister yanking at her hair. "I told him...I told him... He won't listen. *He won't listen!*"

The last was a hurled shriek, and a breath later, glass shattered in the background.

Summer wailed, out of breath. "I can't...I can't do this."

"Calm down, talk to me."

Hysteria bubbled from her sister's mouth. "I heard her, Willow. I heard her. Oh my god....I didn't want this. No, no, no, no, no. I didn't want this. I can't do this."

"What are you saying?"

"I can't...I'm so sorry. I love you, Willow. I love you so much. But I can't take this. Not anymore."

The line went dead.

"Summer!" Willow screamed, voice ripping from somewhere deep in her lungs. "Summer!"

Frantic, she dialed back her sister's number. The line beeped busy on the other end.

Her mama skidded to a stop at her door, blinking away her sleep as she attempted to focus on Willow from across the room.

"I'm scared, Mama."

Grief wrote itself on her mother's face.

stay

She crossed to Willow and pulled her up into her arms. Willow breathed her in. Lilacs and baby powder and comfort. "What do you say we go get her, sweet one? You and me. Bring her home where she belongs."

Relief plowed through Willow, and she nodded against her mama's chest.

"Good. Pack your things."

thirty-five

ASH

"What the fuck do you think you're doing?" Zee pounded the floor behind me, back and forth, gripping at the back of his neck like maybe he was trying to restrain himself from tearing into me.

I shoved a few things into the duffle that was laid out in the center of my bed.

That fucking bed.

"What does it look like I'm doing? Packing." I injected as much sarcasm as I could into the delivery. You know, because I was such a funny guy.

I flung the top closed and zipped it up. Wasn't all that much in there that I needed anyway. It wasn't like I actually *lived* here. All my shit was back in LA where I belonged. The place I never should have left. Where the parties were endless and the women were in no short supply.

Easy.

This place was just a warped fantasy. A sanctuary. An asylum. Couldn't hang out for a second longer.

"And just where is it you think you're going?" Zee demanded.

"Home."

His eyebrows disappeared under his flop of hair. "Home?"

"That is what I said."

He scoffed. "You do realize your ass already has the album eight weeks behind in production?"

I shrugged like it didn't matter while a fresh round of regret went skidding through my system.

"Yeah, well, maybe we've been going at this for too long. Everyone's got their families. Baz and Lyrik have kids. Austin and my sister have one on the way. Seems to me we're just stringing this along for no reason, anyway."

Incredulous, he shook his head. "And you get to make that call? Seriously? You're just gonna toss off everything the guys have put into this band because one day you up and decide it's time to call it quits? What I'd like to know is when *the* Ash Evans turned into such a pussy. Because you and I both know this doesn't have a thing to do with the guys or their families or *Sunder* having run its course. It has everything to do with that girl who just went running out your door."

"Whatever the reason, I'm gone. Can't stay here."

I slung the bag over my shoulder and grabbed my keys.

I strode out my bedroom door. Zee was hot on my heels as I took to the stairs. "And what is it I'm supposed to tell the guys? You know we can't go on without you."

Refusing to look behind me, I hit the landing.

"I'm talking to you," he said as he reached out and grabbed me by the shoulder.

Spinning on him, I took a step forward and got in his face. "We've been spouting those same damned words for what feels like a million years. The band can't go on. And here we've been, desperate to patch it together every time somethin' goes south. I'm tired of it all. Tired of worrying about all this shit. Trying to keep everyone together when everyone's drifting apart."

Stunned, he rocked back on his heels. "Is that what you really think? That this family is weak? Because, from where I'm standing, it hasn't ever been stronger. We all know where we stand. What we want. We still have all the drive and the talent without the bullshit rock-star antics that kept us back for years."

I dropped my eyes to the ground. "Yeah, well I'm not sure what it is I want anymore."

Lie.

Motherfucking lie.

I wanted her.

I met his eye. "Maybe I'm the weak link."

Air jutted from his nose. "Or maybe you're just a pussy. A coward who won't stand up for what you really want because that means you're going to have to drop all the bullshit games. Quit playing. Because I know you want her. And I know you know you're better with her. And then you go and get cold feet and fuck it all away. Is that what you want? To go back to all those chicks who don't give two fucks about anything but what they can get from you? Because then you can turn around and not give two fucks about them? Convenient, isn't it?"

Anger radiated from him.

Clearly the asshole was eager for a fight.

He should have known better than pumping me full of rage.

I'd fight back.

My teeth gritted. "You don't know anything. So back the fuck off before one of us does something we regret."

"Yeah? Like letting that sweet girl, who for whatever insane reason adores you, who just lost her mom, mind you, walk out that door with her heart shattered all over the floor? Or did you mean letting your band down? *Your family?* Because I'm not quite sure what we're talking about here. Why don't you fill me in?"

I was on him in a flash, my fist wound up in his shirt.

He cocked some kind of smirk I wasn't sure I'd ever seen him wear. "Touchy, aren't we?"

The words were grit. "Warning you, Zee."

"Yeah, well I'm warning you." Something that looked like pity flashed on his face. "I've been watching you for years, man. Since the day I stepped up and took my brother's place in the band. Do you know what that's like? Coming in seven years late? Trying to fill up the void of my brother's death, the guy I loved more than this world and looked up to most?"

My hold loosened, and I attempted to swallow around the unbearable rock that lodged itself in my throat.

"I gave up everything for you guys. *Everything.* You, Baz, Lyrik…you were all so tight. Had been through so much together. Couldn't help but feel like an outsider. Wanting to be good enough to be a part of this brotherhood that meant something more than just the music we played. There you were…this easy-go-lucky guy who was always the life of the party. The center of attention. You made me feel at home. Took me under your wing. Showed me I belonged even when I didn't feel it."

Shame had me releasing my hold on his shirt.

Being that easy-go-lucky guy was the only way I survived.

He took a step back, brows pinched together in emphasis. "Through it all, you think I didn't see it, man? All this time? No clue what the fuck it is you're running from, but I see it. And Willow…she's the first thing that has ever made you stop running that crazy race. The first time you ever slowed down. The first time you've ever been at *peace.* And here you go…running again. Just what is it you're running from?"

I lifted my chin. "Don't you see it? I don't get peace. Running is a whole ton better than falling to my knees."

My phone rang in my pocket. I pulled it out, sent it straight to voicemail when I saw it was our manager, Anthony. I'd deal with him later.

My phone rang again, and again I sent it to voicemail. I went to shove it back in my pocket, when a text lit up the screen.

I wasn't surprised it was from Anthony.

But it was the image that popped up on the link he'd attached that blew through me.

This just hit the gossip sites. You need to call me.

I choked on the stagnant air, my vision blurred by the sight of the picture and headline of the article.

"Fuck," I barely breathed, trying to make sense of how the hell this got out. What it meant. The damage it was going to do.

I stumbled back a step, panic and pain soaking me all the way through.

"What's wrong, man?" Zee asked, all his anger shifting to concern.

"I got…" I blinked, dropped my bag to the floor, rushed an agitated hand through my hair. "I've got to get to her."

I raced out the door like a demon was on my heels. One intent to suck me straight back into the pits of hell. I turned over my Navigator, gunned the engine, flew like a madman down the Savannah streets. Desperate to get to her. To explain the unexplainable.

But at least I needed to try before someone else got to her. Before she saw the vile printed on paper.

She deserved to hear this from me even though I knew she wasn't ever going to want to see me again.

Wheels skidding, I took the last turn to her house, my stomach knit in a thousand knots, my chest threatening to bust open wide.

Time stood still when I saw the truck parked in front of her house.

Panic.

Fear.

Those feelings were obliterated by the surge of protectiveness that rose up inside of me.

I careened across the road, slamming on my breaks as my SUV bounced onto the curb, coming to a stop at an odd angle halfway on the sidewalk. My attention barely skated the face of the man sitting in the cab of the truck I'd just cut in front of.

Rage surged.

The need to annihilate.

But all of it was focused on the house. On the girl.

I ran. Fucking ran as fast as I could across her lawn, didn't even pause when I threw open her door.

It all transpired in less than a second.

The scene in front of me.

My girl on her hands and knees. Weeping. Betrayed. The pictures spread out in front of her on the floor. The bastard leering over her shoulder, smug, surely the bearer of the images spread out like a disease.

Old sorrow wrenched through my spirit, slicing new wounds, taking new victims.

I had no clue how he'd even gotten ahold of them.

Willow sobbed and buried her precious face in her hands.

She shouldn't have found out like this.

One second later, I could feel myself splintering. Cracking. My control stripped away.

Bates looked up in the second I lunged. My shoulder connected with his stomach. I rammed him back, the action knocking him from his feet, because my only intent was to get him away from the girl.

The girl.

The girl who suddenly screamed when I straddled him at the waist, cocked back my arm, let loose a fist. It cracked against the side of his face. Hatred poured free. "You think this is a game? Hurting her this way? You bastard. You bastard!"

He spit in my face. "Me hurting her? I think that's all on you."

I fisted his shirt in both hands, lifted him up, and slammed him back down. "Where did you get those pictures?"

Thoughts raced through my head. This asshole had been texting all those pictures to Willow. A sinking realization spread through me. That single pap who'd been following me everywhere probably wasn't a pap at all.

Paid to dig for dirt.

I guess he'd found it.

His grin was smug, his voice grating with the hold I had on

him. "What? You thought you could hide it? Get away with it? I wasn't about to let Willow get tangled with the likes of you. Knew if I dug deep enough, I'd find what I needed. I just needed to open her eyes to who you are. To what you did."

All reason snapped.

Madness swooped in to take its place.

My fists flew.

Fury.

Mayhem.

Flesh split beneath my fists. I couldn't tell if I was angrier with this asshole or with myself. Both of us an obstacle. Both of us unworthy. Neither of us could come close to being good enough for this girl.

Bates struggled to fight back.

Just like I knew all along, the pussy was nothing without a gang of his friends.

Blood splattered, and I grunted as I laid into him harder. Knuckles crunching bone.

Again and again.

Willow screamed, but there was nothing I could do to stop the assault. I'd always wanted to end this fucker. Wipe his stain from her life.

I was lost to it, totally unsuspecting of the sudden crack against the back of my head. Blackness filtered through my vision. I roared, flew around, and stumbled onto my feet, the room spinning when my attention landed on Billy.

The asshole who'd set all this in motion.

I charged him, grabbing him around the waist. We both flew, his back smashing against a bookcase. Books and pictures rained down, glass shattering on the floor, the two of us landing in the middle of it. We struggled for control. I landed three jabs to his side as he landed one to my jaw.

Pain radiated through my face, my head still throbbing from the original blow.

Screams ricocheted from the walls.

Willow. Willow. Willow.

It only made me fight harder. Harder for her. Because I

didn't want to let her go. Didn't want her to hurt. I wanted to take it away.

I flipped him onto his back, my fists nothing but fury and violence and disorder as I pummeled into him again. A foot connected with my gut. The breath shot from my lungs just as Bates jumped on my back.

"Stop!" Willow begged.

Motherfucker.

Apparently neither of these assholes could fight their own fight.

I rammed an elbow into Bates' ribs, going in for another blow to Billy's face.

Willow's voice filtered into my consciousness again, breaking into the disorder. "Get up. Get up now."

They both stiffened, Bates slowly backing off just as Billy slumped down below me.

I turned to face her, the girl's arm shaking like crazy as she held a gun in our direction.

Her words trembled as she spoke, but I was pretty sure she wasn't faking her threat. "Get up, Bates. Get up and get out. Both of you. Don't ever come back and make sure you don't ever cross paths with either me or Ash. Or I promise I'll find a way to prove you were responsible. That it was the two of you who were responsible for the attack outside my store. That you stole from me." She swallowed hard. Resolute. "I'll find a way."

Bates eased himself to sitting. He wiped the back of his hand across his mouth, his lip busted wide, his eye swelling, eyebrow split. He shot me a look that promised I was going to pay. I didn't give a fuck unless this girl was the cost.

"Willow," he demanded.

She looked at him. "Never again, Bates. I don't want to see you. Not ever again."

Don't ever confuse broken for weak.

Billy stood, eyes wide as he looked at her pointing the barrel his way. "Let's get the fuck out of here. They're not worth it. Neither of them."

Bates blinked, still staring at Willow like he wanted to argue, before he harshly shook his head. "You'll regret this, Willow. You'll regret this."

Yeah.

I was fucking certain she would.

But I doubted a whole lot of that regret would have anything to do with him.

Tears streaked down her face when the door slammed behind the two of them.

"Willow," I whispered, warily, hating it had gone down like this. Wishing I'd just manned up and told her the truth. Maybe I'd been trying to protect her, but she'd deserved honesty.

But the truth of the matter was I was terrified.

Terrified of her looking at me the way she was looking at me now.

Her arm shook and shook as she slowly lowered the gun, and I edged forward, carefully unwound it from her fingers, and gathered her in my arms. "Willow."

A cry ripped up her throat.

"How could you?" She fisted both her hands in my shirt. "How could you do this to me? Was it just a game? Was all of this just a sick, cruel game?"

The words locked on my tongue.

"Tell me," she screamed.

I gathered her closer. "I didn't know, Willow, I promise you I didn't know. Not until the day I found her box upstairs."

Willow sagged against me, knees going weak. I sank to the floor with her in my arms. I whispered in her hair, "I didn't know."

"How?" she begged.

My insides trembled. "I met her in LA. *Sunder* had just gotten the label and we found out they were sponsoring a tour. We were out celebrating."

Coffee eyes locked on me as the waitress I couldn't take my eyes off of set a shot the color of licorice in front of me. "My name's Anna. Let me know if there's anything else I can get for you."

"Your number," I said.

She rolled her eyes. "Does that always work?"

"Yeah, most of the time it does."

I grated over the words as every regret I ever had rose to the surface. "I hounded her until she gave in."

Willow shivered in my arms and I hugged her closer as I continued the story I knew she didn't want to hear, but the one I knew she needed. The truth she'd deserved all along. "She warned me right off that I didn't want to date her. I honestly didn't know why, because from where I was sitting, she seemed perfect. Beautiful. Huge smile. Confident."

Willow choked over a sob, and I swallowed around that pain crushing my chest, the words rough as I forced them out. "I fell in love with her, Willow. For the first time in my life, I felt something different about a girl. It scared me because things with the band were happening so fast. But I wanted it. I did."

Her hair was splayed out across my pillow, and she brushed her fingertips over my lips.

"Tell me your dreams," she almost whispered.

Affection pulled at my insides. In a place I hadn't even known existed. "You know, it's crazy, because I feel like I've already achieved everything I've ever wanted. The band finally getting the label. Tour getting ready to start. Didn't really think I needed anything else…wanted anything more. Not until I met you."

A soft smile fluttered on her mouth. "That's what dreams are for. There's always a million of them out there floating around us, just out of reach, waiting for us to catch them. A million more ready to take their place when we find the others."

I gathered her against me, her body so warm, my nose nuzzled in her neck. "Who gave you that soft heart, Anna?"

"It's not soft."

I chuckled. "You're a liar."

Redness flushed her face.

"Tell me yours," I prodded.

Her answer came like a confession. "I just want to be happy."

I shifted to my knees, grinned down at her as I crawled between her thighs. "Think maybe I can help with a little of that happy part."

She giggled, then moaned, and I got the sudden sense I was happier than I'd ever been.

Because that's the way falling in love should always be.

A quick slide straight into bliss.

Willow's words were tortured where she released them against my shirt as she forced them out between her tears. "That's the only thing she ever wanted. To be happy."

I brushed my fingers through her hair. "I know. I didn't understand it then, when I first met her, the desperation behind it. I should have, Willow. I should have. I should have seen the warnings."

A crazed energy spun through my bedroom. A circuit tripped. Chaos ricocheted from the walls. Bounding fast. Gaining speed.

The sheets were stripped from the bed, and the lamp on my side had been knocked from the nightstand. Drawers where pulled out from the dresser and clothes strewn across the floor.

Blackened tears streaked Anna's tormented face.

"How could you? How could you do this to me?"

With both hands, I grabbed my head. Wanting to shake her. Demand that she stop. For the woman I knew to come back to me.

She'd been missing for two weeks.

"What are you talking about?"

"That girl you were talking to. How could you do this to me?"

Frustration and anger tightened my chest, my voice grit. "Haven't touched anyone."

"Don't lie to me," she begged through violent tears. "I heard you...in the kitchen. You told her you loved her."

Confusion crashed through my brain before realization dawned. "Edie?"

"Yes!" she screamed.

"You mean my sister...Edie?" I spit it like my own accusation.

The second I said it, she sagged in relief, and her feet fully went out from under her. I sank with her to the floor.

"I'm so sorry, I'm so sorry," Anna whimpered. "Please, just don't leave me."

I squeezed my eyes closed against the memories I'd just uttered into the air. "I remember being terrified that day...the first time I saw her lose control. It was like...I didn't recognize her. She begged me to forgive her. Promised it would never happen again. I told her it was okay. I wanted to believe it would be."

Willow moaned. "She was sick. She was sick." She gulped. "What happened *that* day? I need to know how it happened."

I pressed a kiss into her hair like it could possibly soothe some of her grief. "It was horrible, Willow. Horrible. I'd do anything to take it back. But I didn't know."

Blood streaked from the corner of Anna's mouth, her lipstick smeared. A bruise marked her cheek and others were blooming across the top of her thighs.

I grabbed her by the outside of the arms. "You need to tell me who did this to you, Anna. Right now."

She blinked, her mouth moving like she didn't want to form the word. "Lyrik."

I jerked back like the word burned me.

Lyrik? No way would he touch her.

But the proof was littered all over her body.

"What did he do?"

"He…he tried…we need to get away from him."

How could he? My fucking best friend who I trusted with my life?

I sucked in a breath. "The second she accused him, I think I knew something was off. But I didn't want to believe she'd lie about something like that."

My hands were in fists when I stormed out the front door. I charged forward, hands ramming against Lyrik's chest just as he was climbing from his bike. "What the fuck did you do?"

Caught off guard, he rocked back, sheer confusion and disbelief written on his face as he rebounded and caught his fall, entire being angling toward me as he returned the shove. "What the fuck, man?"

I stumbled backward a step, bounced right back. "You heard me, what the fuck did you do to her?"

Dark eyes narrowed. "To who?"

"Anna!" I screamed.

I breathed the confession into the top of Willow's head. "There I was, accusing him of trying to rape her, all the while knowing deep down inside that everything was off."

Lyrik pointed a finger in the direction of the small house we all shared.

His voice dropped with a warning. "Listen to yourself, man. Running out here like a madman, making accusations there's no basis for. I know you love her, but there's something there that's not right. Haven't you seen what she's been doing here? She has you wrapped around all her pretty little fingers."

My throat nearly locked. Fuck, I hated putting Willow through this. Putting myself through this. Dredging up the details that'd had me running for the last seven years.

Willow attempted to catch her breath, fingers digging into my shoulders. "She had a good heart. I swear she did. Sometimes she just couldn't find it."

"I know, Willow. I know. It just all came up so fast. Out of nowhere, and I didn't know how to handle it. If I could. I promise you. When I went back inside to confront her...I was so confused. So spun up. Part of me hated her and the other part wanted to save her."

She peeked out at me from the end of the hallway where she was hiding. I pointed at her. "Get the fuck out."

"Ash," she pled, frantic.

"I can't believe what you just tried to pull...blaming my best friend for trying to rape you? Trying to turn me against him? Don't you get how messed up that is?"

"I just...you...you can't go. You can't leave me here. Please, Ash..." That's what this was about? Her trying to get me not to go on tour? Unbelievable.

I searched for a breath, my lungs too tight. "I told her to get out. Get her things and get out. I was furious. She beat herself up, Willow. *Beat herself up.* I had no clue how to handle that."

She jumped on my back when I started to head for the door. "I'm sick, Ash. I'm sick. I don't know how to stop it. I don't know how to stop it."

My mouth parted on a strained breath, and I took her by a wrist and slowly unwound her hold from my neck. Her feet hit the ground.

Not even trusting myself, I turned to face her. She looked to the floor before she sank to it.

"I told you...I'm trying. I'm trying so hard. I hate this part of me, but I don't know how to stop it."

She looked up at me with an expression of sheer torment.

Pain squeezed my chest, this insane love I had for her at odds with the resentment burning through my blood.

I dropped to my knees in front of her.

"I just want to feel. But sometimes I feel too much." She clutched her chest. "And this paranoia sets in…right here…and it's the only thing I can feel and I'm suddenly doing things, saying things that I never meant to say. It's all fueled by this fear that I'm gonna lose something that I might die without."

I felt like I'd swallowed a gallon of broken glass.

"That doesn't make it okay."

She flinched. "Do you think I don't know that? Do you think I don't hate what I just did? That I don't hate myself for being this person? But the thought of you leaving me…I don't know if I can do it, Ash." Desperation weaved its way back into her words. "I need you. I love you so much."

"You need help, Anna. I don't even know you."

"I know…I promise…I'll get it. I'll do anything. Just, don't give up on me. This isn't the real me." She grabbed my hand and pressed my palm against the frantic beat of her heart. "You know the real me. Right here. You know me."

"How am I ever supposed to trust you?"

"I'll prove it. I will. Just…tell me you still love me."

My mouth opened and closed, before I finally sighed and pressed my mouth to her temple, sang the words to the song I'd been writing for her, in those dark moments when I felt her pain and had no clue how to ease it.

Lay me down
Say your peace
Come what may
But you can't hide
The pain behind your eyes

Anna clutched me tighter.

So stay with me
I don't mind
Find your comfort
Right here by my side

I've seen it all before
Want to take it away
So stay with me
I don't mind
Find your comfort
Right here by my side

My voice was grit. "That day…when I went with you to see your mom?"

Willow nodded.

"I sang her that song. It was the song I'd written for Anna. Something compelled me to sing it to her. Thinking it might soothe her. I just had no idea singing it would hurt so bad."

A sob ribbed from Willow, and I continued, breathing the words at her ear. "I think somewhere inside me, I knew I was falling for you. And I was terrified of ever getting back to that place of feeling so helpless. Terrified of loving someone and not being strong enough to help them. Terrified of not being strong enough to be there for them when it really mattered."

"She needed you."

My nod was slow and filled with regret. "And I left her. Right after that happened, I was so shaken up, confused on what to do. The tour kicked off in two days, and here was Anna, desperate and trying to get me to stay. I went to my parents' place because I felt like I needed a breath. To step away and get some clarity."

I squeezed her tighter, pain clenching down as I forced out the admission. "It was the worst night of my life, Willow. I'd gone to my mom and dad's, and I get this text to head over to this guy's house."

Fury lashed as I thought back to the memory. "Somehow, Edie had talked me into letting her go with me to this party."

"No," Willow whimpered, adding it all up. Piecing it together. The night that had destroyed us both.

Music thrummed from within the thin walls. As soon as I knocked, the door flew open to Paul, dude already lit. I made quick introductions, cringed when he gave my sister a beer. But fuck. A red Solo cup was a far cry from the shit I'd already been testing out by the time I was fourteen. Still, she was different. Innocent. She didn't come close to fitting into this sleazy world.

Normally, I'd step into a place like this and instantly glom on to the vibe. Revel in it. Live it up.

Not tonight.

Even though she'd promised she'd keep it together, Anna hadn't stopped texting me since I left. My phone kept going off like a bomb. Constant. Incessant.

Part of me got it. That she was scared I was putting distance between us. The other part was pissed that this was the very reason I wanted the distance.

Truth was, I missed her. That girl who'd become my best friend.

I just didn't know how to handle the dichotomy, the Anna I adored and the one that terrified me.

My sister was laughing and having a good time, so I did my best to relax. I threw back a few drinks, let the world blur and bend and veer.

My phone vibrated in my pocket again. Reluctantly, I dug it out, figuring I couldn't go on ignoring her. Not when I told her I would support her. Taking off like a pussy and not facing what was going down wasn't exactly earning me any gold stars.

I pushed to my feet and moved down the hall where it was quieter, dipped into a vacant bedroom and accepted the call.

"Hey," I said.

She was crying softly. It twisted through me like a dull blade. I hated she was hurting. "I need to talk to you, Ash. Please, come back home."

I sank down on the edge of the bed, rubbed my weary eyes with my thumb and forefinger. "I thought you were going to your apartment?"

"I just…I needed to see you when you got home. Talk to you."

"I'm not up for talking tonight, Anna. I'll go over to your place tomorrow. We'll talk it out. Decide how we're going to handle this, okay?" I tried to keep my voice even, let her know I cared but that I wasn't caving.

A sob broke across the line. "I need to talk to you. Please, Ash, come home."

I sighed. "I'm not doing this shit, Anna. You—"

"I'm pregnant," she suddenly begged.

Everything went silent and the world stopped. Tipped from its axis. Slammed into high gear.

Finally, I caught up.

"You're really gonna pull this right now, Anna?" I gritted my teeth, sympathy blown. "You're going to sit over there, trying to trap me, saying I've got a kid on the way? After what you pulled with Lyrik this morning?"

I wheezed for a breath. "I'm not a fucking toy, and I won't allow you to use me like one. I'm done. When I get home, you need to be gone."

"I am." It was a whimper.

"Just stop, Anna, I can't take any more lies."

I killed the call and pressed my fist to my mouth, wanting to scream, to fucking tear something apart.

This was killing Willow. I could feel it. The anguish that jarred through her body. I wanted to stop. To shield her from the truth. But I kept right on, the words cracking as I offered her my sins. "I didn't believe her, Willow. I didn't fucking believe her. And I just wanted to forget everything. Get back to who I was before I met her."

The bedroom door creaked open, letting in a sliver of light. Casey clicked it shut behind her. She moved across the room, and I let her push me to the bed, let her crawl on top of me.

Because I didn't want to feel anything.

Not the sting of Anna's lies.

Not the loss aching inside of me.

The regret.

The guilt.

But the guilt was there when Casey kissed me, when her hands were on my chest. I squeezed my eyes shut, tried to block it all out, to just focus on the feel of skin on skin. It's what I'd done for all my life. It didn't have to be different now.

It didn't.

But it was.

My phone lit up again, and the guilt bloomed and amplified. I pushed Casey off, the girl smirking at me from where she was twisted sideways on the bed.

Confused, I accepted the call, pushed it to my ear. "Anna."

I wanted to apologize. To tell her we'd make it through this. That we'd figure it out. That I did know her.

On the other end, I heard her crying softly. "I love you, Ash. I need you to know that."

"God, I love you, too. So much."

Casey was suddenly on her knees beside me, voice saccharine sweet. "Aww, isn't that cute, Ash Evans professing his undying love when he just had his tongue down my throat."

"Who was that?" Anna demanded.

"No one."

"Who was that?" she demanded louder. Even from across the miles, I could feel it. The snap. The trigger.

Anna started to hyperventilate on the other end of the line. "Oh my god, oh my god. I knew it. I knew it. You're cheating on me. No, no, no," she stammered. "I can't do this. No."

"Anna, listen," I yelled, coming unhinged.

"I can't do this," she whimpered and the line went dead.

I swore, gripped the phone in my hand, pointed at Casey. "Stay the hell away from me."

I stormed from the room, intent on finding Edie to tell her we were getting out of there when my phone buzzed in my hand.

I nearly threw it against the wall until I saw it was a text from Edie.

Headed home. Don't worry about me.

Part of me wanted to call her and lay into her for just taking off. That shit wasn't safe. The other half was just relieved she'd gone. That she wasn't a part of this mess.

My hands fisted at Willow's back, and I couldn't speak the words. Could barely admit to myself that while I'd been letting that chick crawl all over me, my baby sister was being raped. "I made so many mistakes that night, Willow. So many. But what I did know was I needed to make it right with Anna. Deep down, I knew it wasn't her fault. That she was sick."

I drove back to the house.

Guilt slicked my skin with a sheen of sweat. Couldn't believe I'd let that bitch kiss me. That I'd kissed her back. Touched her.

No fucking wonder Anna didn't trust me. That she was terrified for me to leave for months at a time. Being loyal to her seemed so simple until the second it wasn't.

Did I really have it in me to change? Did Anna have it in her to do the same?

Only thing I knew was I wanted to. That I couldn't bear the thought of leaving this city with things the way they were between us.

Main thing? I knew she was sick. I was certain that was no lie. Even if we didn't end up together, at least I could help her through that. Help her find that happiness she'd been so desperate to find.

I blew out a breath, cracked open my door, and headed for the quieted house. The windows were still blackened with night, the front door locked. I slipped in my key and opened the door.

Profound silence echoed back.

I took a tentative step inside. "Anna?" I called, quieter than intended.

Nothing. I inched down the hall, leaned in and flicked on the light in my bedroom. My attention skated the room, taking in the broken mirror that'd shattered against the wall, pieces falling to the floor, the strewn papers, my drawers pulled from their hinges and my things spilling out, as if she'd been frantic, searching for a secret I hadn't left for her to find.

I raked a hand through my hair. Disquiet bubbled to the surface. Somehow, I was more panicked that she'd actually done what I told her and left.

I straightened, standing back in the darkness of the hall, clutching my phone in my hand, trying to figure out how to apologize. How to let her know I didn't want anyone else. That what happened with Casey was a mistake. A slip in the middle of a moment I couldn't make sense of.

Beg her to forgive me the way I was willing to forgive her.

Fuck it.

I was just going to go over there. Talk it out the way we should have earlier.

I spun and took one step back down the hall, before I froze. Something cold skated down my spine, caught up by nothing but the feeling I got when I saw the burn of lights gleaming from the gap at the bottom of the bathroom door.

Breaths short, I inched forward. I stilled, before I slowly turned the knob and pushed open the door.

Stark white light blazed from above.

My heart stopped and my stomach turned.

Blood.

Splatters.

Handprints.

Smears.

Grief, horror, and shock.

Her body was twisted at an odd angle, cuts lashed open in every direction on her wrists, an empty bottle of pills tipped over on its side next to her bloodied hand.

No.

A bottled sob worked its way out, and I slowly dropped to my knees beside her.

"No. Anna, no," I whispered, before it wound its way into a wail.

I gathered her in my arms, rocked her and rocked her while I begged and pled.

"No."

Body cold. Face ashen.

"No. Anna, no. God, please, no."

Willow wept, struggling to get away. I fought to hold her closer.

"How could you? She needed you. Oh my God. She needed you. She was sick. She was sick."

"I'm so fucking sorry. If you knew how sorry I was."

"She was sick," Willow begged again, slumping back down. Grief pressed down around us. Fuck. I wanted to end it all, but I opened my mouth and gave her the last of her sister's story.

I sat in the hard, plastic chair in the waiting room, fingers trembling as I continuously folded and unfolded the note Anna had scribbled and left on the floor. As if by doing so, the confession pressed into the blood-stained paper might change.

I'm so sorry. I never wanted to be this person. But I can't stop her, and I'm too scared to do this alone. What if I passed it on? That thought? That possibility? It hurts too much. Please forgive me. I need to be free.

The words coiled with my being like a foul, incurable disease, the possibility taunting me from every angle.

She hadn't been lying.

I'd known it in that fleeting second I'd found her lying on the floor and pulled her into my arms. I'd tasted her fear. Felt her sorrow. It was like I could almost reach out and touch the loss.

"Mr. Evans?" a woman asked.

I looked up with a nod.

She sat down beside me. "I'm Dr. Kirklen."

I could barely swallow, because what she was getting ready to tell me was already written in her eyes.

"She's gone?" Grief. Saying it was utter fucking grief.

"I'm sorry. She went into cardiac arrest. Between the overdose and the blood loss, we couldn't get her back. We did everything we could."

It didn't matter that I already knew, sorrow plowed through me.

Blades and ice and fire.

Destroyed.

"The baby?" I could barely croak it out.

She touched my forearm. "The pregnancy was positive."

I blinked, completely numb and in agony at the same time.

I had been going to be a dad. Fuck. I had been going to be a dad. Something I'd never even wanted until the possibility was taken away.

I rammed the heels of my hands into my eyes.

Me.

All of it was on me.

"They told me her name was different on her insurance card. I realized then she'd come to LA and changed her name. Desperate to become someone else. Thinking she was chasing her dreams and she might find them there. I didn't want to know, Willow. I didn't want to know who she was other than that girl I'd fallen in love with. I wanted to erase the rest. So like a coward, I tucked the letter she'd written back into her box and left it. Then I ran.

I'd been running ever since.

Frantic, I jabbed at the elevator button. Desperate to run because there wasn't anything here left for me.

The heavy metal doors closed and the emptiness swelled.

As soon as the elevator landed me on the first floor, I flew out. With each thundering step, I felt a piece of me getting left behind.

The pieces Anna had revealed because all of them belonged to her.

The love.

The loyalty.

The compassion.

Not one of them had been enough. Because I wasn't enough. I was too reckless. Lived too fast.

Thoughts of a child I wouldn't ever get to know overwhelmed me.
The possibilities that never had a chance.
Was it insane I loved someone I didn't even know?
Never fucking again.
I couldn't.
Not when I couldn't be trusted to stay.
I sped up, letting the hold she had on me rip and rend and tear at my back. I was almost at a sprint when I aimed my escape on the glass sliding doors.
Could feel myself being cracked open wide. Splintered.
I had the sudden urge to turn my head as I was flying out the door. My gaze tangled with big, chocolate eyes. I recognized the agony in their search. Like this girl was as desperate to get inside as I was to get out.
I jerked my attention away, not wanting to process anyone else's pain.
Because I'd never again hold a fragile heart in my hands.
Not when the only thing I would do was crush it in my grip.

The familiarity. It was her. My Peaches.

Willow was completely slack in my hold, gutted.

Shame howled through my spirit as I finished the story I'd been too much of a coward to tell.

Both that day I'd taken off from the hospital and left her and her mom with all the questions they'd deserved answered and the day when that familiarity I'd seen in Willow had finally caught up to me.

The question was, just what was it I had recognized?

Because the second I'd left that hospital, for the next seven years, I'd chosen the *easy* route. Refusing to ever get too close. Living for the kind of joy I could find.

Until I'd collided with Willow Langston.

Heart first.

"She was sick, Ash. She was sick."

"I swear to you, I didn't know the extent of it. Not until it was too late," I murmured at the top of her head.

"I can't…" She unwound herself from my arms, climbed to her feet, and I did the same, wanting to wrap her back up and knowing I didn't have the right.

She turned away like she couldn't bear to look at me.

That right there? That was why I'd done what I'd done. Hidden it. Pretended some more. Pretended like I didn't love her when I knew in my gut I could never really have her.

I could feel the quiver that rolled through her body, the pain that laced the accusation. "You knew...when you slept with me today."

My tone was quiet and pleading. "Willow."

Her lips trembled. "You know...somehow I already knew when I got to the hospital she was gone. My mom and I, we'd already been on our way, going there to bring her back because we knew she was spiraling."

Every cell in my body constricted with grief. Grief for her. Grief for Anna. *For Willow's Summer.*

She turned her attention to the ceiling. "They took us in this room, sat us down and told us, and gave us the box and said the man who'd come in with her had left it."

She looked back at me. "I hated that man." The words turned into a hushed whisper. "I hated the man who'd gotten her pregnant then left her. The one who hadn't taken care of her. The one who was too much a coward to even wait for us to get there to tell us what happened."

Her body quaked. "Did you know she was terrified of being a mom? Terrified she'd pass her sickness on? She told me she'd leave that for me. The messy part, she'd tease, because she knew she couldn't take the risk. But she promised she'd be the greatest auntie in the world."

"*Me,*" I told her. Just like I'd told her that night. I was responsible. All of it...it was on me.

She wiped her palm over her wet face. "I need you to go."

Panic seized my heart. "Willow."

She squeezed her eyes closed. "Please...just go."

I dropped my head, nodded slow as I accepted this cruel, sick fate, before I crossed back to the door. I hesitated there, before I gathered the courage to look back, wishing I'd had it all along. I smiled at her. Softly. Sadly.

"It wasn't pretend, Peaches." I touched my chest. "You can't fake this."

stay

"No…but I can't live in my sister's shadow."

I wanted to argue it. But I wondered if she and I had been living in her sister's shadow all along.

WILLOW

The door quietly clicked shut behind him.

I collapsed to the floor. Grief consumed me, agony spreading like a slow, splintering crack as I gathered the pictures to my chest.

I hugged them. A bitter, beautiful treasure I could hardly bear.

Summer smiled back from the stolen moments. Joy and inhibition. Her vibrancy spilled from the glossy sheets, as if she still held the power to command the room. The way she always had.

Wrapped around her was the man I loved. With all of me. Heart. Body. Soul. *Forever.*

I slumped forward and wept.

Crushed by grief.

Swallowed by sorrow.

Weak.

Silence hung like a shroud in the extra room upstairs. I sat in an antique rocker staring out the window. It was the room where I kept all the memories I couldn't endure seeing each day, so I'd steal in here when I wanted to get close to everything I'd lost.

A late summer rain poured it's fury on my backyard. Entranced, I watched as it pelted the roof of the small workshop where I'd fully fallen.

Because falling with Ash Evans had been worth the risk.

Days had passed in a blur as I struggled through a heartbreak more intense than I'd ever experienced. The loss of Ash. The anguish of Summer.

The problem was I couldn't tell if they were one in the same.

Memories of my sister swam through my mind.

"Ring around the rosy

A pocketful of posies

Ashes, Ashes

We all fall down"

Willow and Summer toppled in a pile to the ground, their giggles mounting toward the sky.

Summer linked her pinky with Willow's. Her sister smiled. "Willow and Summer forever."

Willow grinned. "Forever and ever."

Sorrow clawed through my being. For years, I'd wanted to track down the man who I'd believed abandoned her. Accuse and demand. But somewhere inside, after listening to his story, after hearing his regret, I knew his love for her had been just as helpless as mine. That the picture I'd conjured in my mind had been all wrong. Even after I'd done everything I could, it still wasn't enough to save her from herself. And I had to believe that same truth applied to Ash.

Pain intensified. Gripping me everywhere.

Because that hurt, too.

So much.

His love for her.

Did that make me a horrible person?

Summer ran through the tall grasses, wild locks of black hair flying around her smiling face as she turned to look over her shoulder. Willow followed her sister's lead, the way she always did, running down the embankment toward the deep, swollen creek hidden in the bank of trees. Summer jumped in with all her clothes, sinking under, two seconds later shooting up through the water. Her laughter danced through the warm air. She flung her arms above her head.

"It feels amazing, Will. Don't hold back. Don't ever forget what Mama said. The world's waiting for you."

Willow hesitated, wishing she were more like her sister, before she squeezed her eyes closed and jumped in.

But that was the thing about Summer and me. I'd always watched the world with caution while she'd taken it head on, until that world she'd wanted to embrace had slowly tumbled down around her. When the fear had set in.

Willow brushed the tears from beneath her sister's eyes, and Summer clung to her, sobbing at her chest. "It's not supposed to be like this, Will. It's not. I'm supposed to take care of you, not the other way around. I hate this. I hate it so much."

"Shh… It's okay. I'll always, always take care of you."

I swiped at the tears running down my face. I'd tried. God, I'd tried. The hardest part was I couldn't make sense of how we'd ended up here, Ash and I. Why I'd been dealt such a cruel twist of fate. Because I had no clue what was right and if loving Ash was wrong.

He'd been calling me, leaving me messages, begging me to return them. Maybe it was my turn to be the coward. But I didn't know how to face him. How to look at the man I loved wholly and wonder if there was any possibility of him ever loving me.

Twice I'd caught him sitting in his SUV across the street, the presence of that mesmerizing, intoxicating man stretching out to touch me where I wasted away in the loneliness of my house. As I questioned and ached and pleaded for the answers neither of us had.

Memories pressed into my mind, and I hugged her box to my chest. I rocked as I thought back to the conversation we'd had the day before she'd left.

"Bates is…safe," Summer argued, shaking her head at Willow.

Willow continued to work on the old piece, scraping away the decayed to reveal the new. She shook her head. "He said he's gonna marry me. You know that's what I want. A family."

Summer breezed by, whispered in Willow's ear. "Does he make you shake?"

No. Never.

"Love's supposed to be steady. Stable," Willow contended.

Summer laughed, the sound bouncing off the workshop walls. "Oh my sweet, Willow." She grabbed Willow by the cheeks and pressed a kiss to her forehead. "Love never, ever looks like you expect it to. Just wait. When you really feel it? I bet you won't be using any words like stable and safe. Just you wait."

She headed from the shop, before she turned to look back at Willow. Something significant tightened her words. "And when you find it? Promise me you won't ever let it go."

Gasping through my tears, I pressed both hands to my belly, because I'd never, ever expected this love to look like this. I'd never expected it to shatter and shake me through.

Ashes, Ashes, we all fall down.

But my mama…she'd taught me and Summer our worlds were ours to hold. Even when they were in pieces. Even when our dreams were scattered with the wind. Because we never knew where those scattered seeds might land and take root.

ASH

My fingers fumbled on the frets of my bass.

"Goddamn it," I gritted, dropping my head, hunting for that elusive cool that was getting harder and harder to find.

Baz's voice came through the speakers in the booth where I was trying and failing to lay down my track.

Failing would be the key word.

Hard.

"Why don't you take a break. Walk it off. We can come back to this later."

Harshly, I rubbed the back of my hand across my mouth.

"Already have this album weeks behind."

Zee had been right to call me out on my bullshit. Walking out on my band was the last thing I wanted to do. But with this kind of productivity? I might as well have.

"Take a breather," Baz said. This time it wasn't a suggestion.

I set my favorite bass aside, hands clenching and unclenching in vicious fists. Like the action might burn off the aggression and desperation threatening to boil the blood in my veins.

I tore out of the booth, tossing a glare at Baz where he sat at the console, like any part of this was his fault. "Better?" It was all kinds of sarcasm and spite.

He was right behind me as I stormed out where I landed myself in the lounge outside the studio. Zee and Austin were in the far corner, having some kind of hushed, private conversation that probably had everything to do with me. Lyrik and Tamar were on one of the couches, girl draped across his lap and the dude whispering softly as he gazed down at her.

Didn't think the knots laying siege to my guts could twist any tighter.

They did.

I headed for the stairs, needing to get out of there.

Baz stopped me with a hand on my shoulder, his words measured but severe. "You want to take this out on me? Fine. But you know stomping around here like an asshole isn't gonna change a thing. I don't know what the hell happened with Willow, but it's obvious you need to fix it."

Fix it.

I scoffed as I spun to face him. Incredulous. "Fix it? Some things can't be fixed. Not when I was the one who broke them in the first place."

I'd been breaking them all along.

Swore he read it in my eyes, because his voice lowered farther and sympathy edged into his expression. "I know what happened with Anna messed you up, man. It was horrible. Awful. Something no one should ever have to go through. And I know you chose to put it behind you. Live your life the best way you could. Making the best of every day. Do you think I don't know you never quite let any of those days count? But there comes a point in all our lives when that's not enough anymore. When we need the days to matter, because what's the point in living if we don't really have something to live for?"

Emotion welled, too fast, and I was fisting my hands again, struggling to cling to the anger so I wouldn't have to deal with the hurt.

He blinked, jaw going rigid. "God forbid, Ash, *God forbid*, but if I lost Shea today? I'd never regret slowing down, realizing what was important, choosing to make every single one of our days count. One day spent with her is worth more than a million without her."

Grief lashed and scourged. "I'm just not sure I'm worthy of any of Willow's days."

I turned away and staggered up the stairs, head hanging between my shoulders as I ascended. Second I mounted the top, hands landed on my chest, halting my escape.

I looked up. Edie was there, worry and concern bleeding all over her face.

"Edie," I murmured, feeling the last piece of my reserve bust apart.

"You're scaring me, Ash. What's going on with you?"

I gathered her in my arms. "Edie. I'm so sorry. I'm so goddamned sorry."

It was all catching up. Had felt it catching up all along. Ever since that moment a year ago when I'd found out about what I'd let happen to her.

She shook her head against my chest. "I don't understand."

"I fucked up. I fucked up so bad."

She peeled herself away, sympathy on her face as she wrapped her hand in mine and led me over to the living room on the main floor of Baz and Shea's house. She sat me down on a chair and climbed to her knees in front of me.

I scrubbed both hands over my face. "Need to tell you something."

She touched my knee. "You can tell me anything. *Anything*."

"That night…what happened to you…" I couldn't even

form the words.

She nodded.

"There was so much going on behind the scenes. This girl…"

I gathered up my courage and told my baby sister the same story I'd told Willow two weeks ago. I backed up, started from the beginning, from the first night I'd met Anna all the way up to the night when it'd all ended in destruction.

For Edie.

For Anna.

For Willow.

"I was responsible for it, Edie. For what happened to you. I was so wrapped up in what was going on with my life that night, I didn't take care of you the way I should have."

Me.

It'd always been on me.

Tears streaked down Edie's face. "How can you say that? Paul was responsible, Ash. *Paul.* Not you."

"You're wrong."

She shook her head. "I'm not. I spent too many years blaming myself, and I refuse to let you do the same." Her mouth trembled. "It makes me sick to know what happened to you that night. To her. It's horrible and wrong. I can't tell you how sorry I am. I wish I would have known."

My elbows propped on my knees, I threaded my fingers together and lifted my head to peer at my sister. "It kills me I didn't know what was happening to you, Edie. That all those years I didn't have the first clue what you'd gone through that night. To think I was relieved when I'd gotten the text that you'd skated out, thinking at least you were safe, when you hadn't been safe at all."

"We're pretty good at keeping secrets from each other, aren't we?"

"Yeah," I agreed. "Too good. I don't want that anymore. Not for either of us."

Edie turned her attention to the floor, before she peeked back at me. "I can't believe she was Willow's sister."

I rubbed my chin. "It's so fucked up."

"It wasn't your fault, Ash. She was sick. You have to know that."

Part of me did. The other was counting all the mistakes I'd made. The warnings I'd ignored.

"I just...I just wish..." All the unknowns stuck to my tongue.

Edie's face pinched. "Of course you wish you could change it. We all wish we could stop the bad things from happening in our lives. Wish we could take away the hurt from the people we love. Go back and change it. But just because you can't change it doesn't mean you're to blame."

She set her hand on her stomach, affection filling her expression, her eyes so bright when she looked up at me. "I hate what Paul did to me, Ash, and I'd never say it's okay or it was meant to be. But I have to wonder if Austin and I would have found each other if it hadn't happened. If he hadn't have been there for me. Sometimes our greatest gifts are found in our darkest hour."

Her head tilted in emphasis. "What if Willow is that greatest gift for you?"

I gripped the back of my head. "She told me she can't live in her sister's shadow."

"Is she? Standing in her sister's shadow? Is that who you see when you look at her?"

I blew out a breath, honesty floating out. "I worried she might be...when I first realized who she was. Since the second I met her...I felt this...familiarity when I looked at her. Like I already knew her when I shouldn't have. It scared me that I was seeing Anna in her."

"And what do you think now?"

My gaze tangled with big, chocolate eyes. I recognized the agony in their search. Like this girl was as desperate to get inside as I was to get out.

And I knew who I'd been seeing was Willow all along.

I met Edie's gaze. "I think there's no chance of her living in a shadow. Not when she's my sun."

A knowing smile climbed to my sister's face. "You love her."

"So much."

More than anything I'd ever known.

"Does she know?"

Did she?

My mind tumbled through our memories, through the words I'd given her.

"Pretend with me."

"I'm no good for you, darlin'. Can't give you all those things you really want."

"Tell me you love me…the way I love you."

"I can't tell you that."

Realization tightened my chest.

"What if she doesn't feel the same? What if she can't look at me without thinking of her sister. About what I did? About how I let her down? What if I let *her* down?"

Edie touched my knee. "Maybe you need to show her why she should believe in you. That you want her to. None of us missed it, Ash. The way she looked at you. You can't let her go."

A throat cleared to the side, and I looked up as Tamar made her way into the room, obviously catching the gist of our conversation. She dropped an enlarged, black and white photo onto my lap.

One she'd snagged of Willow on my lap in this very spot.

My heart beat an extra beat.

Because my girl…my Peaches…she was snuggled against me, and I had my lips pressed to the top of her head, my hold secure while she melted into me.

Easy.

Not the kind that I'd been seeking for the last seven years.

But something that was simple and real.

Like both of us were exactly where we were supposed to be.

That crazy energy shimmered around us like a palpable thing. That feeling I could never quite put my finger on.

Love.

My Tam Tam squeezed my shoulder. "Just in case you needed proof."

WILLOW

A calm I hadn't felt in weeks filled the space as I let myself get lost in the soothing sound of sandpaper. I ran it over the wood of the old piece again and again.

Revealing the beauty hidden underneath.

I'd finally forced myself to get up and get out of my house. To find a focus for the loss that chased me day by day. Knowing I had to take care of myself. Maybe not to move on, because after Ash Evans, that would be impossible. But to take a step forward.

Emily pressed her hands to the front counter beside the cash register, breaking my attention. Dragging me back to the reality I didn't want to face.

"So that's just it? You're gonna let him go?" A quiet urgency weaved its way into her words.

I attempted to swallow as my chest trembled. "I don't see that there's another solution," I finally grated, my spirit mounting a backlash at the assertion.

I glanced up as her brow twisted in disbelief. "You don't see another solution? Just who is it you think you're foolin'? That other 'solution' is right in front of you. You know the one…that insanely hot rock star you saved? The one who's been savin' you? The one who brought you back to life. Made you believe again? That one."

He was also the one who'd crushed me.

"You know it's not that simple," I said, turning back to the spindles of wood, my hands pouring out their love against the grains. I could almost see it, sitting in that second room where I'd stored all my memories.

No longer would that room bear shame.

"No?" she challenged.

I blinked through the moisture that gathered in my eyes. "He was in love with my sister."

"So what?"

My head jerked up.

"*So what?*" My face pinched in agony and a tremble shook through my body. "How would I ever know if he really loved me, Emily? How? How would I *ever* know for sure that when I laid down with him it was *me* he was looking at and not my sister he was searching for? I could never—"

"Compete with your sister? Is that what you're getting ready to say?"

"No…that's not…"

Was it?

I didn't know. All I knew was I'd loved my sister more than the whole world. Then this man had become my everything.

Guilt swam with the grief. "What if it's a dishonor to her? What if it's a dishonor to all of us?"

Emily slowly approached me, stood on the other side of the rocker and gripped me by both sides of the face. "What if it's a dishonor to ignore *this*? What you've been given."

Sympathy swam in her eyes. "Your sister was amazing, Willow. She was a force. Bright. Talented. A shining star. And I know you loved her with everything you had. But she's not here anymore. But that man? The one who's been going out of his mind trying to reach you? To make you see? To look? From where I'm standing, the only person he's looking at is you."

I dropped my eyes closed. "You were the one who said he was going to break my heart, Emily. You were right."

He'd just done it in an entirely different way than she'd been suggesting.

Soft laughter rolled from her. "I'm not so big to admit when I just might be wrong, Will. And I think right now, you just might be wrong, too. Everything you've ever wanted…everything…those dreams are right there, waitin' on you to reach out and take them."

"I just…I don't know if I can. He doesn't even want any of those things."

We both jerked when the bell jingled over the door. That jingle had been going off more and more since Ash Evans had come into my life, my store no longer a no-name. He'd saved me in more ways than he could ever know, wrecked me all the same.

It was a young man in his uniform, a cap on his head and a digital clipboard in one hand as he balanced a big box on the other. "I have a delivery for a Ms. Langston?"

"That's me," I said, getting to my feet, wiping my hands on my jeans so I could accept the package.

"Sign right here, please."

I scribbled my name in the spot he indicated and he handed me the box, already on his way out the door as he tossed, "Have a nice day," over his shoulder.

I moved over to the counter, grabbed a sharp tool, and raked it across the seal. I pulled out the packing and froze when I came to the small, rectangular wooden box nestled inside. My heart rate sped, a thunder at my ribs, and that horrible lump that'd been living at the base of my throat ached and pled.

With shaky hands, I lifted it out.

It was stained in a whitewash and was who knew how many years old. It was both worn down and beautiful. I set it on the counter and ran my trembling fingertips across the word that had been carved into the top.

The marks were crude and unpolished.

Will.

Emily moved to stand opposite of me. "What is it?" Her brows drew together as she squinted at the raw, unpolished carving.

More tears slipped free. "Ash."

I knew it with every part of me and still felt as if I didn't know a thing.

"Oh, Will," she whispered like encouragement.

I slowly lifted the lid. Old hinges creaked as they exposed an antique silver pocket watch and a piece of paper folded into quarters nestled inside.

God.

What was he trying to do to me?

I frowned at the couple of letters and numbers written across the top, but my attention was stolen by the strong handwriting pressed into the paper.

> **Willow,**
>
> **Where do I even start? You asked me to go and I did because I didn't know how to make sense of our reality. I thought leaving you was for the best. Because I knew I deserved for you to hate me. Then when I realized I couldn't force myself to leave this town—to leave you—I decided what I needed to give you was time.**
>
> **I tried, but I'm honestly not quite sure what giving you time means anymore. All I know is the last two weeks have been the most unbearable of**

my life. Each day that passes is longer than the last, and every second that ticks by feels like an eternity we've lost.

Funny, but I'm pretty sure time didn't start ticking until the day I met you.

Three months ago, I was waltzing down this street like I didn't have a damned care in the world. It'd felt like it. I'd closed myself off to the idea of commitment, to the possibility of ever loving someone again, because I didn't think I could ever take on that kind of responsibility.

I was just...gliding through the days. Letting time pass without it really meaning anything.

I was as close to happy as I thought I could ever get.

That night three months ago? I knew I was close to breathing my last. It was like I could feel death hovering in my periphery. And there you were. Giving me more *time*.

Five days later, I found my way back to this same spot I almost died. I couldn't stay away. Couldn't shake the feeling I had something important to do. Maybe by that moment in time I was already a different man. Maybe between lying in a puddle of my own blood and thinking I'd never see the people I loved again, something had already been loosed inside of me. Maybe that reinforced barrier I'd built around my heart had sustained a crack. But standing there, looking at you the first time? Little did I know you'd already found a way into my soul.

Tears ran hot down my cheeks and the hollow place inside me throbbed. I squinted through the bleariness, trying to make sense of the numbers and letters that sat in place of a finished letter. Hungry for more of his words. Wondering if I was a complete fool for wanting them.

I glanced up at Emily who was grinning at me from the other side of the counter.

"What is this?" I begged.

She'd been on her phone, and she turned the face toward me. "I think...I think they're coordinates." She pointed to the row of numbers and letters at the top of the letter. "These are the exact coordinates for the store."

She inputted the second row. A small gasp shot from her when she retrieved the results. A grin stretched her face when she looked back up at me. "It's the resort where the reunion was."

"Oh my God," I breathed. I swiped away the lingering tears hanging on my lashes and fought to calm my raging heart.

What do I do?

What could this change?

"How will I ever know?"

She reached out and gripped my trembling hand. "We never know for sure, Willow. Not ever. In life there are no guarantees. There are only possibilities. You need to find out where this one takes you."

Emotion spun.

Hope and despair and need.

Tucking the letter back into the box, I grabbed my purse and keys. I started for the door but paused when Emily called after me, "What do *you* see when he looks at you?"

I gave her a somber smile and a nod of my head. I rushed out into the day, unsure where this chase would end. But knowing I couldn't go on ignoring what was screaming out from me on the inside.

I swiped at my tears with the sleeve of my shirt, trying to clear my vision and calm the riot of my heart. I inputted the coordinates myself and followed them to the resort. It guided me through the lobby and out through the back to where the reception had been held beneath the stars and twinkle lights.

A soggy laugh escaped when I found another box had been nestled near a row of flowering shrubs.

I climbed to my knees and pulled it onto my lap. This one was completely square and had the word *You* carved on the top. Again old. Again beautiful. My pulse sprinted as affection tugged a smile onto my lips.

I lifted the lid. Hidden inside was one of the pictures he'd taken on his phone that night when he'd obliterated me. When he'd demanded I see the way he looked at me when all I could see was him.

The image was entirely of my face, my expression both shy and confident. Filled with all the love I'd come to realize in this man.

I unfolded the note he'd left with it.

> **My Willow,**
> **Two months ago, I asked you to pretend with me. To pretend like you belonged to me when a terrified part of me wished there was a way you could. Here was this amazing girl who was so unlike anyone I'd ever met, so far out of my reach because she wanted all the things I could never give her. I couldn't have those things. I was too damned scared to take that kind of risk again. And honestly, I wasn't there yet. Didn't think I needed love or wanted it. But somewhere along the way? In those days that ticked by? You showed me what it was again. Made me remember. Stirred a part of me I'd long since forgotten. A part I mocked as stupid and reckless when, in reality, I'd been living the most reckless life of all. Most of all, you brought out something new. Something *better*. Something I never knew**

was a part of me.

Somewhere in time? Somewhere in time, I fell in love with you.

Love.

It swelled all around me. The warmest embrace against the cold dark I'd been lost in for weeks. I'd been so sure I'd seen it in him…felt it in his touch. But I'd let the shock and grief of Summer convince me it'd been fake.

Ash. With his hard, beautiful exterior and his soft, amazing heart.

I took the letter and box and ran back through the lobby and to my car as this overwhelming emotion bloomed. Spreading through my body. Laying siege to my spirit, heart, and mind.

Chaotic comfort.

My fingers were frantic as I entered the next row of coordinates listed at the bottom of the second letter. I threw my car in gear and let the generic voice wind me back through town and to the old part of the city.

That eagerness I'd been feeling shifted and amplified.

It took a sharp turn into sorrow.

By the time I put my car in park, I was sobbing.

I didn't know if I could do this.

It hurt too much. But there I was, fumbling out the door and stumbling up the grassy hill. Ancient trees stretched their arms across the grounds. As if they were offering their comfort when this place wept with sorrow.

Wind gusted and leaves tumbled.

I dropped to my knees between the two headstones that rested side by side.

Gingerly, I brushed my fingers across my mama's marker that had just been set. Too new. Too brutal. A fresh bouquet of flowers had been set next to the words that branded her days. Her life. Her legacy.

"I love you, Mama. I love you so much. I wish you were here…because I don't know what to do."

The wind howled back, and I gathered my strength, turned my attention to my sister's stone. A stone that had been written far too soon. It also graced a fresh spray of flowers, love and regret left like an omen. Beside it was another box. On the lid, carved in the same crude fashion, was the word *Please.*

This man was breaking me. I wiped my nose with the sleeve of my shoulder, for the first time reluctant to open the box. Petrified of what might be inside. Knowing I needed to see it all the same.

Inside was another folded note. Beneath it was a handful of barren dandelion stems. Like the one marked on his side where his demons rested.

Sadness spun, and I lurched forward, quiet cries tumbling from my mouth as I unfolded the small note I worried might sever the few remaining strands I had holding together my heart.

> **Willow,**
>
> **Asking you to come here is one of the most difficult things I've ever done. Part of it felt cruel. Unnecessary. While the other part felt that bringing you here might be the most important moment in *our* time.**
>
> **You told me you couldn't live in your sister's shadow.**
>
> **I will never downplay what I felt for her. I loved her. I did. But I think your sister and I? We got caught up in each other. Both of us searching for something when neither of us knew what we were searching for. For a moment in time, we found that in each other. Flames destined to burn out. What happened with your sister was a tragedy, Willow. A horrible waste of a beautiful spirit. I'd do anything to go back and change things. Do things differently. I'm willing to bet if your sister had the chance, she would, too.**

She loved life in the only way she could. I think she loved me the same way. It was frantic and fleeting and could never be sustained. But the love she had for you and your mom? It was the truest kind. The kind that scared her the most because it was the only thing that was real to her. If you know one thing…know that. Your light…your love…your peace. That was her constant.

I think maybe…maybe your sister and I were chasing our dreams, and during that search, we collided in the middle. It still kills me that her chase was cut short far too soon when she had so far to go.

But I'm certain now colliding with her somehow sent me chasing after you.

Sobs ripped from my soul. I'd never felt so torn in two. Broken right down the middle. The devotion to my sister and my love for this man.

Barely able to see, I surged back to my feet and ran for my car. I was plugging in the next numbers written on the bottom as I went. I clenched the steering wheel like it might ground me as I followed the directions back out of town.

The road passed through the city before it grew rural, the trees growing tall and proud. A familiarity tugged at my senses, pulled at my heart.

Do you remember, Mama, do you remember?

I pulled off at the small dirt patch at the road's end—an end that led to the place from the story I'd told my mama on the day Ash had gone with me to visit her. When he'd sung her his song. When he'd come to me later and taken me.

The day my heart was no longer mine.

I fumbled up the narrow trail until it broke open to the

meadow.

A meadow where my sister and I had once played. Where my mama would sit with us and we'd cast our dreams into the air.

Dandelions covered every inch of the ground. In the late summer, they'd gone to seed. A breeze blew through. They scattered, lifted and spiraled in the air like tiny white fairies flying off to deliver their dreams.

In awe, I lifted my arms up and spun a circle as all those dreams danced around me.

I pressed my hands to my broken heart. My broken heart that throbbed and moaned. My heart this larger-than-life, arrogant, chaotic man wanted to mend.

It was easy to find, the mismatched collector's box he'd left right in the center. I dropped to my knees and pulled it onto my lap.

I was shaking.

Shaking and shaking as I tenderly brushed my fingertips over the word carved in that same crude sketching on the top.

Stay.

I breathed in as the meaning came together. The message he'd sent.

Will you please stay.

My spirit thrashed and begged. Slowly, I tipped open the lid.

All the air heaved from my lungs. My hand shot to my mouth. Inside was another tiny box. This one wrapped in black velvet. Even then, without touching or opening it, I could tell it was antique, too. I almost couldn't get my hands to cooperate when I reached for the letter waiting inside. Carefully I opened it, my heart at the mercy of his hand.

Peaches,

Peaches.

My palm went to my chest, trying to hold all the emotion in that was desperate to pour out.

You were right. I was a coward the day I left the hospital. I chose the *easy* route. I got on that road and swore to myself I'd never look back.

Then I collided with you. It wasn't until then that I knew what I'd been missing. That I wanted something more. That I wanted my days to count and every single one of them to belong to you.

You are my peace. My light. My definition of love. Yes, it's frantic and chaotic and wild. But it's also soft and quiet and subdued. It's sparks and flickers and a constant flame.

I want to spend all time with you. Eternity. My forever.

Am I scared? Yeah.

But I'm done being a coward. Not when it comes to you. I told you all along that guy was out there waiting on you to find him. I made you promise me you wouldn't settle for anything less than the man who would give you all the things you deserve.

And you?

You deserve everything.

If you'll let me, I want to give you my world.

Because you, Willow, you took over time and became mine.

You...you could never be second place or be hidden in the shadows. You burn too bright. Your faith is too brilliant and your love is too vivid.

You are my sun.

All your dreams...they're spinning around you, just waiting for you to catch up to them.

I'm waiting for you.

My heart beat out ahead of me, urging me home. I didn't even know how I got the little box open, but I did, and my heart that kept screaming at me wanted to burst.

The ring was ornate. Platinum and encrusted with diamonds. Delicate.

So old.

So perfect.

So me.

There was one more word at the bottom of his letter, right beneath the next coordinates.

Stay.

I didn't even need to plug them in. I already knew where they would lead. Still, when I climbed into my small SUV, I had an entirely different destination in mind. I raced back into town and parked in front of the gorgeous house I'd only visited once before.

I rushed up the front porch and pounded on the door.

Three seconds later, a worried Tamar opened it, trying to balance her wiggling little girl on her hip while she focused on me. "Willow…are you okay?"

"I need your help."

Blue eyes flashed. "Of course. Anything."

"We're going to need your camera."

A wicked grin stretched across her face. "I like the way you think."

ASH

I stepped into the vacancy of my huge ass house that echoed back a quiet, hollow void. Funny, how I'd been after the extravagant things. Filling up my life with things that really meant nothing.

Possessions.

Women.

A kind of life that passed at the speed of light.

Now, the only thing I wanted was to fill this place with her *light*. With her laughter and her hope and sweet, sweet soul.

Twilight pressed in on the windows that looked out over the

porch, casting the main floor in shadows and doubt. The entire day had passed and all that *hope* I'd been feeling had been obliterated.

All day, I'd been on edge, waiting for her to come.

For her to choose me.

I'd sat here for close to six hours after that package had been delivered. Pacing. Wanting to claw my hair out with each second that passed.

Then of course because the universe hated me, Lyrik and Austin had gone and called an emergency meeting two hours ago, spouting some bullshit that was going down in LA. They said I had to be there, which was stupid considering I couldn't process anything they said. I was there, but not present. Antsy and uneasy. Checking my phone a million damned times to see if she'd texted or called.

Nothing.

It fucking slayed me.

But like I'd told her, I was done being a coward. I'd laid myself on the line. Offered her my life if she was just willing to reach out and take it.

Pushing out a breath, I headed for the stairs. My hand glided up the railing as I trudged my way toward that room that taunted me with the remnants of her presence. It was only worse tonight. Knowing I'd done all I could and it hadn't been enough.

I edged down the hall and pushed open one side of the double doors. The last of the day spilled inside, giving the room that sang with Willow's spirit a soft, pink hue.

I breathed it in. The lingering scent of peaches filled my senses. Tightened my chest. I blinked, wondering if I just might be losing my mind because it was more intense than it had ever been. That crazy energy that shimmered and played.

I felt myself turning, shifting to look at the barren wall. That vacant place Willow had left like a mark against my name.

Only it was no longer bare.

A row of eight pictures adorned the space. All of them done in black and white and framed in old, vintage wood.

Each huge and utterly profound.

There was just a hint of my girl in each one. A whisper of her shoulder. A profile of her strong face captured like a secret. A tease of black lace.

A shudder ripped down my spine, and the hairs at the nape of my neck lifted in awareness.

Not the dreadful kind.

No. This was the kind that slowed time because you *knew* you were going to want to remember that moment forever.

Hope fisted in my chest.

Slowly, I turned, drawn.

Heart in my throat.

She stood in the doorway to the bathroom.

She was wearing nothing but black lace and one of my white button-ups she'd stolen from my drawer. Undone. All that creamy, soft skin was on display, mounds of mahogany piled on her head, tendrils dripping down to frame that sweet, sweet face.

I swore the room spun.

I could barely speak, my throat too swollen and thick. I managed the only thing that mattered. "Willow."

She edged out into the glimmers of the waning day. Could feel the shyness that wove its way through her body, the redness that flushed her cheeks when she gestured to the pictures on the wall behind me. But her voice was brimming with hope. "You said you wanted to wake to me every day."

Devotion whipped through me, this insane love I had for this precious girl.

I moved toward her, my heart going haywire when I began to breathe her breaths. I reached out and cupped her jaw, her pulse racing beneath my touch. "I do, Willow. I promise…I do. What I told you in those letters…it's all the truth I have to give. You are my sun. My life."

Chocolate eyes glistened, everything I was feeling reflected back. "I thought…I thought maybe by loving you, I was dishonoring my sister. Her memory. *Her dreams*. But she made me promise…the day before she left…that if I found love, the real kind, that I wouldn't ever let it go."

A single tear slipped from the corner of her eye. "I think…I think she'd want us to be happy. I think maybe she was leading us here, all along. Because I found it in you."

I held her face in my hands. "Peaches."

"Tell me it's real," she whispered.

My nose brushed hers. "It's real. There's no faking this—the love I have for you."

A watery smile moved across her mouth, and she clutched her bottom lip between her teeth, hand shaking like an earthquake when she held out the velvet box. "What you said in the last letter…that you want all of it…all of it with me. I need to know that you truly do."

"I want everything. Everything you've got to give, Willow. All of it."

No lie.

Zero reservations.

Her gaze traveled to the far wall. To the spot I'd missed when I'd first come in.

I swore the world shook.

Sitting beneath the window was a wooden bassinet. The old kind built on rockers with carved, ornate slats, Willow's signature style written all over the reclamation.

Shocked, I turned back to look at her, the girl staring up at me.

Hope. Love. Belief.

"Why do I get the feeling this is a sooner rather than later kind of question, darlin'?" My words were clogged with emotion, but that didn't mean there wasn't a grin fighting for claim on my mouth.

"Because I caught a dream. And maybe it looks different than the way I'd always imagined. Different than I expected. But it's real and the only thing I want is to share it with you."

I sank to the floor in front of her, my hands cinched down on her hips, my nose buried in the sweet flesh of her belly. "I want it, Willow. I want it all. I just never knew I did until I met you."

She touched my face, so soft as she ran her gentle fingers through my hair.

Love laying siege, I pressed a kiss there, before I gathered myself and sent my girl a smirk. "Now, where's that box?"

She choked out teary laughter and handed it to me. I pulled out the ring I knew would be perfect for her.

An heirloom.

A treasure.

Priceless.

"Willow Langston, put me out of my misery and tell me you'll marry me."

Tears streaked down her face. Chocolate eyes so wide. Love so clear. "Yes," she whispered.

I slid that ring onto its rightful place, looking between her finger and her face, wondering how I had the right to get something so good, making a silent promise to always cherish it, before I stood up and lifted my girl in my arms. I twirled her round and round.

She threw her head back and laughed. Laughed that perfect, poetic sound that passed through me like a caress. I spun her faster. "Oh my God, Ash, put me down, you're going to drop me."

She squealed when I did just that, right into the middle of *our* bed. I grinned down at her as I peeled off my shirt. "What, you think I can't handle you?" I flexed my arms. "Look how strong I am."

"Oh, it looks like my cocky, arrogant boy has come out to play."

"Your cocky boy always wants to *play*, darlin'. How's that sound, soon to be Mrs. Willow Evans?"

She giggled as I climbed over her. "That sounds like the best thing I've ever heard."

"Does this mean I get to get in this sweet body now? Been dying, baby. Did you know how bad I needed you? How much I was missing you?"

She touched my face.

Sex and comfort.

It tremored around the room.

Staring down at her, I brushed a lock of hair from her

precious face. "I love you. More than you could know."

Her expression softened with all that tenderness only she could give. "I know, Ash. I know. And I promise I'll love you the same…until the end of time."

WILLOW

Above, blue skies stretched on forever. Tufts of pure, white clouds floated on the endless breeze. Birds flittered and chirped, passed from tree to tree.

Laughter lifted to the heavens as they ran through the field of dandelions.
Love, love, love. It bounded all around them.
Ash set a hand on her cheek. "My wife. My sun."
She squeezed his hand closer. "My everything."
Her life. Her joy. Her gift.
That joy spun around her as Willow held a dandelion out toward their son who kicked and giggled in the crook of his daddy's arm.
Willow's heart brimmed with all that love she had to give, her words a

rasp as she whispered to their child, "What do you wish, sweet one? Your dreams, they're out there, waiting all around you. You just have to catch them."

Chasing dreams always came with a risk.

Dreams that scattered and blew and so often seemed out of reach.

But eventually, those dreams?

They settled and took root.

They found the one place they were meant to Stay.

the end

Thank you for reading Stay! Did you love getting to know Ash and Willow? Please consider leaving a review! If you'd like to discuss STAY or any of my stories with other readers, join us in the A.L. Jackson Reader Hangout on Facebook.

Ready for more?

Zee Kennedy was always in the background. Now it's his time to Stand.

Stand, a second-chance romance and the final novel in the bestselling BLEEDING STARS series, is available now.

MORE FROM A.L. JACKSON

stay

ABOUT THE AUTHOR

A.L. Jackson is the New York Times & USA Today Bestselling author of contemporary romance. She writes emotional, sexy, heart-filled stories about boys who usually like to be a little bit bad.

Her bestselling series include THE REGRET SERIES, CLOSER TO YOU, BLEEDING STARS, FIGHT FOR ME, CONFESSIONS OF THE HEART, FALLING STARS, and REDEMPTION HILLS.

If she's not writing, you can find her hanging out by the pool with her family, sipping cocktails with her friends, or of course with her nose buried in a book.

Be sure not to miss new releases and sales from A.L. Jackson - Sign up to receive her newsletter http://smarturl.it/NewsFromALJackson or text "aljackson" to 33222 to receive short but sweet updates on all the important news.

Connect with A.L. Jackson online:

FB Page **https://geni.us/ALJacksonFB**
Newsletter **https://geni.us/NewsFromALJackson**
Angels **https://geni.us/AmysAngels**
Amazon **https://geni.us/ALJacksonAmzn**
Book Bub **https://geni.us/ALJacksonBookbub**
Text "aljackson" to 33222 to receive short but sweet updates on all the important news.

Printed in Great Britain
by Amazon

23248993R00199